MERCURY
SHRUGS

A NOVEL BY ROBERT KROESE

JS KKOEZE

Copyright ©2016 Robert Kroese. All rights reserved. No portion of this book may be reproduced, stored in a retrieval system, or transmitted in any form or by any means—electronic, mechanical, photocopy, recording or other—except for brief quotations in reviews, without the prior permission of the author.

Published by Westmarch Publishing
westmarchpub.com

For Meredith.

....

With thanks to: Joel Bezaire, Mark Fitzgerald, Mark Thompson, and Charity VanDeBerg for their help in improving this book.

Thanks also to those who supported the Kickstarter to get this book published, particularly Julia Balitsky, Kristin Dexter, Colleen Diamond, Christopher Finlan, Brian and Donna Hekman, Justin Jelonek, Andrea Luhman, Steven Mentzel, Kristi Michels, Chad and Denise Rogers, Sean Simpson and Christopher Turner.

This is a work of fiction. If you see any names you recognize, it's probably a coincidence.

AUTHOR'S PREFACE

Welcome, dear reader. What you have in your hands is a novel titled *Mercury Shrugs*. If you were looking for psych 101, it's down the hall.

Mercury Shrugs is the fifth book in the Mercury series, but between you and me it's okay if you haven't read the other four. The plot of *Mercury Shrugs* might not make much sense to you if you haven't read them, but that's probably true either way, and if you read the books out of order at least you have an excuse.

I think of the first three books (*Mercury Falls*, *Mercury Rises*, and *Mercury Rests*) as a more-or-less self-contained trilogy. *Mercury Revolts* is a separate adventure, taking place a few years after the close of Mercury Rests. *Mercury Shrugs* picks up about a year after *Mercury Revolts*, and—kidding aside—I've done my best to make it accessible for new readers and veterans alike. This book also ties up some loose ends from the previous books. Well, maybe it doesn't so much tie them up as tangle them together.

For those keeping score, the chronology goes like this:

"Mercury Begins" (short story)
Mercury Falls
"Mercury Swings" (short story)
Mercury Rises
Mercury Rests
Mercury Revolts
Mercury Shrugs

DRAMATIS PERSONAE

Azrael: Large horned demon, Lucifer's second in command. Also in prison.

Chris Finlan: Former mail-bomber and manifesto writer, currently in federal prison.

Christine Temetri: Former journalist: Last known whereabouts: Northern Africa, c. 5,000 B.C.

Eddie Pratt (Ederatz): A cherub who previously worked for the Mundane Observation Corps.

Jacob Slater: Former scientist for the FBI. Last known whereabouts: Northern Africa, c. 5,000 B.C.

Lucas Jelonek: A fourteen-year-old boy with a rebellious streak.

Lucifer: The devil, currently in a prison somewhere below the Celestial City, in Heaven.

Mercury: A cherub previously employed by Apocalypse Bureau.

Nisroc: A dim-witted but well-meaning angel.

Special Agent Taylor Burton: Head of the FBI Task Force on Beings of Indeterminate Origin.

Suzy Cilbrith: Software tester who worked on the Brimstone Project, now unemployed.

Tiamat: Demoness and former head of Chaos Faction, currently in a rebuilding phase of her career.

PROLOGUE

To Your Holiness the High Council of the Seraphim,

Greetings from your humble servant, Ederatz,
Etc., etc.

Let's dispense with the formalities, shall we?

My name is Eddie. I'm stuck on Earth, AKA the Mundane Plane, with somewhere around a hundred other angels and about seven billion human beings, most of whom don't smell very good.

All things considered, my situation is preferable to never having existed, which seemed to be a distinct possibility for a while there. I suppose it's still a possibility now that I think about it; once you've established the contingency that you may never have existed, anything can happen—or not have happened, as it were. The good news is that if there are any efforts currently underway to erase my existence, I'm unaware of them. That's the way I like it. If I'm going to not have existed, I want it to happen all of a sudden, so I don't have a chance to think about it. "I think, therefore I am," said the philosopher, but he was wrong. Thinking doesn't buy you anything but worry, and it's a seller's market.

It's not just me that almost never existed, of course. I'm nothing in the scheme of things. Nobody is going to go out of their way to make sure I never existed. My near-nonexistence was a mere byproduct of an attempt to rewrite the history of reality itself. But best laid plans and all that, so here I am, along with seven billion sweaty bastards, most of whom are oblivious to both their precarious hold on reality and, evidently, the existence of deodorant.

How did this threat to reality as we know it come about? Well, as usual, it started with good intentions, and I suppose I'm as much to blame as anyone.

As you know if you've read my previous reports, about five years ago the demoness Tiamat attempted to achieve complete mastery over space and time while Lucifer plotted to bring about the destruction of the universe by blowing up the mystical energy source known as the Eye of Providence. Thanks to the intervention of the angel Mercury and a pair of humans named Christine Temetri and Jacob Slater, both plots failed. Unfortunately, due to a fluke accident with a glass apple and a particle accelerator, Christine and Jacob were exiled seven thousand years in the past. Additionally, the primary means of transportation and communication between the Mundane Plane and the other planes was cut off when some knucklehead detonated a nuclear bomb in the planeport.

As a result of this latter event, any angels who happened to be on Earth at the time were stuck here, without any direction from Heaven. With all due respect, though, it isn't entirely clear that the Mundane Plane was any worse off without Heavenly guidance. On one hand, Tiamat and her minions were very nearly successful in taking over the U.S. government and subjecting the entire population of the world to mind control. On the other hand, we had a solid five-year run during which nobody tried to bring about the apocalypse, which did wonders for property values.

In fact, for some time after Tiamat's latest plan for world domination was thwarted, things were eerily quiet on the Mundane Plane. Tiamat's terrorist organization, Chaos Faction, had been disbanded, and Tiamat herself had disappeared. The other prime candidate for the role of global despot, the archangel Michelle, had apparently gone into hiding as well. Lucifer was no threat, as he was still imprisoned in a dungeon beneath the Celestial City of Heaven, completely inaccessible from the Mundane Plane. And the only other angel with the capacity to wreak havoc on a truly epic scale lacked the will and attention span to do so: I hadn't seen Mercury for months, but if history was any indication, he was probably in a bar somewhere in the tropics, using his miraculous powers to cheat some poor schlub at ping-pong.

Never one to leave well enough alone, though, I began to worry that somebody, somewhere, was up to no good. And that's where all the trouble started.

"The results of this study indicate that the month of September of the year 1994 is to be the time for the end of history.... Look, let's put it this way. My wife came to me and said we needed new linoleum in the kitchen. I told her that we should hold off on the effort and the expense of doing it until October or November of 1994."

— *The Reverend Harold Camping*

Ah, my Beloved, fill the cup that clears
To-day of past Regrets and future Fears
To-morrow? — Why, To-morrow I may be
Myself with Yesterday's Sev'n Thousand Years.

— *Rubaiyat*

CHAPTER ONE

The Apocalypse has a way of fouling up one's plans. To its credit, humanity has done its best to anticipate the End of Days, but lacking any basis for a reliable timetable, they've jumped the gun on more than a few occasions. The Apocalypse's stubborn refusal to arrive on schedule has caused no end of trouble for the people who have volunteered to announce its arrival. Those waiting at the metaphorical arrival gate for the Four Horsemen of the Apocalypse are forced to eat a lot of metaphorical crow. And pay for a lot of metaphorical flooring.

Saint Clement I was one of the first to predict an imminent Apocalypse, around 90 A.D. He went around for several years telling the masses that the end was near. The masses responded by making him into a boat anchor. Once he was out of the way, they were free to replace their old linoleum.

A Roman priest and theologian once used the dimensions of Noah's ark to predict that Christ would return in A.D. 500. When 500 ended with a whimper rather than a bang, he was forced to admit it was time to retile his foyer.

Later Christian scholars argued that Christ would wait for the odometer to flip before returning in glory. Never mind that they were using the wrong year for Christ's birth; if it were up to them, there would have been a massive run on flooring materials at the beginning of the second millennium. The Great Linoleum Shortage of 1001 AD was forestalled only by the near universal inability to read a calendar.

Pope Innocent III was convinced that the Apocalypse would arrive on the 666th anniversary of the birth of Islam. The Pope's regard for Mohammed notwithstanding, the mountain failed to arrive. He gave in and replaced the wood flooring in the Vatican with ceramic tile.

In 1669, The Old Believers in Russia barely avoided an expensive flooring upgrade by immolating themselves. This was before the days of zero-interest financing.

The Jehovah's Witnesses nearly single-handedly prompted the rationing of flooring materials at various points in the late nineteenth and twentieth centuries, with Apocalypses scheduled for 1891, 1914, 1915, 1918, 1920, 1925, 1941, 1975 and 1994.

After two thousand years of this, most people had grown a little jaded regarding the prospect of an imminent Armageddon. Predictions of The End became so common by the dawn of the third millennium that homeowners no longer thought twice about installing new flooring weeks or even days before a scheduled Apocalypse.

Installing new flooring is not in itself necessarily a sign of a lack of faith, of course. A perfectly reasonable argument can be made that if installing new flooring shortly before the End of Days is foolish, then hoarding one's cash is even more so. After all, if the bill will never come due, then why not live a little?

On the other hand, some people simply don't have the means to hedge their bets. Such was the case with Emily and Justin Jelonek of Rochester, New York, who had been saving for new carpet in their living room for three years. After catching a late night infomercial proclaiming the impending Apocalypse, Emily and Justin shelved their dreams of knotted pile, withdrew their savings from the bank, got in their 1992 Dodge Caravan, and drove across the country to rendezvous with the Messiah.

Their son, Lucas, like most fourteen-year-olds, was ambivalent about both carpeting and the apocalypse, but he was decidedly opposed to being dragged across the country when he could be at home playing *Call of Duty*. Thus, despite his age, young Lucas had a perspective on the prophesied Apocalypse that his parents lacked.

"It's all bullshit," he said from the rear of the Caravan. His parents had roused him at three in the morning, so he was even grumpier than usual that morning.

"You'd better not let Reverend Jonas hear you say that!" his mother snapped from behind the wheel.

"Reverend Jonas can blow me," Lucas muttered.

"What did you say?" his mother demanded.

"I said Reverend Jonas is a phony."

His mother glared at him in the rearview mirror, but of course she couldn't make out his features in the near total darkness. Earlier in the trip Lucas's outburst would probably have provoked an impromptu roadside prayer session, but he had calculated that they were now close enough to their destination that he could get away with it with minimal repercussions. In fact, as his mother opened her mouth to respond, his father pointed at a sign up ahead, barely legible in the glow from the Caravan's headlights.

"Mentzel Ranch," his father said. "Isn't that the place?"

Emily Jelonek frowned and the minivan began to slow. She put on her left blinker. "Don't think you're getting a pass on this, Lucas," she said. "There will be a reckoning."

Lucas snorted. His mother liked to use Biblical-sounding language in an attempt to control him, and it occurred to him that this meeting with the so-called "Reverend" Jonas Bitters was a perfect opportunity to call her bluff. His parents would see that this whole Apocalypse business was nonsense, and that Bitters was just some deluded blowhard taking advantage of rubes desperate for meaning in their pathetic suburban lives—people like Emily and Justin Jelonek, in other words.

This belief was borne not merely of cynicism, of which Lucas admittedly had no shortage. On the thirty-hour drive from Rochester, Lucas had spent a fair amount of time on his iPhone researching the man responsible for his current situation: the Reverend Jonas Bitters. Lucas suspected, in fact, that he knew more about Jonas Bitters than his parents did. Either that, or they were even more naive than he thought.

Lucas had learned this was not the first time Bitters had predicted the Apocalypse. A little over a year prior, Bitters was humiliated when he summoned a group of nearly a hundred people—the members of an obscure cult known as The Church of the Bridegroom—to the remote Utah desert to witness the return of Christ. The whole sordid episode had been written up in great detail by a freelance journalist named Christine Temetri. Ordinarily, Lucas wouldn't have paid attention to the author's name, but Ms. Temetri's picture appeared at the bottom of the article, and Lucas found her face oddly captivating in a way he couldn't explain.[1] His research into Jonas Bitters was put on hold for some time while he used Google Image Search in an attempt to find more pictures of the somewhat odd-looking though strangely alluring Christine Temetri, but the results were disappointing. His efforts to determine the present whereabouts of Ms. Temetri were also unsuccessful: it was as if, shortly after writing the article on the Church of the Bridegroom, she had simply disappeared off the face of the Earth.

Frustrated with the lack of data on Christine Temetri, Lucas went back to combing the web for information about the man who called himself First Prophet of the Church of the Bridegroom. He learned that Jonas Bitters was a former recreational vehicle salesman who had, through a combination of spurious scriptural exegesis, excessive reliance on Google's automated Hebrew-to-English translation service and mathematical errors that could have been caught by a bright third grader, happened upon April 29, 2012 as the date for the End of the World. He had also pinpointed the location of Christ's return: a plateau on a desolate piece of land belonging to a rancher named Steve Mentzel, just outside of Elko, Nevada.

As Christine Temetri's article—as well as the continued existence of the material world—indicated, Jonas Bitters and his congregation were disappointed: the Messiah did not return as foretold, and Bitters's flock dissipated, their faith shaken.

Under ordinary circumstances, Jonas Bitters might have been forced to give up his illusions regarding his Divine Purpose and go back to selling Winnebagos. But over the next several weeks, some very strange events came to pass—namely, a sizable section of the city of Anaheim, California disappearing, and a third of the Moon imploding—that caused Reverend Jonas to think that maybe he had been on to something after all. He holed himself up in a Motel 6 in Stockton, California, while he went over his calculations one more time.

---

[1] Only about half of this effect was due to the sudden proliferation of hormones in Lucas's newly pubescent body; Christine had this effect on less excitable males as well.

Reverend Jonas emerged three weeks later, claiming to have identified his error.[2] He called in to a local radio show, publicly begging forgiveness from God and his followers for his error, which he blamed on his "sinful nature" and "prideful conceit." He was, he said, "completely wrong" to think that he could predict the end of the world by relying on "human reason." It was foolish to think the Messiah would return on April 29, 2012. The actual date, he had now been reliably informed, was one year later: April 29, 2013. He insisted that the location, although also presumably determined through the use of "human reason," remained accurate.

It was a testament to the human need to believe in something that Jonas's revised date was rejected out of hand by only 99.2% of those listening. Given that the radio program had an audience of roughly six thousand people, that gave Jonas forty-eight people willing to hear him out. Those forty-eight people become the seed of the newly reconstituted Church of the Bridegroom, which at first met in a defunct Krispy Kreme location in Stockton. With the general unease arising from the quasi-apocalyptic events of the next few weeks, the church grew rapidly and soon had to move to the abandoned Pizza Hut next door.

The most recent article Lucas could find on Reverend Jonas, from a few weeks earlier, indicated that the Church had grown to perhaps three hundred people. There was no telling how many of these people would actually show up in Nevada, of course. It was one thing spend a couple of hours on Sunday holding hands and singing hymns in an old Pizza Hut; it was quite another to haul your ass to a desolate spot in a remote desert in the middle of the night. Lucas would have been surprised to see more than two hundred people there.

So when the Caravan crested a hill and its headlights showed hundreds of cars parked in neat rows ahead of them, his jaw dropped. He had seen smaller turnouts at Bills games his father had dragged him to. Lucas had always possessed a deep suspicion for the tribalistic impulses underlying sports fandom—a sentiment that was reinforced by his father's inexplicable passion for a team that hadn't made the playoffs since before Lucas was born.

---

[2] He had in fact discovered *an* error, but the sheer volume of errors he had committed made that almost inevitable.

"We're late!" his mother fretted, pulling into an empty space between two other minivans. "If we miss Jesus because you had four pieces of sausage for breakfast..."

This imprecation was aimed at Lucas's father, who had insisted they stop at an all-you-can-eat breakfast buffet in Salt Lake City two hours earlier. That indulgence had resulted in an extended stop at a rest area shortly thereafter, during which Justin Jelonek's wife and his digestive system cooperated to remind him that free will is an illusion.

Emily Jelonek turned off the engine and they climbed out of the car. Lucas and his father stood for a moment yawning and stretching in the cold desert air. There didn't seem to be anyone else around.

"Should we get the—" Justin Jelonek started, gesturing toward the lawn chairs and other supplies they had packed in the back of the Caravan.

"We don't have time!" Emily snapped. "It could be starting!" She aimed the small flashlight from her keychain on the ground in front of her and hurried off through the sea of cars. Lucas and his father scurried after her, afraid of being left alone in the dark.

The cars were parked some six rows deep. Just beyond them the driveway was blocked by a gate that had been chained shut. A sign on it read:

MENTZEL RANCH
TRESPASSERS WILL BE SHOT

Lucas's mother squeezed through the gate opening, stepping over the chain, and his father followed.

"So we're just going to, like, ignore the sign?" asked Lucas, pausing in front of the gate. He strongly doubted whether anyone cared enough about this remote parcel of scrub land to waste bullets defending it; his objection was prompted mostly by a desire to irritate his mother.

"Move it, Lucas!" his mother snapped, briefly shining the little flashlight in his eyes before turning and continuing on her way. Momentarily blinded, Lucas scowled and felt his way through the gap. He jogged to catch up to his parents, who seemed more than willing to leave him behind if it came down to it. He'd never seen his mother so worked up.

As they made their way up the low hill beyond the gate, Lucas wondered what it was that his mother thought she was missing exactly. Was she just worried about committing a faux pas, walking in late during Reverend Jonas's presentation? Or did she really believe that Jesus Himself was going to descend from the clouds and call His followers home? He tried to picture the logistics of this scenario. In his research, he'd run across a painting of Jacob's Ladder with angels traversing it, some going up and some going down. Judging by the number of cars he had seen, it would take hours to get all the attendees up a stairway like that, even if Heaven was located at a relatively low altitude. So if that's what she was hoping for, there was no hurry—unless they were only admitting a limited number of people, which seemed pretty un-Jesus-y to Lucas.

The skies were clear, though: no sign of any sort of staircase, elevator, spaceship, or any other mode of transportation that might facilitate the ascension of the faithful. Cynical as he was, some part of Lucas had hoped he would see something, that it wasn't all just bullshit. But of course it was. If there was one thing Lucas had learned in his fourteen years on planet Earth, it was that *everything* was bullshit.

They crested the hill and Lucas found himself looking down on a massive throng of people, several thousand at least, arranged in a rough circle around a low, flat plateau about thirty feet in diameter, which served as makeshift stage. Standing near the edge of the plateau nearest to Lucas was a man whose arms were raised over his head. Ringing the plateau were a dozen electric lanterns on poles, showering the assembly with a garish blue-white light. The man was speaking in assured, comforting tones, although Lucas couldn't make out what he was saying from this distance. Reverend Jonas Bitters, he thought. Lucas had to admit he was impressed. It took balls to pull off something like this, fleecing a bunch of dipshits into following you into the middle of nowhere, employing nothing but charisma and an empty promise.

"Hurry!" his mother called, as he lagged behind, taking in the scene. After a moment, Lucas ran after his parents. He had nearly caught up to them when suddenly they both stopped in their tracks. As they were still a good fifty feet from the edge of the crowd,

Lucas was at first confused. But as he came alongside his father, he saw the reason for their trepidation: something very strange was happening below.

A sort of aura had come over Reverend Jonas, a light that shone directly on his face but which lacked any discernible source. Jonas himself seemed oblivious to the effect, but an eerie hush had overcome the crowd, broken here and there by gasps and murmurs. As the aura brightened, the crowd's agitation increased. Then, apparently prompted by their reaction, Reverend Jonas stopped speaking and held his hands in front of his face, observing the strange glow.

Reverend Jonas at first seemed startled by the effect, but then a smile came over his face. "Beloved!" he exclaimed. "It is happening! The time has come at last!"

"We made it!" Emily Jelonek gushed. "We made it in time!"

Justin Jelonek nodded silently, his mouth open.

Cheers and exultations went up from the crowd. Lucas and his parents stood in awe. Was it true? Lucas wondered. Had Reverend Jonas been right after all? Was this strange transfiguration a sign of the Messiah's impending return?

Reverend Jonas spread his hands, his palms facing the crowd, and the audience fell silent. By now he was glowing so brightly that Lucas had to shield his eyes. "What you are witnessing," Reverend Jonas went on, "is the manifestization... the manifestisizing... mandifizing..." The brilliant figure of Jonas Bitters staggered across the plateau as he tried to regain his train of thought.

"What is happening to him?" Justin Jelonek asked.

Emily Jelonek shook her head.

"What you are witlessing..." Reverend Jonas murmured, barely audible. Then he groaned and clutched his chest as if having a heart attack. Confused murmurs arose from the crowd, and Lucas's parents exchanged frightened glances.

An unpleasant but not unfamiliar sense of disappointment came over Lucas. For a moment, he had allowed himself to believe in Reverend Jonas, to think that this man really did have some sort of mystical connection to an unseen spiritual realm. But it was becoming very clear that Reverend Jonas had not foreseen whatever was happening to him and was helpless to control it. Lucas's momentary disappointment, however, soon gave way to excitement and then morbid fascination. For although the so-called First Prophet had obviously not foreseen what was happening, *something* was happening. Something terrifying—and, Lucas thought, wonderful.

Reverend Jonas was being torn in half.

CHAPTER TWO

Somewhere in a dungeon far below the Celestial City of Heaven; July 10, 2015

"Just do it, you big pussy," said Lucifer.

"*You* do it," retorted Azrael. "Have you ever been run through with a flaming sword? It hurts like hell."

The two demons were conversing in the bowels of Heaven's most secure prison, which was located in a football stadium-sized cavern several hundred feet underground. The cavern, dimly lit by lanterns suspended on long chains from the ceiling, was mostly empty; the two demons were in a roughly fifty-foot-square alcove off the main cavern, which was separated from the main cavern by a wall of thick steel bars. Other than tunneling through three hundred feet of solid rock, the only way out of the prison was to open the man-sized sliding gate in the middle of the wall of bars, traverse the main cavern, open a heavy steel door, climb a steep, winding staircase to the surface, and then open a steel hatch on the surface. The three doors were, of course, locked and could theoretically only be opened from the outside.

These impediments were, however, mostly for show. The real barrier to escape was the coffee-cup-sized obsidian cube that rested on a pedestal twenty paces from the cage opening. Known as a Balderhaz Cube after its eccentric inventor, this device neutralized any attempts at harnessing interplanar energy to perform miraculous feats such as bending steel bars or supernaturally manipulating lock tumblers. So Lucifer and his faithful servant Azrael languished in a dank cave, counting the days of a ten-thousand-year sentence.

That fate was unpleasant enough, but to make matters worse, Lucifer and Azrael shared the cage with six other demons, who spent most of their time bickering, whining, and trying to kill each other.[3] One of these, a demon named Drekavac, was a newcomer, but the others were all long-time minions of Lucifer who had been there since Lucifer's sentencing. Well, would-be minions. There wasn't much in the way of diabolical scheming to be done in a cage inside a cave far underground, and lately Lucifer's grip over his fellow inmates was starting to seem tenuous. Azrael's insubordination was only the latest example.

"That's not how this works," said Lucifer to Azrael, glancing at the group of demons sitting in a circle behind him. "I'm the Prince of Darkness. You do what I say, not vice versa." Lucifer was acutely aware that if he lost control of Azrael, it was only a matter of time before the others turned on him. Fortunately, the rest of the demons were preoccupied at present: they sat in a circle near the back wall, playing some sort of game involving a variety of oddly-shaped dice and an ungodly number of very thick rulebooks.

"I backstab Gurien," announced one of the demons, who was named Pazusu.

"What?" gasped the one called Gurien, who sat across from Pazusu. He turned toward a demon named Drekavac, who was poring over one of the rulebooks. "Can he do that?"

Drekavac shrugged, his eyes still on the book. "You guys can do whatever you want, but Gurien comes first in the initiative order."

"Then I backstab Pazusu," said Gurien, with a grin.

"You can't backstab Pazusu," said Drekavac tiredly. "He's behind you."

"Then I regular stab him."

"Wait!" cried Pazusu to Gurien. "Why are you stabbing *me?*"

"Because you tried to stab me!" Gurien yelled back.

"Yeah, but you don't know that," said Pazusu.

"You just told us, dummy," said Gurien.

"No I didn't," Pazusu protested. He turned to Drekavac. "He's only stabbing me because I was going to stab him, but he can't know I was going to stab him because I haven't had a chance to do anything yet, because it wasn't my turn."

"It's your own fault for not waiting your turn!" shouted Gurien.

---

[3] The latter was technically impossible, as all demons are immortal, but it didn't stop them from trying.

"Oh, so now I can do stuff out of initiative order whenever I feel like it?" said Pazusu. "Fine, then I backstab Gurien again."

"You can't backstab him *again*," grumbled Drekavac. "You haven't done anything yet. It isn't your turn."

"Exactly," said Pazusu, with a smug smile on his face.

Lucifer sighed. On some level he knew it was his own fault he had been thrown in with this gang of idiots; his own paranoia prevented him from hiring any underlings with the intellect to mount a conspiracy against him. Azrael was the closest thing to a strategic thinker of the group.

"Looks to me like you're Prince of Jack and Shit," said Azrael, "and Shit left town." He spoke quietly enough that the others didn't overhear, but the threat was implicit in his words. Lucifer knew it was time to act.

"Watch it," said Lucifer. "You can be replaced, you know."

"Promise?" said Azrael.

"I meant when I get out," said Lucifer through gritted teeth. "I'm going to need a second in command, and I won't brook this sort of insubordination."

"*If* you get out."

"Oh, I'll get out," sniffed Lucifer. "I've got a plan. You think it's just a coincidence the new guard showed up? It's all part of my plan."

Lucifer spoke of the angel who was slowly pacing the perimeter of the area outside the cage, swinging a fiery sword in lazy arcs in front of him. The guard, who went by the name Malcazar, was garbed in the uniform of the Heavenly Incarceration Corps. He had appeared that morning in place of another guard, an angel named Fornaeus. The scuttlebutt was that Fornaeus had gotten in some trouble and had been reassigned.

"What are you saying?" asked Azrael dubiously. "You were behind the change in guards? I don't believe it."

"I've still got spies in Heaven's organization. It took some doing, but I was able to get a personnel change made."

"So this new guy is one of yours?"

"No," said Lucifer, frowning. "They vet these guards too carefully. I can get occasional favors by bribing them,[4] but there's no way any of these guys would knowingly help us escape."

"So what was the point of getting Malcazar appointed in Fornaeus's place?"

"Malcazar is one of the Senate's favorites," Lucifer replied. "Big hero in the Battle of Eden II. They gave him that sword to reward him for his service. It doesn't look familiar to you?"

"Should it?"

Malcazar reached the right wall of the cavern, turned on his heel and began walking toward them.

"That gem in the pommel is a shard of Ubiquium," Lucifer said. "Our new guard is wielding the Sword of Eden."

"You mean the one...?" Azrael began.

"Yes, the one used by the angel to guard the Garden of Eden after God kicked out Adam and Eve. That's the story, anyway. It's mostly rubbish. But the point is, that's a very special sword. If I can get close to that sword, I can get us out of here."

"If you need to get close to the sword, why don't you make him stab *you*?"

"Because, you dolt, I need to be able to concentrate. I'm not going to be able to do that if I'm in excruciating pain from having my insides sliced open." After a moment's thought he added, "Not that, you know, it will be that bad."

Azrael grimaced. "You really think you can get us out?"

"I *know* I can," said Lucifer. "I've memorized an incantation to activate the Ubiquium. If I can get within a few inches of the sword, I can harness the power of the gem to temporarily neutralize the Balderhaz Cube. He gestured toward the black cube on the pedestal on the other side of the cage wall.

"Why does it have to be me?" asked Azrael. "Why not one of these jerks?" He motioned to the group of demons behind them. Lucifer's eyes were drawn to one of the rulebooks in front of Drekavac, the cover of which depicted a motley group of

---

[4] Angels in Heaven have no need of money or most other material things, but Lucifer had wisely hidden several caches of Cuban cigars, single malt whiskey, and Silver Age comic books around Heaven in case of the eventuality that he was ever incarcerated there.

adventurers with medieval weapons gathered around a huge statue of some kind of demonic entity. Two of the adventurers were trying to pry a massive ruby from the statue's right eye. Lucifer vaguely remembered helping to co-author the game sometime in the late 1970s as part of his largely failed effort to corrupt American youth.

"I backstab Gurien and Pazusu while him and Gurien are arguing," said the demon sitting to Drekavac's right. His name was Amalech.

"You aren't even in the same room as them, Amalech," groaned Drekavac.

"I'm in the same room as Amalech, right?" asked the demon on the other side of Drekavac. He was called Salamar.

"Yes," said Drekavac.

"Okay," said Salamar. "I backstab Amalech."

"What did *I* do?" Amalech protested.

"Nothing, said Amalech. But Pazusu backstabbing Gurien is making me suspicious."

"He hasn't done that yet. It's not his turn. And you would have no way of knowing about it if he had. Also, you're unconscious. And giant rats are eating your face," said Drekavac.

"Oh yeah," said Salamar. "Stupid giant rats."

Drekavac turned back to Pazusu and Gurien. "You know, you guys could try attacking the owlbear that's bearing down on you from across the room."

"I don't feel like attacking the owlbear would be true to Pongo the Magnificent's motivations," said Pazusu. "He's chaotic evil."

"You're *all* chaotic evil," Drekavac groaned. "Even chaotic evil characters occasionally have to cooperate. Like when there's a rabid owlbear about to devour you all."

Pazusu thought it over. "I'm not feeling it. I think Pongo would backstab Gurien."

Drekavac began to pound his forehead with his fist.

As the bickering continued, Azrael turned to face Lucifer again. "All right, point taken," he said. "You wouldn't want to rely on these guys for a delicate operation."

"Precisely," said Lucifer. "It has to be you, Azrael."

Azrael sighed, glancing at Malcazar, who was now halfway across the cavern and getting closer. "What do we do after we get past you-know-who? Even if we get out, we're still stuck in Heaven. The planeport was destroyed."

"I'll find us a way off this plane," said Lucifer. "Overcoming the Balderhaz Cube is the hard part. The rest is cake."

"What about these guys?" said Azrael, indicating the demons behind them. "Do we have to take them with us?"

"Unfortunately," said Lucifer, with a distasteful glance at the group of bickering demons, "we're going to need them. Balderhaz has an old lab not far from here where we can hole up and work on getting off this plane. I don't think the authorities know about it, but if they find us we'll need some demons to play defense."

Azrael nodded. Outside the Celestial City, the plane known as Heaven was largely uninhabited, and technically construction of anything larger than a thousand square cubits outside the city limits violated Heaven's notoriously strict zoning ordinances. Some leeway had always been given to the eccentric genius Balderhaz, however, and it was rumored that centuries ago he had set up an underground laboratory in the hills a few miles away.

"How is it you know where this lab is, when the authorities never found it?" asked Azrael.

"I've got better intelligence than they do," Lucifer replied. "Even in here. More foresight as well. I knew Balderhaz had built secret labs on dozens of planes, and some time ago I put some effort into locating as many of them as I could, in case the information ever became useful."[5]

"So your plan is to hide out in Balderhaz's cave while we build a portal to escape Heaven," said Azrael. "You know they're going to send every angel they can find after us, right? You really think this gang of idiots can hold them off?"

"Not for long," said Lucifer, "but they can buy us enough time to get off this plane. Balderhaz's lab should have everything we need to build a portal generator. We just need a few days to put it together." Lucifer glanced through the bars at Malcazar, who

---

[5] Balderhaz himself was thought to be stranded on the Mundane Plane, but his legacy lived on throughout the multiverse, in the form of secret facilities, Balderhaz Cubes, and various other artifacts of his eccentric genius.

continued to approach, now whirling the flaming sword in front of him. Behind Lucifer, the demons continued to bicker.

"His name is Valbard the Destroyer!" Gurien snapped. "If you're going to backstab my character, at least use his name."

"Fine," said Pazusu. "Pongo backstabs Valbard the Douchebag."

Drekavac sighed. "Okay, but Pongo has to wait his turn. And while you're waiting, Pazusu, you might want to reconsider your course of action, since Valbard is the only thing between you and an angry owlbear." He turned to Gurien. "Okay, Gurien. Your turn. What does Valbard do?"

Gurien frowned, evidently uncertain whether he should attack his ersatz teammate or face down the rampaging owlbear. "I think," he said at last, "it would be, um, true to Valbard's motivizations to attack Pongo."

"He can't do that!" Pazusu shrieked. "I charge Valbard with stealing my character's motivations!"

"That's not a thing," said Drekavac.

"Well, it should be," said Pazusu. "I also charge him with acting on information obtained out of initiative order."

"Also not a thing," said Drekavac.

"This game is stupid," Pazusu grumbled. "All the good rules are missing."

"All right, Gurien," sighed Drekavac. "Roll to see if you hit Pongo."

"Wait!" cried Pazusu. "I've had a change of heart. I want to attack the owlbear."

"For like the tenth time, Pazusu," Drekavac groaned, "*it's not your turn.*"

"I know," said Pazusu. "But I just wanted to say, for the record, that when it's my turn, I intend to attack the owlbear."

"So you're not going to backstab me?" said Gurien.

"Nope," said Pazusu. "Pongo has had a change of heart. Much as it pains his chaotic evil heart, he has decided that in this case it is in his interest to cooperate with Valbard to kill the owlbear. Pongo advances to stand alongside Valbard. I mean, he will, when it's his turn."

"For real?" said Gurien. "You're not just saying that?"

"Don't be so paranoid, Gurien," said Pazusu. "I was just fucking with you. I'm not going to backstab you while you're facing down a ravenous owlbear. That would be stupid. If you die, the owlbear is going to attack me next."

"Yeah..." said Gurien doubtfully.

"Oh for fuck's sake, Gurien. I'm not going to backstab you. It was a joke. We're fighting a goddamned owlbear."

Gurien turned to Drekavac. "You heard him. He's not going to backstab me. He's going to attack the owlbear."

"I heard him," said Drekavac.

"Okay, then it's settled," said Gurien. "No more infighting and backstabbing. We're all going to cooperate, at least until the owlbear is dead. Right, Pazusu?"

"Yes, Gurien. Just do your turn."

Gurien nodded and took a deep breath. "I attack the owlbear with my pike."

"Good," said Drekavac. "Roll to see if you hit."

Gurien rolled a die. "Seven," he said.

"Miss," said Drekavac. "Pazusu, your turn."

"Sweet," said Pazusu. "I backstab Gurien."

CHAPTER THREE

Berkeley, California; October 12, 2016

The little red rented Chevy Cruze pulled into a vacant parking space in front of an old Victorian house in residential neighborhood not far from downtown Berkeley. The car's two occupants sat for a moment regarding the house. It wasn't what they expected.

"You're sure this is the address?" asked the slight, nervous-looking man in the passenger's seat. If their intelligence was correct, this was the home of a very old, very rich man.

"It's right there on the house, boss," said the purple-haired woman behind the steering wheel.

The slight man nodded. "So what do we do now?"

"This was your idea, Eddie," said the woman. "I just wrote the algorithm."

"Yeah," said Eddie unenthusiastically. It was true; this whole thing had been his idea. Somehow when he had devised his plan, he had pictured someone else executing it. But it was still just him and Suzy. Suzy was nearly as socially inept as he was, and she was even less personally vested in the project. Eddie suspected Suzy was helping him primarily because she had had trouble finding a job after the Brimstone Incident.[6] Half of the companies she'd interviewed for thought she was a hero and the other half thought

---

[6] Suzy had inadvertently uncovered an illegal government program to develop a so-called 'suitcase nuke.' The bomb was stolen by a terrorist organization called Chaos Faction, led by the demoness Tiamat, who nearly destroyed a medium-sized Midwestern city with it. For more details, see my previous report, titled *Mercury Revolts*.

she was a traitor, and evidently HR departments frowned on both qualities in their software developers.

"It's fine, Eddie," Suzy said, and Eddie smiled. Coming from Suzy, that sentence counted as enthusiastic encouragement, and for a moment he felt better. But then she added, "I mean, what's the worst that could happen?"

Eddie shuddered as he thought about the worst that could happen.

"Sorry," said Suzy. "It's just something people say."

Eddie nodded. "They say it when the worst that could happen is something less extreme than being burned alive. Or eviscerated. Or turned inside out. Or—"

"I get it, Eddie," said Suzy. "I know what demons are capable of. I've met my fair share. But to be perfectly honest, you're just not terribly threatening. Nobody is going to go to the trouble of turning you inside out. And even if they do, you're immortal, right?"

"Being immortal is not actually a selling point when you're inside out," said Eddie.

"I'm just saying, eventually you'd be okay. It might take a few days for your internal organs to slowly work their way back inside, but—"

"Okay, pep talk over!" said Eddie, who was starting to get nauseous.

"Seriously, Eddie," said Suzy, putting her hand on his shoulder. "You'll be fine. Whoever this guy is, if he was up to no good I seriously doubt he'd be hanging out in a residential neighborhood in Berkeley. We don't even know for sure that he's an angel."

"True," said Eddie. "He could be a perfectly ordinary two-hundred-year-old."

"Maybe our information is wrong."

"It's not," said Eddie. "You checked it."

Suzy nodded. "Do you want me to come with you?"

Eddie sighed. "No," he said. "Too dangerous for a mortal. I'll take care of it. Park down the street a ways. If I'm not back in half an hour—"

"You will be, Eddie. It will be fine."

Eddie nodded. He threw open the car door, took a deep breath and stepped out onto the sidewalk. After taking a moment to calm himself, he walked up the steps to the house and rang the bell. A minute or so later he heard footsteps, and then the door opened. A gaunt, pale, wispy-haired young woman answered the door. She had an anxious, almost desperate look about her, like someone in hock to the mob opening an envelope from Publisher's Clearinghouse.

"Hello?" said the woman, blinking in the afternoon sunlight. "Can I help you?"

"Hi," said Eddie. "My name is Eddie Pratt. I'm looking for Marcus, um, Uittenbroek?" Suzy had told him how to pronounce the name, but he still wasn't sure he was getting it right.

"What for?" the woman asked. She glanced behind her nervously.

"Um," said Eddie again. "I'm a journalist doing some research on a company called Hermeticorp. Mr. Uittenbroek seems to be the biggest shareholder of the company, and I was hoping to ask him a few questions. I'd have called, but—"

"No," said the woman. "That won't do. Your name is Glibber Gabilard and you're a palm reader from Neptune."

"Um," said Eddie. "What?"

"Look," replied the woman impatiently, "do you want to see Mr. Ottenbocker or not?"

"Uittenbroek," Eddie corrected.

"Yeah, him. If you want to see him, you're from Neptune, and your name is Bamber Nuttershoots."

"Not Glibber Gabilard?"

"Ooh, that's even better!" the woman exclaimed, suddenly hopeful. "You're good at this. There's a spare room upstairs if you can keep him occupied for a couple of hours. Tony is working on a puppet show for this afternoon. Please, come in!"

Eddie followed the young woman inside. "I'm afraid I don't—" he started.

"My name is Rhonda, by the way. I'm on after the puppet show. I'm going to eat a live eel."

"Good heavens, why?" asked Eddie.

"Boredom," said Rhonda. "It's why we do everything around here."

"You're going to eat a live eel because you're *bored*?"

"*I'm* not bored," said Rhonda. "I'm just lazy. What was your name again?"

"Eddie."

"No!" Rhonda snapped. "You're Gooey Gooblegurkin! Eddie is a *boring* name. You're not allowed to do anything boring. Okay? I know you'll slip eventually and eat a bowl of Cheerios or watch an episode of *The Big Bang Theory*, but try to do it with a hubcap on your head. It doesn't have to be a hubcap. You get the idea."

Eddie didn't get the idea. At all.

"I think there's been some sort of misunderstanding," he said. "I need to see Mr. Uitten—"

"Yeah, I heard you," said Rhonda impatiently. "You want to interview Mr. Boringname about something boring with Boring Company, Limited. It's not going to play, okay? We're right on the edge here. You know what happened the last time Mr. Curry got bored."

"Mr. Curry?" Eddie asked. He didn't think he knew anybody named Curry. Why did that name sound familiar?

"I assume he's your Mr. Neuterbook. People show up once in a while looking for him. He's got a lot of aliases. Usually I just send them away, but frankly I'm a little desperate right now. I mean, Mr. Curry is always a little demanding, but lately—"

"Who was at the door, Rhonda?" called a man's voice from the next room. "Does he have Twinkies?"

"He's got something even better!" Rhonda yelled.

"I do?" asked Eddie.

"Look, you just need to bluff him until the puppet show. Hey, do you play ping-pong?"

"Not well," said Eddie. "Wait a minute. Why do you ask?"

"Mr. Curry loves to play ping-pong. It doesn't really matter if you're any good. He cheats anyway. Of course, it's better if you can make it a challenge for him. Challenges make him drink. And he likes to nap after he drinks. Naps are our friends."

This was all starting to seem oddly familiar to Eddie. "Do you work for Mr. Curry?" he asked.

"Work," said Rhonda, as if she had heard the word somewhere before. "Not unless keeping him entertained is work. And honestly it's getting to the point where I'm thinking it might be easier just to get a real job."

"So that's what you do all day? Try to keep Mr. Curry entertained?"

"*Entertained* isn't really the word," said Rhonda. "Distracted, maybe. He gets in trouble if he has too much time to think."

"I think I know this guy," said Eddie.

"Yeah?" said Rhonda, unimpressed. "Look, if you're going with the journalist ploy, I'm telling you, it won't fly."

"It's not a ploy!" Eddie protested. "I really do want to ask Mr. Uittenbrook—that is, Mr. Curry—about his interest in Hermeticorp."

"You're not hearing me," said Rhonda. "Maybe Mr. Curry is your Mr. Otterbox. Maybe he does own this Hermit Company. But he's not going to want to hear about it. You're going to bore him, and that's a problem, because if he gets bored, he's going to leave. Or worse. And then me and Tony have to find another place to live."

"That's what this is all about?" asked Eddie. "You're freeloaders?"

Rhonda shrugged. "There was a party here like three weeks ago, and some of us just never left. Mr. Curry has been mopey ever since, and he keeps threatening to leave. Or blow the place up. That would actually be better, because then I wouldn't have to get a job. He's done it before, you know. At least that's what my friend Mickey says. They said it was a natural gas explosion, but Mickey was there. We've been trying to keep him distracted."

"Mickey?"

"What?" Rhonda said. "No, Mickey is in Long Beach. We've been trying to keep Mr. Curry distracted. Anyway, you have to leave now."

"Rhonda!" yelled the man from the next room. "Twinkies!"

"I'm telling you," said Eddie, "I know this guy." He made to move to the door, but Rhonda blocked his path. He could easily have moved her out of the way by harnessing interplanar energy to give her a little push, but Eddie tried not to use miracles when it wasn't absolutely necessary.

"Look," he said. "Just let me talk to him for one minute."

"Not if you're going to talk about Boringstock in Boringcompany. We can't risk it." She made an elaborate gesture that somehow communicated the idea of a house exploding.

Eddie sighed. He figured there wasn't any point in trying to be subtle. "Fine," he said. "I wasn't going to do this, but you've forced my hand. Rhonda, I'm an angel. My real name is Ederatz. I used to work for the Mundane Observation Corps. Maybe I still do. It's hard to say, because communications with Heaven have been cut off since Mercury blew up the planeport with the Wormwood nuke. That's your boss's real name, by the way. Mr. Curry is actually Mercury. You know, the Roman god? He got in some trouble with the Apocalypse Bureau for that. They like their agents to keep a low profile, but Mercury has never been very good at that. Not since that business with those oily Trojans inside the wooden horse. He's the one who wrecked the Moon, you know."

Rhonda stared at him for a moment. "Hmm," she said, "I think this just might work. If you can keep up this angel business for a couple of hours, the spare room is yours. At least until…" She made the house-blowing-up motion again.

Eddie nodded and slipped past her. Taking a deep breath, he turned the door handle. He hoped he was right about Mr. Curry. If Mr. Curry wasn't who he thought he was, he was obviously some kind of very dangerous psychopath. Actually he was probably a dangerous psychopath either way. Hopefully the thing about blowing up the house was just his idea of a joke.

The door opened into a large room with a badly scuffed oak floor and walls that were painted a depressing pale grayish-blue. The room was devoid of furniture except for a ping-pong table in the center. It would have been impossible to play ping-pong on the table at present, however, because the table was almost entirely covered with a towering model of a Babylonian ziggurat built out of Twinkies. Leaning over the model, making minute adjustments to the third tier of the impressive structure, was a very tall, silver-haired man.

Mercury.

CHAPTER FOUR

Mentzel Ranch, just outside Elko, Nevada; April 29, 2013

The top half of Reverend Jonas' body seemed to have shifted a few inches to the right, so that it was out of sync with his lower torso. Lucas blinked several times, but the strange effect remained, like a picture that had been torn in half and then sloppily taped back together. From the audience's horrified gasps, it was clear they were seeing the same thing. Reverend Jonas seemed to be puzzled and in some discomfort, but was keeping it together remarkably well for a man who was being split in two.

Between the upper and lower halves of Reverend Jonas, just above his waistline, a sort of rift now appeared, like the ragged edge of the taped-together photo. Through the rift came a glaring white light, like the glow of an acetylene torch—a hundred times brighter than the aura that still lit up Reverend Jonas's face. The rift continued to grow, both in length and in width, and there was a sound like hurricane-force winds tearing through a window. But the air was still, and soon the sound morphed into something like the shearing of a hundred steel beams. Reverend Jonas seemed to be screaming, but it was difficult to make out his face against the glare of the widening rift, and Lucas could hear nothing but the deafening tearing-metal sound.

Transfixed by the scene, Lucas realized he was viewing it through the cracks in his fingers, as some part of his brain had registered the danger of staring into a light of such intensity. Many of those in the crowd, even closer to the phenomenon, had shut their eyes and clamped their hands over their ears. But as Lucas watched, the intensity of the light seemed to diminish a bit even as the rift continued to expand, enveloping more and more of Reverend

Jonas, who was now frozen in place, like a character on a paused video. The volume of the shearing sound faded as well.

Soon the figure of Reverend Jonas had been obliterated completely. It was unclear what had happened to him exactly; it seemed to Lucas as if he had been staring at a photograph of Reverend Jonas behind which someone had been holding a match. The flame had broken through the paper at Reverend Jonas's torso and burned outward, erasing Reverend Jonas and everything in the vicinity. Lucas didn't get the sense that Reverend Jonas had been killed; it was more like he had just stopped *being*. Lucas found himself shuddering at the thought.

"Run!" someone below screamed, and the crowd below began to split up. Lucas was puzzled at first, but he soon realized what was happening: if the rift continued to grow, it would soon engulf those in the front rows of the audience. Evidently having decided there were some limits on the extent to which they were willing to emulate their leader, the assembled members of the Church of the Bridegroom had begun, en masse, to flee. Already some on the periphery had tripped on the uneven ground and were scrambling to avoid being trampled by those in more imminent danger.

Lucas viewed the scene with some amusement. If this really was the end of the world, what did these people hope to accomplish by running away? Did they think God or the Devil had opened a matter-obliterating rift in the cosmos only to spare them if they could manage a respectable time in the hundred-yard dash?

As the terrified congregants began to work their way back to the road, though, Lucas's detached cynicism gave way to concern for his own survival. If he was going to be obliterated by a rift in the space-time continuum, so be it, but he wasn't about to be trampled by a stampede of terrified fanatics.

"Run, Lucas!" his father cried. Lucas nodded and the three of them set off running back to the car. His mother still had her flashlight out, but it was practically worthless, as the road was lit from behind them by the dazzling glow emanating from the rift. Their shadows stretched out before them, obscuring rocks and dips in the road, and the flashlight seemed to do nothing to dispel them. Lucas tried to be cautious, but the crowd was gaining on them, and he made the mistake of glancing back. His foot struck a jagged rock sticking out of the road and he fell.

It was a few seconds before his parents noticed, and the wind had been knocked out of him, preventing him from calling after them. He managed to get to his knees, but as agitated shadows washed over him, he realized the throng was almost upon him.

And then, suddenly, the shadows were gone. Or, more precisely, they were lost in a sea of even bigger shadows: the light behind them had gone out.

The fleeing throng, now blinded, lost its momentum and devolved into a mass of individuals trying to get their bearings in the near-total darkness. Lucas got to his feet and turned to look behind him. It took a moment for his eyes to adjust, but after a few seconds he could make out several dots of light in the distance. He realized it was the lanterns ringing the plateau; from his vantage point higher on the hill, he could just see over the heads of the congregants.

"Lucas, come on!" his mother yelled. She sounded frightened and, Lucas thought, guilty—like a mother who knew her family was in mortal danger, and that it was her fault.

But Lucas felt no need to do her bidding and even less need to reassure her. While his mother continued to bark at him from behind and the crowd milled about confusedly in front of him, he kept his eyes on the area in between the torches. The rift had disappeared, but as his eyes adjusted to the dim light, he could see three figures standing there, in the exact spot from which Reverend Jonas had just vanished. What the hell was going on?

"Lucas!" cried his mother again, now closer to him. Lucas continued to ignore her. He dived into the crowd, his small frame dodging congregants left and right as he worked his way back toward the plateau. Confusion reigned in the crowd; no one seemed to know whether to continue fleeing, return to the plateau to see what had happened, or simply wait for something else to happen. Lucas managed to navigate the chattering masses of people and soon emerged from the other side of the crowd. It was far easier than he expected; apparently the congregants had taken the most direct route away from the plateau rather than try to escape via the road. In the distance, Lucas saw vague shadows of hundreds more people scattered across the desert, apparently just as confused as the group on the road. Some of them seem to still be trying to put more ground between them and whatever had just happened; others had paused to talk or assess their situation. Only one person was walking boldly back toward the plateau: Lucas Jelonek.

Lucas thought that he might find, when he got through the crowd, that the light had been playing tricks on his eyes, but to his surprise he now saw four figures on the plateau. He couldn't make out their features, but he was certain that none of them was Reverend Jonas. All four appeared to be men, but three of them were much taller than Jonas and the third was too short and squat. They had appeared from out of nowhere.

The four figures stood uncertainly, peering into the darkness. The crowd had dispersed too far to be seen from the plateau, but presumably the four figures could hear the uncertain murmuring in the distance. Lucas imagined that wherever they had come from, it had to be rather unsettling to suddenly materialize in the middle of a ring of torches on a desert plateau, surrounded by the confused murmurs of hundreds of people.

A strange sort of cold clarity came over Lucas. Sensing the fear of the people behind him and the fear of the three strange men who had just appeared below, he realized that something momentous was happening, and that whatever happened over the next few seconds would determine how it played out.

"Lucas!" he heard his mother call again from behind, but he pressed on, not listening. He stopped a dozen paces from the base of the plateau and, before the nagging doubts at the back of his mind had a chance to take over, opened his mouth to speak.

"Hey!" Lucas called. "Who are you?"

One of the tall men peered out of the darkness at him. Lucas was just now barely inside the penumbra of light cast by the torches. The tall man turned toward the others and the four conversed for a moment. Then the tall man turned toward Lucas again and took a few steps his direction. Lucas took a deep breath and clenched his fists at his side, expecting at any moment to be vaporized by some powerful alien death ray.

But the man simply walked to one of the lanterns, removed it from its pole, and held it out in front of him. Lucas breathed a sigh of relief: this man was definitely human. He was very tall and his hair had a weird, silvery sheen, but the latter might have been an artifact of the unnatural blue-white light of the lantern. Peering at

Lucas, the man cleared his throat and said, "Is this planet Hooston?"

Lucas frowned, unsure how to respond. The crowd murmured uncertainly in the dark beyond the lanterns.

"Um, what?" said Lucas after a moment.

"I asked if this is planet Hooston," said the tall man. "It's a joke."

"Oh," said Lucas. "I, um, don't get it."

"Can't you see the kid is like twelve?" said one of the other tall men, coming up next to him. Lucas couldn't see the second man very well, but judging from his frame and his voice, he could very well be the first man's brother. The second man went on, "When *Superman II* came out, he wasn't even..." He trailed off and the two men exchanged glances. Then they said, in unison, "Wait, what's the date?"

"April 29," replied Lucas.

"The year!" cried the first tall man. "Tell me the year!"

"Um, 2013," said Lucas.

The two men were visibly relieved by this information. A third man came up alongside them, and they briefly exchanged words. The three had uncannily similar builds. Triplets?

"Then it worked," said the third tall man.

"That was the easy part," said the first tall man.

"Why are all you people on our land?" said the shorter man, coming up behind them. His face was shrouded in shadow as well.

"It's not ours yet," said the first tall man.

"Get out of our yard!" yelled the shorter man, ignoring him.

The first tall man turned and said something to the shorter man, and the shorter man grumbled and walked away. The first tall man held the lantern out in front of him again, peering at the throng of people that was slowly beginning to re-coalesce around the plateau. "Say, what's going on out here?" he said.

"Some kind of campout?" asked the second tall man, as if completing the first man's thought.

"Um, it's a kind of religious thing, I guess," said Lucas. "Supposed to be the end of the world. But I think it's over now."

"Oh yeah," said the third tall man. "The big Apocalypse scare. I almost forgot."

Where did you guys come from?" Lucas asked.

"Not *where*," said the second tall man. "*When*."

"We're from the future," said the third tall man. "But don't worry, we don't intend to stay long. This is just a pit stop."

"We'll be out of your hair in a jiffy," said the first tall man, "and you can get back to your apocalyptic ritual. Although, spoiler alert: the world is still here four years from now."

"We can't go on," said a man's voice behind Lucas.

"Sure you can," said the first tall man. "Seriously, we'll be gone as soon as we get the shard adapter connected to the portal generator. Twenty minutes, max. Then you can get on with your primitive dumbfuckery. Not that I'm judging."

"You killed our leader," said the man, emerging into the light to Lucas's right. "First Prophet Jonas Bitters. I'm his brother, Noah. Technically I'm Second Prophet, but he was entrusted with divine secrets to which I am not privy. We can't continue the ceremony without him."

"Well," said the third tall man, "That sucks. Usually the portal generator will adjust its target location to avoid solid objects. The universe must have had it in for your leader."

"If it's any consolation," the first tall man said, "killing him was an accident. We honestly thought this whole area would be uninhabited."

"Who are you people?" demanded Noah Bitters.

The first tall man, still holding the lantern, walked to the edge of the plateau and stepped off. Gasps went up from the crowd. It was only fifteen feet or so down, but a fall from that height could easily break a leg. The man floated gracefully to the ground, landing a few paces in front of Lucas. The other three men stepped off a moment later, the second tall man on his right and the other two on his left.

"Behind me," said the man with the lantern, indicating the shorter man, who was still on the plateau, "is the famed inventor Balderhaz."

The shorter man gave a wave from the plateau.

"My name is Mercury." Then he moved the lantern in front of the tall man on his left and Lucas saw that there was good reason he suspected the two tall men were brothers: they were identical. The man with the lantern said, "This is my friend Mercury." He moved the lantern in front of the tall man on his right, and Lucas saw that he was identical to the other two. "And this," said the tall man, "is my other friend Mercury."

CHAPTER FIVE

Lucifer's cell; July 10, 2015

"God damn it, Pazusu!" shrieked Gurien, and launched himself over the stack of rulebooks toward Pazusu.

Azrael took a step as if intending to break up the struggle, but Lucifer shook his head. Azrael shrugged and stepped back to continue his conversation with Lucifer. "You're sure the authorities don't know the location of the lab?" asked Azrael.

"If they did," Lucifer replied, "they'd have built a new portal generator themselves by now. You know how desperate they are to reestablish contact with the Mundane Plane and the other planes."

"Maybe they lack the expertise."

"Possibly," said Lucifer. "But if that's the case, they'd have still less interest in locating the lab. Either way, it's unlikely they've found it—and even if they have, it's doubtful they will look for us there."

"But you don't have the expertise to build a portal generator either," said Azrael.

"No," said Lucifer. "But *he* does." He nodded toward Drekavac, who was trying to extricate one of the rulebooks from underneath Pazusu, who was being pummeled in the face by Gurien. Drekavac managed to get the book free but accidentally elbowed another demon in the process, who retaliated by punching Drekavac in the jaw. Drekavac, dazed, swung back, but missed his attacker entirely and stumbled into another demon. Soon the entire group was embroiled in the fracas, each demon punching and kicking whoever happened to be nearby. The quarrel between Pazusu and Gurien had merely been the match on the pile of oil-soaked rags;

demons—particularly those who had been locked in a cage for several years—didn't really need an excuse to engage in violence.

"Who?" asked Azrael, raising his voice slightly to be heard over the fracas. "The new guy?"

"Indeed," said Lucifer. "Believe it or not, our longsuffering Dungeon Master over there is something of a savant with interplanar physics." He motioned toward Drekavac. "I pulled some strings to get him thrown in here with us. If anyone can figure out how to get off this plane, it's him." Drekavac had only been in the cage with them for the past week; an archivist at the Heavenly library, he had been shocked to find himself dragged away from his job without warning, arrested on trumped-up charges and thrown into a cage with Lucifer and his minions. He'd been doing his best to fit in since then, but it was clear he didn't belong with this gang of miscreants.

"I thought he was a librarian," said Azrael doubtfully.

"He was," replied Lucifer. "But five hundred years ago or so, he worked for Balderhaz. They had a falling out, and since then he's worked at the Heavenly Library. At one point, though, he was intimately familiar with the workings of the planeport."

"And you think he has the expertise to build another planeport?"

"Not an entire planeport," said Lucifer. "Just a single portal generator, with a single destination."

"I assume you have another plane picked out," said Azrael. "Where do you plan to go?"

Pazusu had managed to turn the tables on Gurien, having gotten him into a headlock. The other demons continued to brawl around them. Malcazar was now only about twenty paces away, but the acoustics in the cavern were such that even though Lucifer and Azrael were speaking at normal volume, the guard would have a hard time making anything out over the bickering going on behind them.

"Not where," replied Lucifer with a grin. "*When*."

Azrael snorted. "Time travel? It's a myth, Lucifer."

"Not true," said Lucifer. "Balderhaz figured it out. The authorities have suppressed most of the evidence, but I've managed to determine, in theory, how it could be done."

"You're a liar, Lucifer. If you knew the secret of time travel, you wouldn't be stuck in here with us."

Malcazar, flaming sword in hand, stopped in his tracks and turned to study escalating melee, frowning as if he were uncertain whether to intervene. Lucifer and Azrael continued to take no notice of him.

"I said I know in theory how it could be done, not that I can do it at will," Lucifer said, a hint of irritation in his voice. He was doing his best to be tactful with Azrael, but he was more accustomed to intimidating his underlings into submission than having to cajole them into action. He calmed himself and went on, "I've always suspected it was possible, but I never had time to look into it before."

"So that's what you've been doing?" said Azrael. "Researching time travel?" Lucifer had spent much of the past two years poring over ancient tomes from the Heavenly library that he'd bribed guards to deliver to the prison. In fact, it was—ironically—these deliveries that had gotten Drekavac tossed into the pokey with them. Lucifer had arranged for one of the guards to get caught with a sensitive book on the metaphysics of interplanar energy channels, and the guard had rolled over on Drekavac, blaming him for not following proper security procedures. Drekavac was thrown into prison and the guard was replaced by Malcazar—evidently another element in Lucifer's escape plan.

"In part," answered Lucifer. "The key is the—"

He broke off as a Gurien stumbled into him, having been shoved by Amalech. Without taking his eyes off Azrael, Lucifer gripped Gurien's throat with his right hand and hurled him back into the fray. The brawl showed no signs of abating; in fact, it seemed to be intensifying. These free-for-alls happened once every few days, and they tended to go on until Azrael put a stop to them. Inside the Balderhaz Cube's sphere of influence, the demons were incapable of performing miracles, but they remained demons— which is to say, short-tempered, thin-skinned, and capable of absorbing an infinite amount of physical punishment. It wasn't uncommon for them to literally tear each other's limbs off over some minor slight. All their wounds would heal eventually, but in the meantime the scene could get pretty gruesome.

Azrael sighed, observing the escalating violence. "I guess I'd better step in." Azrael was by far the largest and most intimidating of the demons; he tended to dominate the other demons through sheer force of will.

"No," said Lucifer, holding up his hand as Azrael took a step toward the fracas. "This is our chance."

As the melee went on and neither Lucifer nor Azrael showed any signs of stepping in, Malcazar grew impatient. "Get your lackeys under control, Lucifer," growled the guard, holding his flaming sword in front of him.

Lucifer waved his hand dismissively toward Malcazar without making eye contact. "Nothing I can do," he said. "They get rambunctious sometimes."

"Then have your enforcer do it," Malcazar said, pointing the sword at Azrael.

Azrael glanced at Lucifer, who gave him a slight nod. Azrael sighed. "It's not my job to keep your inmates quiet, Malcazar," he said. "Why don't you try doing your job?"

"My *job*?" Malcazar snapped. "Do you know what I was doing before I got summoned down into this rat hole to babysit you goofballs? I was the head of security for Cravutius's security detail. Cushiest job in Heaven. Then one day they tell me I've got to spend the next hundred years in this mother-loving cave."

"Such language, Malcazar!" Lucifer jeered, turning to face the angel. "Careful, boy. If you fall any farther out of the good graces of the Heavenly authorities, they might throw you in here with us."

"You wish," said Malcazar. "In fact, I've already filed an appeal to get reassigned. I never should have been stuck down here in the first place. Some kind of bureaucratic snafu. I'll be out of here in a week."

"Not if you can't keep control of your prisoners," said Lucifer. "Have you considered that this is a test? Your bosses have this cave under surveillance, you know. They're watching you right now, wondering when you're going to get off your ass and do something about this brawl."

Malcazar's eyes went to the ceiling, apparently looking for hidden cameras. Azrael shot a questioning glance at Lucifer, who shook his head. Malcazar returned his attention to the cage. "You in there!" Malcazar he yelled. "Stop that!"

The demons, oblivious to the command, continued kicking, pummeling, scratching, and choking each other. Pazusu still had Gurien in a headlock and was slowly squeezing him unconscious.

"Good show," said Lucifer. "You've practically got them eating out of your hand."

"I don't need your commentary, Lucifer," Malcazar snapped.

"Nobody *needs* my commentary," said Lucifer. "But you have to admit, it adds color. Speaking of which, have you ever seen anyone's face turn that shade of purple?"

As they watched, Gurien's body went limp, but Pazusu continued to squeeze.

"I heard the Senate was going to summon Gurien for questioning today," Lucifer remarked to Azrael. "Of course, that's going to be difficult if his—" As he spoke, Gurien's head popped off his body, his neck torn in half by Pazusu's brawny arm. Pazusu gripped the head by the base of the skull and jaw, tore it completely free and hurled it against the bars of the cage. It bounced off the bars with a clang, then rolled into the center of the fracas. Another demon picked it up and hurled it at one of his fellows. Meanwhile, blood continued to spray from Gurien's severed neck arteries. Pazusu gave a triumphant screech. "Try backstabbing me now, bitch!" he howled, then turned and attacked another opponent seemingly at random.

"Feel free to intervene anytime you think things have gotten out of hand," Lucifer said to Malcazar.

"Tell them to stop!" barked Malcazar. "They listen to you!"

"Tell them to stop or what?" said Lucifer.

"Or," Malcazar said, pointing the fiery sword at Lucifer, "Or you know what!"

"A tough guy, huh?" said Azrael, glancing at Lucifer with a *this-had-better-work* look on his face. "Why don't you try that sword on me?"

"Don't think I won't!" snapped Malcazar.

"You wouldn't dare," said Lucifer. "You don't have the balls to stab Azrael in the abdomen with that sword. Not even through the bars of this cage. I heard about you in the Battle of Eden II. You hid behind a bush for most of the battle and then came out when the fighting was over. Accidentally stumbled over the enemy general's corpse. You almost fainted because you can't stand the sight of blood. Maybe your bosses heard the same story."

"That's a lie!" Malcazar cried. "I slew a hundred men in that battle! They gave me this sword as a reward!"

"I wouldn't get to attached to it," said Azrael. "Anyone who won't even stab an unarmed man in a cage doesn't deserve a fancy sword like that."

"Oh yeah?" said Malcazar, eyeing Azrael. "Watch this!" He took a step forward, drawing his sword back along his side in preparation to attack.

Azrael winced as he saw the blade coming, but rather than back away, he gripped the bars and gritted his teeth. Malcazar thrust the sword through the bars, right below Azrael's solar plexus. The point emerged from Azrael's lower back and he screamed. The sound was remarkable, somewhere in between the roar of a lion and the bellow of a foghorn. The combatants behind them suddenly stopped what they were doing and turned to see what had made that sound. Azrael's face was contorted, and he was now staring wordlessly at Malcazar, who seemed nearly as shocked as he was.

Only Lucifer retained full control of his faculties. He lunged forward, reaching through the cage to get his hand on the pommel of the sword. To his surprise, Malcazar's hands went limp, and Lucifer had no trouble getting the hilt away from him. Glancing at Malcazar, Lucifer saw that the angel's face had gone white as chalk. Could it be? Were the rumors true? Apparently the brave Malcazar really *did* get queasy at the sight of blood. This was going even better than expected!

Malcazar reeled, looking as if he was about to pass out. Meanwhile, Azrael, with the sword still protruding from his midsection, stumbled backwards toward the other demons, who dumbly retreated. It was one thing to see Gurien's head ripped clear of his body; it was another to witness the invincible Azrael impaled by a flaming sword.

"I've got you, Azrael," said Lucifer comfortingly, taking a step toward the big demon. But if Azrael was hoping for gentle treatment, he was disappointed. Lucifer planted his right heel on Azrael's hip, gripped the sword hilt with both hands, and gave it a jerk.

Azrael screamed again. The sword, its flame sizzling with blood and Azrael's intestinal juices, came free, and Azrael's eyes rolled up into his head. The giant demon fell like a tree to the floor of the cage. The other demons continued to stare, uncertain what to make of the situation. On the other side of the cage, Malcazar was sitting on the cave floor with his head between his knees, apparently trying not to lose consciousness.

Lucifer held up the sword triumphantly. "Witness the fruits of months of planning!" he cried. "I present to you the Sword of Eden!" He held the sword in the air momentarily for effect.

"I don't get it, boss," said Pazusu after a moment. "What good is a sword going to do in here?"

Lucifer grinned at them, lowering his arm. He turned the sword upside down and stuck his thumbnail under the gem on the pommel. With some effort, he wrenched it free, and then tossed the sword aside. It clattered to the ground next to Azrael, who lay moaning and clutching the wound in his belly.

"The sword is worthless," said Lucifer. "But this!" He held the gem between his thumb and forefinger, closing his left eye to regard it with his right. "This is a piece of..." He trailed off, examining the gem. "Shit!"

"What... what's wrong?" Azrael gasped. His eyes were open and some of the color had returned to his face. Even inside a Balderhaz Field, angels healed quickly.

"It's a fake!" Lucifer shrieked. "You son of a bitch! All that planning for nothing! The gem is a fake!" He hurled the gem through the bars of the cage, and it landed with a clatter somewhere in the cavern. He turned and picked up the sword, examining its length closely. "This isn't even the real Sword of Eden!"

Malcazar's shoulders began to quiver, and after a moment Lucifer realized the guard was laughing.

"What the hell is so funny?" Lucifer demanded. "They cheated you! Your sword is a fake!"

Gripping one of the bars, Malcazar slowly pulled himself to his feet, still chuckling to himself. "Of course it's a fake, you blockhead," he said. "You think the Senate would give me the real Sword of Eden, even if they had it? I'm a big deal, but I'm not *that* big a deal. Gosh, I guess it really is true what they say."

"Oh," said Lucifer coldly. "And what's that?"

"The devil is in the details," replied Malcazar with a smile. "Sorry, Lucifer. You and your pals are going to be here for a very, very long time."

CHAPTER SIX

Eddie breathed a sigh that expressed equal parts relief and resignation. His hunch was correct. "Mr. Curry" was his old friend Mercury.

"So it is you," said Eddie, observing the impressive structure. "I should have known."

"Are you the Twinkie guy?" Mercury asked, without looking up. "I need three hundred more to finish the top."

"Sorry, Mercury," said Eddie. "I don't have any Twinkies."

"Well, it's going to be a pretty sad-looking ziggurat," said Mercury, still not looking up. If he recognized Eddie, he showed no sign.

"Yeah, that's too bad," said Eddie. "So, I wanted to ask you about some stock that you—"

"I say it's going to be a sad-looking ziggurat," said Mercury.

"I heard you," said Eddie. "Suzy is in the car outside. You remember Suzy, right? We tracked you down by—"

"Yep, pretty sad looking ziggurat."

"Uh-huh. Seriously, Mercury, I know this is important, but Suzy and I have been working on—"

"You're not going to ask me why it's a sad-looking ziggurat?"

Eddie sighed. It was pretty clear he wasn't going to get Mercury's attention until he had paid appropriate homage to the Twinkie edifice. "Why is it a sad-looking ziggurat, Mercury?" he asked, and then winced in anticipation.

"Because it's in tiers!" Mercury exclaimed. He grinned at Eddie. "Hey, do I know you?"

"Yeah, we've saved the world together a few times. Well, you did most of the work. I helped occasionally."

"Cool, cool," said Mercury. "You're not one of those hubcab-wearing freaks, are you? I like this town, but what is it with the people wearing hubcaps on their heads? And the interminable puppet shows! I try to be accommodating to the mentally challenged, but I swear on this stack of Twinkies that if have to sit through another puppet show..." He made the house-blowing-up gesture.

"Are you seriously threatening to blow up this house because of a puppet show?"

"Blow up the house?" Mercury asked, examining his hands. "I thought I was threatening to make banana bread."

"You might want to work on your hand signals. You're frightening the natives."

"Eh," said Mercury. "Fuck those guys. Freeloaders, all of them."

"Why do you keep them around then?"

"I'm terrified of being alone," said Mercury.

"Really?"

"No, not really," replied Mercury. "But somebody's got to do the Twinkie shopping, don't they? Also, between you and me—" His voice dropped to a whisper. "—I kind of like some of the puppet shows. I get bored sometimes."

"So I hear," said Eddie. "Ennui got you down again?"

Mercury shrugged. "You know how it is. The first seven thousand years are always the toughest. Hey, aren't you that MOC guy?"

"Yeah," said Eddie. "Ederatz. Of course I haven't had any contact with Heaven for a while. Or any other angels, really, since we thwarted Tiamat's last plan for world domination."

Mercury nodded. "Good times. I thought you looked familiar. What time is it?"

"Uh," said Eddie. "Around eleven?"

"Okay, cool," said Mercury. "Puppet show isn't until one. Let's get drunk." He turned and went through another door. Eddie followed, and found himself in a much more luxuriously appointed room. Lush carpet covered the floor and burgundy leather armchairs sat around a glass coffee table. Mercury flopped into one of the chairs. "Rhonda!" He barked.

Eddie sat down across from him. A moment later, Rhonda appeared with a Sierra Nevada bottle in each hand.

"You read my mind, Rhonda," said Mercury. "Have you met Eddie? He helped me save the world once."

"Four times," Eddie muttered. "Not that I'm counting."

"That's fantastic!" exclaimed Rhonda in a patronizing, pseudo-enthusiastic tone. "Do you know where I can get a live eel?"

"If I did, I wouldn't tell you," said Mercury. "Where's your hubcap?"

Rhonda put a hand to her head, reddened, and ran out of the room.

"So, what brings you to the neighborhood, Eddie?"

"An algorithm, actually," said Eddie. "You remember Suzy Cilbrith?"

"Sure," said Mercury. "Cute girl. Purple hair. A little extra padding where it counts. Programmer on the Brimstone project."

"Yeah," said Eddie, a bit nonplussed by Mercury's comprehensive recall regarding Suzy. Eddie had known Mercury for literally thousands of years, and every time they met he had to re-introduce himself. "Anyway, I got to thinking, after the Brimstone thing, that maybe it would be a good idea to catalog all the angels and demons still on the Mundane Plane. I mean, Tiamat and Michelle seem to have gone underground, but I don't want to get surprised again. If we can reestablish contact between the good angels, maybe we can forestall the next evil plot before it hatches."

"Hmm," said Mercury, taking a swig of his beer.

"Anyway, I asked Suzy if she could help me find the other angels. I figured that there had to be signs, ways of identifying patterns in a person's behavior that would mark them as an angel."

"Like what?"

"Well, I've been watching the news for miracles, but there's so much ridiculous tabloid reporting these days that it's almost impossible to tell when an actual miracle happens. Suzy's been helping me narrow the results by cross-referencing news reports with other data. The problem is that other than miracles, the main sign is actually a *lack* of data, specifically no birth record and no death record. So we had to—"

"Gaaahhhh!" Mercury suddenly cried. "The crushing boredom has returned! Rhonda, beer!" He downed the rest of the bottle and set it down next to him. A moment later, Rhonda ran into the room with a hubcap on her head and a beer in her hand.

"Good girl, Rhonda," said Mercury. "Take that hubcap off your head. It looks ridiculous."

Rhonda nodded, removed the hubcap, and retreated from the room.

"The point is," said Eddie, "it turns out to be incredibly difficult to find an angel unless he does something really out of the ordinary, and there's some kind of paper trail. For example, if an individual somehow bought three hundred shares of a company in 1837 and still owns them."

"The great thing about this story," said Mercury, "is that just when you think it can't get any more boring, it totally does." He took a swig of beer.

Eddie went on, undeterred. "In 1837, a man named Marcus Uittenbroek bought three hundred shares of a company called Quicksilver Fabrication, which was later renamed to Hermeticorp. SEC records indicate that this Marcus Uittenbroek is still the owner of these shares, one hundred eight years later. Since the initial purchase, the stock has split sixteen times. Would you like to guess how much those shares are worth today?"

"Not unless you're going to give them to me."

"Mercury," said Eddie, "you're Marcus Uittenbroek."

"I am?" asked Mercury, staring at his knees as if they held the key to his identity.

"I'm fairly certain," said Eddie. "This is the address I found for Mr. Uittenbroek. Also, if I'm not mistaken, the name Uittenbroek is Dutch for 'out of his pants.'"

Mercury chuckled. "Yeah, I thought it would be funny to... hey, you're right! I did use that name for a while! I *am* Marcus Uittenbroek!"

"Yes," said Eddie. "And you're rich."

"How rich?" Mercury asked.

"800 million dollars, give or take," said Eddie.

"Wow," said Mercury. "I'm no monetologist, but that sounds like a lot."

"It is," said Eddie.

"Huh," said Mercury. "I don't even remember buying that stock."

"Maybe you won it in a bet or something."

Mercury nodded. "That sounds like me."

"Anyway," said Eddie, "I'm relieved to find it's you. We figured Marcus Uittenbroek was an angel, but we didn't know which one. Could have been Lucifer for all we knew."

"Except he's still in prison, right?" asked Mercury, unable to completely hide his concern with his facade of disinterest.

"As far as I know, yes," said Eddie.

Mercury nodded and took another swig of beer. "Of course he is. He'll never get out." Mercury sounded like he was trying to convince himself as much as reassure Eddie.

"I would think not," said Eddie. "But Lucifer's not the only demon to worry about. There's Tiamat, for starters. And we don't know what Michelle or Gabrielle are up to."

Mercury shrugged.

"As I was saying," Eddie continued, "We didn't know who Marcus Uittenbroek was, but we knew he was an angel and that he had a lot of money. A sympathetic angel with a lot of money could be a great ally to us."

"Hmm," Mercury said again.

"Yes, well," Eddie went on. "I realize you're not really a team player, but your fortune could really help us in our efforts to locate the other angels on this plane. It's just been me and Suzy for the past six months, and finding you is the first break we've had. I think if we could hire more people—researchers, investigators, programmers, et cetera—we'd have better luck. We've been working out of a tiny office in Baltimore, and the only way I can even afford that is by selling a gold brick every few weeks."

"Transmogrification," Mercury said. "The oldest trick in the angel book. They'll catch up to you eventually, you know."

"That's what I'm saying," said Eddie. "I've got no other way to make money. I mean, other than actually *making* money."

"Counterfeiting is even worse," said Mercury. "Governments hate competition."

"So you see the problem. Your eight hundred million dollars would be a huge help. And since you don't seem to be using it...."

"Why are you so interested in connecting with the other angels, Eddie? Why not just leave well enough alone?"

"I told you," said Eddie. "Eventually Tiamat or Michelle or somebody is going to start getting ideas again. You know how these people are. We need to be ready."

"To do what? Play the hero? Haven't you had enough of that, Eddie? Has it occurred to you that these angels are less dangerous when they're scattered all over the world with no way to contact each other? By reconnecting them, you might create the very conspiracy you're trying to prevent."

"I guess I'm not that cynical," said Eddie. "Most angels are well-intentioned."

"Ugh," said Mercury. "The well-intentioned ones are the worst. Give me a power-hungry psychopath over a well-intentioned angel any day."

"Well, take your pick," said Eddie, who was starting to get irritated. "We've got one of each."

Mercury sighed and glanced at Eddie. Mercury knew exactly what he was talking about: Tiamat, with her psychotic drive for world domination, was bad enough, but now Michelle had gotten it into her head that it was her destiny to be Earth's benevolent despot. Michelle's intentions were always good, but the end result was the same.

"I know you don't want to think about it, Mercury," said Eddie, "but if we don't set up some kind of organization to thwart the next attempt at world domination, nobody is going to do it. You know how most angels are. They're lost without direction."

"Good point," said Mercury, nodding. "And that's exactly why this is a terrible idea."

CHAPTER SEVEN

Philadelphia, Pennsylvania; October 12, 2016

True to form, at the very moment Eddie was pleading for Mercury's help, Tiamat was in a warehouse in Philadelphia, hatching her latest plan of world domination. If Eddie had known the nature of the plan or whom she was sharing it with, however, he might not have been so anxious to counter it.

"I'm going to buy up all this worthless land here," Tiamat said, pointing at a highlighted area on a blurry photocopied map of California and Nevada. "The nukes will hit here and here. If we hit the fault line just right, the land to the west should fall into the ocean, and we'll be sitting on a million acres of oceanfront property."

Two men and a woman sat on crates around the discarded cable spool Tiamat was using as a table, studying the map with interest. As most of Tiamat's minions had been apprehended by the federal authorities after the Brimstone Incident, she had never worked with these three before, so she was acutely aware of the need to impress them with the boldness of her plan. When she finished speaking, an awkward silence filled the vast, empty warehouse. The three glanced at each other uncertainly.

"Well," said Tiamat at last. "What do you think?"

After another long silence, one of the men spoke up. He was a burly, swarthy-skinned man who wore an adhesive name tag that read:

Hello!
My name is
Zicandar

Tiamat had made them all wear nametags so she could keep them straight.

"Do you *have* two nuclear bombs?" he asked.

"Not yet," said Tiamat. "We're going to steal them."

"From who?" the man labeled Zicandar asked.

Tiamat waved her hand dismissively. "Details," she said.

"I don't think that's how fault lines work," said the other man, a pale, lanky guy apparently called Iriblis. "California isn't just, like, a sheet of ice floating on the ocean. If you detonate nukes on a fault line, California will still be there. You might move it an inch or two, I guess."

"And aren't you worried about fallout?" said the woman, who was labeled Mermera. Mermera was compactly built and had a stern face. Her shoulder-length black hair was pulled tightly into a ponytail behind her head. "You can't just detonate a couple of nuclear warheads and then build a five-star resort at ground zero. It'll take hundreds of years for the radiation to get down to a tolerable level."

Tiamat glared at them for a moment, but then allowed her visage to soften. "Very good!" she said. "That was just a test to see if you three had the smarts to execute the actual plan, which has nothing to do with nuclear weapons or fault lines at all. Congratulations, you all passed!"

The three shrugged and exchanged glances, clearly not appreciating the value of Tiamat's praise. "So what's the real plan?" asked Zicandar.

"Excellent question," said Tiamat with a nod. "Very good. Right down to business. Let me ask you gentlemen a question: do you know anything about computers?"

The three stared at her. "You mean like programming?" asked Zicandar. "Or hardware engineering, or what?"

"I know some Javascript," said Mermera.

Tiamat sighed and shook her head. "I can see I will need to start at the beginning." She pulled a sheet of paper from a manila folder in front of her and placed it on top of the map. It was a sheet that appeared to have been torn from a very old book, perhaps an encyclopedia. Most of the page was taken up by a black and white photo of a young woman in go-go boots feeding a punchcard into a machine the size of an industrial freezer. "This, gentlemen," Tiamat said, pausing for effect, "is a *computer.*"

The three exchanged nervous glances again, as if uncertain whether they were expected to laugh.

Tiamat went on, "You see, large corporations use computers to allocate funds to different accounts. In many cases, the amount being transferred can't be expressed as an exact dollar value, so the computer has to round the value to the nearest penny. Nobody notices the rounding because the amount being added or subtracted is so small, but these transactions occur millions of times a day, and it adds up to a lot of money. So what we're going to do is—"

"Program the computers to transfer all those fractions of a cent into an account that we control," said Iriblis.

Zicandar nodded. "This is like the oldest scam ever. You'd never get away with it."

"Also, it's bullshit," said Mermera. "I mean, maybe computers forty years ago didn't have the capacity to store amounts beyond two decimal places, but these days it's trivial. Hell, my phone can do it. You'd be shaving off billionths of a cent, *at most.* If you had root access to every computer used by every Fortune 500 company in the world, you might make a nickel a week. If you didn't get caught, which you would."

Tiamat stared daggers at Mermera. She was so angry she was shaking. But she forced herself to close her eyes for a moment and take a deep breath. "Very good," she managed to mutter after some time. "That too was a test."

"Why don't you just tell us the actual plan?" said Zicandar. He and the others were clearly getting bored.

"Yes, yes," said Tiamat. "The actual plan. I suppose the time for tests has passed. Very well. What we are going to do is create an entirely new continent in the middle of the Pacific Ocean. You see, all we have to do is locate a substance that causes matter to duplicate—"

"Out of curiosity," said Iriblis, "Do you have any nefarious plans that *weren't* stolen from Superman movies?"

"I haven't a clue what you mean," Tiamat sniffed.

"Why doesn't that surprise me?" muttered Mermera.

There was a buzz from inside Zicandar's jacket, and he held up his finger and pulled out a phone. Tiamat glared at him.

"Burton," he said into the phone. "Yeah, she's here, but I don't think she's... of course I've got the box. Take it easy, D'Angelo. I can follow orders. I'm just saying, unless you want a recap of *Superman Returns*, I don't think she has anything to offer us... No, that's *Man of Steel*. Brandon Routh. How the fuck should I know? Check Rotten Tomatoes for fuck's sake. Amy Adams. Yeah, I'm with you. Cute as a button. All right, I should go, she's getting pretty pissed. See you back at the office." He slid the phone back into his jacket. When his hand appeared again it was holding a Glock nine millimeter semiautomatic pistol. With his other hand, he produced a wallet, flipping it open to show a badge that read: FBI. The other two men produced guns as well.

"Oh, how amusing," said Tiamat, but she sounded more irritated than amused. "An FBI sting operation."

"I'm Special Agent Taylor Burton," said the man labeled *Zicandar*. "These are agents Chad Rogers and Kristin Dexter. You're under arrest, Ms. Midford. Or whatever your name really is."

Tiamat sighed. "I supposed I should have known posting a Craigslist ad for demonic henchmen would attract the wrong element. Are you guys even demons?"

"No," said Burton. "The FBI doesn't hire demons, to my knowledge."

"Where did you get the names?"

Burton reached into his backpack, pulled out a dog-eared paperback book, and tossed it onto the table. The cover read: *Demonology for Total F***ing Imbeciles.*

"Should have known," Tiamat muttered. "That damn book causes me more problems. It's the only one on the market that actually has some solid information about demons."

"Demons aren't real," said Burton. "Sorry to disappoint you."

Tiamat leaned back in her chair—and then remembered that her chair was actually a wooden crate. She caught herself before tumbling to the floor, and made an admirable though ineffective effort to pretend she had been stretching. When she had recovered her composure, she replied, "Oh, but they are, Special Agent Burton. And you're also wrong to think I'm disappointed. Do you recall what the ad said would happen to non-demons who responded?"

"Of course," said Burton. "The ad promised that any mortal beings who showed up would be—and I quote—'turned inside out'. I assumed it was a figure of speech."

"You assume too much," replied Tiamat with a smile. "Turning people inside out is one of my favorite punishments. I never get tired of it. I'm just surprised that any human being would volunteer for the treatment."

Burton shrugged. "Give it your best shot," he said.

Tiamat smiled at him. "You know," she said, "they say that pain is the best teacher. I'm going to make a believer out of you, Special Agent Burton." She raised her right hand as if about to cast a spell. "For the ten seconds you have left on this planet, you're going to know that demons are real."

CHAPTER EIGHT

Eddie frowned at Mercury. "I don't understand," he said. "Why is organizing the angels a terrible idea?"

Mercury sighed. "What are we going to do with these angels once we get them all together? As long as they're scattered all over the world, they're mostly harmless. But if we recruit them to join Eddie's Angels, suddenly we've got to have something for them to do. If you don't, someone else will. So what's that going to be, Eddie? You going to retrieve cats from trees? Stop earthquakes? Intervene in wars? Prevent genocide? Thwart a coup, or maybe foment one? With that kind of power, you're going to have to make some pretty tough calls. And like it or not, you're going to end up involved in politics. People are going to look to you for solutions. Do you want that responsibility, Eddie? Do you think you can handle it?" Mercury took a swig of beer and shook his head. "If it's true that I've got $800 million in the bank, I'm going to give it away. I'll donate it to Doctors Without Borders or Nurses Without Boundaries or something. I don't want that kind of power."

"I get what you're saying, Mercury," said Eddie, "but we don't have the option of doing nothing. You know that Tiamat is working on something right now. Probably Michelle too. We'll find out about it after the nefarious plot is already well underway. You'll try to stay uninvolved, like you always do, but in the end your conscience will overcome your apathy and you'll save the day. You're not as unpredictable as you like to think you are. I'm just asking you to put a little planning into what you're going to end up doing anyway. You save the world, Mercury. It's your thing."

"No," Mercury corrected, "my thing is saving the world begrudgingly, with minimal forethought and an immense amount of style."

"It's really the first part that matters," said Eddie.

"Says you," replied Mercury. "I'm sticking with the full package. It's worked for me so far."

"So far, yes," agreed Eddie. "But what if this time you're too late? Is it really worth it to risk the world just so you can maintain your slacker image?"

"It's not an image," said Mercury. "I'm fully devoted to the slacker lifestyle." He let out a groan. "You know what we need?"

"What?" asked Eddie.

"An adult."

"You're seven thousand years old, Mercury. I think you qualify."

"Only on paper. I'll admit that I'm the smartest, bravest, most heroic, and apparently richest angel on Earth. But I don't want to be in charge of anything. I'm not cut out for it. I'm not sure any of us are."

"What are you saying?"

"As much as I hate to admit it," said Mercury, "Heaven is a stabilizing influence on this plane. Yes, there was the whole apocalypse thing, but that was an anomaly. For seven thousand years, the authorities in Heaven kept pretty good tabs on this place. Michelle has an authoritarian streak, but you have to admit she's largely been a positive influence. She just needs guidance."

"You want to try to reestablish contact with Heaven," said Eddie.

"I don't *want* to do anything," said Mercury. "But it's like you said. If we don't do it, someone else will. Imagine if Tiamat figures out a way to travel to other planes while the rest of us are still cut off from Heaven, with no way to call for reinforcements. Sure, she could do some damage if she managed to rebuild Chaos Faction with whatever demons are still running free, but the real risk is that she finally discovers the secret to interplanar travel. She could recruit demons from all over the multiverse and bring them here."

Eddie nodded, his brow furrowing. "But nobody knows how to build a portal generator except Balderhaz, and he's disappeared as well."

"'Disappeared' is a subjective term," said Mercury.

"You know where he is?"

"I think I could get a hold of him if I needed to."

"Okay," said Eddie, thinking it over. "I can see the value of focusing on building a portal generator rather than trying to locate the other angels. But if you really think it's a good idea, why haven't you started on it yet? Why haven't you already contacted Balderhaz?"

"Denial, I guess," said Mercury. "Also, a project like this will take a lot of money. And I didn't know I was loaded until five minutes ago."

Eddie nodded again, rubbing his chin. Mercury was actually making some sense. If Balderhaz really could reestablish contact with Heaven, it might be their best bet for keeping Tiamat under control. Suzy would probably be a little disappointed they wouldn't be using her algorithm after all—but at least it had gotten them to Mercury, and Eddie was sure they'd find some other use for her.

"All right," Eddie said. "Let's do it your way. When can we get started?"

"Well," said Mercury. "First we need to find Balderhaz."

"Okay, how do we do that?"

"You have to understand," said Mercury, "he may not want to be found."

"I understand," said Eddie. "But you have some way of reaching out to him?"

"Well, yes," said Mercury. "It's not a foolproof means of communication by any means, but I can give it a shot."

"Got it," said Eddie. "So... should we come back tomorrow? Or, like, next week?"

"What?" asked Mercury, furrowing his brow. "No. It shouldn't take that long. It's not that big of a house." He took a deep breath and bellowed, "Balderhaz!"

"Hang on," said Eddie. "You're saying that he's—"

"Shh!" Mercury hissed, cocking his head as if to listen.

There was no sound for some time. Mercury sighed. "That's what I was afraid of. He doesn't want to be found. You take the upstairs, and I'll take this floor. And if you find him, don't make any sudden movements. He spooks easily."

Eddie nodded, getting up from his chair. Before they reached the door, it opened and Rhonda came in. "Did you say something, Mr. Curry?" she asked.

"Yes," said Mercury. "We need to find Balder—I mean, Mr. Baldwin. You check the basement."

Rhonda nodded and turned to leave.

"Oh, and Rhonda?" said Mercury. She stopped and turned to face him.

"If we don't find him in the next twenty minutes..." Mercury said, and then made the house-blowing-up motion.

Panic came over Rhonda's face and she turned and fled from the room.

Mercury gave Eddie a puzzled glance. "What is it with people and banana bread?" he asked.

CHAPTER NINE

Tiamat's smile faded, and was replaced with a look of exasperation. "How are you doing that?" she asked.

"Doing what?" asked Burton.

"Interfering with my ability to harness interplanar energy! You shouldn't be able to do that!" She paused. "Unless..."

"Unless what?" asked Burton.

"Unless you have a Balderhaz Cube."

"Is that what it's called?" asked Burton. He reached into a backpack that lay against the crate he was sitting on and pulled out a metal box about the size of grapefruit. As Tiamat watched in dismay, he set the box on the spool, flipped a catch, and opened it. He pulled out fist-sized obsidian cube and set it on the spool next to the box.

"Where did you get that?" Tiamat growled.

"I got it from my boss. He said it would render you harmless. Frankly, though, you look pretty harmless anyway."

"Do I?" said Tiamat with a smile. She almost tried to lean back in her chair again, but caught herself in time. "In that case, perhaps we can agree on a friendly wager. Do you work out, Special Agent Burton?"

Burton shrugged again. "I try to stay in shape."

"It shows," said Tiamat. "How would you like to arm wrestle me?"

Burton frowned. "I'm not going to arm wrestle a middle-aged woman."

"Why not? Afraid you're going to lose? Tell you what, if you win, I'll come with you willingly and tell you everything I know. If I win, you let me go."

"And what do you know that's so valuable?" asked Burton.

Tiamat smiled. "Nice try, Special Agent Burton. You find that out *after* you beat me. Obviously your boss thinks I know something or he wouldn't have sent you after me."

"My boss thinks you had something to do with the Myrmidon plot. Says you spearheaded the whole mind control chip thing. But then, my boss didn't just hear you pitch us the plots from three different Superman movies."

"I'm in a regrouping phase," Tiamat said, trying not to sound defensive.

"Clearly," replied Burton. "As you've been reduced to posting 'minions wanted' ads on Craigslist."

Tiamat chuckled. "Oh, you are precious, Special Agent Burton. Do you really think I posted that ad in an attempt to attract demonic henchmen to my cause? This was merely a ruse to gauge the FBI's response. The fact that you are here tells me that you have no clue about the actual plot that is unfolding even as we speak."

"You're bluffing," said Burton.

"Am I?" asked Tiamat. "Only one way to find out. Beat me at arm wrestling and I'll tell you everything I know." She pulled up her right sleeve and leaned forward, planting her right elbow on the spool.

"Fine," said Burton. He holstered his gun and rolled up his sleeve. "Watch her." Rogers and Dexter held their guns steady on Tiamat.

"Only one condition," said Tiamat, glancing down at the Balderhaz cube next to her. "You have to get rid of this."

Burton shook his head. "No sale. My boss said to keep that thing near me at all times."

"And you're always the good little special agent, aren't you?" Tiamat said. "You always follow orders, no matter how silly they are. Your boss tells you to apprehend a crazy woman spouting ridiculous world domination schemes and you do it. He says, 'oh, and make sure you have your magic box with you, or there's no telling what she might do!'"

"You did just threaten to turn me inside out," Burton noted.

"And how on Earth would I do that, Special Agent Burton? Voodoo? You're smarter than that."

"A lot of strange things have been happening lately," said Burton. "The Anaheim incident, the Moon imploding, the Myrmidon project... Also, there's the fact that there's no way you could have known I had this—he glanced at the cube—Balderhaz whatsit on me. I don't believe in magic, but something isn't right. If you don't want that black cube around, then I'm for damned sure keeping it in sight."

Tiamat sighed. "You honestly believe that little black cube is the only thing keeping me—a woman half your size—from beating you at arm wrestling? And you're so certain of this that you're willing to forgo the possibility of obtaining critical information on an active terror threat?"

Burton shrugged. "If you've got that kind of information, then my boss was right about you being a threat. And if he's right about you being a threat, then he's probably right about this cube. Logically speaking, you're either completely harmless and therefore useless to me, or extremely dangerous, and therefore not to be trusted."

"I suppose that's true," she said. "All right, then. Take me in." She held out her hands as if expecting to be handcuffed. "But first, tell me if you would: if you had to say, what would be your guess? Am I extremely dangerous or harmless?"

Burton regarded her for a moment. "I get the feeling," he said, "that you could be dangerous under the right circumstances. It follows that you could be useful under the right circumstances. But at present, your circumstances don't favor you."

"You're dodging the question, Special Agent Burton. Do you believe in demons?"

"Beliefs are a liability in my job," said Burton. "They get in the way of facts. I will tell you this, though: I *hope* there are demons."

"And why is that?" asked Tiamat.

"Because the greater the evil out there, the more necessary a man like me is."

"Ah," said Tiamat, smiling, "so you're an opportunist."

"Exactly," said Burton. "Word around the office was that this meeting was a fool's errand. Following up on a Craigslist ad for demonic henchmen. Nobody wanted to do it. But my boss insisted it needed to be done."

"And that made you suspicious."

"Yeah," said Burton. "Made me think there was more to it than he was letting on. I had heard through the grapevine that he was looking for someone to head up a special division having to do with... unusual threats to national security."

"A real-life *X-Files*."

"Something like that. Anyway, I put two and two together. Figured worst case scenario, I waste a few hours apprehending some harmless nut. Best case, I neutralize one of these threats and put myself at the head of the line for the new division."

"So you do believe in demons."

"I suspect my boss believes in demons. If I act like I believe in demons, I've got an in with him. Like being a member of the same lodge, but without the silly hat."

"Quite the schemer, aren't you, Special Agent Burton?"

"I don't scheme," said Burton, shaking his head slightly. "I just try to stay alert to the scheming going on around me, and react accordingly. For example, right now you're thinking about grabbing that cube and hurling it across the warehouse. My boss said it has a range of about fifty feet, so you could conceivably throw it far enough to escape the effect—assuming there *is* an effect. Of course, if you do, I will shoot you." He produced his pistol from his coat.

"You'd shoot an unarmed 45-year-old woman?" Tiamat asked. "Won't that be difficult to explain to your superiors?"

"I'm not going to have to explain anything," said Burton. "You're a narcissistic sociopath, but you're not delusional. And you clearly know more about that cube than I do. So if you pick up that cube, it's because you know it really does have some kind of mystical power over you. And if that's true, then I have to assume you are not what you appear. Which, given my boss's level of concern, presumably means you really are some sort of malevolent supernatural entity. In which case, I suspect that it's going to take more than bullets to put you down."

Tiamat stared at him coolly. "You're going to feel differently when you're standing over the bleeding corpse of the unarmed woman you just murdered in cold blood."

"Maybe," said Burton. Before he finished the word, the cube was already in Tiamat's hand. She pushed her seat back and twisted to the right, bringing the cube to her shoulder to hurl it across the warehouse. Six shots rang out in the vast space, tearing holes in the back of her jacket. The cube clattered to the concrete floor and Tiamat collapsed face down, not moving. A pool of blood spread out from underneath her.

The three agents got to their feet and studied the scene for a moment. Rogers and Dexter holstered their guns. Burton did not.

"So, do you?" asked Dexter, after some time.

"Do I what?" asked Burton.

"Feel different."

Burton walked to the Balderhaz cube and picked it up with his left hand, as he was still holding his gun in his right. He walked to the table and put the cube back in the box, keeping one eye on Tiamat the whole time. By the time the box was back in the backpack, the fingers on her right hand had begun to move.

"I feel like you should handcuff that bitch," he said.

CHAPTER TEN

Mentzel Ranch, just outside Elko, Nevada; October 22, 2016

Mercury, Eddie, Suzy and Balderhaz stood on a small desert plateau a few miles outside of Elko, Nevada. The dry air was cool, but the sun climbing the sky to their left cast a warm glow on their shoulders, promising to bake the shit out of the already parched ground before the day was done. A tiny dust cloud on the horizon indicated that a car was headed their way.

"What a Godforsaken place," said Suzy. "Does it really have to be so remote? Are we worried about radiation or something?"

"I am," said Balderhaz, who was slathering some sort of thick gray cream on his mostly bald pate. He had applied the cream unevenly, so that while most of his thin hair was now cemented against his scalp, a few errant wisps still undulated in the breeze, reminding Suzy of seaweed on an ocean floor. "Zinc oxide with lead shavings," said Balderhaz, holding the jar out to Suzy. "SPF eight hundred."

"You know lead is poisonous, right?" said Suzy.

Balderhaz frowned, staring at the glob of gray goo he had just scooped up with his fingers. He gave the glob a sniff and then stuck his fingers in his mouth.

"Tashtes okay to me," he said, working the stuff around his mouth.

Suzy grimaced and forced herself to look away. Despite his brilliance, Balderhaz was the sort of person who would long ago have been eliminated from the gene pool were he not immortal.

"Not radiation," said Eddie. "Prying eyes. Building regulations. Zoning regulations."

"That and the possibility of an uncontrolled surge of interplanar energy, sucking everything for miles around into another dimension," said Mercury.

"You mean like what happened in Anaheim?" Suzy asked.

"Same principle, yes," said Mercury. "Interplanar energy channels can be capricious beasts. Although obviously we'd have safeguards to avoid something like that."

"Safeguards designed by him?" asked Suzy. She indicated Balderhaz, who was now on his hands and knees, dragging his tongue across the parched ground. Evidently he had decided he wasn't enamored of the taste of the gray goo after all.

"Don't let him fool you," said Eddie. "He really is a genius. Nobody on Heaven or Earth knows more about manipulating interplanar energy than Balderhaz."

Mercury nodded. "And frankly, if we have an uncontrolled energy surge, being a few hundred miles away from civilization probably won't help much. I mean..." He glanced at the misshapen Moon that was still visible in the western sky.

"Holy shit," said Suzy. "Are you saying *that* could happen on Earth?"

"Could and almost did," said Mercury. "You know, I get a lot of shit from people about imploding the Moon, but they don't realize how close the Earth came to—"

"Mercury," said Eddie. "I don't think you're helping to reassure Suzy."

"Oh, is that what we're doing?" asked Mercury, regarding Balderhaz, who was now sitting up on his haunches, pawing at his tongue.

"Did you guyth bring any water?" Balderhaz asked.

"In the car," said Eddie, pointing to the Lincoln Navigator they had driven out to the ranch. Balderhaz nodded and ran to the car. He opened the rear door and climbed inside, slamming the door after him.

"Maybe this isn't a good idea," said Suzy, watching the dust cloud in the distance. She could now just make out a red pickup truck at the front of it. "I didn't realize it was so dangerous."

"Danger is relative," said Mercury. "As much as I hate having to be the responsible one, Eddie is right about Tiamat and Michelle. They're always scheming, and for once we have a chance to get out ahead of them. If we don't reestablish interplanar communications, someone else will."

"Hmm," said Suzy.

"What?" said Eddie. "If you have doubts about this plan, you should let us know."

"Hey, I'm just a hired gun," said Suzy. "I'll order materials, apply for permits, pay off local officials, whatever you need me to do to get this thing built. I'm happy to have any job after the Brimstone debacle.[7] But all this interplanar portal stuff is above my pay grade. You guys are the angels."

"No," said Eddie. "We're a team. If something's bothering you, you need to tell us."

The red pickup was now only a hundred yards or so away.

"Well," said Suzy, "it does occur to me that maybe you two haven't been completely honest about your motivations."

"Meaning what?" asked Eddie.

"Meaning that although my understanding of celestial politics is limited, from what I gather you two have been on the outs with the Heavenly authorities for some time now. Mercury in particular has been playing pretty fast-and-loose with the rules. He screwed up the Apocalypse, wrecked the Moon, blew up the planeport—"

"Saved the world, saved the world, saved the world," Mercury muttered.

"Look, I get it," said Suzy. "I'm on your side. But I know a little something about how bureaucracies work. And if Heaven works anything like Washington, D.C., when the dust settles the higher-ups are going to be looking for a scapegoat—or scapegoats—to pin all these debacles on."

Eddie shook his head. "I've documented everything. We had no choice. Even blowing up the planeport was the least bad option. The Senate will see that."

"You're not listening, Eddie. Bureaucratic finger-pointing has its own logic. Somebody is going to have to pay."

"Spit it out, Suzy," said Mercury. "Eddie can be a little dense."

---

[7] Brimstone was the name of the secret, illegal government project to build a nuclear bomb to replace the one that was built by the secret, illegal government project called Wormwood.

"Fine," said Suzy. "Eddie, I think Mercury talked you into building this plane generator because when contact with Heaven is reestablished, he wants to be in control of it. He wants to have a monopoly on interplanar travel so that the Heavenly authorities won't dare try to punish him."

Eddie frowned and looked at Mercury. "Is that true?" he asked.

Mercury shrugged, watching the red pickup come to a halt in front of them. "Does it matter? It doesn't change anything. You know this is our best chance at forestalling Tiamat's schemes."

"It matters," said Eddie, "because the whole point of this project is to thwart the plans of a power-hungry despot. It doesn't help to stymie Tiamat if another despot steps into her place."

Mercury laughed. "Me? A despot? I think you overestimate my ambition, as well as my attention span. Look, even if we can get the portal generator to work, it's going to be capable of opening a single portal, connecting this spot to one particular place in Heaven. That's it. It's hardly going to give us absolute control over time and space. Might it someday lead to the construction of another planeport? Maybe. Would it be cool if the authorities decided to name the planeport after me out of gratitude, and perhaps commission a gigantic bronze statue of me in the center of it? Sure. But that's as far as my ambition goes. I'm not cut out to be a dictator. All right, everybody, pipe down. Let me do the talking."

A leathery, weather-worn old man had gotten out of the red pickup and was walking toward them. Mercury took a step forward and held out his hand.

"Marcus Uittenbroek," he said, shaking the man's hand.

"Good to meet you, Marcus," said the man. "I'm Steve Mentzel. I understand you're interested in buying my land."

Mercury opened his mouth to reply, but was distracted by a knocking sound coming from his left. Looking to the Navigator, He saw Balderhaz's face pressed against the glass.

"I've got it," Suzy said, and walked to the car.

"Who is that?" asked Mentzel, watching as Suzy opened the door and climbed into the backseat next to Balderhaz.

"That's Uncle Stan," said Mercury. "He's got an eight-inch stainless steel bolt in his head."

"Oh my God," said Steve Mentzel, staring at Balderhaz in horror. Balderhaz now had his head in Suzy's lap, and was sobbing uncontrollably. "Construction accident?"

Mercury shook his head. "No, he was born that way," he said. "Weirdest thing."

Steve Mentzel regarded him speechlessly.

"So," Eddie interjected, "I assume our offer is acceptable to you, Mr. Mentzel?"

Mentzel nodded. "More than acceptable," he said. "Suspicious, even. You're offering double what I asked."

"We didn't want to get outbid," said Mercury. "The family is building a house for Uncle Stan, and we let him pick the location. He doesn't get to make a lot of decisions, so this was kind of a big deal for him. Look how excited he is."

Mentzel frowned, looking at Balderhaz and Suzy in the backseat of the Navigator. Balderhaz was still weeping, and Suzy was wiping gray goo from his scalp with Kleenex. "*He* picked this spot?" Mentzel asked.

"Well," said Mercury, "he drooled on a map, which is about as about as clear an indicator as you're going to get from Uncle Stan."

"I see," Mentzel said uncertainly. "You know, I'm not sure how I feel about taking advantage of a man who is clearly... mentally defective."

"Don't worry about that," said Mercury. "Uncle Stan is broke. I'm the one with the money."

"You're the one I'm talking about," said Mentzel.

"Oh," said Mercury.

Eddie chuckled nervously. "We're an eccentric family, Mr. Mentzel. But we're honest people. This is where Uncle Stan wants to spend the remainder of his days, so this is where we're going to build. Assuming you accept our offer. We can pay in cash."

Mentzel nodded slowly. "Well, that's all good. I wanted to ask you one other thing, though."

"Sure," said Eddie.

"You're not religious nuts, are you?"

"Uh," said Eddie. "No. Why do you ask?"

"I've had some problems with these oddballs from California. End of the world types. I put up signs, but it doesn't keep them out.

I haven't seen them for a few years, but I keep expecting them to show up again someday."

"Well, you won't have to worry about them anymore," said Mercury. "Once you sign the land over to us, they'll be our problem."

"Unless you're them," said Mentzel.

"We're not," said Eddie. "But even if we were, like Marcus says, it wouldn't be your problem anymore."

"Thing is," said Mentzel, "I'm a little concerned you're going to go all Heaven's Gate on me. I don't want to get a call from a TV reporter in six months and have to talk about how you all seemed like nice people and I can't believe you all drank cyanide because you thought some damn comet was going to take you to Heaven."

"No worries there," said Mercury. "Next major comet sighting isn't until 2037. What you should really be worried about is asteroids. Did you know that the Tunguska meteor knocked down 80 million trees? And it might have been less than a hundred yards in diameter. An asteroid the size of—"

"What Marcus is trying to say," Eddie interjected, "is that we have no suicidal or otherwise destructive intentions. We just want to build a nice place where we can cherish our remaining years with Uncle Stan."

"While he slowly dies of natural, non-comet-related causes," added Mercury.

"That's right," said Eddie.

"Fine," said Mentzel. "What you do on your own property is your business. I mean, as long as you aren't trying to open some kind of mystical portal to Heaven."

"Absolutely not," said Eddie.

"Wouldn't dream of it," said Mercury.

"So when can we start on the mystical portal to Heaven?" asked Balderhaz, who had wandered up behind them.

"Sorry!" said Suzy, grabbing Balderhaz by the shoulder. "Uncle Stan, let's get you something to eat. There are sandwiches in the car."

"Good idea," said Balderhaz. "I'll need to eat something before I start working on the mystical portal we're planning to build here."

Suzy smiled weakly, pulling Balderhaz back to the Navigator.

"He's confused," said Eddie. "Sometimes he repeats things without knowing what they mean."

"The confluence of interplanar energy at these coordinates is really quite remarkable," Balderhaz was saying. "We'll still need proximal transducers to help inhibit the noise in the chaotic vector matrix, but any time you can leverage the topography to stabilize the metagenic field, I call it a win."

"See?" said Mercury. "Pure gobbledygook. We've taken him to the best doctors in the world, but they all say the same thing. He needs an MRI."

"So why don't they give him one?" asked Mentzel.

"They can't, because of the bolt in his head. It's ironic, I suppose."

Mentzel nodded. "All right, then. Why don't you all follow me back to my office and we can sign the paperwork."

"Excellent!" said Eddie. "We're eager to get started. On the house for Uncle Stan, I mean."

"Mystical gateway to Heaven, here we come!" yelled Balderhaz from the backseat of the Navigator. Suzy got in next to him and slammed the door.

"Are you sure he wouldn't be better off in some kind of institution?" Mentzel asked.

"Nah," said Mercury. "This is the best place on Earth for him to be."

CHAPTER ELEVEN

FBI Headquarters, Washington, D.C.; October 24, 2016

Tiamat sat at a metal table, her hands cuffed in front of her. A chain ran through the handcuffs, securing her to a metal ring bolted to the table's surface. In front of her, just out of reach, was the Balderhaz cube. She sat in silence, waiting. She had been in the small, windowless room for nearly two hours, having been escorted from a holding cell early that morning. After nearly two weeks in FBI custody, she had begun to think that Special Agent Burton and his superiors had forgotten about her.

The door to the opened and a man in a dark blue suit entered. He smiled at Tiamat.

"Special Agent Burton," she said. "You're looking dapper today."

"First day in a new job," he said, sitting down in the chair across from her. He placed a manila folder on the table in front of him. "You're looking at the Director of the Task Force on Beings of Indeterminate Origin."

"Euphemisms," sniffed Tiamat. "Not an auspicious start. How do you expect to face your enemies if you can't name them?"

"Again, you assume too much," said Burton. "We're a task force *on* BIOs, not *against* them."

"If I'm not your enemy," said Tiamat, "you could demonstrate that fact by unchaining me."

"You're a dangerous woman with a history of subversive activity," replied Burton, "irrespective of your nature or origin."

"Then charge me with a crime."

"The courts can't be trusted to deal with the likes of you. Fortunately, I've been granted the authority by the President himself to hold you indefinitely without trial. It's the opinion of the White House lawyers that the Constitutional right to due process only applies to human beings."

"I see," said Tiamat. "But what proof do you have that I'm not human?"

"Good question," said Burton, reaching into his jacket pocket. He pulled a metal object from his pocket and set it on the table next to the manila folder.

"What the hell is that?" Tiamat asked.

"Pruning shears," said Burton. "I intend to remove one of your fingers."

Tiamat reflexively pulled her hands back, straining against the chain. "Why on Earth would you do that?"

"To see if it grows back," Burton answered matter-of-factly. "If it does, I'll have documented evidence that you are a supernatural being." He pointed at a tiny camera peeking out from the wall their left, just below the ceiling.

"Or you'll have documented evidence of yourself using violent coercion against an unarmed suspect who has been charged with no crime."

"After your miraculous recovery in the warehouse," said Burton, "that's a chance I'm willing to take. Unless you'd prefer door number two." He reached into his jacket and withdrew a smaller object, setting it next to the shears.

"A pen?"

Burton opened the folder and turned it so the document inside faced Tiamat. "An admission that you are a Being of Indeterminate Origin, which effectively negates any claim you have to due process."

"So I sign this or you cut off my finger."

"Correct."

"I could always say I was coerced."

"You can say whatever you like. Nobody is going to hear it but me. Don't get the idea that this is some kind of momentous decision on your part. It's just a formality. Legally, the result is the same either way."

"Unless my finger doesn't grow back."

"Sure," said Burton. "But we both know it will."

With a sigh, Tiamat picked up the paper and signed it.

Burton picked up the document and inspected it. The line at the bottom read "Katie Midford AKA Tiamat." Tiamat had simply signed it "Tiamat."

"Is this your full name?" asked Burton.

Tiamat shrugged. "It's what I go by on this plane," she said.

"What do you mean when you say 'this plane'?"

Tiamat sighed again.

"Look," said Burton. "Here's how this is going to work. You help me, I help you."

"And how are you going to help me, Special Agent Burton?"

"For starters, I can make you more comfortable. Get you a bigger cell. Books and TV."

"Internet access?"

"Maybe eventually. If you prove yourself reliable, I might even let you come with us on field trips occasionally."

"Oh, goody," said Tiamat. "Field trips to apprehend other angels, you mean."

"Possibly," said Burton. He paused a moment, then continued, "I'm going to level with you, Tiamat. I'm a bit out of my element here. I've done as much research as I can about these 'angels' or whatever you want to call them, but frankly the reports I've come across are sketchy and often contradictory. Don't get me wrong; the higher-ups are definitely believers. This task force was created at the request of the President himself. The problem is at the lower rungs of the bureaucracy. You see, law enforcement agents are trained not to see the supernatural. In this job, ninety-nine percent of the time the simplest explanation is the right one. An agent who goes looking for fanciful, complicated explanations is soon going to be unemployed. So even when I interview agents I know have had first-hand experience with angels, I get nowhere. They make up the most ridiculous explanations you can imagine to avoid admitting they've come across something completely inexplicable. I've talked to civilians as well, but they're just as bad. They've got no training in observing details, so half the time you can't even tell what they're trying to explain away. And the other half of the time, they get so carried away with their own theories that you can't separate conjecture from what they actually saw."

"So you want a crash course in angelology." said Tiamat. "What's in it for me? And don't tell me bon-bons and Netflix. I can't be bought so cheaply."

"Fair enough," said Burton. "I'll admit I have little to offer you in terms of material rewards. I can make you a bit more comfortable, but you and I both know that I can never let you go free."

"If this is your idea of sweet-talking me, you might want to rethink your strategy," said Tiamat.

Burton went on, "But it occurred to me on my way over here that what you really want isn't material anyway."

"Oh?" said Tiamat. "And tell me, Special Agent Burton, what do I really want?"

"Power," said Burton.

"And you're going to give that to me?"

"No," said Burton. "But I fully expect you to take it. You see, Tiamat, whether you realize it or not, you're actually in a very privileged position. You are the only angel on Earth in the position to influence FBI policy. The U.S. government is fully committed to getting control over the BIO menace. How we go about that and what angels we target first is largely up to you."

"Why, Special Agent Burton, are you suggesting that I would use my influence to settle petty grudges with other angels?"

"Yes," said Burton.

"Then we understand each other," said Tiamat with a smile. "What do you want to know?"

"You can start by explaining what you mean when you talk about 'planes.'"

"Unchain me," said Tiamat.

Burton thought for a moment, then reached into his pocket and withdrew a key. He reached over the table and unlocked the handcuffs.

Tiamat took them off and rubbed her wrists. "Thank you," she said, glancing at the Balderhaz cube. "Planes are like alternate dimensions. Everything you experience, what you consider the 'universe,' is actually just one of many planes."

"Does this have something to do with the Many Worlds hypothesis in physics?"

Tiamat shrugged. "I don't really keep up with Mundane Science. The idea has been around a long time. It's had many different names."

"So there's another Earth on each of these planes?"

"I couldn't say," said Tiamat. "I haven't been to all of them."

"How many have you been to?"

"A few dozen, maybe? The ones I've been to have all had a version of something like Earth, but it's often almost unrecognizable. One thing you have to understand is that the so-called 'laws of physics' are only laws here on the Mundane Plane. Everywhere else, they are more like suggestions. Maybe originally all the planes were identical, but a few thousand years of minor violations of the laws of physics can have some pretty dramatic consequences."

"Are you saying that these different planes have only been around for a few thousand years?"

"That's a conjecture based on the amount of variation I've seen in the planes. Nobody knows for sure how old they are, but the consensus seems to be that the known planes split off from each other about seven thousand years ago. Your turn, Special Agent Burton. What are you trying to accomplish with this task force?"

"The main purpose of the task force is to identify, catalog and track every angel on Earth, to assess the potential threat level of each, and to make recommendations regarding how to handle them. Every angel will either be apprehended and neutralized or be converted into an asset."

"Fine," said Tiamat. "But I didn't ask the purpose of the task force. I asked what *you* are trying to accomplish."

"I plan to turn this task force into a new division of the FBI, and eventually a cabinet-level department."

"With you in charge."

"Of course," said Burton.

"What if the angels don't cooperate?"

Burton smiled. "That's the beauty of this task force," he said. "Angels who resist being converted give me justification for requesting more funding and more power.

"Nicely done, Burton. Are you sure you're not a schemer?"

Burton shrugged. "I never force things, but I'm always ready when the stars align. An opportunist, as you said. How many angels are there on Earth?"

"My best guess is around a hundred."

"Where do they come from? Is there really a place called 'Heaven?'"

"There's a plane called Heaven, although it's not all it's cracked up to be. And no, it's not where you go when you die."

"Where *do* people go when they die?"

"Schenectady. How should I know?"

"How many known planes are there?"

"The exact number is classified. Honestly, I'm not sure Heaven even knows. My best guess is around five hundred. Theoretically, there could be an infinite number of planes. But most of them are inaccessible. You can't get to a plane unless you can pinpoint its location, for lack of a better term. You need a sort of address."

"Like an IP address on the Internet. Not a physical location, but a unique identifier."

"Something like that."

"But it takes more than just knowing the address. You have to have some kind of portal, right?"

"Yes," said Tiamat. "And to create a portal, you need to have a portal generator. But the only one in existence was the one that powered the planeport. It was destroyed by a nuclear explosion four years ago."

"The planeport? What's that?"

"Like an airport, but for connecting planes. Basically one big portal generator, with a bunch of portals open between various planes. Theoretically you can open a portal from anywhere, on any plane, to anywhere else, but it's much more difficult in some places than in others. It all depends on the configuration of the interplanar energy channels. Anyway, the key point is that right now, nobody can open a portal anywhere, because the only portal generator in existence has been blown to smithereens."

"So all the angels on Earth—that is, on the Mundane Plane—are stuck here."

"Correct."

"Who blew up the planeport? And why?"

"An angel named Mercury. He's a bit of a troublemaker."

"Sounds like somebody we should look into. Do you have any idea how to locate him? Or any other angels?"

"Sadly, no," said Tiamat. "Mercury is hard to pin down. And after the failure of the Myrmidon project, my minions all scattered. If I had any idea where they were, I wouldn't have had to resort to posting Craigslist ads."

Burton frowned. "So you're saying you can't actually help me find any other angels."

"Oh, I didn't say that," replied Tiamat. "My predicament was due mainly to my lack of resources. I assume you don't have that problem."

"If I can make a case that it will help us find the other angels, I can probably get it."

"Good," said Tiamat. "I'll need a lab. Nothing fancy, just some room to work and some basic fabrication tools. I'll get you a list. And three or four assistants."

"Any particular skills you're looking for? A background in chemistry or physics maybe?"

"Heavens no," said Tiamat. "I don't want them to have to unlearn all that nonsense. I need people who are good with their hands but don't have a practical thought in their heads. Art students are always a good choice. Let's see, what else? A photonic crystal laser. Ten grams of tritium. A hundred yards of thirty-gauge platinum wire. A Siamese cat."

Burton was furiously jotting all of this down. "A Siamese cat? Really?"

"They help create a soothing work environment."

"What are you going to be doing with all this stuff?"

Tiamat grinned. "We're going to build a miracle detector."

CHAPTER TWELVE

The former Mentzel Ranch, just outside Elko, Nevada; April 29, 2017

It was the ugliest building Suzy had ever seen. Squat and rectangular, its steel siding painted a dull greenish-gray, it seemed like the perfect sort of place for a bunch of religious nuts to hole up while waiting for the Apocalypse. She hoped Steve Mentzel never found out what they had done with his property.

She hadn't intentionally gone for the cult compound look when she'd commissioned the construction; she had simply been trying to get an airplane-hangar sized building put up as quickly as possible. Money had been no object; even after buying all the materials to build the portal generator, they had spent less than a quarter of Mercury's fortune. The facility's official name was the Hermeticorp Institute for Universal Awareness, a name deliberately selected for its vagueness. They didn't want to frighten Mentzel or the other locals with a name that was explicitly religious, but they also didn't want to give county or state officials the idea that they were operating some kind of illegal manufacturing operation. "Hermeticorp Institute for Universal Awareness" gave the impression of a bunch of some kind of new age-infused corporate retreat center, hinting at harmlessness as well as potential sales tax revenue from bored executives.

Mercury, finding the acronym HIUA completely unmanageable, simply referred to the nondescript square building as the Box. The name caught on with Eddie and the others, and Suzy found herself powerless to resist. In order to appease her organizational nature, she reverse-engineered this into an acronym for Building for Otherwordly Transport. Dropping the preposition was no big deal, and after a few beers one night she convinced herself that "X" was a perfectly reasonable abbreviation for "Transport." Thus the HIUA became the Box, and the Box became the BOX. The four of them had lived in hastily constructed apartments on the southern side of the BOX for the past three months.

"Beautiful, isn't she?" said Mercury. The two of them stood on a nearby ridge admiring the recently completed structure.

Suzy turned to regard Mercury for a moment, just to make sure they were both looking at the same building.

"I mean, I'll grant you the BOX is not an architectural wonder," Mercury went on. "But the potential it represents is beautiful. Just imagine, by this time tomorrow we're going to be in Heaven!"

"*You're* going to be in Heaven," said Suzy. "I'm staying here."

"Suit yourself," said Mercury. "You could be the official representative for humanity at the historic reestablishment of communications between the Mundane Plane and Heaven."

"Meh," said Suzy.

"I hear you," said Mercury. "To be honest, I'd avoid it myself if I could. But I started this damn project, so I guess I have to see it through. Eddie and Balderhaz will go too, of course, but Eddie gets nervous in stressful situations and, well, Balderhaz...."

"Yeah," said Suzy. She had managed most of the construction over the past six months, but that was nothing compared to babysitting Balderhaz. When he was on task, he had incredible concentration, often working for several days nonstop. But she had to keep constant tabs on him for fear that he would wander away and get himself crushed by an earth mover or sealed inside a concrete footing. They had spent one anxious night scouring the desert for him only to find that he had fallen asleep on the roof.

Yet, for all his eccentricities, it was clear that Balderhaz knew what he was doing. The capacious building was filled with hundreds of bizarre-looking devices, none of which resembled anything Suzy had ever seen before, but which Mercury and Eddie assured her were critical to the construction of a portal generator. The actual portal generator was only about the size of a large suitcase; the rest of the doohickeys and thingamajigs were only necessary to build other doohickeys and thingamajigs that had been used for constructing other doohickeys and thingamajigs that were required to build the doohickeys and thingamajigs that had been used to create the portal generator. The way Mercury explained it, interplanar portal technology used an entirely different sort of physics than the stuff she had learned in high school. According to Mercury, trying to build a portal generator with human technology was "like trying to build a television set starting with chopsticks and a bucket of sand."

"You really think he'll be done tomorrow?" Suzy asked.

"He's done now," said Mercury. "We're just waiting for the batteries to charge."

"Seriously? It uses batteries?"

"Not, like, electric batteries," said Mercury. "They're specially designed cells that soak up interplanar energy. Interplanar energy is all around us, and there's a particularly strong confluence in this area, which is one of the reasons we picked this place. Once the batteries are full, we'll be able to open the portal to Heaven."

"But only to Heaven."

"Why? Did you want to go somewhere else?"

"No, just curious if you could use the portal to go to any other planes. I've never been anywhere but here."

"Theoretically we could, with enough power," said Mercury. "But in practice we're largely dependent on the configuration of the interplanar energy channels. In short, Heaven is the easiest place to get to from here."

"That's not what I learned in Sunday School," said Suzy.

"You should have paid better attention," said Mercury. "'Knock and the door shall be opened.'"

"So this is really happening? We're finally done? We're really going to open a portal to a whole other world?"

"Looks like it," said Mercury. "I have to admit, I was a little concerned that when Balderhaz activated the batteries, we might attract...." He trailed off.

"What?" asked Suzy.

"Shhh!" Mercury hissed. "Do you hear that?"

Suzy listened for a moment. "I don't hear... oh." She now noticed a barely audible, rumbling sound. Like thunder, but with an odd sort of rhythm.

"Damn it!" Mercury shouted. "She found us." He took off running toward the compound. "Turn them off! Turn the receptors off!"

Trying to locate the source of the sound, Suzy scanned the horizon. There. Three black specks in the distance, slowly growing larger. Helicopters.

"Who?" she called to Mercury. But he had already vanished inside. Suzy followed. By the time she got inside the building, the sound of the helicopters was loud enough that she could hear it through the walls. Not knowing where the receptors were located, she ran through the maze of strange contraptions and machinery toward the center of the building, where the portal generator was. She figured that if Mercury failed to get the receptors shut down in time, she might be able to grab the portal generator and get it out of the building. She had a feeling she knew who the "she" was Mercury thought had found them—and it was vital that the portal generator not fall into her hands.

Suzy walked down an aisle between two rows of machinery toward the open area where she had last seen Balderhaz working on the portal generator. As she rounded a corner, the device came into view. To Suzy, the portal generator seemed like the physical manifestation of anticlimax: all this work had gone into building something that looked like a small steamer trunk with a dinner-plate-sized satellite dish protruding from the top of it. A black conduit about the thickness of a garden house ran from an aperture near the bottom of the case across the floor, disappearing to somewhere else inside the BOX. That part was new—she assumed it was the connection to the batteries that Mercury had mentioned. As Suzy approached, she noticed something else different about the device: the dish was angled toward the concrete floor a few feet in front of it, and although no visible light was emitted by the dish, a faint blue-white ellipse had formed on the floor and was slowly becoming brighter. Someone had turned it on.

Suzy stepped into the open space, wondering if it was safe to try to move the thing. But as she left the cover of the machinery, the thought of escaping with the portal generator left her mind: just around the corner, a few paces from the device, was the figure of Balderhaz. He was facing away from her and had his hands in the air. A stack of boxes between her and Balderhaz blocked her view of who was threatening him, but she was fairly certain that she didn't want to meet them.

Suzy stopped in her tracks and began to slowly back her way out of the open area. Once she was again hidden by machinery on either side, she turned around—and nearly walked head-on into the barrel of an assault rifle. The burly man behind the rifle, who wore a lot of scary-looking black gear on his person, grinned at her.

"Got another one," the burly man shouted. Then, more quietly, he said, "Hands up. Turn around. Walk."

She did as instructed, walking back into the open area. The man gave her a nudge in the back with his rifle barrel, and she stepped past the stack of boxes toward Balderhaz. To Balderhaz's left stood Mercury and Eddie, with their hands raised as well. At the gunman's prompting, she stepped up next to Eddie.

Three more men wearing the same heavy black tactical gear stood a few yards in front of them, their guns raised. Next to these men stood a black-haired man in a blue suit. He had a gun in one hand and a black cube in the other. Next to him stood a middle-aged woman Suzy had met before.

Tiamat had taken control of the BOX.

CHAPTER THIRTEEN

Tiamat was smiling. Suzy hated it when Tiamat smiled.

Mercury greeted Suzy with a grim nod.

"This is a twist, eh, Mercury?" said Tiamat. "Me foiling your nefarious scheme, I mean."

"Don't flatter yourself, Tiamat," said Mercury. "It's pretty clear you're not the one in charge. Also, it isn't so much a nefarious scheme as a pernicious connivance."

"So," the black-haired man interjected, "you're the notorious Mercury. You've caused an awful lot of trouble on this plane, you know."

"Not just this plane," Mercury protested. "I've caused trouble in places you've never even heard of."

"Well, those days are over," said the man. "I'm Special Agent Taylor Burton, director of the FBI Task Force on Beings of Indeterminate Origin. That's 'angels' to you. We're taking control of this facility, and taking you all into custody. I assume you're all angels?"

"Not that one," said Tiamat, pointing to Suzy. "She's human."

"Fine," said Burton. "We'll process her separately."

"You're making a mistake," said Eddie. "You can't control Tiamat with that cube. She's using you."

"I appreciate your concern," said Burton, "but I'll take my chances."

"Don't you see?" said Eddie. "She has a grudge against Mercury. She's using you to eliminate her enemies."

"Of course she is," said Burton. "But it just so happens that our interests in this case are aligned. Now, somebody shut that thing off." He was referring to the portal generator, next to which the blue-white ellipse on the floor was now glowing brightly. Suzy saw now that the ellipse was actually comprised of two different colors: a maze-like blue pattern etched onto a white background. Was that it? Suzy wondered. The portal to Heaven?

At Burton's command, Balderhaz stepped toward the portal generator.

"Wait," said Burton, holding up his hand. Balderhaz paused uncertainly. Burton turned to Tiamat. "Can we trust him?"

"I wouldn't," said Tiamat.

"You can't trust *her*!" Eddie yelled, clearly frustrated with Burton's apparent obtuseness. "She's using you! You're going to—"

Burton made a minute gesture with his hand, and Suzy heard a loud crack. Eddie fell to the ground, not moving. Turning her head, she saw the man who had escorted her in, his rifle butt raised. She glanced at Mercury, who shook his head almost imperceptibly at her. "Face front!" the gunman snapped at her, and she complied.

"In case I haven't made myself clear," Burton said, his voice even, "I'm not particularly interested in your opinions. I'd appreciate it if you'd keep quiet unless I speak to you." He turned to Balderhaz. "You built this thing?"

Balderhaz nodded. "And that thing," he said.

Burton looked quizzically at him for a moment. "Ah," he said, looking at the cube in his hand. "Yes, this is a handy little device. Levels the playing field between angels and humans. You have my gratitude."

Balderhaz shrugged, uncertain how to respond.

Burton turned to Tiamat. "He seems harmless," he said.

Tiamat snorted. "He may be the most dangerous angel in existence," she said. "There's no telling what he might do if you let him touch that thing. He may have it rigged to self-destruct. He might transport us all a million miles into deep space. He might open a rift in the space-time continuum and annihilate Earth."

"Is that true?" Burton said to Balderhaz.

"Well," said Balderhaz, "it depends on how you're using the modal auxiliary verbs 'may' and 'might.' Essentially, you're setting up hypothetical situations in which one particular event out of several possibilities—some of which would have required advance planning on my part—takes place. Additionally, some of these scenarios seem to presuppose certain motivations, or at least the establishment of some subjective hierarchy of available options, to wit—"

"That's enough," said Burton, holding up his hand again.

"I know he seems like a buffoon," said Tiamat, "but he really is quite clever. I wouldn't let him near that machine."

"What if we just leave it?" asked Burton.

"It's an open portal," said Tiamat. "Assuming it's working properly, there's another one just like it somewhere. Heaven, presumably."

"It goes both ways?" asked Burton.

"That's how portals work, genius," replied Mercury.

Burton regarded him coolly, then turned to Balderhaz. "Where is the other side of that portal?" he asked.

"Heaven," Mercury answered. "Like Tiamat said. It's the only plane we can get to from here."

Burton looked to Tiamat, who nodded. "It would take too much power to go anywhere else," she said.

"Why did you turn it on?" Burton asked.

Balderhaz glanced at Mercury, as if uncertain how much to say.

"We heard the helicopters," said Mercury. "We were going to shut down the receptors, but it was too late. Balderhaz thought maybe we could go through before you showed up."

"We hoofed it in," said Burton. "I only called for backup once the advance team was safely inside the building. Your security is somewhat lacking, by the way. You might just as well have left the door open for us."

Suzy grimaced. Their "security" consisted of little more than locked doors and a chain link fence. She had been counting on their remote location to keep them safe from burglars and vandals; the idea of keeping out the FBI—to say nothing of demons—simply hadn't occurred to her. Not that she would have been able to do anything about it anyway. Maybe that's why Mercury had never mentioned the possibility.

"Speaking of open doors," said Mercury, "there's no telling who's on the other side of that portal right now. I imagine they're wondering why somebody bothered to open an interplanar portal if they weren't going to use it."

"It may have gone unnoticed," Burton suggested.

"Not likely," said Mercury. "Balderhaz specified the coordinates for the central square in the Celestial City, right in front of the Eye of Providence. Somebody's seen it by now for sure. They've probably alerted the Heavenly authorities. I wonder how long it will take for them to send an expeditionary force through."

"Expeditionary force?" asked Burton.

"Probably a score of combat-trained cherubim with flaming swords," said Mercury. "Even with a Balderhaz cube, your men are no match for them. My best suggestion is this: drop your weapons and try to look nonthreatening. I'll go through the portal and explain what's going on. We probably have a few minutes before things get out of hand."

Tiamat snorted. "The last thing we need is you scheming with the Heavenly authorities against us. We need to shut that thing down. Now."

As she spoke, Suzy heard footsteps and the rustle of clothing behind her. Glancing back, she saw another two dozen men in tactical gear pouring into the open space. They spread in a circle around the assembled group, guns at the ready. It occurred to her that at some point the sound of the helicopters had ceased. Apparently these were the reinforcements. She wondered how the score of cherubim with swords would do against all these men.

Burton glanced at Tiamat, and then at Balderhaz. "You," he said, pointing his gun at Balderhaz. "Step back."

Balderhaz did as instructed.

"Tiamat, shut down the portal generator. And don't try anything."

Tiamat nodded and moved toward the device, gracefully sidestepping the glowing ellipse. However much Tiamat resented her current position as FBI lackey, Suzy realized, she would be much worse off in Heaven. If Tiamat suddenly appeared in the Celestial City, she'd be thrown in an underground cell to rot for the next seven thousand years.

The top of the portal generator's case was angled slightly, and embedded in the angled panel was a small LCD screen. Just below the screen was a fold-out tray on which a keyboard rested. Tiamat studied the screen for a moment and then tapped a few keys.

"What's taking so long?" Burton asked.

"Relax," said Tiamat. "This is a sensitive device. It has to be shut down in the proper way to avoid side effects."

"Side effects?" asked Burton dubiously. "Like what?"

Suzy heard Eddie groan on the floor next to her. "She's doing something," he murmured. "Don't trust her."

Suzy glanced at Mercury, who was studying Tiamat with interest. He seemed bemused, like someone anticipating the punchline to a joke but not certain whether or not he wanted to blurt it out.

"This is only going to take longer if you don't let me concentrate," said Tiamat.

"Concentrate on what?" Burton demanded, taking a step toward her. He held his gun pointed at her chest. "What are you doing? Just shut it down!"

"Done!" said Tiamat with a smile.

"Good," said Burton. "Now step away from the—"

"See you soon," said Tiamat, and stepped onto the glowing ellipse.

Burton opened fire, hitting her three times. Her scream faded as if someone had turned down her volume knob, and then she was gone.

CHAPTER FOURTEEN

"None of this makes any sense," Lucifer said with a frown. "How can the goblin attack me when he has only one hit point?"

"Hit points don't affect a monster's ability to attack," said Drekavac tiredly. "It's the same with your characters. It's a concession to playability."

"Well, it's silly," said Lucifer, studying a big black rulebook whose cover was dominated by a giant scimitar-wielding demon menacing a trio of adventurers. "Who wrote these rules?"

"I thought you did," said Drekavac. A few of the other demons in the circle nodded.

"I think I would have remembered that," said Lucifer. "Oh, wait. This does seem familiar: THACO." He pronounced the acronym *Thay-co*. The rest of the demons in the circle groaned. Lucifer chuckled.

Suddenly Gurien yelped as if something had bit him.

"What the hell's gotten—" Pazusu started, but then trailed off, following Gurien's gaze. In the middle of the circle of demons, a faint blue-white ellipse had appeared, glowing in the dim light of the cavern. It seemed to be getting brighter as they watched.

The rest of them now saw it as well.

"What in Heaven's name...?" asked Drekavac.

"It's a portal!" Azrael cried. "Someone is breaking us out!"

Lucifer seemed less enthusiastic, although his interest was certainly piqued. He stood up and took a step back. "Careful," he said. "We have no idea who might be coming through that thing."

The other demons heeded the warning, getting up and stepping back from the brightly glowing portal.

"Hey!" called Malcazar from across the cavern. "What are you guys doing in there?"

"Don't let him see the portal!" Lucifer snapped. "Move!"

The demons congregated together, putting their bodies between the wall of bars and the portal.

"Just playing a game, Malcazar," called Lucifer. "No need to get up from your nap."

But Malcazar was already halfway across the cavern, his fiery sword drawn.

Lucifer heard a high-pitched scream behind him, and he turned to see a figure flicker into being on the glowing ellipse. No sooner had she fully materialized than she tumbled to the cage floor, moaning in pain.

"Turn her over!" Lucifer barked. The woman had landed face-down.

Two of the demons complied, carefully moving the woman onto her back. Her shirt was drenched with blood.

"Tiamat!" Lucifer exclaimed. "What the hell are you doing here?"

"No... time... to explain," said Tiamat. "Go... through the portal."

Lucifer frowned at her. "You're breaking me out?"

"Yes," gasped Tiamat. "Be ready."

"For what?" asked Lucifer.

But Tiamat had lost consciousness.

"What's going on in there?" Malcazar growled, now nearly to the bars. "Step to the back of the cage, all of you!"

"You think it's a trap, boss?" Azrael asked.

"Probably," said Lucifer. "But it can't be worse than this. Go!"

Azrael nodded. He took a step onto the portal and vanished.

"The rest of you too! Go, go, go!"

One by one, the demons stepped onto the portal and vanished. Soon only Lucifer, Gurien and Tiamat were left.

"Lucifer!" Malcazar yelled, struggling to keep his hands steady enough to get the key into the lock. "Step away from that portal!"

"What about her?" asked Gurien, indicating Tiamat.

Lucifer looked at Malcazar and then regarded the bloody figure of Tiamat lying on the stone floor a few feet away. "Follow me," he said. "Take her with you."

Lucifer stepped onto the portal and disappeared.

CHAPTER FIFTEEN

The BOX, just outside Elko, Nevada; April 29, 2017

"God damn it!" Burton growled. "Where the hell did she go?"

"Don't worry," said Mercury. "She went to a farm where she can run and play with all the other aspiring tyrants."

"I tried to warn you," said Eddie, getting to his feet and rubbing the back of his head. "I did, you all heard me."

"Everybody shut up!" Burton shouted. He turned to Balderhaz. "You! What did she do?"

Balderhaz took a step toward the portal generator. He frowned as he scanned the LCD screen. "She seems to have changed the coordinates slightly."

"To a different plane?" asked Burton.

"Not enough power for that," said Balderhaz. "She just moved the destination portal... this can't be right."

"What?" demanded Burton. "What did she do?"

"If I'm reading this correctly, she moved it about a hundred feet underground."

"*Underground?*" asked Burton. "Why?"

"Lucifer," said Mercury. "Oh, man. I'm such an idiot. This is my fault."

"What?" asked Suzy. "What did you do?"

"Tiamat must have found out where they're holding Lucifer. She's going to break him out."

"Lucifer?" asked Burton. "You mean...?"

"The devil himself, yes," said Mercury. "Burton, if you've got any sense in your head, you'll order your men to aim every weapon they have at that portal."

"Shut it down!" Burton said. "Close the portal!"

"She locked me out," Balderhaz said. "I can get around it, but it's going to take me a few minutes."

"What if we just wreck the generator? A few hundred rounds—"

"The portal will persist for a few minutes if the generator is shut down without closing it," said Balderhaz.

"There's no time," said Mercury. "Aim your guns at the portal and be ready. Suzy, take cover."

Suzy nodded and took a step toward the bank of machinery to her left.

"Don't move!" Burton snapped. "Take one more step and I'll—"

But as he spoke, a massive horned demon suddenly materialized on the portal. The demon paused a moment, taking in its surroundings.

"Shoot that thing!" Burton cried. "Kill it!"

In the split second it took them to aim their guns at the demon, it launched itself toward Special Agent Burton, nearly reaching him before being cut down in a hail of bullets. Another demon appeared on the portal behind him to take his place, and another after that.

Suzy was so stunned that all she could think of to do was put her hands over her ears to shield them from the deafening sound of gunfire. A strong hand gripped her arm, and after a moment's confusion she realized it was Mercury. She followed him as he pulled her down an alley, then made several quick turns through the maze of contraptions, boxes, and instruments. He shoved her into a narrow spot between two large metal machines. "Stay here!" he barked, barely audible over the constant gunfire.

"What are you going to do?" Suzy asked.

"Get shot, most likely," said Mercury, and disappeared from view.

Suzy crouched in her hiding space, her eyes closed and her hands clamped over her ears, for what seemed like an hour while the shouts, screams and gunshots went on and on and on. The smell of smoke—like the smell of firecrackers mixed with machine oil—permeated her nostrils. Then, suddenly, the cacophony stopped. After a moment she heard voices, low and muffled. She removed her hands from her ears, but still couldn't make out who was speaking or what was being said. She cautiously peeked out of her hiding space, and saw that the aisle was clear.

Keeping her head low, she worked her way back to the open area where the portal generator was. Peering through a crack in two boxes, she saw that the portal generator had been knocked on its side, and its casing was riddled with bullet holes. The portal itself was gone. Next to the portal generator, half-obscured by a blue-gray fog of smoke that hung in the air, stood a tall blond man wearing an orange jumpsuit and holding an automatic rifle. Suzy scanned the area as well as she could through the gap in the boxes but saw no one else. It wasn't until she craned her head so that she could see the floor that she realized where everyone had gone.

There were bodies everywhere. About half of them wore black tactical gear and the other half wore orange jumpsuits. There was an awful lot of blood spattered around, but it was hard to tell which blood belonged to whom. At least some of the FBI men were clearly dead, while others were merely unconscious or wounded. The demons, for the most part, looked even worse off, but Suzy knew that they'd be as good as new in a few hours. Not so much the men in black who were missing limbs or large chunks of brain matter. Suzy had to look away and take several deep breaths to keep from gagging. Groans and whimpers filled her ears.

"Wow!" she heard someone say—presumably the blond man, who seemed to be the only one in the condition to speak. "That was exciting, wasn't it?" He seemed to be the winner of the battle by default.

The only response was more moaning. Having calmed her stomach a bit, Suzy peered through the crack again, but was unable to locate Mercury or the others. All she could see was the blond man standing over a chaotic mass of black, orange, and red.

"Now, does somebody want to tell me where we are?" the blond man said. "You there," he said, poking his rifle barrel at one of the men in black, who seemed to be trying to get up. "Where are we?"

"Desert," the man mumbled. "Nevada."

"Nevada!" cried the blond man. "I love Nevada! Anywhere near Vegas?"

The man in black shook his head.

"No matter," said the blond man. "Ah, it's good to be back on the Mundane Plane. Although frankly it's good to be anywhere besides that damn cage. Tiamat, I could kiss you on the lips. Tiamat?" He looked around at the mass of bodies. "Gurien!" he snapped. "Where's Tiamat?"

"Here, boss," said a weak voice somewhere to the left of Suzy's field of vision. "She's underneath me."

"Well, get off of her, you cad," snapped the blond man, who was apparently Lucifer. Somehow he wasn't what Suzy had expected. "Tiamat!"

"I hear you," groaned Tiamat. "But I'm in no mood to be kissed on the lips or anywhere else. Help me up."

Lucifer moved out of sight for a moment. Several of the men in orange began to get slowly to their feet, beginning to recover from the wounds they had suffered.

"Search them all," said Lucifer. "Make sure they're completely disarmed. Then dump the dead ones somewhere and tie up everybody who's still alive."

"Wouldn't it be easier just to kill them?" Gurien asked.

"We might need hostages," said Lucifer. "Now do what you're told."

"What about the wounded ones?" asked another demon.

"If you can keep them from moaning, tie them up with the others. Otherwise, put a bullet in their head and throw them in the pile."

Most of the moaning stopped.

"And these three?" said another voice, over to Suzy's right. "They appear to be civilians."

"Those three are angels," said Tiamat, still out of sight. "Tie them up. Where's Burton? He's got a Balderhaz cube. Where's the girl?"

"Who?" asked Lucifer.

"There was a pudgy girl with purple hair. No matter. Just be careful with those three. Especially the tall one."

There was some scuffling and moving about as the men in black were sorted into categories of living, dead, and mostly dead. Two gunshots later, the moaning stopped completely and the middle category had gained a couple of members. The corpses were dragged out of sight, and the others—including Mercury, Eddie and

Balderhaz—were prodded into the center of the open area, where they had their hands and feet secured with regulation FBI zip-ties. Only four of the FBI agents were still alive, Burton among them. He seemed to have been grazed on the right shoulder and left cheek, but was conscious and alert. Balderhaz and Eddie looked unharmed, but Mercury seemed dazed and his shirt was soaked with blood.

"They're not going to stop, you know," said Burton. "There are only a handful of you, and the federal government has virtually unlimited—" The demon called Pazusu punched Burton in the gut and the man doubled over and fell to the floor. Tiamat nodded in approval. No one else spoke up after that.

By the time the captives were tied up, the demons were all on their feet, although several of them were limping or nursing other wounds. The only exception was the massive horned demon who had come through the portal first. He seemed to have taken the brunt of the gunfire, and his mutilated, barely recognizable form still lay on the concrete floor, half-covered with the bloody remnants of his jumpsuit.

Lucifer retrieved the Balderhaz cube from Burton's pocket and then turned and walked directly toward Suzy. For a split second, thinking he had seen her, she considered running, but she froze and held her ground. Lucifer stopped in front of the stack of boxes, set the cube down on top of the stack, turned, and walked back toward the captives. It occurred to Suzy that if she could get to the cube, Mercury and the others might have a chance to escape. But Lucifer was a good eight inches taller than she; she wouldn't be able to reach the top of the stack of boxes without a ladder or something else to stand on. And that commotion would likely draw attention. She decided to remain where she was for now.

"So," Lucifer said, walking back to Tiamat, "what have you been up to?"

"I've been working with the FBI for a few months now, just for something different," said Tiamat, with an obvious effort to appear nonchalant. "They're paranoid about angels. So I built them a miracle detector."

"Did you?" said Lucifer, intrigued. "May I see it?"

"Sure," said Tiamat. "Check Burton's other pocket."

Lucifer walked to Burton, who glared coldly at him. Ignoring him, Lucifer reached into Burton's pocket and pulled out a device that was only a little larger than an iPhone. "Compact design," said Lucifer. "I'm impressed. What's the range?"

"Ten miles or so, depending on the size of the surge. There's a much more powerful one in D.C., but of course that one isn't portable. These morons were drawing so much interplanar energy that we were able to pinpoint them to within a few miles of here. This baby got us the rest of the way."

"What kind of cat did you use?"

"Siamese."

"Good choice." Lucifer walked around the portal generator with an admiring look on his face. "So the great Balderhaz decided to try to reestablish contact with Heaven. Do you think it can be repaired?"

"I'm sure it can," said Tiamat. "But why would you want to? The only place you can go is Heaven. You know, where you just escaped from."

"You think too small," said Lucifer. "This portal generator is just the thing I need to reestablish my dominion over this plane."

"You mean *our* dominion," said Tiamat. "I broke you out. We're partners now."

"Of course!" said Lucifer, with a disarming smile. "Of course we are. I'm eternally indebted to you, my dear. We've had our differences in the past, but it's time to put that behind us."

"Good," said Tiamat cautiously. "Now what is this plan of yours?"

"Well," said Lucifer, "to be honest, it's a bit sensitive. I'd rather not divulge too much at this point. Nothing personal, but there are a lot of contingencies and I don't want to get ahead of myself."

"I see," said Tiamat. "So what's the next step?"

Lucifer bent down and righted the portal generator. The LCD screen was cracked and the casing had at least a dozen bullet holes in it. Lucifer absently felt at the holes with his fingertips. "How long do you think it will take to repair it?" he asked.

"Depends what's wrong with it," said Tiamat. "But they seem to have all the tools we would need to fabricate replacement components. I wouldn't think it would take more than a few hours."

"Good, good," said Lucifer. "With a working portal generator, we're most of the way there. But I'm missing one piece of the puzzle. A certain artifact that has unique properties. I know where it is; I just have to go get it."

"And how long do you expect this to take? We can't remain here indefinitely. Somebody is going to miss these agents."

"If my suspicions are correct, I shouldn't need more than four hours," said Lucifer. "You can hold off the feds until then. Just tell them you've got hostages. It'll be like Waco all over again."

"Didn't everybody in the compound at Waco get incinerated?"

"Yes, *eventually*," Lucifer replied. "But they held out for almost two months. All I need is a day."

Tiamat seemed unconvinced.

"Look, I'll leave my minions here with you. You saw how they did against these guys. You'll have no trouble holding off the feds for a day. Hear that, Azrael? Tiamat's in charge until I get back."

A faint moan emerged from Azrael's bloody form.

"You see?" said Lucifer. "Everything is going to be fine. Get that portal generator working. I'll be back as soon as I can."

CHAPTER SIXTEEN

The BOX, just outside Elko, Nevada; April 29, 2017

It had been only three hours since Lucifer disappeared, and the sound of helicopters had returned with a vengeance. There were no windows in the building, but the rumbling whine of rotors was all around them. Whether the helicopters belonged to the media or some governmental agency was impossible to say. All Suzy knew was that their remote desert facility had definitely drawn some attention. Occasionally an amplified voice identifying itself as "the FBI" would break through the droning of helicopters to demand that Tiamat release the hostages and come out with her hands up, but Tiamat had shown no interest in doing either of those things. The voice of the FBI called her by name, so whoever was out there had some idea what they were dealing with, although the voice seemed to be unaware of the involvement of Lucifer or any other demons.

Tiamat was agitated but trying not to show it. She had released one of the more badly wounded FBI agents to warn the authorities outside what would happen if they tried to enter the building, but she didn't seem terribly worried about this possibility. Tiamat's main concern seemed to be getting the portal generator working. She had assigned Balderhaz to this task, threatening to start shooting FBI agents if he tried any "funny business." Balderhaz was busy at work on the device, although if Suzy knew Balderhaz, he was motivated more by the idea of repairing his damaged creation than by the threat of more dead FBI agents.

Meanwhile, Suzy had managed to drag a sturdy plastic storage container to the stack of boxes in front of her without being seen, and now was waiting for the right moment to climb on top of it to grab the Balderhaz cube. Unfortunately, Tiamat had taken to pacing back and forth on the other side of the boxes, barely twenty feet away, and Suzy didn't dare move for fear of alerting the demoness of her presence. So far Tiamat had been so preoccupied—or unconcerned with Suzy's disappearance—that she hadn't even bothered to send a demon looking for her.

The captives sat on the concrete floor, their hands and feet tied. Only Balderhaz had been allowed to roam free, and he was under constant surveillance by the demon known as Pazusu. Balderhaz had replaced the broken screen and opened up the bullet-ridden casing to examine the device's innards. He had made a few adjustments, closed it back up again, and was now tapping at keys and staring at the screen.

"Is it working yet?" asked Tiamat. "What's taking so long?"

"What's your hurry?" asked the big horned demon, who sat on a crate nearby. "Lucifer said he'd be back in—"

"I didn't ask for your input, Azrael," Tiamat snapped.

Azrael shrugged. He had been put in charge of watching the captives, and he was clearly bored. He had spent the past three hours sitting on the crate, holding a rifle across his lap and waiting for his numerous wounds to heal. His condition had improved, but he was still shaky and pale. Tiamat had instructed the rest of the demons to patrol the inside perimeter of the compound, in case the feds tried to sneak somebody inside.

"I think it's working," said Balderhaz. "But I won't know for sure until I finish the self-test. A few more minutes."

Tiamat nodded. "Well, get to it. I want that thing working by the time Lucifer gets back." Then she mumbled, almost inaudibly, "That bastard better get his ass back here quick. If he double-crosses me, he's going to find out—"

A deafening blast rang out somewhere in the building, to Suzy's left. It was followed by shouts and automatic gunfire.

"Gurien!" Tiamat said into a walkie-talkie she had appropriated from one of the FBI agents. "What was that? What's happening?"

The only answer was a garbled squeal of feedback. More gunfire followed.

"Damn these incompetent fools!" Tiamat snarled. "Azrael, stay here and watch the hostages. If the FBI gets in, start executing them."

Azrael nodded and Tiamat ran off, disappearing into the maze of junk.

She had been gone for only a few seconds when Special Agent Burton got to his feet and launched himself toward Azrael. His ankles were still tied together, but somehow he had gotten his hands loose. A small piece of scrap metal lying on the floor where he had been sitting attested to his method.

Azrael tried to get his rifle pointed at Burton, but there was no time. Burton threw his arms around Azrael and slammed into him, knocking him off the crate. The demon probably had fifty pounds on Burton, but Azrael was still recovering from his wounds and Burton had both momentum and desperation on his side. Azrael yelped as he hit the concrete floor, the weight of Burton coming down on top of him.

Burton had obviously put some thought into his attack: staying on the offensive after Azrael hit the floor, he repeatedly pummeled Azrael in the chest, where the majority of his bullet wounds were clustered. Azrael howled in pain, holding up his arms in an attempt to protect himself. The two grappled on the floor, momentarily disappearing from view behind the crate. Then suddenly Burton had the rifle in his hand and was rolling away from Azrael. Azrael pulled himself onto his hands and knees, trying to get to Burton, but he was too late. Burton, still prone, aimed the gun at the demon's head and fired. A hole appeared in Azrael's forehead and he fell to the floor, still. Suzy knew an angel could recover even from a bullet to the brain, but it would take a while—particularly inside the radius of the Balderhaz cube.

Realizing she wasn't going to get a better opportunity, Suzy climbed on top of the plastic container, grabbed the cube, and jumped down to the floor. She had intended to run with it to the far side of the building to give Mercury and the others a chance to escape, but she wasn't sure the angels could sense the cube's absence—and it wouldn't do any good to give them a chance to escape if they didn't *know* they had a chance to escape. Since the captives were momentarily unguarded, she decided to leave the matter up to Mercury. She went around the stack of boxes, emerging into the open area.

Burton had gotten a large knife from Azrael and had removed his gag and the zip-ties on his hands and feet. He saw Suzy

117

approach but he ignored her. Burton went to the nearest of the FBI agents, who had gone ashen from blood loss. He cut the man's bonds and then cut the hands free of another man nearby. Handing the knife to the man, he said, "Get everybody free. Be quick about it." Burton then turned his attention back to the wounded man.

Suzy crouched down next to Mercury. "Are you okay?" she asked.

In the distance, automatic gunfire erupted again.

"I haven't felt this bad since I sat through the director's cut of *Avatar*," Mercury said, "but I'll survive." He glanced at Burton, who was still busy attending to his own men. "Go find a knife."

Suzy nodded, getting to her feet. Burton was too preoccupied to worry about them now, but she wasn't going to count on his help to escape. She found a box cutter on a workbench not far away, and returned to Mercury. She cut Mercury's hands loose and then handed him the Balderhaz cube. ""I thought you might want this."

"Good thinking," Mercury said. He took the cube and bent down to cut the zip-tie on his feet. "Balderhaz, turn the portal generator back on."

"What?" asked Suzy. "Why?"

"I'm going to get us some reinforcements."

Balderhaz frowned. "But I haven't tested it yet. There's no telling what might happen to you if you try to go through the portal now."

"I know it's risky," said Mercury. "But we've got no choice. The FBI doesn't have a chance against demons. Like Burton said, they aren't going to stop. They'll keep sending men, and the demons will keep slaughtering them. We need help." As he spoke, he cut Eddie's hands apart and handed him the box cutter.

Balderhaz nodded and stepped toward the device.

"Hold on," said Burton, stepping between Balderhaz and the portal generator, rifle in hand. "Nobody's going through that thing. You saw what happened last time."

"You're out of your league, FBI dude," Mercury said, taking the Balderhaz cube from Suzy. "Get your men out of here while you can."

"That isn't going to happen," said Burton, pointing his rifle at Mercury. "As far as I'm concerned, you and your friends are still potential threats. I'm not leaving here without you."

Suzy glanced at the other FBI agents, who stood watching this exchange. They were unarmed and in pretty rough shape; several of them could barely stand. However much loyalty they might have to Burton, she didn't think there was much chance of them getting involved in a fight between Burton and Mercury—particularly now that they had seen what angels could do.

"You're adorable, Special Agent Burton," said Mercury. "But you're powerless as long as I'm holding this." He held the Balderhaz cube in the air, a few inches above his shoulder.

Burton frowned. "That isn't how the cube works," he said. "It doesn't have any effect on—"

Mercury hurled the cube at Burton, smacking him hard right between the eyes. Burton took two steps backward and then collapsed on the floor. The Balderhaz cube landed at Mercury's feet and he picked it up. "They're also pretty good paperweights," Mercury said. "Eddie, take his gun."

Eddie, who had just gotten his feet loose, scrambled over to the unconscious Special Agent Burton and grabbed the rifle. He spun to face the other agents, but needn't have been concerned. None of them had moved.

"Balderhaz, get that thing fired up," said Mercury.

Balderhaz stepped up to the portal generator and began tapping keys. "I'm going to reset the destination parameters," he said. "But I can't guarantee this is going to work. The portal could shut down halfway through the transfer, stranding you in the void, or you could be torn in half, or—"

"None of this is helping my mood," said Mercury, wincing and holding a hand to his belly. "Just do it. Tiamat could be back any second."

Balderhaz bit his lip and went back to work. Soon, a faint blue-white ellipse glowed on the floor in front of them.

"Mercury, you're insane," said Eddie. "You can't go through that thing. Just look at it!" As he spoke, the glowing pattern went fuzzy around the edges, flickered, disappeared momentarily, and then reappeared.

"No choice," said Mercury, handing Eddie the cube. "Balderhaz, is it ready?"

Balderhaz held up his hands helplessly.

"I'm going to go ahead and take that as a yes," said Mercury.

"Don't do this, Mercury," Suzy pleaded. "It isn't safe."

"True," said Mercury, with a grin. "But it's certainly not boring." He stepped onto the glowing ellipse and disappeared.

CHAPTER SEVENTEEN

Florence Administrative Maximum Facility (Supermax), Fremont County, Colorado; April 29, 2017

Lying in bed, Chris Finlan heard footsteps in the hall and he frowned. Visiting hours were over and the footsteps were too soft and light, not the rhythmic thud of the guards' thick rubber soles. A lawyer, maybe? But lawyers didn't usually come to the prison this late, and everyone in this cell block had exhausted all of their appeals. Death row was one cell block over; Finlan's lawyer had cut him a deal for life.

Some deal, he thought as the footsteps grew louder.

Chris Finlan wondered how long it would take them to figure it out—and what they would do when they did. Would they really keep him in prison forever? The Florence Administrative Maximum Facility—affectionately known as "the Alcatraz of the Rockies"— was only twenty years old; he figured a building like this would probably stand for another hundred years or so. Eventually, though, it would be decommissioned and he'd be moved to some new, higher-tech facility—maybe something like those cool glowing hula hoop rings from the old *Superman* movie. Or would the United States itself fall first? Then what? What would happen to the millions imprisoned by that corrupt empire in institutions such as this one? As much as he wanted to hope for revolution, a storming of the Bastille, it was a fool's hope. In all likelihood, a violent overthrow of the federal government would result in all the inmates of this facility slowly starving to death.

All except one, at least. Chris Finlan wasn't sure he *could* starve to death. He knew he could get very, very hungry: he'd had a run of bad luck during the Great Depression, occasionally not eating for weeks at a time. But no matter how hungry he got, his body just kept going, as if subsisting on some mysterious energy drawn from the aether. He supposed even his body might eventually succumb to hunger, but he wasn't eager to find out. If it looked like that was the way things were going, he'd have to find some other way to end himself. But then, that meant getting rid of *it*.

No, he said to himself. It won't come to that. There had to be some other way out.

As the footsteps continued to get louder, Chris Finlan sat up in bed. He was somehow certain that the mysterious visitor was coming to see him. Most of the other prisoners were asleep, their snores echoing in the concrete hall. Occasionally he would hear one of them wake up and offer some sort of challenge—ranging from guardedly friendly to blatantly hostile—to the visitor, but the visitor quieted each man in turn with a few words. Chris Finlan couldn't make out what the visitor was saying, but he sensed an eerie power in the man's tone. It was a mode of speaking mastered by some of the Victorian spiritualists he had met, similar to hypnotism—a way of exerting one's will over others through simple voice commands. He'd never heard anyone use it to such astonishing effect, though.

"Hey, who—" started the man in the cell next to him.

"Go back to sleep," said the visitor.

Seconds later, the man was snoring again.

A few more steps and the visitor was standing in front of Chris Finlan's cell, a svelte silhouette with blond hair ablaze in the fluorescent illumination behind him.

"Chris Finlan," said the visitor.

"That's me, chief," said Chris Finlan, attempting to affect an air of nonchalance, but his voice cracked in the middle of the last word. He cleared his throat. "Who the devil are you?"

"You know," said the visitor, "I was planning on giving you an alias, but I expect you're the sort of man who appreciates the truth. Chris—may I call you that?"

Chris Finlan shrugged.

"Good," said the visitor. "I... hold on." The visitor put his hands on the bars in front of him and slowly pulled them apart, until there was just enough room for him to squeeze through. He did so, and was soon standing in front of Chris. "There, that's better," he said. "I don't like talking through bars. Bad memories."

Chris Finlan nodded, still staring at the gap in the bars. Was this actually happening? Was he dreaming?

The visitor held out his hand and Chris Finlan shook it. He sure felt real.

"As I was saying," the visitor said, "My name is Lucifer. And before you ask: yes, *the* Lucifer. Satan himself."

Chris Finlan swallowed hard. "Do you... want my soul?"

Lucifer burst into laughter. "Your soul!" he barked, then clapped his hand over his mouth, remembering where he was. "You mortals and your souls. What would I want with your soul, for Pete's sake? Do you people think I wear them on a necklace? No, Chris, I have no interest in your soul. In fact, I suspect you know exactly what I want. Where is it?"

"I don't know what you're talking about," Chris said, backing away slightly.

"Oh, come now, Chris. You know better than to play this game. You've been around a long time. A *very* long time, by human standards."

"You don't know anything about me."

Lucifer sighed. "It's your own fault, you know. You should have kept a low profile. As good as my surveillance network was at its peak, I never would have found you if you'd have just kept your head down. In fact, until a few months ago I was still under the impression the shard was still in Heaven, attached to the Sword of Eden. But when—after months of plotting, mind you—that turned out not to be the case, I spent some time pondering where the shard might be. Clearly Heaven didn't have it, and if another demon had gotten his hands on it, I would have heard about it. So presumably it was in the hands of a mortal."

"Please," said Chris Finlan, "I don't know anything about a shard. I'm just a guy who got fed up and—"

"Knowing something about the properties of ubiquium," Lucifer continued undeterred, "it occurred to me that a person who had been exposed to it for a long period of time would have developed some... eccentricities. Not just longevity, of course, although that's a given. How old are you, by the way? Two hundred? Three?"

Chris Finlan regarded Lucifer for a moment, unsure what to say.

123

"Drop the coy act, Chris. It'll do you no good to withhold details from me. I know all the important stuff anyway. I'm just curious."

"I was born on January sixth, 1823."

"Almost two hundred, then," said Lucifer. "Yes, that's when the ennui starts to set in. The ennui turns to anger, and that coupled with the introversion and obsessiveness... well, here you are."

"I wrote a manifesto," said Chris Finlan tentatively.

"Of course you did. You thought you had it all figured out. The solution to all mankind's problems. You wanted to tell everyone."

"But nobody would listen."

"They never do. So you started sending bombs in the mail."

Chris Finlan nodded.

"And you wound up here. Made the news, which is how I heard about you. I had actually been planning on getting in touch before I... well, I had a bit of a setback. Of course, back then I thought you were a just a garden-variety psychopath. I didn't realize your psychosis had a supernatural cause. But after my failed attempt at acquiring the shard, I did some thinking and came up with a profile for a person suffering from UOD."

"UOD?"

"Ubiquium Obsessive Disorder. The more I thought about it, the more certain I was that you had the shard."

"I don't know what you're talking about."

"Please, Chris. Let's not waste time. You've had a good run, but surely you can see it's over. You don't want to rot in here for the next thousand years, do you?"

Chris Finlan shook his head. Then hope momentarily surged inside him. "You could break me out! Together we could—"

"No, Chris. Understand that it's not personal, but I simply have no need for you. If you'd come by your psychosis honestly, there might have been a time when I could have found a place for you in my organization, but these days things are tight. And to be honest, you're just a guy who stumbled upon a magic gem. Without it, you're nothing. Useless."

"I'm not useless!" Chris Finlan shrieked. "I've figured it out! If I just could have gotten them to listen to me, I could have changed things!"

"Enough!" Lucifer growled, and Chris Finlan cowered from him. "I've wasted enough time here. Give me the shard."

Chris Finlan shook his head.

"Give. Me. The. Shard."

"I... can't," said Chris Finlan.

"You think you can't, because you've grown attached to it, but it's a delusion. It will hurt for a while, being without it, but eventually you'll be fine. And then you can slowly die of natural causes in your cell, like the rest of the losers in here."

"No," said Chris Finlan. "I mean, I *can't*. They wouldn't let me have it in here, so I..."

Lucifer groaned. "You swallowed it, didn't you?"

Chris Finlan nodded.

"But don't they check your cell? How do you... I mean, when it comes out...?"

"I have to swallow it again every couple of days."

Lucifer grimaced. "How long ago did you last swallow it?"

"Um. This afternoon, I think."

"Good," said Lucifer, taking a step toward Chris Finlan, who was now backed against the wall of his cell.

"What are you—" Chris Finlan started. And then he screamed. Lucifer had reached into his belly, and was now rooting around inside of him with his fingers, a mildly disgusted look on his face. Chris Finlan could do nothing but stare at him in horror. After a moment, Lucifer pulled his hand back and held up something small and hard. His arm was covered with blood halfway to his elbow.

"There!" Lucifer cried triumphantly. "That wasn't so bad, was it?"

Chris Finlan slumped to his knees, his eyes still fixed in horror.

"I want you to know how much I appreciate this," said Lucifer. "And I also wanted to tell you... Chris! Pay attention, this is important."

Chris' eyes had gone glassy, but were now once again fixed on Lucifer's face.

"Good. Chris, I want you to know that you didn't figure anything out. You're delusional, Chris. There's no meaning for you to find, in two hundred years or two thousand. Everything is pointless."

Chris Finlan fell face-first to the cell floor, dead.

"Good talk," said Lucifer, wiping his arm on Chris' bedsheet. He put the shard in his pocket and slipped out of the cell.

CHAPTER EIGHTEEN

The BOX, just outside Elko, Nevada; April 29, 2017

Mercury had just vanished through the portal when Suzy heard a woman's voice to her left. "Drop it, Eddie," the voice commanded. Suzy turned to see Tiamat approaching, rifle in hand. Eddie, still shakily holding Azrael's gun on the FBI agents, hesitated.

"Look, if you're going to shoot, shoot," said Tiamat. "I don't have all day."

Eddie slowly set the rifle down next to the still motionless body of Azrael.

"Oh, hell," said Tiamat, frowning at Azrael. "What did you do to Azrael?"

"It wasn't me," said Eddie. He glanced at the still-unconscious Burton.

"Why are you all out of your zip-ties?" Tiamat said, sounding more flustered than angry. "Why is the portal on? And where the hell is Mercury?" When no one answered, she held the barrel of the gun up to the nearest man's head. "Somebody better start talking," she said coldly.

Suzy gave a sigh of defeat. It had obviously been too much to hope for that the FBI would successfully storm the building and rescue them. The perimeter of the building was outside the reach of the Balderhaz cube, which meant the demons guarding the building had a huge advantage over the mere humans trying to get in. Evidently the demons had dispatched the immediate threat.

"He went to get help," said Suzy.

"From Heaven?" said Tiamat. "Damn him. Balderhaz, shut that thing down."

Balderhaz got to his feet.

"Wait," said Suzy. "Tiamat, you're not thinking this through. I realize you were desperate to escape the FBI, but we can't let Lucifer run free on Earth. We need help."

Tiamat sneered. "Lucifer gets all the press. He's not so bad. I've come up with more elaborate schemes for taking over the world than he ever has."

"That may be," said Eddie, "but you of all people should know better than to trust him. You don't even know where he's gone. Do you really think he's going to let you in on his master plan when he gets back? You're smarter than that, Tiamat."

"He needs me," said Tiamat. "If it weren't for me, he'd still be in prison."

"You're counting on Lucifer to be *grateful?*" asked Eddie incredulously. "Please, Tiamat. Think about it. His minions are loyal to him, not you. When he gets back—"

As he spoke, a figure began to materialize on the portal. It flickered for a moment, then became solid: Mercury had returned.

But it was clear that something was wrong. He was dressed oddly, in a torn, dingy gray tunic and matching pants that were a good three inches too short for him. On his feet were badly scuffed leather boots. And he was hurt—far worse than he had been when he had stepped onto the portal less than two minutes before. His clothes were stained with blood and his face was pale. He stumbled off the portal into Suzy, who did her best to keep him upright. Eddie rushed to her side, grabbing Mercury's arm.

Tiamat watched with interest, her rifle still at the ready, but she didn't intervene.

"Mercury!" Suzy exclaimed. "What happened to you?"

"Shut it down," Mercury gasped, his voice hoarse and barely audible. "Shut the portal down!"

"You heard him, Balderhaz!" Suzy said. "Shut it down!"

Balderhaz nodded and stepped back to the keyboard. He glanced at Tiamat, and she gave him a nod. Balderhaz began tapping at keys.

Everyone else simply stared at Mercury. Tiamat was doing her best to maintain an illusion of control, but she clearly had no better idea of what had happened to Mercury than anyone else. While she watched, Suzy and Eddie helped Mercury to the crate Azrael had been sitting on.

"What happened to you, Mercury?" Eddie asked. "Did you make it to Heaven?"

Mercury stared at him uncomprehendingly. "Heaven?" He asked. "No. Lucifer... coming here. Shut it down. This is what I've been... waiting for."

"Mercury, you're not making any sense," said Suzy. "You've only been gone for two minutes. What do you mean, this is what you've been waiting for?"

"Seven thousand years," Mercury gasped. "I've... waited. To stop him. Shut it down."

"Lucifer?" asked Eddie. "He's already here, Mercury. He just left a few hours ago."

Mercury looked momentarily stunned, then shook his head. "No, different Lucifer. Alternate timeline. Lucifer in control... of everything. Coming... here."

One of the FBI agents let out a yelp, and Suzy turned toward the portal just in time to see another figure flicker into being. For a moment, everyone remained in stunned silence. Tiamat's eyes went wide with fear as the man's features came into focus. But then confusion came over her face. This man was too tall to be Lucifer, and his hair was silver, not blond.

It was Mercury. Again.

Suzy stared at the man, then looked at the man sitting on the crate, then turned back to the man on the portal. The Mercury on the portal seemed stunned, as if he had seen a ghost. This Mercury was dressed the same as the Mercury who had just disappeared a couple minutes earlier.

"Mercury?" asked Suzy. But if *this* was Mercury, then who was the man sitting on the crate a few feet away?

"You need to shut that thing down," said the newly arrived Mercury to Balderhaz.

"You don't have to keep telling me!" snapped Balderhaz, who was furiously tapping at keys. He hit the Enter key with a flourish and the portal began to fade. An air of relief came over the group as those assembled realized no one else was coming through.

The Mercury sitting on the crate fell forward, collapsing on the floor. Eddie and Suzy, distracted by the appearance of the second Mercury, had released their grip on him.

"Mercury!" cried Suzy, dropping to the floor to help him. She and Eddie struggled to turn him over.

"That jerk was going to leave me behind," the Mercury standing next to the portal generator said. He shuddered. "You should have seen that place. It was awful. Like the post-Judgment Day scenes from *Terminator 2*, but without the cool robots."

"He has no pulse," said Suzy, her fingers on the prone Mercury.

"Give him a slap on the cheek," said the standing Mercury. "He'll be fine."

Suzy slapped him and checked his pulse again. She shook her head.

The other Mercury frowned and stepped toward the Mercury on the floor. He knelt down next to him, grabbed the front of his dingy tunic, and shook him. "Hey!" he shouted. "Wake up!"

The Mercury on the floor did not wake up. The more recently arrived Mercury gave him another slap across the cheek. Still the man on the floor did not stir. "Holy shit," said the Mercury crouched next to his prone doppelganger. "I think I'm dead."

"That's impossible," said Tiamat. "You can't die. You're an angel."

"Also, you're talking," said Suzy. "Who is this guy? He's not you."

Mercury stood up slowly, regarding the corpse. "As near as I can tell, he's another iteration of me."

"Like a clone?" asked Eddie. "What do you mean, another iteration?"

"Well," said Mercury, "you guys remember when you told me it was a really bad idea to go through the portal?"

"Yes," said Eddie, Suzy and Balderhaz simultaneously.

"Turns out you were totally right," said Mercury. "Something went wrong with the portal. I didn't go to Heaven. I went *here*. But not *here*, here. Another here. Not a different plane, but a different version of this one. Lousy place. Zero stars. Do not recommend."

"What the hell are you talking about, Mercury?" Tiamat demanded.

"Another Earth. Just like this one, but far, far worse. Imagine a place where the *Star Wars* prequels exist but the original *Star Wars* trilogy doesn't. A place where all the chocolate chip cookies are actually raisin cookies. A place where the Beatles don't exist but Wings does, and all the dental floss is unwaxed."

"You were only gone for two minutes," said Suzy. "How do you even know all that?"

"I'm extrapolating," Mercury replied. "Point is, it's not a nice place. Somehow Lucifer took control of the whole plane a long time ago and nothing has been the same since. Not our Lucifer. An alternate Lucifer. I'm in charge of the resistance. I mean, not me. Him." He pointed at the other Mercury. "Was in charge. Somehow he knew I was coming. Lucifer knows too. He was right behind us. He wants to take over this plane too."

"But why?" asked Eddie. "Doesn't that Lucifer already have his own plane?"

"Yeah," replied Mercury, "but as I think I mentioned, it's kind of a shithole. He wants a new one."

"So this is a completely different Lucifer?" asked Suzy. "Not the one who just left here?"

"Yes," Mercury said. "I think so? I haven't really had a chance to process it all. But we have bigger problems. We need to stop Lucifer. Our Lucifer, I mean. I know what he's after. Some kind of artifact that he plans to use to travel back in time."

"How do you know that?"

"Mercury told me. The other Mercury. He was kind of rambling, but I got the gist of it."

"Why does Lucifer want to go back in time?" asked Eddie.

"He plans to rewrite history. Undo everything that's ever happened, ever since the dinosaurs climbed down from the trees."

"Dinosaurs never lived in trees, Mercury."

"Gaaahhh!" Mercury cried, overcome with panic. "It's happening already!"

"Calm down," said Suzy. "Think it through. Nothing has happened yet. What is Lucifer trying to do?"

Mercury nodded, taking a deep breath. "All I know for sure is what he—" Mercury motioned toward the other Mercury, dead on the floor— "told me. That our Lucifer is going to try to go back in time and erase history. It makes sense, if you think about it. Lucifer knows his days are numbered. Eventually somebody is going to reestablish contact with Heaven, and he doesn't have the organization or clout to resist the authorities for long. It's just him and a handful of minions. So he's going to erase it all and start over—with him in charge."

"Time travel," said Suzy, shaking her head. "Is that even possible?"

"Of course it's possible," said Balderhaz. "If you can travel in space, you can travel in time. Time, space, it's just different ways of looking at the same thing. Otherwise, how do you explain him?" He was gesturing toward the dead Mercury on the floor.

"What do you mean, Balderhaz?" Eddie asked.

"Isn't it obvious?" Balderhaz said. "Lucifer's already done it. The alternate timeline is the result of Lucifer having gone back in time and changing history."

"But..." Eddie said, with a frown. "If Lucifer did rewrite history, then why are we still here?"

"I'm not entirely convinced we are," Balderhaz answered.

"Of course we're here!" exclaimed Tiamat. "Don't be foolish. Evidently, there was an unknown plane where alternate versions of Mercury and Lucifer existed, and somehow by damaging the portal generator we managed to access it. The portal is closed now, and there's no need to worry about it further. It was a fluke, that's all. Time travel is impossible."

"So the alternate reality wasn't the result of Lucifer going back in time?" asked Suzy.

"That's right," said Tiamat. But Balderhaz was shaking his head.

Eddie turned to him and said, "You think Lucifer did go back in time, Balderhaz?"

"Yes and no," replied Balderhaz. "All possible realities exist in theory. Somehow the damaged portal generator opened a rift to a different reality. The same reality that Lucifer created by going back in time."

"None of this makes any sense," Suzy groaned.

"However the alternate reality came into being," said Mercury, "the important thing is that we stop Lucifer before he does the same thing here. Tiamat, you have to let these people go. We need to join forces to stop Lucifer."

Tiamat shook her head. "No," she said after a moment. "This is one of your tricks."

"No trick, Tiamat. I've seen a universe where Lucifer is in charge. And unless you want this place to turn into that place, we need to stop him."

"How can you stop him from doing something he's already done?" Suzy asked.

Mercury shook his head. "I don't know. But why would the other Mercury tell me to stop him if it had already happened?"

"Maybe you can undo what he already did the same way he's trying to undo everything else," Eddie suggested.

"How did the other Mercury even know what our Lucifer was going to do?" asked Suzy.

"And how do you know you can trust him?" said Eddie. "You only knew him for two minutes."

"I have a good feeling about him," said Mercury. "He has a trustworthy face. Had. Can somebody cover him up? It's a little creepy."

Suzy nodded and walked to a tarp that had been thrown over a piece of equipment. Tiamat gave her a nod, and she pulled the tarp off and covered the body.

"I don't understand how he could die," said Eddie. "If he really is you, he should be immortal."

"Maybe he was a mortal version of me," said Mercury.

Suzy shook her head. "He said he'd been waiting for this for seven thousand years."

"Well, I don't know," said Mercury.

"I have a theory," said Balderhaz.

"Let's hear it," said Tiamat.

"I think our Mercury killed him."

CHAPTER NINETEEN

"I didn't kill him!" Mercury protested. "He was already shot when I met him! He was in pretty rough shape, but I assumed he would be fine in a few hours. Because, you know. Immortal."

"Ordinarily he would be," said Balderhaz. "But when an angel's body dies, its spirit has to connect with the source of his energy, the Eye of Providence, in order to regenerate. In this case, that circuit was already busy."

"You mean because there was already a Mercury here," said Eddie. "The other Mercury's spirit reached out to the Eye, but couldn't make the connection because this Mercury was already connected."

"That's the theory," said Balderhaz.

"Well, I didn't do it on purpose!" cried Mercury. "How was I supposed to know there could only be one immortal version of me at a time?"

"You couldn't have known," said Suzy.

"And I'm not sure what you could have done differently even if you had," Eddie added.

Mercury nodded glumly, regarding the sheet-covered corpse. He turned away with a shudder. "I guess there's nothing to do now but try to stop Lucifer from doing what he was warning us about. Balderhaz, what would Lucifer need to convert your portal generator into a time machine?"

Balderhaz thought for a moment. "The main thing he'd need is much more powerful batteries. He'd need a thousand times the power we have here."

"Our batteries take up that whole section of the BOX," said Mercury, waving at a massive bank of dozens of metal cylinders, stacked three high, each of them the size of a large refrigerator. "So unless Lucifer's got several truckloads of batteries socked away somewhere, there wouldn't seem to be much danger."

"Not necessarily," said Balderhaz. "Our batteries take up a lot of space because we're using xenon difluoride-based cells. It's a rather inefficient way of storing interplanar energy. There are substances that are better for this purpose, but they're extremely rare. The rarest of all is ubiquium."

"Isn't that what the Eye of Providence is made of?" asked Eddie.

"The Eye of Providence is the only known source of ubiquium in the multiverse," said Tiamat. "Lucifer would have to go to Heaven and crack a piece off. Impossible."

Eddie nodded. "If that was his plan, he would have used the portal to get to Heaven."

"He wouldn't stand a chance of getting near the Eye," said Mercury. "That can't be his plan. You said there were other substances that would work, Balderhaz. What are the other alternatives?"

"Any sort of compound comprised of tightly bound three-dimensional metallic network structures would work," said Balderhaz. "But they're all extremely rare, and none of them has anywhere near the potential of ubiquium. He'd need a truckload of any of the others."

"We're missing something," said Mercury. "He's got to be after ubiquium. But where would he find a piece on Earth?"

"The shard," said Eddie.

Mercury rubbed his chin thoughtfully.

Tiamat scowled. "It's a myth," she said. "There is no shard."

"The what?" asked Suzy. "Can somebody tell me what the hell you're all going on about?"

Eddie pulled a wrinkled bill from his pocket and unfolded it. He pointed at the pyramid on the reverse. "The Eye of Providence," he said. "Source of all the interplanar energy in the multiverse. It doesn't actually have a big eyeball on it. That part is symbolic. Like if I wrote a book about angels and put wings on the angels on the cover, even though—"

"Yeah, I get it, Eddie," said Suzy. "I'm a little behind on my metaphysics homework. I'm not retarded."

"That story is bunk anyway," said Tiamat. "If there really is a piece missing from the Eye, and if Lucifer was the one who broke it off, why doesn't he still have it?"

"The story is that he lost it," said Eddie. "He had a special sword commissioned, with the shard as the gem in the pommel. It was still being fabricated when he was kicked out of Heaven. The sword was given to the angel who guarded the entrance to the Garden of Eden, but at some point it was lost. It's never been recovered."

"He must have figured out where it was while he was in prison," said Mercury.

"This is all pointless theorizing," said Tiamat. "Whatever Lucifer's up to, it's not time travel. We'll find out when he gets back."

"When he gets back, it will be too late," Mercury snapped. "You think he's going to take you back in time with him? He's going to rewrite history without you in it."

"He's not going back in time!" Tiamat snarled. "It's impossible!"

"Even if you don't buy the time travel bit," said Mercury, "you have to realize that Lucifer is going to ditch you as soon as he no longer needs you."

"Your concern is touching," replied Tiamat. "But I can handle Lucifer."

"That you can, my dear," said a familiar voice behind Suzy. She turned to see Lucifer stride into the open area, smiling broadly. He held his right palm open in front of him. It held a glittering azure gem.

"Is that...?" Tiamat began.

"The shard of the Eye of Providence," said Lucifer.

"Told you," said Mercury.

"I have to say," Lucifer went on, "you guys sure know how to throw a party. There must be three hundred FBI guys and cops outside. I had to cause an explosion on the other side of the building as a diversion just to get back in."

"Damn it, Lucifer," said Tiamat. "We thought the FBI had broken in."

"Couldn't be avoided," said Lucifer. "But don't worry; the FBI is still terrified you're going to execute their agents. I'd say we have a few more hours at least before they storm the building."

137

A groan went up from the floor near the crate, and for a moment Suzy thought they had been mistaken about the other Mercury being dead. But it was only Azrael.

"Who shot Azrael?" asked Lucifer, regarding the body of the massive demon, who was once again still. He leaned over to pick up Azrael's rifle.

"Escape attempt," said Tiamat, glancing at the still unconscious Special Agent Burton. "We took care of it."

Lucifer nodded absently. His eyes alighted for a moment on the boots sticking out from under the tarp, but he made no discernible reaction. Tiamat and Mercury exchanged glances, but neither spoke. Tiamat was still ostensibly allied with Lucifer, but she had evidently decided not to inform him of the warning from the alternate Mercury, so there remained some hope for a crack in their alliance.

Lucifer turned his eyes to the others assembled. "Where's Drekavac?" he asked.

"Perimeter duty," said Tiamat.

"I need him here," said Mercury. "He's the only one who knows how to modify the portal generator."

Balderhaz cleared his throat.

"Apologies," said Lucifer. "The only one I can trust to make the necessary modifications."

Balderhaz shrugged, evidently satisfied with the correction.

"I'll go find Drekavac," said Tiamat. "Watch these guys while I'm gone." She turned to leave.

"But of course," said Lucifer, leveling his gun at Suzy. Suzy cursed herself for coming out of hiding. Mercury and Eddie would at least have a chance to escape if they didn't have to worry about her being killed.

"I'm curious," Lucifer said once Tiamat had left. "How did you figure out I was going to retrieve the shard?"

"It was a logical conclusion," said Balderhaz. "Converting the portal to a time machine would require a high capacity—"

"He's just conjecturing, of course," Mercury interrupted. "We have no reason to think you're planning on going back in time, erasing the past, and installing yourself as the absolute despot on this plane. We were having a freewheeling spitball brainstorming type session to pass the time and you just happened to walk in during the time travel slash absolute despot portion. Pure coincidence."

"Uh huh," said Lucifer, eyeing Mercury suspiciously. "Well, no matter. As it happens, though, I *am* planning on going back in time, erasing history, and installing myself as the absolute despot on this plane."

"Wow!" exclaimed Mercury, nodding appreciatively. "That's pure genius. I don't know where you come up with this stuff."

As he spoke, Tiamat returned with Drekavac in tow.

"There's the guy!" said Lucifer, clapping his hand on the mystified demon's back. "So, Drekavac. I need you to convert this portal generator into a time machine."

Drekavac stared at Lucifer, dumbfounded.

"You can do it, right?" Lucifer said. "After all, time is just a different way of looking at space."

"Well, sure," Drekavac said uncertainly. "I mean, theoretically. But you'd need an immense amount of power. The portal would have to be on a nexus of interplanar energy channels and you'd need a battery capable of holding at least a billion Balderhazes. Something like—"

"Like this?" said Lucifer, holding out the shard to Drekavac.

"Is that... ubiquium?" asked Drekavac, staring at the shard. "Where on Earth...?"

"Funny story," said Lucifer. "I promise to tell you earlier if you get the time machine working."

"I don't know," said Drekavac. "Time travel. It's problematic. Causal loops, ethical quandaries, problems of free will... Are you sure you want to mess with that stuff?"

"Wow," said Lucifer. "You know, when you put it that way, it gives rise to questions like 'why are you still talking?' and 'have you ever met me?' Build the fucking time machine or I tear year ears off with a pair of pliers. And then, when your ears grow back? I tear them off again. Are we on the same page?"

Drekavac, suddenly pale, nodded. He took the shard from Lucifer and walked toward the portal generator.

"Everything's coming together," said Lucifer, with a smile on his face. "I almost regret that in a few hours, none of this will ever have happened."

CHAPTER TWENTY

The next several hours passed without incident. Tiamat had found more zip-ties and re-secured the captives. She guarded them, gun in one hand and the Balderhaz cube in the other, while Lucifer helped Drekavac with the portal modifications. Mercury, Suzy, Eddie and Balderhaz huddled together on the cold concrete, silent except for Balderhaz's mumbled commentary on the shoddy job Drekavac was doing. From what Suzy could hear, though, his complaints were mostly about the "inelegance" of Drekavac's engineering, not actual incompetence. Lucifer seemed pleased with the progress Drekavac was making; as the helicopters droned on outside Suzy began to lose hope that the FBI would intervene before Lucifer's plan came to fruition.

Tiamat had disposed of the dead Mercury, dragging the corpse off somewhere while Lucifer was distracted. An unspoken agreement seemed to have manifested that no one present would mention the existence of an alternate universe where Lucifer was the unquestioned despot; it was hard to imagine such a warning doing anything but encouraging him.

Their only hope, Suzy thought, was that Tiamat and Lucifer would turn on each other. It was hardly a remote possibility; the two had been at each other's throats for most of the past several thousand years and had now formed an alliance out of necessity. Lucifer assured Tiamat that not only would she and all the other demons be going back in time with him but that she would be his second in command, but she seemed unconvinced. Suzy's impression was that Tiamat was simply biding her time until she could make her move against him. What that move would be, and whether it would be an improvement on Lucifer's plan, was anyone's guess.

Azrael was now conscious, the bullet having worked its way out of the hole in his forehead. He sat in a corner and held his head, occasionally moaning. He'd heal faster outside the radius of the Balderhaz cube's power, but Lucifer insisted on keeping the big demon close. So Azrael sat and moaned, his angelic biology slowly knitting together damaged brain tissue. Occasionally he would open his eyes long enough to shoot a resentful glare at Lucifer. It was pretty clear Azrael was getting tired of being shot, punched, stabbed, and whatever else had happened to him lately.

"How far back do you intend to go?" asked Tiamat.

"All the way," said Lucifer.

"You mean...?"

Lucifer nodded. "To the Epoch."

"Is that possible?" asked Tiamat. Lucifer looked to Drekavac, who frowned, regarding the portal generator.

"It'll push the shard to its limits, but I think I can do it," he said.

"What's the Epoch?" Suzy whispered.

"Beginning of angelic history," Eddie replied. "The moment when angels, Heaven, and all the other planes came into existence. Around seven thousand years ago."

"Take it as far back as you can," said Lucifer. "I need to assert control while Michelle and the others are still disorganized."

"I'll do what I can," said Drekavac. "The shard can only hold so much energy."

"I realize that," Lucifer snapped. "Just get as close as you can."

Drekavac nodded and went back to work.

"I thought angels were eternal," Suzy whispered. "How could they have come into existence at a particular moment in time?"

"Honestly," said Eddie, "I'm a little puzzled about it myself." Mercury and Balderhaz remained silent.

Suzy frowned. "Weren't you guys there?"

"Most angels don't like to talk about it," said Mercury.

"I don't understand," said Suzy. "Was there a moment at which you all suddenly came into existence or not?"

"How would we know?" asked Balderhaz. "Do you remember when *you* suddenly came into existence?"

"Don't be obtuse," Suzy replied. "I mean, did you…" she trailed off, realizing she had no idea how to finish the sentence. "I guess what I mean is, what are your first memories?"

"Quiet down over there!" Tiamat snapped. "No plotting!"

They were quiet for some time. "It's fuzzy," Mercury whispered at last. "We all remember the beginning a little differently. Like Eddie said, we don't like to talk about it."

Suzy took this as a hint and dropped the matter. To her, it seemed like kind of an important point to nail down, since history was soon going to be rewritten starting from that moment in time, but it was pretty clear she wasn't going to get the sort of answers she was hoping for.

For the next hour, Drekavac worked on the portal generator while helicopters droned on outside. The captives waited in silence. At last, Drekavac announce that he was finished.

"So," said Lucifer, looking at the portal generator. "It's a time machine now?"

"Yes," said Drekavac.

Lucifer regarded the device. "It doesn't look any different."

Drekavac pointed at the aperture on the base of the machine. The long conduit to the battery had been disconnected. In its place was a conduit only about five feet long, which was connected to a plastic box about the size of small microwave oven. Suzy had seen Drekavac put the shard inside the box earlier. "All I did is build a cradle for the shard and connect it in place of the battery. It's not fancy, but it will work."

"No style at all," muttered Balderhaz.

"It's fine," said Lucifer. "You've set it to the Epoch?"

"With a small margin of error, yes."

"And the shard is fully charged?"

"Yes. Ubiquium is so efficient, it takes less than five minutes for it to soak up a full charge when it's on a nexus like this one."

"Good. Activate the portal generator."

Drekavac tapped a few keys and the portal generator began to hum. A white-blue ellipse appeared on the floor.

"This is it," said Lucifer, regarding the portal with excitement in his eyes. He turned to Azrael. "Okay, buddy, you're up."

"Uh, what?" asked Azrael, who was still sitting on the floor holding his head.

"You're going through first," said Lucifer.

"Me?" Azrael groaned. "Why don't *you* do it? It's your evil plan."

"Too dangerous," replied Lucifer. "I need a point man."

"You mean a guinea pig."

"A very brave and handsome guinea pig."

"Why not Pazusu? Or Gorkin? Or any of the other demons? Somebody who didn't just get *shot in the head?*"

"It's gotta be someone I can trust," said Lucifer. "Come on, Azrael, you should be honored I chose you. Anyway, all you have to do is go through and scope the place out. Make sure there aren't, you know, erupting volcanoes or sabretooth tigers waiting for us. Take a look around and come right back here. If everything checks out, the rest of us will go through."

Azrael groaned again.

"Come on, you big wimp," said Lucifer. "You'll be fine."

"Easy for you to say," Azrael said, getting slowly to his feet. "You're not the one who keeps getting shot and stabbed and punched."

"Look," said Lucifer, "just go through the time machine and I promise you'll never have to do anything like this in the future."

"Really?" asked Azrael.

"Cross my heart," said Lucifer. "Starting tomorrow, you can take it easy."

Azrael thought it over. "All right," he said at last. "What do I do?"

"Just go through the portal, have a look around, and come right back."

"That's it?"

"That's it."

"Okay," said Azrael. He took a step toward the portal.

"See you in a few minutes," said Lucifer.

"Hang on," said Tiamat. "If the portal is set for a specific point in time, then won't he return at the same moment he left?"

Drekavac shook his head. "Temporal slide."

"What he means," said Lucifer, "is that the temporal distance between the two points remains constant, but time continues to move forward at both ends."

"Like *Bill and Ted's Excellent Adventure*," Suzy offered.

Lucifer, his face suddenly contorted with anger, turned to rebuke Suzy. He opened his mouth and then paused. "Well yes, actually," he admitted begrudgingly. "Like *Bill and Ted's Excellent Adventure.*" He turned back to Azrael. "Okay, pal. Time to go."

Azrael nodded, took a deep breath, and stepped onto the portal. He flickered and winked out of existence.

"Isn't it dangerous to leave that thing open?" asked Suzy. "I mean, what if a caveman wandered through?"

"It's pretty unlikely there's anybody immediately on the other side," said Mercury. "And animals are generally smart enough not to get near mysterious glowing ellipses."

"How long do we give him?" asked Tiamat.

"Five minutes," said Lucifer. "If he's not back by then, we'll figure he's been torn apart by velociraptors."

"And then what?"

Lucifer shrugged. "Send somebody else through."

They didn't have to wait that long. Less than a minute after he'd left, Azrael re-materialized on the portal. He stumbled forward, looking dazed and disheveled. His face was bloody and bruised, as if he'd been hit in the head with a large rock.

"Shut it down," he gasped. "Shut... the portal down."

"You know," said Mercury, "I'm starting to think this portal thing is not such a good idea."

Drekavac tapped a series of keys and the portal began to fade.

"What happened?" Lucifer demanded. "Were you attacked?"

"Cavemen," said Azrael. "Attacked me."

Lucifer frowned. "You mean actual people living in caves? You know you're a demon, right? Why didn't you just slaughter them all?"

Azrael shook his head slowly. "No time... hit me with rocks." He sank to the ground, holding his head.

"You were surprised by prehistoric people with *rocks?*" said Lucifer. But Azrael simply stared straight ahead, apparently too dazed to respond.

Lucifer threw up his hands. "I don't even know why I bother to have minions," he said. "Drekavac, change the temporal coordinates by a few hours and try it again. This time I'm going through."

Drekavac nodded. "A few hours forward or back?" he asked.

Lucifer regarded him sternly. "I thought you said you had set it as far back as you could."

"Right," said Drekavac. "With a small margin of error, in case—"

"Damn it," Lucifer snapped. "I said set it as far back as you can. Did you not hear me say that?"

"Well, yes," replied Drekavac. "But I assumed you wouldn't want to—"

"As far back as you can, Drekavac," Lucifer said coldly. "Do you understand?"

"Yes, sir."

"How long will it take?"

"A few minutes?"

Drekavac nodded and went back to tapping at keys. After a few minutes the blue ellipse once again appeared on the concrete.

"Is it done?" Lucifer asked.

"Uh…" said Drekavac, looking at the screen. "No. The coordinates haven't changed. Sorry, I'm getting more resistance than I expected as I approach the Epoch."

"Get it done," Lucifer snapped. He turned to Tiamat. "Perhaps while we have some time we should discuss our strategy for seizing power over this plane."

"Good idea," said Tiamat. "I think we should start by attempting to recruit as many angels as possible, before Michelle can—"

Lucifer put his finger to his lips. "Let's discuss the matter in private."

Tiamat shot him a quizzical look but then said, "As you like." She handed her rifle to the still-dazed Azrael. "Watch them while we're gone," she said.

Azrael nodded dumbly, taking the gun. Tiamat followed Lucifer and the two disappeared from view.

Drekavac muttered a curse as he regarded the screen. The portal remained open next to him.

"Close that thing down," said Azrael. "It freaks me out."

"I'm trying!" Drekavac growled. "Whoever wrote this software doesn't know a damn thing about UI design."

"ID-Ten-T error," Suzy muttered.

Balderhaz chuckled. "Pebkac," he said.

146

Suzy giggled. Eddie and Mercury looked at each other and shrugged.

"Can you keep them quiet, Azrael?" Drekavac said. "I'm trying to... Azrael?"

Azrael had gotten to his feet and started across the open area in the opposite direction Lucifer and Tiamat had gone.

"Where are you going?" asked Drekavac.

"Away from here," said Azrael. "If you were smart, you'd do the same. You're messing with stuff you don't understand."

"You can't leave!" cried Drekavac. "What am I supposed to do with all these people?"

But Azrael just kept walking, leaving Drekavac, alone and unarmed, with the captives.

Drekavac smiled weakly at the group of hostages. "All right," he said, in a quavering voice. "Lucifer and Tiamat will be back shortly. No funny business!"

But Mercury was already on his feet. Ankles still tied together, he began hopping toward Drekavac.

"This looks a lot like funny business," said Drekavac disapprovingly.

Mercury stopped a few feet in front of Drekavac. "Move," he said.

Drekavac stepped aside and Mercury took another hop toward the steel shelving unit behind him. He turned around and leaned down, and Suzy realized he was picking up the box cutter from where Tiamat had left it.

"I'm not sure I should let you have that," said Drekavac. "You could... see, this is exactly what I was concerned about."

Mercury had gotten his hands free and was working on his feet. Drekavac seemed to be trying to get the courage up to intervene. "Don't even think about it," said Mercury, brandishing the box cutter at Drekavac. It wasn't a very intimidating weapon, but it was enough to cow Drekavac.

Drekavac frowned a Mercury. "Let the record show that I'm completely opposed to this current course of action on your part," he said.

"Noted," Mercury replied. He went to Suzy and cut her hands free, then handed her the box cutter. "Start working on the others," he said. "And do it fast. Lucifer could be back any second." While

147

Suzy freed Eddie and Balderhaz, Mercury looked through the shelves for another knife. He didn't find one, but he pocketed the Balderhaz cube and Tiamat's "miracle detector."

Suzy cut the zip-tie on Special Agent Burton's wrist and then handed him the box cutter. "Good luck!" She said, and turned back to the others. "Let's go."

They set off toward the exit.

"Wait!" cried Drekavac. "Come back!"

But Mercury and the others were already gone.

CHAPTER TWENTY-ONE

Mercury led the way through the maze of equipment, with Suzy, Eddie and Balderhaz right behind him.

Mercury stopped and held up his hand as they approached the perimeter of the building. "Careful," he whispered. "Lucifer's minions are—"

His words were interrupted by the sound of an explosion from somewhere behind them. The fluorescent lights overhead flickered out, and the building was suddenly dark except for minimal battery-powered emergency lighting—Suzy had skimped on lighting requirements to save time. Another explosion sounded just ahead, followed by shouts and the clattering of debris on the floor.

"Another diversion?" asked Suzy.

"Lucifer's already inside," said Mercury. "I think the feds got sick of waiting." He glanced back the way they'd come.

"What's the problem, Mercury?" asked Eddie. "Keep going!"

Mercury handed the Balderhaz cube to Suzy. "You go, Eddie," said Mercury. "Keep Suzy safe. Balderhaz!"

Balderhaz, who seemed to have gotten lost down an adjoining alley, turned to look at Mercury.

"Stay with the group, please," said Mercury.

Balderhaz shrugged and shuffled back toward them.

"Where are you going, Mercury?" Suzy asked.

Somewhere in the distance, another explosion sounded.

"I have to destroy that portal generator before Lucifer causes any more trouble," said Mercury.

"I think the FBI is going to take care of that for you," said Eddie.

"Can't count on it," said Mercury. "It won't take long. Get the Balderhaz cube away from here and I can melt the thing to slag in a second."

"But all our work..." Balderhaz protested.

"I know," said Mercury. "It sucks. Maybe we can build another one someday."

Balderhaz grumbled something indecipherable.

"I'll catch up to you guys shortly," said Mercury, slipping past them in the direction they had come. "Just go."

"Wait!" cried Suzy. "Mercury!"

But Mercury, intent on finding his way through the maze of equipment in the dark, paid no attention. Were he not inside the Balderhaz field, he would convert a small amount of interplanar energy into light, but for now he had to stumble through the dimly lit building, cursing each time he banged a knee or elbow into a piece of errant machinery.

As Mercury approached the open area, he saw the familiar bluish-white glow of the open portal on the floor. Next to it, visible only because of the reflected light from the portal itself, was the portal generator, still intact. Drekavac still stood in front of it, regarding the screen. He turned as Mercury approached.

"Good, you're back," Drekavac said. "The shard is fully charged. I managed to set the portal generator a few hours farther into the past, but..." His face fell as he turned and saw that it was Mercury approaching. "You again! Why don't you leave me alone?"

Not sure what to make of this odd greeting, Mercury ignored it. "Step aside, Drekavac," he said. "I need to disintegrate that thing."

Drekavac sighed and shuffled away from the portal generator. "I just wish you would make up your mind."

Mercury took a step toward the portal generator, hoping that Suzy was far enough away with the Balderhaz cube for him to use interplanar energy to perform a miracle. He would only need to weaken the molecular bonds of the portal generator's components momentarily and the thing would collapse into a pile of dust.

As he approached, two more explosions sounded nearby. So far, whatever explosives the feds were using didn't seem to be doing much damage, but Mercury suspected that was because the demons were using interplanar energy to minimize the effects. Even with the Balderhaz cube inside, it would be easy enough to create a dome-shaped barrier that would cause any bombs to detonate prematurely. Of course, that would only work until the feds decided to use something really powerful, like a nuke. And since they'd evidently already decided to sacrifice three of their own agents, Mercury suspected the nuke was on its way. The feds were starting to get an idea what they were up against, and they were going to use every weapon in their arsenal.

Mercury raised his hand, attempting to harness enough interplanar energy to destroy the portal generator. At first the energy seemed to be flowing freely, but then he felt some resistance. Was Suzy returning with the Balderhaz cube?

No. The resistance was too sudden. Someone was actively interfering with his attempt to perform a miracle. But Drekavac showed no interest in stopping him. Mercury turned to see a tall, thin figure approaching, barely visible in the dim bluish light. Lucifer.

"You know," said Lucifer, "if you had any sense, you'd be miles away from here by now."

"I got to thinking about that," said Mercury. "It occurred to me that it doesn't do me any good to be sipping piña coladas in the Azores if I've never existed."

"You won't feel a thing," said Lucifer. "One moment you'll exist, and the next you won't."

"Is that what you told Tiamat?"

Lucifer chuckled. "Tiamat's fine."

"Of course she is. But she's not going back in time with you, is she?"

"No," said Lucifer. "Tiamat's not very good at playing second fiddle. I hit her over the head with a pipe and tied her up."

"I figured. Azrael has abandoned you, you know."

Lucifer shrugged. "Don't need him. Where I'm going, there will be plenty of potential converts."

Another explosion sounded overhead.

"Can't let you do that, Lucifer," said Mercury. "You had your chance at world domination. You lost. No do-overs."

"I've changed the rules," said Lucifer. "Try to keep up." He launched himself toward the portal, but Mercury, anticipating the move, tackled him around the waist. The two crashed into the steel shelving unit behind the portal generator, knocking tools and other equipment to the ground. Seizing the advantage, Mercury took a swing at Lucifer's face, but he misjudged the distance in the dim light and merely grazed the demon's jaw with his knuckles. Lucifer backed away and then altered his trajectory, heading back toward the portal.

But when Lucifer was only a few feet away, another blast sounded, shaking the ground so hard he was thrown to floor. Mercury, gripping one of the steel shelf supports, barely remained on his feet. As Lucifer crawled toward the portal, Mercury dived at him, grappling him around the waist and rolling away from the portal. Mercury landed hard on his back, with Lucifer on top of him, and barely moved his head in time to avoid being punched in the face. Lucifer's knuckles hit the concrete with a crack and he yelped in pain. He rolled off Mercury, holding his right hand in his left and groaning, while Mercury tried to catch his breath. For a moment, the two lay there, side by side, looking straight up at the ceiling. Except the ceiling was missing: one of the bombs had apparently torn a gaping hole in the roof and they were now staring at the dark canopy of the desert sky, dotted with the pinpricks of thousands of stars.

"Wow," said Mercury after a moment.

"Yeah," said Lucifer. "Makes you feel pretty insignificant."

"Sure does," said Mercury. "Like, we're just two people out of billions on one little planet orbiting one star out of billions and billions."

"Makes our differences seem kind of petty," said Lucifer.

"Right?" said Mercury. "Like, what are we even fighting about?"

"Well," said Lucifer, "I wanted to go back in time and erase history and you're trying to stop me."

"I know *that*," said Mercury. "I meant, like, in the grand scheme of things, what does it really matter?"

"Oh," said Lucifer. "Yeah, I see what you mean. But that's just the human condition writ large, isn't it? I mean, what's the point of doing *anything*? You can't think that way."

"I suppose not," said Mercury. "Still, I think it helps to stop and get some perspective once in a while. Hey, can I ask you a question?"

"Shoot," said Lucifer.

"Well, I don't want to give you any ideas," said Mercury. "But I'm curious. If the shard is so valuable, why don't you take it back in time with you?"

"Trust me, I would if I could," said Lucifer. "But you can't take charged ubiquium through a portal. It's too unstable. It'll blow up and probably tear a hole in the spacetime continuum, obliterating me and everything else for miles around. I could drain the shard of energy, but it has to be charged to power the portal."

"Catch-22," said Mercury.

"My favorite kind," said Lucifer. "So, my hand is feeling a little better if you want to get back to it."

"Okay," said Mercury. "I'm never going to let you get away with it, you know."

"We'll see about that," said Lucifer, sitting up.

Mercury pulled himself into a crouch, ready to launch himself at Lucifer as soon as he made his move. Lucifer got to his feet and took a step toward the portal. Mercury launched himself at Lucifer again, spreading his long arms to tackle him. But Lucifer twisted away at the last moment, and at the same time another explosion rocked the building. Lucifer caught himself against the shelving unit but Mercury, badly off balance, stumbled forward, trying not to trip over his own feet. Just as he regained his footing, another explosion went off behind him, there was a roaring in his ears and then everything went black.

CHAPTER TWENTY-TWO

Somewhere in North Africa; c. 5,000 B.C.

Mercury awoke face-down with the smell of dirt and decaying leaves in his nostrils. He pulled himself into a sitting position and looked around.

At first he wasn't sure where he was. Then he wasn't sure *when* he was. And then he was sure neither where nor when he was.

He had gone through the portal and ended up somewhere—and somewhen—else. The portal was nowhere to be found. Sometime after he had gone through, the portal had been shut down. Had Lucifer come through as well? Mercury was fairly certain he had not. Mercury didn't think he'd been out for more than a minute; if Lucifer were anywhere nearby in this desolate landscape, he'd see him. Also, he doubted Lucifer would have left him alone if he'd come across him lying face down in the sand. The jerk would have pantsed him at the very least.

Mercury stood up and surveyed the area. A jungle, he thought. A canopy of trees hung overhead, broken only by occasional cracks of daylight. The rustling and squawking of birds and other animals could be heard. But something was wrong: the animal sounds were sparse and lethargic, and the smell of decaying leaves and sight of wilted vegetation around him attested that it had been some time since this rain forest had seen any rain. But there was something else: the cracks of daylight overhead were too big and well-defined. These weren't gaps in the foliage; they were actual *cracks*. He was looking at a ceiling. But there were no walls, just an endless ceiling that extended to the horizon. A dome.

No, he thought. It couldn't be.

Mercury had heard Balderhaz's theories about what had happened to Horace Finch's insane vanity project in the North African desert, but as with nearly everything Balderhaz said, he hadn't taken it seriously. Balderhaz thought the entire facility—along with Christine Temetri and her friend, what's-his-name, the explosion guy—had been transported several thousand years back in time. It was a cheery thought, that Christine had lived out the rest of her life in some other time, but Mercury had never really allowed himself to believe it. But as he strolled under the massive dome, his feet crunching on dead leaves that had fallen from the dying trees, he realized it was true. He had gone back in time through the portal and somehow ended up in the precise location where Eden II had been transported.[8] How was that possible? And where was he, exactly? Still in Nevada, or at the remote North African site of Eden II? Or somewhere else entirely?

He strolled outside through a door that had been left open and stood blinking for a moment in the bright desert sun. The landscape superficially resembled the Nevada desert he had just left, but it was clearly a different place. It wasn't just that the building was missing; the vegetation was different, and the sand was a different shade of brown. The real clincher, though, was the mountain range in the distance that hadn't been there before he came through the portal, 7,000 years later in the world's history. He couldn't be in Nevada; seventy centuries of erosion wouldn't erase those mountains. The vista matched his memories of the North African plain where Horace Finch had constructed Eden II.

He puzzled on this for some time. Why had the portal transported him ten thousand miles across the planet's surface, rather than just causing him to materialize in the same spot he had just left? The answer came to him when he remembered that the portal would be using the geometry of the interplanar energy channels rather than an ordinary reckoning of geography. The Nevada site was the location of a nexus of energy channels, so it

---

[8] Eden II was a self-contained ecosystem built by the eccentric billionaire Horace Finch. The actual purpose of the vast domed structure was to hide the existence of a huge underground particle accelerator that Finch believed would give him absolute mastery over time and space. Unfortunately, due to unforeseen circumstances, the entire facility was accidentally sent 7,000 years back in time.

made a perfect spot for a portal location. But the interplanar energy channels had undergone a realignment in 2012,[9] which meant that the Elko nexus likely hadn't existed before that. Drekavac probably hadn't taken the realignment into account, which meant the channel he'd opened up simply followed the path of least resistance between the present and the past. Thus the destination portal would appear at the location of another nexus, possibly hundreds or even thousands of miles away. So here he was, in North Africa.

That was *where* sorted. The bigger question, though, was how long had Eden II been here? Judging from the sorry condition of the jungle, it had been several weeks at least since the life-support systems of Eden II had shut down. Had the systems worked for a while and then shut down, or had they stopped working the moment the place was ripped out of Africa? As Mercury understood it, most of the infrastructure for Eden II was underground; it was hard to see how the machinery required to keep this place going could have been transported back as well without displacing a whole lot of ground. Most likely only the above-ground part of the facility had been sent back in time, which meant that the jungle would have started dying almost immediately. Assuming that it had been at most a year since Eden II appeared, Christine and what's-his-name might still be alive.

He needed to find her. After all, there had to be a reason he was transported to this particular place and time, didn't there?

He frowned as it occurred to him that the reason might be to foil Lucifer's plot to rewrite history. And that train of thought prompted another question: why hadn't Lucifer followed him? The obvious answer was that the portal generator had been damaged in the FBI's attack. A wave of despair washed over Mercury as he realized this might very well mean he was trapped in the past forever. Well, for the next seven thousand years anyway. The good news was that Lucifer's plan had been thwarted—at least for now. Mercury just hoped Suzy and the others had gotten free.

Of course, there was always the possibility that Lucifer would repair the portal—or eventually even build another one—and try again. But Drekavac had set the portal generator for as far back as he could, and time was still moving forward... which meant that he

---

[9] The result of another of Lucifer's attempts at world domination.

couldn't possibly travel farther back than Mercury had. Mercury smiled as the realization dawned on him: he was uniquely situated to prevent Lucifer's plan from ever coming to fruition. All he had to do was wait for Lucifer to show up. But that could be hours... or years. Mercury didn't relish the prospect of camping out here for the next God-knows-how-many years waiting for the devil to show up. It would be like that time he tried sitting through that horrible French play with the two guys bickering for three hours. There had to be a better way.

If only he had some way of knowing when the portal had reopened, then he could go look for Christine and not have to worry about missing Lucifer. Also, it might be a good idea to try to find some other angels to alert them of Lucifer's plan. But if it really was the Epoch, then angels might not even be around yet. It was odd to think about: somewhere on Earth, another Mercury had recently materialized, or was about to. A Mercury who had no idea what sorts of adventures were in store for him on this strange plane. Poor bastard, he thought.

His memories of this time—like those of all angels—were a little fuzzy. Every angel had some vestigial memories of being in Heaven before the creation of the Mundane Plane, but they were vague, like a half-remembered dream. The first few years— decades?—on the Mundane plane were fuzzy as well, as if the angels had been awakening from that collective dream. Or maybe it was like Balderhaz said: before the angels had come into being, they had existed like newborns, fully conscious but unable to process and store their experiences as memories. What remained from before that time was a mainly a sense of loss, a shared notion that they had come from somewhere better, and were returning there some day.

Mercury sighed and put his hands in his pockets, his right hand touching something that felt like a cell phone. He pulled it out: the miracle detector. The device was simply a plastic box with a screen and a single button on the side. Mercury pressed the button on the side and the screen came to life, displaying an hourglass icon. After a few seconds, the icon was replaced by the words:

NO ANOMALY DETECTED

It figured. Tiamat said the range was only a few miles, and even if there were other angels on Earth, it was pretty unlikely any of them would be that close or would be using interplanar energy at this very moment. It occurred to him, though, that the miracle detector would also alert him if the portal re-opened. He could go looking for Christine and come back here if the portal re-opened.

He wondered if he should use the miracle detector to try to locate the other angels. The device wouldn't detect angels per se; it could only detect the warping of the energy channels that was caused by an angel's conscious manipulation of them. Still, if he went airborne and covered a lot of ground, he'd undoubtedly find one of them eventually. He might even run into the earlier version of himself. That would be weird—although not as weird as seeing an alternate version of himself die before his own eyes.

If he did find other angels, he could warn them about Lucifer's plan and they could help him watch for his arrival. Was there another Lucifer out there somewhere too? There had to be. He wondered what the future Lucifer's plan was for dealing with prehistoric Lucifer. Nothing good, in all likelihood. He doubted very much Lucifer would exhibit any sentimental attachment to his younger self; he would simply be another threat to be eliminated.

Mercury spent the next several hours waiting for Lucifer to appear, but the portal didn't reopen. His boredom finally getting the better of him, Mercury went back outside and leapt into the air, soaring above the desert plain. He flew toward the mountains in the East, thinking they might lead him to a river or some other water feature near which humans—or angels—might congregate. But still he saw nothing but sparsely vegetated desert plain. The local fauna—gazelles and various rodents—confirmed that he was somewhere in Africa, but there were no humans to be found. As he neared the mountain range, he turned south, continuing for several miles. Occasionally he would check the miracle detector, but it continued to insist:

NO ANOMALY DETECTED

When he was a little over ten miles from Eden II, he decided to turn back, as he was unsure the miracle detector would register the portal opening from this distance. But as he checked the device once more, the familiar message disappeared and was replaced by a small arrow pointing to the southeast. It would occasionally switch to a different direction or disappear entirely, but it was pretty clearly pointing to a disturbance in the interplanar energy channels of some kind.

Mercury hesitated for a moment, uncertain how long he should leave the portal location unattended, but the anomaly would dissipate as soon as the miracle had been performed, so he might not get another chance to locate its source for some time. Ultimately his curiosity got the better of him. He veered slightly to the right and increased his velocity, heading in the direction the arrow pointed.

CHAPTER TWENTY-THREE

Somewhere in North Africa; c. 5,000 B.C

Christine Temetri and Jacob Slater huddled behind a bush, watching from a distance as their village burned. There wasn't much cover in this terrain, but so far the two of them seemed to have escaped notice. The same couldn't be said for the other members of their adoptive tribe, who had been slaughtered or rounded up by the Detroit Pistons.

That wasn't the belligerent tribe's real name, of course. Its real name in the local language was some combination of lingual clicks, humming, and impossibly complicated hand gestures. Jacob and Christine and mastered a few basic words and phrases over the four months they had been among the Lakers, but amongst themselves they still used English exclusively—including coming up with their own names for the local tribes. There were six other tribes that the Lakers—their own tribe—had contact with, and it was hard enough to keep them straight without having to remember which one was a hum and three clicks and which one was two clicks, a hum and thumbs-up. Christine had suggested naming the tribes after schools of Western graphic art (the Pre-Raphaelites, the Impressionists, the Cubists, etc.), but even she couldn't remember if the group to the southeast were Dadaists or Modernists, and Jacob's scheme of matching tribes to NBA teams won out.

Most of the tribes—the Lakers, the Nets, the Bulls, the Celtics, the Heat and the Jazz—coexisted more or less peacefully in the region, but recently the Bulls and the Celtics had formed an alliance against the Pistons, who had been on an expansive tear. The chief of the Pistons, Isiah Thomas, had apparently gotten it into his head that it was his divine destiny to subjugate all the other tribes in the

161

region. This sudden belligerence was so out of character for these people that the other tribes had failed to recognize the threat until the Nuggets and Trail Blazers, farther north, had already been wiped out. Even after that slaughter, the Bulls-Celtics alliance remained an informal agreement characterized not so much by any actual strategic cooperation as it was by the hope that the Pistons would pick on one of the non-allied tribes next. That hope proved unfounded.

The Lakers were in talks with the Heat and Jazz about what to do about the Piston threat, but these tribes were fiercely independent and exhaustively deliberate in their decision-making; nothing firm had been decided by the time the Pistons emerged en masse from the scrub and chased the Lakers from their huts. Most of the men had been killed; the women and children had been captured. The Pistons had set fire to the Lakers huts and returned to their own village, leaving only a handful of men behind to look for stragglers.

Christine and Jacob had escaped the carnage only because they had been assigned by the tribe to gather blackberries that morning. It was rare for the Lakers to send two members of the tribe off by themselves, but they made an exception for Christine and Jacob, who were hopeless at hunting, weaving baskets, and just about every other task the tribe needed done. Jacob was fairly certain it wasn't even blackberry season; the two of them had been gone all morning and still hadn't found any. They couldn't help wondering when the Lakers' charity was going to run out, but that was a moot question now.

"Do you think it's safe?" Christine asked.

"For—*unck*—what?" asked Jacob. Jacob had a chronic verbal tic that had mostly subsided since their arrival in prehistoric Africa, but it tended to return in high stress situations.

"To go back to the village. Maybe we can scrounge enough food to make it to the Timberwolves." The Timberwolves' village was about forty miles to the south.

"I'm pretty sure the Timberwolves are cannibals," said Jacob. "We would—*unck*—have better luck with the Heat."

"The Heat are even farther," said Christine. "We'll never make it. There are lions down that way."

"There are lions *everywhere*," said Jacob. "That's why I didn't use NFL teams."

"M'boutoo [click click]!" said a voice behind them, and they spun around to see a man with a spear watching them. He bore the tribal markings of the Pistons.

"Son of a bitch," said Christine. Jacob nodded. For a moment, he considered running. These tribesmen were ridiculously fast, but this guy looked fairly old and gaunt by local standards, and Jacob thought he could outrun him. But that would leave Christine alone, and in any case, there was no place for him to go. Better to be killed quickly now than to be eaten by a lion. Or a Timberwolf.

"[Click click] Mootoo [click]," the man said, pointing his spear to their right. They got to their feet and began walking in the direction he indicated. After a few minutes, they encountered another Pistons tribesman. This one was younger and healthier looking, and the sheer surface area of his tattoos seemed to suggest some importance. He and the man who had taken them captive engaged in a long exchange, punctuated by silences in which they would stare curiously at their two captives. Christine and Jacob were used to this; they were the lightest-skinned people any of these tribesmen had ever seen. Even Jacob, who was considered "African American" in twenty-first century America, was an anomaly with his coffee-and-cream complexion. In fact, it was Jacob who appeared to be of most interest to these two men—it seemed to Jacob that they were having trouble categorizing him. Christine was obviously *different*, but what was Jacob? And how would their determination affect his fate? He wasn't sure he wanted to know the answer to that.

After some time the two men seemed to come to a decision, and the old man again click/hummed an order at them and pointed in the direction they had been traveling. Christine and Jacob started walking, with the two men following close behind, their spears at the ready.

Coming over a small ridge, they found themselves looking at a group of several dozen people standing huddled together, guarded by half a dozen men with spears. Christine and Jacob were prodded toward the group, whom they recognized as members of their adoptive tribe, the Lakers. Jacob realized with some discomfort that he was the only man among them. The warriors of their tribe had all been killed—even poor old James Worthy. Why hadn't they killed Jacob? Was it merely because they didn't think he was a threat?

After a few more stragglers had been added to the group, someone click/hummed another order, and the group began shuffling to the north. Christine and Jacob went with them.

They spent the next five hours walking across the desert with the other captives. It was hot, but not unbearably so, which was good because the attackers had apparently only brought a minimal amount of water with them. Once an hour or so, they would stop and pass around a skin of water, each of them getting a single swallow. Occasionally one of the women would collapse. The first time this happened, several of the others went to her aid but were mercilessly attacked by the captors. One young woman was impaled with a spear and left to die alongside the woman she had been trying to help. The next time someone fell, she was left to die on her own. The Pistons didn't seem concerned that the women might be faking; everybody knew that being left out here alone was a death sentence.

Eventually they reached the Pistons' village, which could easily have been mistaken for the Lakers' village except for one major difference: in the center of this village was a roughly circular stone altar, about three feet tall and ten feet in diameter. The surface of the altar was stained with blood.

The captives all around Christine and Jacob were variously seized and prodded, disappearing to other areas of the village, until only Christine and Jacob remained, encircled by a ring of men with spears. They stared uneasily at the altar.

"I don't suppose we've been—*unck*—selected to be guests of honor at some sort of welcoming ceremony," said Jacob.

"That's one way to phrase it," said Christine.

To their left, a pair of men wearing elaborate headdresses exited a large hut. They walked to the altar and stood, one on either side, their spears planted on the ground in front of them.

Then a third man emerged from the hut. He was older and heavier than the other two, and wore an even more elaborate getup. Jacob could only assume this was the chief of the Pistons tribe, the man he knew as Isiah Thomas. He was a little disappointing, truth be told. Even the actual Isiah Thomas was more intimidating than this guy. But then the actual Isiah Thomas didn't have a flaming sword. This guy did.

"Shit," said Christine.

"Well, now we know what happened to Nisroc's sword," said Jacob. Nisroc was the angel who had chased them out of Eden II four months earlier. He was supposed to be guarding the entrance to the garden with a flaming sword, but he claimed to have lost it on the way over. The last Christine and Jacob knew, he was still scouring the plains looking for it. Apparently Chief Isiah Thomas had found it. He stopped in front of the altar and whirled the sword in front of him in an obviously practiced manner.

"I wonder if this explains the Pistons' sudden belligerence," said Christine.

"What do you mean?" asked Jacob.

"These tribes were so peaceful before. Maybe the sword inspired them to violence, like—"

"Like the monolith in *2001*," said Jacob.

"I was going to say the Coke bottle in *The Gods Must Be Crazy*."

Jacob shook his head, still watching the chief twirl the sword. "The noble savage is a myth," he said. "These people were peaceful because their environment checks their population growth, making it largely unnecessary to quarrel over resources. Also, they don't have the technology to administer a political unit larger than a village. No roads, no written language…"

"So how do you explain this sudden turn toward violence?"

"Aberration," said Jacob. "Possibly precipitated by the acquisition of the sword."

"That's no answer," said Christine. "Did the sword turn them evil or not?"

"Not in the way you're thinking," said Jacob. "It's not The One Ring."

"The Evil Thing," Christine corrected.

"Whatever," said Jacob. "The point is, you're regressing into animism, the belief that inanimate objects have spiritual properties. Besides, violence is not in itself necessarily—"

The chief had ceased his show and was now pointing the fiery sword directly at Christine. He click/hummed an order and one of the spearmen stepped toward Christine.

"You were saying?" she said.

165

The man grabbed Christine by the arm and dragged her toward the altar. Jacob protested, but the other spearman growled at him and pointed his spear. All around him were other men, also with spears at the ready. There was going to be no escape this time.

Christine tried to resist, but it was no use. She was already weak from hunger and thirst, and there was nowhere to go even if she could break free. The man dragged her forward and threw her down on the altar. She raised her hands as she fell, catching herself as she hit the hard stone. She could smell the blood of those who had died there before.

The chief was clicking and humming something fierce behind her, and she rolled onto her back to face him. He was walking toward her, swinging the fiery blade over his head. As Christine tried to scurry away, two men approached, one on either side of the chief. Each man grabbed one of her ankles while the two more ornately festooned men took hold of her wrists. The four of them pulled her flat on the stone surface while Jacob watched helplessly, a man barring his way with a spear. He'd never felt more useless in his life. He could only hope that the chief killed him as soon as he was done with Christine; Jacob didn't think he could live with himself after failing to protect Christine from these psychopaths.

The chief stood next to the altar, uttering some sort of prayer to a god or gods that would die out thousands of years before Jacob was even born. When the chief finished, he raised the fiery sword over his head. Christine clamped her eyes shut and turned her head away.

He brought the sword down in a decisive arc toward her neck.

Jacob closed his eyes as well, unable to watch. He wasn't sure what cue he was waiting for; some kind of bloodthirsty hum/click of exultation, he supposed. But it didn't come. All he heard was the equivalent of confused muttering. He opened his eyes to see the chief, sword outstretched mere inches from Christine's neck. A look of frustration had overcome him; he seemed to be trying to drive the sword downward, but without success. Finally he pulled the sword back over his head and made a second attempt, swinging once again at Christine's neck. Again Jacob grimaced and turned away. But this time, Jacob kept his eyes open, and he saw the blade halt three inches from Christine's neck, just as it had before. It was as if an invisible barrier was protecting her. After a few seconds,

Christine opened one eye and then the other, staring at the blade. The men around her clicked and hummed in confusion and fear.

Jacob heard someone speaking behind him—it sounded like the local language, but a dialect he hadn't heard before, as if the speaker was not a native. At the man's words, the men released Christine. The chief turned toward them, clicking angrily, but whoever the newcomer was, the men seemed more frightened of him than they were of the chief. Turning to see their mysterious stranger, Jacob literally didn't believe his eyes.

No, he thought. It can't be him. He's ten thousand miles and seven thousand years from now. This is some kind of fantasy my subconscious has concocted because I can't deal with the thought of Christine being executed. But as he turned back to look at Christine, he could see she was just as stunned as he was.

"I'd leave now if I were you," the tall, silver-haired man said. "I'm not entirely sure if I told them I'm a god who is displeased with the chief's choice of sacrifice or if I'm a constipated gazelle who wants to date the chief's sister."

CHAPTER TWENTY-FOUR

Mercury led them away from the village while the Pistons were still arguing about how to deal with this silver-haired stranger. When they had gotten a safe distance from the men with spears, Mercury stopped and turned, smiling at them.

"Hey, Christine," he said. "Hey, Christine's weird friend."

"Mercury!" Christine screamed, and threw her arms around him. As she embraced him, she realized there were tears running down her cheeks. Surprised by her own emotion, she forced herself to let go. She regarded Mercury with amazement. "You're here!" she exclaimed. "And you recognize us!"

"Of course I recognize you," said Mercury. "Why wouldn't I... oh, because I might not have met you yet. No, it's me. Well, it's 2017 me. You haven't met any earlier versions, have you? No, forget I asked. I would remember. I see you met the locals."

"You came back from 2017?" asked Jacob. "Five years have passed for you?"

"Yeah," said Mercury. "Don't worry, though, they mostly sucked. How long has it been for you?"

"About four months," said Jacob. "It actually hasn't been too bad up until today. Did you come back to rescue us?"

"Well, no," Mercury admitted. "I didn't actually mean to come back at all."

Christine frowned. "You time-traveled accidentally?"

"That's how *we* got here," said Jacob. Christine shrugged.

"It's complicated," said Mercury. "The planeport got destroyed by, um, me. So the planes are all cut off from each other. Some other angels and my friend Suzy got the idea to build a new portal generator to reconnect them, but then Tiamat showed up, and she used it to free Lucifer, and he converted it into a time machine using a shard from the Eye of Providence. His plan is to erase history and start over with him in charge."

"Not really *that* complicated," Jacob observed.

"I guess not," said Mercury. "Pretty standard Lucifer stuff."

"But Lucifer didn't come back with you?" Christine asked.

"No."

"You stopped him then."

"Well, so far. I'm expecting him to reopen the portal eventually and try again. In fact, I really should get back there in case he shows up."

"How did you find us?" asked Jacob.

"Oh," said Mercury, pulling the miracle detector from his pocket. It still registered only one anomaly, in the direction of the village they'd just left. "I used this thing. I wasn't actually looking for you, in all honesty. I was just going where this thing pointed. Apparently there's some kind of supernatural artifact in that village that's disrupting the interplanar energy channels."

"The sword," said Christine.

Mercury shook his head. "It's true that a flaming sword is a supernatural artifact, but the amount of power it draws is negligible. There's no way something like that would register on a miracle detector from miles away. It would have to be something like... oh."

"What?" Jacob asked.

"It's not the sword," said Mercury. "It's the gem in the sword's handle. The shard."

"*That's* the shard you were talking about?" asked Christine. "The one Lucifer uses to build a time machine?"

"I'm afraid so," Mercury said. "I didn't put it together until just now."

"So we can stop him," said Jacob. "We just take the shard from Isiah Thomas and destroy it. Oh, Isiah Thomas is what we call the chief. You see, I've named the local tribes after—"

"Great story," said Mercury. "Here's the problem: I can't destroy the shard. I mean, maybe I could, but ubiquium is an insanely powerful substance. If I start banging on it with rocks, I might accidentally implode everything for miles around."

"Okay," said Christine, "then just drop it in the ocean or something."

170

Mercury sighed. "This is the other problem. Time travel is a tricky thing. You find yourself in a lot of causal loops. If we take the shard from Isiah Thomas, we might find that in seven thousand years we were the cause of Lucifer getting his hands on it."

"But if we don't take it, then not taking it will have caused Lucifer to get it."

"Exactly," said Mercury.

"So," Jacob said, "time will find a way around our efforts to prevent an occurrence that's determined to happen."

"You're anthropomorphizing time," said Mercury. "Time doesn't want anything. It just is."

Jacob shrugged. "It's a—*unck*—metaphor. Deal with it."

"Well, we can't do nothing," said Christine.

"Why not?" Mercury replied. "The result is the same either way, and doing nothing is less work."

"You don't know that," said Christine. "Maybe we can pull a fast one on time."

"How?" Mercury asked.

"What if we replace the shard with a fake? Could you do that? Make a dummy shard?"

Mercury shrugged. "I could transmute some sand into glass. Cut it and polish it, and give it a blue tint to make it look like the shard. I still think it's pointless though."

"Why?" asked Christine. "If you can sneak in and replace the shard without anyone noticing, then maybe history will unfold the way it did the last time around, except this time Lucifer will end up with a fake shard."

"I don't think that's how it works," said Mercury, "but it's worth a try, I suppose."

"Can you make us some water while you're at it?" asked Jacob.

"Sure," said Mercury. "Scoop up a handful of sand."

Christine and Jacob each scooped some sand into their hands.

"Boom," said Mercury, pointing an index finger at each of them. The each found their hands full of water. Christine immediately drank hers, but Jacob was so surprised that he accidentally pulled his hands apart, spilling the water on the ground.

"Um," said Jacob, regarding his wet hands. "Can you make me some more?"

171

"No more till we get to camp," said Mercury. "Come on." He turned and began walking away.

"Camp?" asked Jacob, as he and Christine hurried after Mercury. "Where's that?"

"Not far. I just need to get close enough to Eden II that the miracle detector will alert me if the portal reopens."

They walked nearly another three miles before Mercury proclaimed that they had reached camp, Jacob grumbling the whole way about how thirsty he was. By this time, the sun had set, and a chill had crept into the air. Mercury dug a large bowl-shaped impression in the ground, fused the sand on the bottom into glass, refilled it with sand, and then transmuted the sand into water. Jacob got on his hands and knees and slurped enthusiastically at it.

"Good enough?" Mercury asked.

Jacob gave him a thumbs up.

"Swell," said Mercury. "For my next trick, fire!" He pointed his finger at a boulder, and it burst into flame. The three of them sat around it, warming themselves.

"I don't mean to complain," said Christine after some time, "but we haven't eaten anything since—"

"There's a ram in the thicket over there," said Mercury.

"Where?" asked Christine.

Mercury motioned vaguely in the distance. "Best I could do," he said. "Food is harder than water. You can't just make it out of rocks. Well, you can, but it's awful. Whoever coined the phrase 'manna from heaven' never tried the stuff. It's like eating granola made with dryer lint and chalk dust. Also, you're going to have to prepare it yourself. I'm busy." He was rubbing his hands together over a lump of sand he had picked up.

"Okay," said Christine uncertainly, "but how do I...?"

Mercury set down the lump and picked up another handful of sand. He poured some of the sand from his right hand to his left, and then pulled his right hand away as if stretching a rubber band. He spun the elongated object around and held it out to Christine: a knife made out of glass.

"Careful of the blade," said Mercury. "It's crazy sharp, but brittle. One quick sweep across the throat."

Christine stared at the knife. "You're going to make me kill a wild ram?"

"I'm not going to make you do anything," said Mercury. "But if you want to eat, you're going to have to kill the ram. Now leave me alone. This is delicate work." He had gone back to rubbing the lump between his palms.

"I'll do it," said Jacob. "You can help me gut it."

Christine nodded and handed Jacob the knife. She followed him as they went off in the direction Mercury had indicated. It wasn't hard to find the ram; it was flailing about trying to get its horns disengaged from the branches. Jacob put it out of its misery with the knife. He felt a little bad about it, but not as bad as he felt hungry. With Christine's help, he dragged the carcass back to the fire. They didn't bother to gut it; there was far too much meat for them to use anyway. They just removed one leg, skinned it, and got it roasting on a makeshift spit. The whole process took nearly two hours. Jacob took the first shift at the spit while Christine slumped to the ground, exhausted. "What do you think, Mercury?" she asked.

"I think," said Mercury, holding a blue gem up to the light between his fingers, "it just might pass."

"Wow," said Jacob, looking up from the spit. "That's amazing."

"Yeah," said Mercury, getting to his feet. "And probably futile. Save some of that meat for me. Oh, and you'll need this." He scooped up a handful of sand and bent over to Christine. "Hold out your hand."

She did so, and he poured the contents of his hand into hers. "Sand?" she said.

"Taste it," Mercury replied. "I'll be back." He walked off into the darkness.

Christine took a pinch between her fingers and tasted it. She smiled. "Salt."

CHAPTER TWENTY-FIVE

Mercury returned less than twenty minutes later, holding a stone that looked to Christine identical to the one he had been carrying when he left.

"So?" she asked.

"I did it," said Mercury. "Slipped in and out unseen. Replaced the shard with the fake."

"So that's the real shard," said Jacob, regarding the gem in Mercury's hand. "What are you going to do with it?"

"Drop it in the ocean, I guess," said Mercury.

"Now?"

Mercury shook his head. "I can't leave you two alone that long this close to the Pistons. Those guys are persistent. Ran into a slew of them on the way over. A slew of Pistons? A passel of Pistons? Anyway, Isiah Thomas seems to have decided I'm closer to the constipated gazelle than the angry deity, and he wants his sacrificial lambs back."

"Can't you just wipe them out with your miracle powers?" asked Jacob.

Mercury shot him a dubious glance. "Easy there, Josef Stalin. I'm not really supposed to use my 'miracle powers' for genocide. Also, that would kind of defeat the whole Prime Directive approach we're taking to replacing the shard. I'll get you guys to Eden II tomorrow. That place is a long way from the Pistons' village, so it should be safe. You can keep an eye on the portal location in case Lucifer shows up. Don't try to stop him, just hide and watch. Hopefully he won't show up until after I get back. Once I do, we'll figure out what to do next."

Christine frowned, trying to make sense of the perverse causal schema in which she found herself. "But what if this is how Lucifer gets the shard? What if he shows up right when we get to Eden II?"

"That's not how it works," said Mercury. "If Lucifer from 2017 manages to travel back to now, he already has the shard."

"Why don't we go right now then?"

"Because you two are starving, exhausted, and in no shape to travel. The world isn't going to end if we camp here for the night. Probably. Anyway, I don't need to sleep. I can stay up and watch the shard. Hey, let me do that. You're burning one side." Mercury took over the spit from Jacob and Jacob lay down across the fire from Christine. "Get some sleep," said Mercury. "I'll wake you up when it's done."

Christine nodded lazily, then lay her head back on the ground. She was just thinking how nice it would be to have a pillow and wondering if that was within the range of Mercury's transmutation abilities when suddenly it was daylight. She sat bolt upright in a panic, thinking something must have happened to Mercury.

"Relax," said Mercury, who was sitting on a rock a few feet away. "I didn't want to wake you. There's plenty of food, if you're hungry. I'm afraid it's cold though."

Christine nodded dumbly and made her way to the water bowl, shivering as she left the warm glow of the fire. As she drank, she noticed a large black scorch mark on the ground a few yards from their camp. She looked at Mercury questioningly.

"Burnt offering," said Mercury. "Had to dispose of the rest of the carcass. Figured it was a better option than attracting hyenas."

Christine nodded again and walked back to the campfire, which was now just smoldering rocks. She gave Jacob a gentle kick in the ribs, waking him up, and then tore into the hunk of meat Mercury had left on a slab of rock next to the fire.

When they had eaten and seen to their other immediate needs, they set off toward Eden II. Mercury thought they could make it there by mid-afternoon. Jacob mentioned the possibility of flying there, but Mercury wasn't keen on the idea. Carrying one person while flying was hard enough, he said; carrying two was downright dangerous, not to mention extremely uncomfortable for everyone involved. So they walked.

Occasionally they would stop for water, which Mercury miraculously created out of sand. Around noon, they took a break under the shade of a small stand of trees and ate some salted ram meat, which Christine had packed in the basket she and Jacob had taken for collecting berries. Even after a hearty lunch, there was still enough left over for one more meal.

As the day wore on and the heat intensified, they had to stop for water more frequently, and Christine began to wonder if they were going to make it. A small cloud had been following them since the late morning, blocking much of the sun, and Christine suspected it was Mercury's doing. Even so, the heat was oppressive. She wanted to just lie down and let the buzzards finish her off.

But as they surmounted a small rise, a large dome-shaped structure came into view on the plain below: Eden II. It really was an impressive structure; she supposed that if it weren't for the thing's remote location in the middle of this patch of worthless desert, one of the tribes of the region would have set up shop there. But it was just too far from any source of fresh water or food to be of much practical use. So it sat abandoned, its once lush jungle dying, its expertly constructed dome slowly crumbling. In seven thousand years, there would be no trace of it.

"Who's that?" Jacob asked, and Christine redirected her gaze to where Jacob was looking. It took her a few seconds to discern the figure in the distance, barely distinguishable amid the waves of heat emanating from the desert floor. At first she thought it was an animal of some sort, an anteater or a hyena, but then she realized it was a person, hunched over as if looking for something.

"Nisroc," she found herself saying.

They stared for several seconds longer. "No," said Jacob at last. "It can't be. He's still looking for the sword?"

"He's looking for something," said Christine.

"Hold on," said Mercury. "That's Nisroc? The demon that I spray-painted and dropped onto the roof of the Vanden Heuvel building?"

"You did *what?*" Christine asked.

"Oh, you weren't there," said Mercury. "Long story."[10]

---

[10] For an explanation of how this came about, see *Mercury Revolts*.

"I don't think he's a demon yet," said Christine. "He's still working for Heaven at this point. He kicked us out of Eden II. Said he was supposed to be guarding it with a flaming sword, but he lost it."

They watched for a moment longer and the tiny, hunched-over figure of Niscroc continued to scour the desert.

"Should we tell him?" said Jacob.

"He'll probably keep looking for the next thousand years if we don't."

"All right," said Mercury. "Let's go." He set off down the slope toward Nisroc, Christine and Jacob following close behind. Some ten minutes later, they were standing a few paces from Nisroc, who continued obliviously scanning the ground. He gave no indication of having seen them.

"Hey there," said Mercury at last.

The man stopped and looked up at Mercury momentarily. "They just checked on me yesterday," he said. "It doesn't help to keep pestering me, you know." He went back to scanning the ground.

"Did they?" asked Mercury. "We must have gotten our signals crossed. How goes the search?"

"It would go better if you people would leave me alone and let me look. Or help. You can look over there." He pointed vaguely in the direction he had just come from.

"I think you already looked there," said Mercury.

"So now you're going to tell me how to do my job?" said Nisroc. "I've been doing this for four months, you know. I think I have some idea how to do it."

"Ah," said Mercury. "A proponent of the labor theory of value."

"I have a system," Nisroc sniffed. "I go East-West on Tuesdays, Thursdays and Saturdays, and North-South on Mondays, Wednesdays and Fridays."

"What about Sundays?"

"Sundays I go in circles."

Mercury nodded. "That definitely bears some superficial resemblance to a system," he said. "However, I've got some good and/or bad news, depending on how attached you are to your current occupation." He held up the shard between his fingers.

178

"What's that?" asked Nisroc.

"It's what you're looking for," said Mercury.

"No, no. I'm looking for a sword."

"Right, but this is what your bosses really care about. This is the shard from the Eye of Providence."

Nisroc frowned dubiously. "I'm pretty sure I lost a sword."

"This is the gem from the handle," said Mercury. "The sword isn't important. Look." He pulled the miracle detector from his pocket. "See, this thing is... uh oh."

"What?" Christine asked, craning her neck to see the display.

"Two blips," said Mercury. "The portal is opening. Come on!" He took off running toward the dome in the distance.

CHAPTER TWENTY-SIX

"Let's go," said Jacob. Christine nodded, and they set off together after Mercury. Christine heard Nisroc close behind. They went through an open door and followed Mercury to a clearing in the wilted jungle. When they got there, Mercury was on his hands and knees in front of it, combing through the dirt.

"Mercury," Christine gasped, out of breath. "What are you doing?"

"Looking for something to use as a weapon. A rock, anything."

"Can't you just use, you know, miracles?"

"Sure. So can Lucifer. But a nice big rock would give me an edge."

"How about, *unck*, this?" asked Jacob, stepping into the glow of the portal holding a rock a little larger than his fist.

"Perfect!" cried Mercury, seizing the rock. As he did so, a massive horned demon flickered into being on the portal. Christine recognized him; she had met him once before: Azrael, a minion of Lucifer. He was still standing on the portal, trying to adjust his vision to the dim light, when Mercury smacked him in the forehead with the rock. Azrael staggered backwards and fell to the ground.

"Woohoo rock!" exclaimed Mercury. "Nothing beats rock!" He drew the rock back over his shoulder, ready for someone else to come through. Christine, Jacob and Nisroc waited breathlessly.

And waited.

And waited.

Azrael groaned.

"Nisroc," said Mercury. "Make sure he doesn't get up. Hit him with another rock if you have to. Jacob, find Nisroc another rock."

"Is Lucifer coming through?" asked Christine.

"I would think so," said Mercury. "He must have sent Azrael through to check things out. It's funny, because when I left, Azrael had... oh."

"What?"

Mercury's brow furrowed. "This is... he sent Azrael through first. Before I went through. Then he reset the portal for later, so I got here before he did."

"I'm not following."

"Azrael went through the time portal before I did, but it was set for a few hours later, so he's just showing up now."

Azrael groaned again.

"I thought I told you to hit him with a rock," said Mercury.

"We can't find any," said Nisroc. "Can we borrow yours?"

"Why did you hit me?" asked Azrael, sitting up and rubbing his head.

"You're working for Lucifer," said Jacob.

"Sure, but I don't mean any harm," said Azrael. "I'm just checking things out. Hey, how the hell did *you* get here?" Azrael had apparently recognized Mercury.

"Long story," said Mercury, taking a step toward Azrael, rock still at the ready.

"Wait!" cried Azrael. "You don't have to hit me! I'm not going to do anything!"

"Okay, listen," said Mercury. "I need you to go back through the portal and tell Lucifer the portal didn't work."

"But it obviously did work," said Christine. "I mean, Lucifer is going to know he went *somewhere*."

"Right, right," said Mercury. "Okay, tell him it's not safe. Tell him you were attacked. But not by me. You can't tell him I was here."

"Why not?"

"Look, Azrael. Lucifer is messing with stuff he doesn't understand. Paradoxes, causal loops, impossibilities. You know what I'm talking about. I shouldn't even be here. And if we let him get away with this, it's going to get worse. We could all just disappear and it would be like we never existed."

"How do you know all this?"

"I've seen it," said Mercury. "I'm from the future."

"And I don't exist?"

"Nope."

"You mean I just vanished?"

"No, you never even existed. I never even heard of you."

"Then how did you know who I was?"

"I didn't," said Mercury.

"But you called me by my name."

"No, I didn't," said Mercury. "See, now you're remembering things that never happened. It's the first step in the annihilation process."

"Gaaahhh!" cried Azrael. "What do I do? How do I stop it?"

"Calm down," said Mercury. "Just go back through the portal. Tell Lucifer it's not safe here."

"Not safe how?"

"Who cares? Tell him you were attacked by cavemen."

"Cavemen?" said Azrael, frowning. "Like, actual people living in caves?"

"I feel like you're getting a little bogged down in the details here, Azrael. Just tell him you were attacked. It's not safe."

"Then what do I do?"

"Damned if I know. Whatever you want, I guess. If I were you, I'd get the hell away from Lucifer, but that's your call. Just do it quick, before Lucifer sends somebody else through."

Azrael nodded slowly and got to his feet. "Okay," he said. "I guess I'll see you later."

"Yep," said Mercury. "Have a nice trip."

Azrael stepped onto the portal and vanished.

Christine turned Mercury. "Okay, now what?"

"Now Lucifer has Drekavac set the portal back a few hours, and I go through and show up here."

"No, I mean now what do we do? Should Jacob and I go through the portal?"

"I wouldn't recommend it," said Mercury. "You'd be walking into a hostage situation. Being stuck in 7,000 B.C. is better than being dead."

"Maybe you should go through," said Christine. "Stop Lucifer from ever coming back."

"Oh, no," said Mercury. "I just got *out* of a hostage situation. Besides, I'm already there. Another of me isn't going to help things any."

"This is all very confusing," said Nisroc, shaking his head.

"Also, I still have this." Mercury held up the shard. "Lucifer's already got one shard. Imagine what he might do with two."

"But..." Jacob said, "if you bring the shard into the future, after the time machine was built, then the shard wasn't in the past when Lucifer found it. And if Lucifer never found it, the time machine would never have been built."

"So," said Christine, "you can foil Lucifer's plan by giving him the one thing he needs to complete his plan."

Jacob frowned. "Unless Lucifer uses the—*unck*—time machine to take the shard back in time so that he will have it to build the time machine."

"I can't see Lucifer doing that," said Christine. "He's a narcissistic megalomaniac. He's not going to willingly help someone else take over the world, even if that someone is an earlier version of himself."

Mercury nodded. "I tend to agree. Lucifer is the sort to go back in time and murder his own grandfather, even if it means he'll never exist."

"You're saying we should take the shard to the future," said Christine.

Mercury shook his head. "Too many variables. I still think we're better off—" As he spoke, the portal suddenly faded, leaving them in the near-darkness. "Well, I guess that's decided," said Mercury.

"And we aren't going home after all," said Christine.

"Sorry," Mercury replied. "The good news, though, is that Lucifer hasn't come through yet."

"But he still could," said Jacob. "At any second."

"Yes," said Mercury. "So you all need to hide. I'm going to fly to the middle of the ocean and drop this shard off, like that decrepit door-hogger Kate Winslet."

"No!" cried Nisroc, and for a moment they were all startled, having forgotten he was there. "I will get in so much trouble if you do that!"

"Look, Nisroc," said Mercury. "It's not safe to keep this thing around. Lucifer is going to get his hands on it eventually and wipe out history."

"It belongs in Heaven with the proper authorities," declared Nisroc. "It's the safest place for it."

Mercury, Jacob and Christine traded glances.

"What do you think?" asked Christine. "Would it be possible for Lucifer to retrieve that thing from the bottom of the ocean? Like if he had one of those things?" She indicated the miracle detector Mercury was holding.

Mercury sighed. "I suppose so," he said. "Even the Mariana Trench is only six miles deep. Any place I could hide it, he could find it, given enough time. And he's got seven thousand years."

"Then Nisroc is right. Heaven is the safest place for it. And while you're there, you can tell them about Lucifer's plan and maybe get some reinforcements."

Nisroc nodded, emboldened by this show of support. "I will call for a portal and we can bring it there together."

"Fine," said Mercury. "Nisroc and I will deliver the shard to the authorities. You two stay here in case Lucifer shows up. I'll be back as soon as I can."

As he spoke, a portal once again appeared on the ground in front of them.

"Um, Nisroc...?" Mercury asked.

"That's not me," said Nisroc nervously. "I haven't even called yet."

"It's the same as the last one," said Christine. "Quick, grab your rock!"

"Hold on," said Mercury, watching the portal. "This could be your chance."

"What do you mean?" asked Christine.

"Nobody's coming through," said Mercury. "If you go now, you might be able to sneak through while Lucifer is distracted."

"You mean—"

"Go!" exclaimed Mercury. "You're not going to get another shot."

"What about the shard?"

"I'll have to stay behind with Nisroc. You and Jacob go."

"Can't Nisroc take care of it?" asked Christine. "All he's got to do is call for a portal and bring it to Heaven. You can do that, can't you, Nisroc?"

Nisroc nodded. "Easy-peasy," he said.

"Come on!" Jacob exclaimed. "Let's go!"

"Can't risk it," said Mercury. "I need to stay. You two go."

"I'm not leaving without you," said Christine.

"You'll be stuck seven thousand years in the past!"

"So will you!"

"Yeah, but I've done it before."

"Well, I'm going," said Jacob. "With or without you." He took a step onto the portal and vanished.

"Your turn," said Mercury.

"You first," said Christine.

"Damn it, Christine!" Mercury snapped. "Fine." He turned to Nisroc. "Nisroc, call for a portal immediately and take this to the authorities in Heaven. Do not stop, do not pass go, do not collect $200. You have one mission in life: get this shard to Heaven. Do you understand?"

Nisroc nodded, taking the shard from Mercury. "Piece of cake," he said.

"Godspeed," said Mercury. He grabbed Christine's hand. "Let's do this." They stepped onto the portal together and vanished. A split-second later, the portal was gone as well.

Nisroc stood alone for a moment, staring at the shard. "I don't know why nobody thinks I can do anything," he said. "If they'd just give me a—" He felt something strike his back and looked down to see a spear protruding from his abdomen. "Oh," he said, and fell to the ground. Before he lost consciousness, he felt someone take the shard from his hand.

CHAPTER TWENTY-SEVEN

We can only speculate as to what happened to the shard after it left Nisroc's hands. The most likely scenario appears to be something like this:

Three members of the tribe known as the Pistons had been stalking Mercury's group for some time, finally seizing on their chance to attack when most of the group disappeared through the portal. Perhaps they knew Nisroc had the shard and killed him to get it back; perhaps they were just grumpy after a day-long trek through the desert. In either case, they took the shard and left Nisroc for dead, unaware that he would in short order recover physically, if not emotionally, from his ordeal.

Unfortunately for the three Pistons, on the way back to their village they encountered a hungry lion, which devoured a significant portion of their party along with the shard itself. The lion was later injured in an inconclusive struggle with a bull elephant and limped off to die alone of starvation. Its body was picked apart by vultures, one of whom swallowed the shard.

The vulture survived for several weeks with the shard in its belly, but the added weight eventually made it easy prey for a crocodile while the bird was bathing in the headwaters of the Nile. The crocodile carried bird's carcass in its belly, along with the shard, all the way to the Nile delta, where it was attacked by hunters. The crocodile escaped after suffering a fatal blow from a spear; it sank to the bottom of the river where its corpse slowly rotted over the next several months. The shard remained on the bottom of the delta for the next three hundred years.

During an uncharacteristic drought one year, the waters in the delta receded enough that a child playing in the river spotted the shard. He swam down to recover it. Realizing it was very valuable, the child ran to bring the shard to his father, but in his excitement he tripped on a tree root and fell on his face, dropping the shard. The shard was picked up by a passing merchant, who insisted he had bought the shard from a street vendor in Khartoum. As there were no witnesses to the contrary, the merchant's claim was sustained.

That night, however, the child's father broke into the merchant's home to recover the shard. The merchant awoke and put up a struggle; the child's father killed him and ran with the shard. He was apprehended shortly by a soldier, who delivered the shard to the local strong man-cum-mayor. At the time, a young prince was attempting to unify the towns in the area into a single kingdom, and the strong man-cum-mayor, fearing attack from the neighboring provinces, gave the shard to the prince in an effort to buy his protection.

The shard remained in the prince's family for seven generations, while his small kingdom gradually grew to encompass most of modern-day Egypt. The prince's great-great-great-great-grandson was buried with the shard in an elaborate tomb protected with all manner of traps, ruses, hidden doors, and truly stomach-churning curses. It remained inviolate until the late 18th century, when tomb robbers broke in and stole virtually everything. The only thing they missed, in fact, was the shard—which remained safely ensconced in the mummy's right hand. It remained there, undisturbed, for another 40 years.

In 1831, an Irishman named Darius Finlan borrowed $80,000 to launch an Egyptian treasure-hunting expedition. Sadly, Finlan arrived after most of the easily-accessible tombs had already been raided and he failed to uncover any previously untouched tombs. After six months, facing the prospect of having to return to Britain with nothing to show for his venture, he made a final sweep of a tomb long since thought to be picked over. The mummy once respectfully enshrined in the tomb had been dumped in a corner, its headdress and other accoutrement removed. On a hunch, Darius Finlan checked the mummy's left hand, which was clamped shut. He had to break off three of the fingers, but he was rewarded for his efforts with a stunning gem of the purest blue. He slipped it into his pocket to hide it from his employees, who were owed six weeks of back pay, and managed to skip town, hopping on the next train

188

to Damascus. Three weeks later he was back in London, where he was promptly beaten to death by his creditors. He was found bleeding to death in the street, not ten paces from his front door, by his eight-year-old son, Christopher. Darius Finlan handed the shard to his son, murmured, "Here's something," and died.

Chris Finlan kept the shard on him from that moment on, never revealing its existence to his mother or anyone else for fear that his one keepsake from his father would be taken from him. Over the next several years, the previously friendly and gregarious Chris Finlan developed an unnatural attachment to the shard; he began to eschew relations with other people and could often be seen walking the streets of his neighborhood addressing a person or persons unseen. Chris Finlan attended university in London, eventually graduating with a degree in mechanical engineering. He spent the next thirty years pursuing a stable if unremarkable career at a London firm, where it was often remarked by his coworkers that he hadn't appeared to have aged a day since he was hired. When the tone of these comments began to change from amusement to bewilderment bordering on fear, he put in his notice and moved to Boston.

Over the next hundred years, he continued to work as a mid-level engineer, changing cities every ten years or so in order to avoid suspicion regarding his unnatural youthfulness. His antisocial tendencies worsened with each move; he found it harder and harder each time to go through the motions of initiating friendships. Ultimately he stopped trying. A few months later, he quit his job and bought a shack in a remote area of Montana, where he started mailing bombs to public figures and writing a manifesto that would, he believed, "explain everything."

Unfortunately, Chris Finlan's manifesto was universally misinterpreted as a cry for help, specifically the sort of help that can only be delivered by an FBI SWAT team with a shitload of automatic weapons. He was arrested, given a trial in which he threw himself on the mercy of the court. Mercy was granted in the form of seventeen life sentences, to be served in sequence. He was only a year into this sentence when he died in prison, under highly suspicious circumstances. He was not missed.

CHAPTER TWENTY-EIGHT

The BOX, just outside Elko, Nevada; April 29, 2017

Christine found herself in a large warehouse-like building that was filled with odd-looking devices and machinery. Next to her stood Mercury, and standing a few feet in front of her was Jacob. Wherever they were, one thing was clear: they were no longer in prehistoric Africa.

"Hey," said a man's voice behind them. "How did you get back here?"

Christine turned to see a small, balding man standing next to a contraption that looked like a steamer trunk with a satellite dish on top of it.

"Move," said Mercury, ignoring the man. Christine felt him grabbing her arm. "Quick, while Lucifer's distracted."

"Where?" asked Jacob, regarding the maze of boxes and equipment.

"Anywhere," said Mercury. "Just go!"

Jacob set off down an aisle between two rows of machinery, Christine and Mercury following.

"Who was that?" Christine asked, looking behind her.

"That's just Drekavac," said Mercury. "He's harmless. Keep moving."

They made their way through the maze. Christine had no idea where they were or how big this building was; she could only hope they would eventually reach an exit. But just when she began to suspect Jacob was leading them in circles, an explosion sounded somewhere behind her. The fluorescent lights overhead flickered out, and the building was suddenly dark except for minimal battery-powered emergency lighting. Another explosion sounded farther away, followed by distant shouts and the clattering of debris on the floor.

Jacob stopped, holding his hands over his head. "What's happening?" he asked.

"FBI is attacking the building," said Mercury. "We need to get out of here."

"Where?" asked Jacob. "I can't see anything!"

"Just keep going as straight as you can. We'll hit the perimeter wall eventually."

But as he spoke, someone came around a corner just ahead of them and stopped short. His face was obscured in the dim light.

"There you are!" exclaimed the man. "Sorry, got turned around."

"Who the hell...?" Jacob started.

"Balderhaz?" asked Mercury, slipping past Christine toward the small figure, who was barely visible in the dim light. "What are you doing back here?"

"Wait," said Christine. "You mean this is Balderhaz? *The* Balderhaz? As in—"

"Who are these people, Mercury?" asked Balderhaz. "What happened to the other angel and the girl with the purple hair? I like her, she smells like cinnamon."

"It's complicated, Balderhaz," Mercury replied. "I'll explain later. For now, we need to get out of here."

"You went through, didn't you?" Balderhaz asked excitedly. "You went back in time!"

"Yes," said Mercury. "Again, if we could just move toward the exit—"

"Pity," said Balderhaz.

"What?" asked Mercury. "What are you talking about?"

"You should have found the shard and gotten rid of it while you were back there. Then Lucifer would never have been able to hook it up to the portal generator."

"We did!" said Mercury. "It's all taken care of. I gave the shard to... oh, shit."

"What?" asked Christine.

"You're saying Lucifer hooked up the shard to the portal generator?"

Balderhaz nodded.

"Then we failed. Somehow Lucifer got the shard despite our efforts."

"You mean *because* of our efforts," said Jacob. "You were right, Mercury. It was pointless to meddle. Whatever we chose to do, we would have ended up causing him to get the shard. *Did* end up causing him to get it. So much for free will."

"Ha!" cried Balderhaz. "Free will. The nutty ideas you people come up with. You're stuck in a causal loop. Free will is an illusion. Right now, an earlier version of you is somewhere in this building, about to go back in time and go through everything you just went through to wind up here."

"Figures," said Mercury. "Let's just get out of here before the FBI levels this place."

"What if Mercury stops him?" said Christine. "Stops the other Mercury, I mean. Keep him from going back in time."

"I wouldn't try it if I were you," replied Balderhaz. "The universe is pretty stubborn about this sort of thing. You'll probably get yourself blown to pieces."

"Well that's just fucking fantastic," said Christine. "So we did all that work for nothing. Nothing we do makes any difference."

"Cool your jets, princess," said Balderhaz. "I said free will is bullshit, not that nothing you do makes a difference. The trick is to beat the universe at its own game."

"Seriously," said Mercury. "Can we have this discussion outside? It's getting kind of explodey in here."

"This will just take a second," Balderhaz said, pulling something from his pocket.

"What's that?" asked Jacob.

"What's that?" asked Jacob. It was a disk made of some silvery metal, rather larger than a quarter. As Balderhaz held it up, Christine saw that it seemed to catch the light in a strange way, swirling and pulsing as if the coin had a mind of its own.

"A quoin," said Balderhaz. "My own invention.""My own invention."

"A coin?" said Christine. "You didn't invent coins."

"*Quoin*," said Balderhaz. "Kwuh-oin. As in quantum coin. You flip it, but the final resting position of a quoin is determined by subatomic quantum phenomena. It's truly random."

"How is that different from a regular coin?" asked Christine.

193

"Coin tosses aren't truly random," said Jacob. "Their behavior can be described using classical—"

"Can we have the philosophical discussion later?" asked Mercury. "We get it. Truly random. So what?"

"So we pick two actions, one associated with heads and the other with tails—"

"We know how a coin toss works, Balderhaz. Please get to the freaking point."

Balderhaz sniffed. "Heads, Mercury goes and warns himself not to go back in time. Tails, Mercury doesn't warn himself and leaves with us. Two incompatible results. Mercury can't both cause Lucifer to get the shard by going back in time and cause him to get the shard by not going back in time. The quantum randomness allows us to break free from the causal loop. There's a fifty percent chance he will succeed in preventing Lucifer from getting the shard."

"And a fifty percent chance he will fail," said Christine.

"Yes, sweetie," said Balderhaz. "That's how percentages work."

"This is insane," said Jacob. "We can't leave the fate of the universe to a coin toss."

"Quoin toss," said Balderhaz. "And if you don't, you have a hundred percent chance of failing."

"What the hell," said Mercury. "It's not the craziest thing I've ever done. Let's try it. Whatever happens, the rest of you get the hell out of this building."

"Excellent," said Balderhaz. "Here goes nothing!" He tossed the quoin in the air and caught it in his palm, then slapped it onto the back of his other hand. He pulled his hand away and looked at it.

"Well?" said Christine. Mercury and Jacob stared dumbly at Balderhaz, unable to see the quoin's surface in the dim light.

Balderhaz looked up at them and grinned.

CHAPTER TWENTY-NINE

"Tails!" Balderhaz announced.

"Great," said Mercury. "So I let myself go back in time and everything happens just like it already happened. Truly a groundbreaking strategy. Now let's get the hell out of here."

"Good luck!" said Balderhaz, ducking down a side alley.

"Where are you going?" Christine called. But Balderhaz was already gone.

"Should we go after him?" Jacob asked.

"He's fine," said Mercury. "Keep going."

Another explosion sounded somewhere to their right. Jacob, Christine and Mercury continued straight until the aisle widened into a larger open area. The lighting was a bit better here.

"There!" said Mercury, pointing to their left. An EXIT sign glowed in the distance. Mercury looked to his left and then to his right, but saw no signs of Lucifer's minions. "The coast appears to be clear," he said. "I'll go first. Stay right behind me. And when you go out the door, put your hands up. Ready?"

Christine and Jacob nodded. Mercury took a deep breath and sprinted toward the exit. He slammed into the door, throwing it open, and stumbled outside, his hands in the air. He grimaced, anticipating a hail of bullets. But it didn't come.

"STEP AWAY FROM THE BUILDING," the voice of the FBI said from somewhere behind a bank of blinding floodlights. Mercury, Christine and Jacob did so, their hands still in the air. When they were fifty feet or so from the building, dark-clad men appeared and seized them. They were dragged into a large black trailer which looked ominous from the outside but turned out to resemble an upscale dentist's waiting room on the inside, complete with black leather couches and outdated copies of *Cosmopolitan* and

Sports Illustrated. John Mayer's "Waiting on the World to Change" leaked almost inaudibly from unseen speakers.

The black-garbed men instructed them to sit, and they did so. The black-garbed men left.

"I don't get it," said Jacob. "Are they arresting us? What's going on?"

"Not arresting us," said Mercury. "Charming us. They know I'm an angel, and they probably think you two are as well. They've lost control over Tiamat, so they're desperate for allies. That's why we're getting the soft touch. They're going to try to convince us to cooperate with them against Lucifer."

"And are we going to?" asked Christine.

"The question," said Mercury, "is whether they are going to cooperate with us."

As he spoke, the door to the trailer opened and three more people—two men and a woman—shuffled in, prodded by more black-garbed men. Christine recognized the men. The first was a cherub named Eddie, who was a sort-of friend of Mercury's. The other was Balderhaz. The woman was cute, in pudgy, purple-haired sort of way.

The black-garbed men instructed the newcomers to sit, which they did. The black-garbed men then left again.

The three angels, one man, and two women sat for a moment, regarding each other nervously.

"Wow," said Mercury after a moment. "This is really awkward. And I say that as someone who recently witnessed his own death. Okay, let's do this. We'll go around in a circle, clockwise. Say your name, a sentence or two about yourself, and your favorite *Gilmore Girls* character. I'll start. My name is Mercury, I'm an angel probably best known for imploding the Moon, and I refuse to answer the question on the grounds that there are too many great characters on that show to pick just one." He turned to Christine, on his left.

"Uh, Christine Temetri," she said. "I used to be a journalist. Then I was sort of a focal point for the Apocalypse for a while. Lately I've been focusing on hunting and gathering."

"I'm Balderhaz," said Balderhaz. The group sat for a moment, staring at him, but it became clear he wasn't going to say anything else.

"Oh," said Eddie. "I'm Eddie, AKA Ederatz. I'm a cherub. I used to work for the Mundane Observation Corps. I, um, helped Mercury save the world a few times. And, um, Rory I guess?"

"Suzy Cilbrith," said Suzy. "Former software developer turned whistleblower turned girl Friday, I suppose."

"I'm—*unck*—Jacob Slater," said Jacob. "I was a forensic analyst for the FBI. Lately I've been hanging out in prehistoric Africa with Christine, mostly just trying to survive. Oh, and I always kind of liked Luke."

"I forgot to answer that part," said Suzy. "I like Luke too." She smiled sheepishly at Jacob, who smiled back.

"Glad we have that settled," said a man entering the trailer. "I was always partial to Sookie."

"Special Agent Burton," said Mercury. "Surprised to see you up and around, considering how determined your coworkers seem to be to kill you."

"Don't get up," replied Burton, sinking into a plush chair. "We're going for a ride."

"Where?" asked Christine.

"Not far," said Burton. "Just outside the blast radius."

"Blast radius of—*unck*—what?" asked Jacob.

"Ten kiloton bunker-buster," said Burton. "Non-nuclear, but it has a hell of kick."

"You're making a mistake," said Mercury. "Even if that thing gets through Lucifer's defenses, you won't kill him. You'll just scatter him and his minions to the wind. They'll reincorporate somewhere else and go back to their evil plans." As he spoke, the trailer began to move slowly over the rough ground.

"But without the portal generator," said Burton. "And now that we know what to look for, we can prevent them from building another one."

"Also," Jacob interjected. "*Unck.*"

"It's a bad idea," said Mercury. "Let me go back in there. Maybe I can still stop him from going back. Failing that, I can follow him back in time and thwart his plan there. I always do."

Jacob tried again, "And didn't you say, *unck*, that—"

"Out of my hands," said Burton. "I only brought you all here because I thought you might be interested in working as consultants for the new division of the FBI that I'll be heading. From what I've been able to gather, you've all had quite a bit of experience with—"

"Unck!" Jacob shouted, and everyone turned to face him. He held up his hand and took a deep breath. "The shard," he said finally. "Mercury said that—"

"Oh shit," said Mercury. "He's right. If you blow up that place, you'll destroy the shard."

"Meaning what?" asked Burton.

"Meaning you might tear a hole in the space-time continuum. At the very least, you're going to kill everyone within several miles."

"Ubiquium," said Balderhaz, nodding thoughtfully. "Powerful stuff."

Burton looked from Mercury to Jacob to Balderhaz, a dubious look on his face. "That's what Tiamat said before she escaped and freed Lucifer from prison."

"And the fact that you can't tell the difference between an actual threat and one of Tiamat's bluffs is a compelling argument for keeping the FBI the hell out of things you don't understand," said Mercury. "Call off the attack."

"Nothing I can do about it," said Burton. "The order comes from the President himself. Neutralize the threat at any cost. We've tried smaller scale explosives, but Lucifer has put up some kind of invisible barrier. Nothing gets through it."

"That's the problem!" cried Mercury. "This isn't a conventional enemy. You can't neutralize him by—"

Half a dozen explosions sounded outside, in rapid succession. The trailer continued to roll slowly away from the scene.

"What was that?" asked Suzy.

"Sounds like RPGs," said Jacob.

"They're distracting him," said Mercury. "Trying to lull him into a false sense of security, so when the bunker buster comes, he'll let it detonate on the shield like the rest of the bombs."

"Except the bunker buster will detonate twice," said Jacob. "Once when it hits the shield, and then again, a split-second later— with a hundred times the force. It'll level that place."

"How long do we have?" Mercury asked.

Burton glanced at his watch. "The bomber is three minutes out."

Mercury leapt from his chair and gripped Burton by his lapels. "Call it off, you psychopath!"

"Sit down," said Burton coolly. He was pointing a gun at Mercury with his right hand. In his left was the Balderhaz cube, which he had evidently retrieved from Suzy.

Mercury sighed and stood up, nearly losing his balance as the trailer went over a bump. "So the veneer of civility turns out to be pretty thin," he said. "One little bump and the pistol comes out. I don't see a future in this relationship, Special Agent Burton."

"Sit down and we'll talk it over," said Burton.

"You know what your problem is, Burton?" said Mercury, still standing, his head brushing the ceiling of the trailer. "You're a reactor. You react to situations based on previous experiences. And you're a quick learner, I'll give you that. But your methodology prevents you from reacting appropriately to unprecedented situations. And what we have here—" As he spoke, the trailer went over another bump, causing Burton's aim to drift wide for a moment. Mercury went limp, spinning around and falling into Burton's lap while seizing Burton's wrist with his right hand. He squeezed hard, and there was a crack. Burton grunted and the gun fell out of his hand into Mercury's. "—is an unprecedented situation," Mercury finished. He kissed Burton on the cheek, stood up and shot the latch on the trailer's rear doors twelve times. The doors fell open, revealing the portal facility against the night sky. A dirt road rolled away beneath them.

"It was unlocked," Burton said.

"Also?" Mercury said, taking a step toward the opening. "You have no style." He tossed the gun to Burton and leapt out of the truck.

CHAPTER THIRTY

Mercury sprinted at top speed toward the portal facility, praying nobody took a shot at him until he was out of range of the Balderhaz cube—which was still receding along the road along with Special Agent Burton and the others. Fortunately, the feds didn't seem terribly interested in a madman running toward the target of the bunker buster bomb; they were preoccupied with getting out of the way of the blast. The helicopters too were arcing away from the scene. As far as Mercury could tell, the only human beings still present were two dozen or so agents ringing the building at a distance of about a hundred yards, firing rocket-propelled grenades from shoulder launchers. They seem to firing at random locations; the grenades mostly exploded harmlessly a few yards from the roof or somewhere near the perimeter of the building. Occasionally one would get a little closer, doing minor damage to some section of the building. Lucifer didn't have enough demons inside to maintain a full barrier; they were having to shift their efforts from place to place to react to the attacks. There was no way they were going to be able to repel the bunker buster. Maybe if they knew it was coming, one of the demons could redirect the bomb away from the building, but that required more effort than simply putting up a semi-solid shield for the bombs to detonate against.

Lucifer had to know that the FBI would eventually graduate to weapons he wouldn't be able to repel. That's all the feds knew how to do: escalate the situation until was resolved, one way or another. Lucifer's goal was obviously to go through the portal before there was nothing left of the facility but gaping crater. Mercury could only hope the portal was too damaged for him to escape. Of course, it didn't really matter what Lucifer did if the bunker buster destroyed the shard, annihilating the Earth. If Mercury couldn't stop Lucifer, he had to at least get the shard out of harm's way.

Mercury ran past the fleeing vehicles and down the dirt road to the facility, reaching the door without incident. As he entered, shots rang out. He was ready for this; it was no great difficulty to cause the bullets to alter their trajectory around him. The Balderhaz cube was now far enough away that he could once again perform miracles.

Ignoring the surprised minions who continued to fire ineffectively at him, Mercury ran down an aisle toward the center of the building. The light was dim here, but there was no time to slow down. He kept running, trusting his memory of the maze to get him to the portal generator without incident. Behind him he heard one of the minions in pursuit, but a loud crash followed by a moan indicated the demon had made a wrong turn. By some miracle not of his doing, Mercury managed to avoid running into anything, and he emerged into the open area just as the portal flickered to life. Drekavac stood at the controls of the portal generator, and Lucifer was a few steps away.

"You again!" exclaimed Lucifer, taking a step toward the portal. "How do you keep showing up just as I'm about to go back in time and rewrite history?"

"It's kind of a funny story," said Mercury, sidling toward the shard receptacle. "After the last time I stopped you, I returned before I left and—"

"I don't actually care," said Lucifer. "Anyway, I owe you a debt of gratitude. While I was unconscious, Drekavac managed to get a few more weeks out of the portal generator. So whatever damage you may have done by going back, I can undo by going back even further. Anyway, I should get out of here before the FBI blows this place." He stepped onto the portal and vanished.

"Drekavac!" Mercury said. "I need to go stop Lucifer. Take the shard and—"

But as he spoke, Drekavac turned and ran away, disappearing into the darkness.

"Son of a bitch," Mercury growled. He could go after Lucifer, but if he carried the shard through the portal, there was no telling what would happen. Something pretty bad, considering that Lucifer had deliberately left it behind. And if Mercury went after Lucifer without the shard, the feds would blow it up—and something else, also pretty bad, would happen.

"There he is!" a voice yelled in the darkness behind him. "Shoot him!"

Mercury ducked down, flipped open the shard receptacle's lid, and grabbed the shard. It was cool to the touch but still glowed bright orange with interplanar energy. Automatic weapon fire rang out and Mercury ducked and ran down an alley, gripping the shard tightly. Overhead there was a sudden barrage of explosions, almost masking the hum of an approaching airplane. The FBI was getting ready for the grand finale.

Mercury ran through the maze, dodging gunfire and trying to get to the nearest exit. Explosions continued to sound all around him. He made it to door and threw it open, barely slowing down. He could hear the bomber overhead; it would be releasing its payload any second. He didn't know how much longer it would take for the bomb to reach its target, but he suspected it was a matter of seconds. He could only hope he was clear of the blast area in time.

Flickers of light in the distance signaled the ongoing launches of RPGs at the facility; the poor saps behind them had no idea Lucifer was already gone. Mercury heard gunshots behind him and was vaguely aware of bullets thwicking into the sand just ahead, but he didn't dare expend any energy trying to repel them. All his effort was channeled into running as fast as he could away from the building.

Then, suddenly, he realized the RPG firing had stopped, and the men firing them had taken cover—preparing for the imminent detonation of the bunker buster. The split-second warning of a flash of light on ground around him gave Mercury just enough time to dive to the ground and throw up a barrier of interplanar energy between him and the building.

The sound of the bomb was like a mountain punching another mountain. Wind whipped past Mercury's face, pelting him with sand, rocks, and occasionally a small chunk of the building. But after a few seconds of this, Mercury realized that he was still intact. The shard was still in his hand, undamaged—no thanks to that Special Agent assface Burton. The shard's orange glow began to fade as its stored energy dissipated.

Mercury got to his feet and brushed himself off. The desert sand flickered with light, and as he turned, he saw dozens of small fires flickering amid the rubble. Pieces of sheet metal and machinery lay strewn across the ground in every direction. So much for all their hard work—not to mention most of Mercury's fortune. People today have no respect for private property, he thought. You can't build anything these days without somebody coming along and wrecking it.

And that wasn't the worst of it. Now Lucifer had gone back in time to rewrite history, and there was no way of stopping him, because the portal generator was in a million pieces thanks to the overzealous efforts of the FBI. Mercury sighed. It was shit like this that made him want to just throw in the towel. At least he could sort of understand Lucifer's motivations. Evil you could work with. But there was no reasoning with bureaucratic stupidity.

But as he wandered through the ruins, surveying the extent of the destruction, the familiar blue glow of the portal appeared once again. "How the hell...?" Mercury murmured, staring at the glowing ellipse. Had Lucifer gotten bored with the prehistoric past and decided to come back? But that was impossible. He'd have to have built another portal generator—and found another shard.

A man materialized on the portal. He was tall—taller than Lucifer. Another, shorter man materialized right behind him. The tall man surveyed his surroundings in apparent horror and then turned to the shorter man. "What the hell happened?" he said. "It looks like a bomb went off."

"Uh-oh," said the shorter man. "I think it did."

CHAPTER THIRTY-ONE

The BOX, just outside Elko, Nevada; April 29, 2017

"Heads!" Balderhaz announced.

"Great," said Mercury. "Just to be clear, that's the option where I try to prevent myself from going back in time?"

"Correct," said Balderhaz. "Good luck!" With that, he turned and ducked down a side alley.

"Where are you going?" Christine called. But Balderhaz was already gone.

"Should we go after him?" Jacob asked.

Another explosion sounded somewhere to their right.

"He's fine," said Mercury. "Just keep going that way until you hit the outer wall, then turn left. You'll come to a door. Go outside with your hands up and generally do your best not to get shot. I'll catch up with you shortly, assuming I don't tear a hole in the space-time continuum." Mercury turned and went back the way they had come, threading his way through the maze in the near-darkness. He emerged into the open area to see Lucifer standing a few feet away from the portal, facing away from him.

"You know," Lucifer was saying, "if you had any sense, you'd be miles away from here by now." He was addressing someone Mercury couldn't see.

"I got to thinking about that," said an eerily familiar voice. "It occurred to me that it doesn't do me any good to be sipping piña coladas in the Azores if I've never existed." Chills went down Mercury's spine as he realized who was talking.

"You won't feel a thing," Lucifer was saying. "One moment you'll exist, and the next you won't."

"Is that what you told Tiamat?" said the voice.

Lucifer chuckled. "Tiamat's fine."

"Of course she is. But she's not going back in time with you, is she?"

"No," said Lucifer. "Tiamat's not very good at playing second fiddle. I hit her over the head with a pipe and tied her up."

"I figured. Azrael has abandoned you, you know."

Lucifer shrugged. "Don't need him. Where I'm going, there will be plenty of potential converts."

Another explosion sounded overhead.

"Can't let you do that, Lucifer," said the voice. "You had your chance at world domination. You lost. No do-overs."

"I've changed the rules," said Lucifer. "Try to keep up." He launched himself toward the portal, but someone dived out of the darkness, tackling him around the waist. The two crashed into the steel shelving unit behind the portal generator, knocking tools and other equipment to the ground. Lucifer's opponent took a swing at his face, but missed. Lucifer backed away and then altered his trajectory, heading back toward the portal.

It occurred to Mercury, watching this scene unfold, that he could help his alternate self apprehend Lucifer, thereby negating the need to travel back in time in the first place. He wasn't certain his actions weren't somehow going to cause what happened the first time to happen again, but it was worth a try. He ran to Lucifer, barreling into him just as another explosion rocked the ground. They fell to the floor together. Mercury managed to get to his knees while Lucifer was still stunned; he punched Lucifer hard in the jaw, and his head struck the concrete with a crack. Lucifer lay motionless on the floor.

"Thanks," said Lucifer's opponent, who was leaning against the shelving unit, trying to regain his footing. "I had him on the ropes, though."

"No, you didn't," said Mercury. "In five seconds he would have knocked you back seven thousand years. Trust me, I've seen this movie before." He got to his feet and regarded his double in the near-darkness.

"Hey!" cried the other man, with sudden recognition. "You're me!"

"You really are a genius," said Mercury. "I don't think I tell you that often enough."

The two Mercurys stood regarding each other for a moment.

"I suppose you're another alternate version of me?" said the other Mercury. "Don't tell me you're the evil Mercury, because that puts a lot of pressure on me."

"Not evil," said Mercury. "Just a bit more experienced. You were about to go back in time and try to stop Lucifer from getting the shard. But you failed. In fact, your actions caused Lucifer to get the shard, allowing him to convert the portal generator into a time machine. So nice going, dickhead."

The other Mercury thought for a moment. "If that's true," he said, "then *you* did that, not me. That makes you the dickhead. I'm completely innocent. An ingénue, really."

"An ingénue is a girl," said Mercury.

"What's the male version?" said the other Mercury.

"Dope, I think," said Mercury.

"I like ingénue better."

"Suit yourself, sweetheart."

"So what do we do now, dickhead?"

"Look, if you get to be Ingénue Mercury, then there's no way in hell I'm going to be Dickhead Mercury. I want to be Red Mercury."

"No fair!" cried Ingénue Mercury. "*I* want to be Red Mercury."

"Of course you do," said Red Mercury. "Red Mercury is a badass name. But I called it. Anyway, you already have a name."

"Ingénue Mercury is stupid. I picked that when I was just a naive young lass. I want to be Blue Mercury. It keeps the symmetry."

"What about Green? Then we'd be like Hulks!"

"No, we'd be like Christmas angels."

"Oh," said Mercury. "Good point. Okay, I'm Red, you're Blue."

Mercury nodded, and was suddenly struck by the weirdness of having his identity split in two. From now on, he would no longer be just Mercury; he would be the Mercury who stopped the other Mercury from going back in time. Part of him wanted to insist that he was *the* Mercury, but that claim implied that the other Mercury was some sort of impostor or knock-off, which wasn't the case. The other Mercury had just as much claim to be the real Mercury as he did. On the other hand, thought Mercury, *I* created *him*. He wouldn't exist if it weren't for me stopping him from going through the portal. This realization made him feel a little better, but somehow he doubted the other Mercury would see it that way. So, for now at least, he would resign himself to being Red Mercury, in deference to his counterpart.

"So what do we do now, Red?" asked Blue Mercury.

"Beats me," said Red Mercury. "This is all fresh territory, now that I've fucked up the past. But it would seem we no longer have to stop Lucifer from getting the shard, since I knocked him out cold. I like it when things resolve themselves without logical paradoxes."

"Except for the part where you both did and didn't go back in time, and now you're talking to yourself."

"Well, yeah. Okay, I'll watch Lucifer. You go find Tiamat. We'll drag them out of here and turn them over to the FBI."

"The FBI?" said Blue Mercury. "Really?"

"It's the best we can do for now. Hopefully Balderhaz can reset the portal for Heaven and we hand the demons over to the appropriate authorities, but I'm mildly terrified of using the portal right now."

"Fine." Blue Mercury left. While he was gone, Red Mercury removed the shard from its sconce and put it in his pocket. Blue Mercury returned a minute later dragging Tiamat behind him by her ankles.

"Good, she's still out," said Red Mercury.

"Um, yeah," said Blue Mercury. "'Still.'"

Lucifer groaned and began to get up.

"Here," said Blue Mercury, handing Red Mercury a foot-long piece of iron pipe. Red Mercury rapped Lucifer on the top of his skull and the demon's body went limp.

"There, now he's still out too," said Blue Mercury, with an approving nod. "Let's get them out of here."

Red Mercury led the way, dragging Lucifer through the maze of equipment, and Blue Mercury followed close behind with Tiamat.

"Hey," said Red Mercury as they made their way down an alley, "I wanted to tell you I'm sorry things didn't work out with Christine."

"What are you talking about?" asked Blue Mercury, as Tiamat's head clanged against a shelf support. "What happened with Christine?"

"Nothing," said Red Mercury. "I just meant that it's too bad about her being stranded seven thousand years in the past. I think you had a real shot with her."

"What has gotten into you?" asked Blue Mercury. "I'm an angel. We're an angel. We can't... you know, with humans."

"Well, we *could*. We just generally don't."

"In any case, it's not like that with me and Christine. She's just, like, some girl. You should know that."

"I did," said Red Mercury. "I mean, I do. Of course. Sorry, time travel is doing weird things to my head. Obviously you have no romantic interest in Christine."

"None."

"Good," said Red Mercury. "Then we're on the same page."

Blue Mercury furrowed his brow but said nothing. The two Mercurys made their way toward the exit.

CHAPTER THIRTY-TWO

The two Mercurys reached the end of an aisle. The outer wall was a dozen or so paces away, and to their left Red Mercury could see the green glow of an EXIT sign. There was no sign of Lucifer's minions, but they could be anywhere along the perimeter. The two Mercurys turned to face each other.

"I'll drag them to the door," both Mercurys said in unison. "You cover me."

Each shrugged in deference to the other. "Okay," they both said. "You drag them to the door and I'll cover you."

A long pause followed. "It doesn't matter to me," they both said. "But we can't..." They broke off, revealing they were at an impasse. Red Mercury regarded blue Mercury, knowing exactly what the other was thinking.

"Buridan's ass," said Red Mercury.

"Duck," said Blue Mercury.

"No, it was an ass," said Red Mercury. "It starved to death because it couldn't decide between—"

"Duck, asshole!"

Red Mercury ducked. As he did so, gunfire rang out behind him. Blue Mercury put up his hand and for a moment, glancing over his head, Red Mercury saw a series of bullets hanging in mid-air. The bullets came to a halt and then fell to the ground, clinking on the concrete.

"Thanks," said Red Mercury. "Nice of that guy to break the impasse."

"Take cover," said Blue Mercury, grabbing Red Mercury's arm and pulling him back into the aisle. "I was barely able to stop those bullets."

"The Balderhaz cube," said Red Mercury.

211

Blue Mercury nodded. "It's getting closer. The FBI is about to make their move. We need to finish this, quick."

"Did you see where that guy was shooting from?"

"Yeah. I'm going to flank him. You stay here and draw fire."

"Oh, good," said Red Mercury. "I love drawing fire."

Blue Mercury disappeared in the darkness. After a moment, Red Mercury leaned out into the open space, but couldn't see anyone. He tried creating a burst of light in the direction the shots had come from, but Blue Mercury was right: the Balderhaz cube was nearby and getting closer. Now that the hostages had gotten free, the FBI had probably received the green light to storm the building. They'd win the firefight eventually, by virtue of superior numbers, but a lot of them were going to die in the process. The good news was that if the FBI was going in on foot, then they weren't yet considering an airstrike.

Shots rang out in the darkness, and then somebody was moving toward him. It was Blue Mercury, holding the demon's rifle.

"Nice work," said Red Mercury. But then Blue Mercury stopped about twenty feet away and leveled his rifle. Red Mercury began to think maybe Blue Mercury was the evil one after all—or at least he'd had a very bad reaction to finding out he wasn't one of a kind.

Red Mercury winced as Blue Mercury let loose a burst of gunfire. The bullets were so close, Red Mercury could hear them zipping past his ear. Behind him someone yelped and fell to the floor. Opening his eyes, Red Mercury saw the demon, who had been approaching from behind him. It was the one called Gurien.

"Let's get out of here before more show up," Blue Mercury said.

Red Mercury nodded. He grabbed Lucifer's ankles and Blue Mercury grabbed Tiamat's. The two Mercurys dragged the demons to the door. Red Mercury let go of Lucifer and opened the door, stepping outside with his hands up.

"STEP AWAY FROM THE BUILDING," the voice of the FBI said from somewhere behind a bank of blinding floodlights.

"Okay," said Mercury. "But we've got a couple of demons you guys might want to take a look at."

Blue Mercury stepped into the light next to him, also with his hands up. There was a pause for several seconds during which nobody behind the lights seemed to have any idea what to do.

"Mercury?" said another voice from the megaphone. "This is Special Agent Burton. Are you saying you have Lucifer and Tiamat in custody?"

"Not so much in custody as lying on the floor unconscious," shouted Red Mercury.

"Can you bring them outside?"

"Not with our hands up," the two Mercurys said in unison.

There was another pause.

"Okay," said Burton. "Go get them."

The two Mercurys dragged their respective demons outside.

"Step away from the demons," said Burton.

The Mercurys took a step away and several black-garbed men ran forward. They gagged and handcuffed the demons, and then carried them away. As they were doing so, Burton stepped forward into the light.

"You've got the Balderhaz cube?" asked Red Mercury.

Burton held up the black cube. "We were about to go in. So, I noticed there are two of you."

"Long story," said Red Mercury. "Is Suzy safe?"

"Yes, she's resting comfortably. The others as well."

"Others?" said Blue Mercury.

But before Burton could respond, another black-garbed man approached. "Sir," he said, "we just had three men surrender at the West gate."

"Very good," said Burton. "That's everybody, assuming nobody else has duplicated themselves...?" He looked to the Mercurys, who shook their heads.

"Not that we know of," they said in unison. Red Mercury added, "You have Drekavac and Azrael?"

Burton nodded. "They surrendered a few minutes ago." He turned to the black-garbed man. "Take this," he said. "Keep all the suspects together, gagged and handcuffed. Under constant watch, and never let any of them get more than fifty feet from this cube. Guard the cube with your life." He rubbed his forehead and glared at the Mercurys.

"Got it, sir," the man said. "I'll put them the prisoner transfer truck." He took the cube and began to walk away.

"Wait," said Burton. "Put them back in the building."

"Sir?"

"I want that cube near the portal generator until we can figure out what to do with it. If anybody else comes through that thing, I want to have the upper hand."

"Yes, sir." The man turned and jogged away.

"Come on," said Burton, walking toward the lights. "I'll take you two to see your friends."

"Both of us?" said Red Mercury. "That might be a little unsettling to the others. Maybe you should keep us separate. Take me to that dank old trailer you've got around here somewhere, and take this handsome gentleman somewhere nicer. He needs to be debriefed. And between you and me, he could use clean socks as well."

"Whatever you're trying to pull," said Blue Mercury, turning to face his counterpart, "you're not going to get away with it. I'm you, remember? I can see right through your smartass tricks." He turned to Burton. "If he's going to the trailer, that's where I'm going. I admit to being a little confused why you aren't arresting us though."

"Need to pick my battles," said Burton. "I know how dangerous Tiamat is, and if that really is *the* Lucifer, my guess is that I'm going to need all the help I can get. I'm willing to consider you two and your friends allies—for now."

"That's the first halfway intelligent thing I've heard you say," said Red Mercury. He sighed, glancing at Blue Mercury. "All right, take us to the trailer."

Burton escorted them to the large black trailer that Red Mercury had escaped from a few minutes earlier. They went inside, where Suzy, Eddie, Balderhaz, Jacob and Christine sat on couches waiting for them. They were speechless as the two Mercurys entered. Blue Mercury's jaw dropped as he saw Christine and Jacob.

"Hi, gang," said Red Mercury. "This is my new pal, Blue Mercury. Don't let the name fool you, he's actually not any more suicidally depressed than I am. Oh, I'm Red Mercury now."

"Um, hi," said Christine, looking from one Mercury to the other. Balderhaz waved. The others simply stared.

"You didn't tell me...." Blue Mercury murmured, pulling Red Mercury aside.

"About Christine and Jacob being back," whispered Red Mercury. "Yeah, I ran into them when I went back in time. But it's no big deal to you, right? You have no romantic interest whatsoever."

"You tricked me, you son of a bitch," said Blue Mercury. "You knew as soon as I saw her—"

"We should probably discuss this later," said Red Mercury, smiling at the others, who were still staring at them.

"I'm going to get you for this," Blue Mercury said.

CHAPTER THIRTY-THREE

"How are there two of you?" Eddie asked at last. "Is one of you from an alternate reality, like..." He trailed off.

"Like Gray Mercury?" asked Red Mercury. He had decided on this name for the now-deceased Mercury who had come through the portal fleeing from the alternate Lucifer. It just seemed to fit, for a number of reasons. "No. Well, I don't think so. I'm not sure what the difference between an alternate timeline and an alternate reality is."

"No difference," said Balderhaz. "Realities, timelines, universes, planes, dimensions... all different names for the same thing."

"But Blue Mercury is identical to me," said Red Mercury. "The only difference between us is that he didn't go back in time. Gray Mercury was a whole different person. He came from a completely different universe."

"All that means is that the Gray universe diverged from ours much earlier," said Balderhaz. "Maybe thousands of years ago. The divergence that created the Red and Blue Mercurys was only a few minutes ago."

"What divergence?" asked Blue Mercury. "We're both here in the same reality. We're two different people, but we occupy the same universe."

Balderhaz nodded. "Yes, but there's also a universe where Mercury didn't stop himself from going back in time. That decision point created a divergence. Part of that divergence is a causal anomaly."

Christine frowned. "What do you mean, 'causal anomaly'?"

"An event occurred in our universe that had no cause."

"Which was?"

217

"Why, your appearance, of course," said Balderhaz, as if he couldn't understand how there was any confusion on the matter.

"*My* appearance?" asked Christine.

"Yours and that of Red Mercury and the other gentleman."

"His name is Jacob," said Suzy. "He's sitting right next to you." Jacob gave Suzy an appreciative nod. Balderhaz shrugged.

"When you say 'appearance,' you mean our return to the present?" asked Christine.

Balderhaz snorted. "You didn't 'return' anywhere. You just appeared, *ex nihilo*. Mercury never went back in time, so he couldn't have brought you back to the present with him. The three of you just materialized for no discernible reason."

The two Mercurys regarded each other, deep in thought.

"That's insane," said Christine. "Mercury went back in time, just like Jacob and I did. We met him there. I mean, then. And then we returned to the present."

"Wrong," said Balderhaz. "In this universe, Mercury never went back in time. There is another universe where he did, but it diverged from ours. There is no causal relation between the two."

"Then why do I remember going back in time?" asked Red Mercury.

"Why does a chair dream of being an antelope?" asked Balderhaz. "Meaningless question."

"You're contradicting yourself," said Christine. "You said that our return—that is, our sudden appearance—was inexplicable. That it had no cause. But then you said that the decision point created a divergence. So there *is* a cause."

Balderhaz shrugged. "It's a semantic issue. Yes, the decision point precipitated the divergence, and one result of the divergence was you showing up here. That doesn't make your appearance any less arbitrary or inexplicable. I wave a magic wand over a hat and a rabbit jumps out of it. You ask, 'How did you do that?' And I say, 'With my wand. Weren't you paying attention?' Such an answer makes a mockery of the idea of cause and effect."

"So we appeared by magic?" asked Christine.

Balderhaz shrugged again. "Semantics," he said.

"What I hear you saying," said Blue Mercury, "is that I'm the *real* Mercury. I belong in this universe. He's just an interloper." He pointed his thumb at Red Mercury.

"That's one way to look at it, I suppose," said Balderhaz.

"A really stupid way," said Red Mercury.

"This is all fascinating," said Special Agent Burton, who had been standing just inside the door watching this drama unfold. "But if you're all done solving the mysteries of the universe, perhaps somebody could tell me what to do with the two demons I have tied up in the next trailer."

"Well," said Blue Mercury, "I don't recommend putting them on the payroll, which seems to have been your first instinct with Tiamat."

Red Mercury nodded. "They're both completely insane, and extremely dangerous. The only place they can safely be detained is Heaven."

"You're suggesting we use the portal generator again. You realize that every time somebody turns that thing on, something horrible happens."

"We won't be using it as a time machine," said Blue Mercury. "Just to open a portal to Heaven. We only ran into problems last time because Tiamat interfered. If you can keep them from causing trouble while Balderhaz resets the portal generator, we should be fine. We'll deliver them to the authorities in Heaven, and Bob's your uncle."

"And then what?"

"Then Blue Mercury and I arm wrestle," said Red Mercury. "What do you mean, 'and then what'?"

"I mean, do we establish some sort of diplomatic relations with Heaven? How does this work, now that we know you guys exist?"

The Mercurys shrugged. "Beats me," said Blue Mercury. "Politics isn't really our thing. We were just going to reestablish contact and then let the bureaucrats do their thing."

"I imagine, though," said Red Mercury, "that handing over Lucifer and Tiamat would be a pretty good start to the U.S. government's official relationship with Heaven. You'll be the guy who made that happen."

Burton nodded. "All right," he said. "You two come with me. And you, Balderhaz. The rest of you stay here." He added, after a pause, "Please."

The two Mercurys and Balderhaz followed Burton outside and back to the building. The lights had gone back on; the FBI had probably cut the power when the hostage situation started. They found their way through the maze back to the open area near the center of the building. They found Lucifer, Tiamat, Azrael and all the other demons bound and gagged, not far from the portal generator. The black-garbed man Burton had talked to earlier stood guard, along with three other agents.

"Well, this is an interesting reversal," said Blue Mercury. The eyes of the assembled captives went wide at the site of the two Mercurys.

"Jesus Christ, Dexter," said Burton. "We're supposed to be resolving hostage situations, not creating new ones."

"Sorry, sir," said Agent Dexter. "There was no other place within fifty feet of the portal thing where I could keep an eye on them all. This place is a mess."

"Never mind," said Burton. "If all goes well, we'll be sending these BIOs back home in short order." He turned to Balderhaz. "Can you set that thing back to Heaven?"

"Sure," said Balderhaz. "Piece of cake." He went to work on the machine.

"Good," said Burton. He turned to the two Mercurys. "You two should probably go through first, explain the situation. Come back here and give us the green light to send the demons through."

"Okay," said Blue Mercury. "But only one of us should go. The authorities don't know there are two of us, and they tend to get spooked by things they don't understand."

"Then we have something in common," Burton deadpanned.

"I'll go," said Red Mercury. "I've seen everything Blue Mercury has seen and then some."

"What are you, like eighteen hours older than me?"

"It was an eventful eighteen—oh, shit. Not again."

"What?" Blue Mercury asked. He and Burton turned to see what Red Mercury was looking at. "Oh, shit," Blue Mercury agreed.

The familiar blue-white ellipse of the portal had once again appeared.

"What did you do, Balderhaz?" Burton demanded.

"Nothing!" Balderhaz cried, stepping away from the portal generator. "It isn't even turned on!"

"Somebody is opening a portal to here from somewhere else," said Blue Mercury.

"Or somewhen else," added Red Mercury.

As they watched, a tall, lean figure materialized. He was wearing a crimson robe with flared lapels and an odd-looking pyramid-shaped hat that seemed to be made of velvet. The getup was so strange that it took a moment for the watchers to recognize him.

"Greetings, dwellers of this fair plane!" the newcomer exclaimed. "It is I, Lucifer! I have spent the past three hundred years trying to open a portal between our two worlds. Many said it was not possible, but ever since the loathsome traitor Mercury disappeared through a strange rift in the spacetime continuum, I have devoted all the resources of my realm to reopening it. And now the momentous moment is here, and I am proclaiming my dominion over this plane as well. Bow before me!"

The two Mercurys, Special Agent Burton, and the bound captives sitting on the floor stared at the crimson-robed figure.

"Bow!" screeched Lucifer. "Or I shall bring you to your knees with my miraculous... why isn't this working?"

Burton held up the Balderhaz cube.

"What's that?" asked Lucifer.

"You've never seen a Balderhaz cube?" asked Red Mercury.

"A what?" asked Lucifer.

"It prevents the performing of miracles. I guess you have no Balderhaz where you're from, so no Balderhaz cubes. Interesting. Of course, you should really be more concerned about *that*."

Lucifer turned just in time to get smacked across the head with an iron pipe. He fell to the floor unconscious.

"You really enjoy doing that, don't you?" asked Red Mercury.

Blue Mercury shrugged, letting the weapon clatter to the ground. "It's not every day you get to whack the devil in the face with a pipe."

"Tie him up," said Burton. "Put him with the others."

Dexter nodded and went to work on Lucifer.

Burton turned to Red Mercury. "Can I surmise that this is the alternate Lucifer that the now-deceased version of you was running from?"

"So it would seem," said Red Mercury, watching as Burton's men tied the newcomer up and dragged him next to his shocked counterpart.

"Gray Lucifer," said Blue Mercury. "Do you think he really worked on his portal generator for three hundred years?"

"Wouldn't surprise me," said Red Mercury. "That plane was right out of the Dark Ages. Completely backwards from a technological standpoint."

"And every other standpoint," said Blue Mercury. "That's what happens when Lucifer is in charge of the place. No freedom, no creativity, no innovation. Just millions of people scrabbling to get by, for thousands of years."

"No Balderhaz either," said Red Mercury. "Gray Lucifer was starting from scratch, trying to understand interplanar technology. It's kind of amazing it only took him three hundred years."

Balderhaz nodded, in some combination of appreciation and agreement.

Burton frowned. "But if three hundred years have passed on his plane since Gray Mercury came here, then why did he show up now, rather than three hundred years from now?"

"Who knows?" Blue Mercury said. "Maybe he accidentally invented time travel too."

"These were the only coordinates he had," said Balderhaz. "If he built a portal generator from scratch, using brute force methodology, it may actually have been simpler for him to build the time travel component into his device. It's all a matter of perspective."

"So does he have a shard as well?" asked Red Mercury.

"Or something like it," Balderhaz said. "With enough time and resources, you could build a battery with as much energy potential as the shard. If it was made of something other than ubiquium, though, it would have to be gigantic. And of course you'd need some sort of amplitude modulator, or the rift would be unstable and the gravitational vector would tear apart anything going through the portal. Man, would I love to see how they handle the torque shear problem on that scale!"

"You may very well get to," said Blue Mercury, regarding the still open portal.

Burton shook his head. "Nobody's going through that thing. We have no idea what's on the other side."

"Somebody needs to go through and shut that thing down at the source, permanently," said Blue Mercury. "Nothing good can come from leaving a portal open to that place."

"I don't like it," said Burton. "We need to get these demons to Heaven before anything else goes wrong."

Balderhaz frowned. "I'm not sure I can even open another portal while that one is open."

"Then it's settled," said Red Mercury. "Balderhaz has to go through the portal to the Gray timeline to shut down the portal there."

"Whoohoo!" cried Balderhaz. "I can't wait to get a look at the oscillation matrix on that baby!"

"We don't have time for you to satisfy your intellectual curiosity, Balderhaz," said Blue Mercury. "We just need you to set the thing to self-destruct and come back here so we can open the portal to Heaven. Can you do that?"

"Hmph," Balderhaz grumbled. "You people come across a marvel of interplanar engineering and your first thought is to blow it up. I have half a mind just to stay in the Gray timeline."

"I'll go with him," said Blue Mercury.

Burton frowned. "Can we trust him?"

"He gets like this sometimes," said Red Mercury. "He just needs adult supervision." He turned to Blue Mercury. "Are you sure you want to do this? I can go."

"I've got it," said Blue Mercury without looking at his counterpart. "Come on, Balderhaz, let's go."

Balderhaz nodded. He took a step toward the portal and disappeared.

Blue Mercury stepped up behind him, then paused to turn and look at Red Mercury. "In case I don't make it back," he said, "tell Christine... well, you know. Don't fuck it up."

Red Mercury nodded as Blue Mercury took another step and vanished.

CHAPTER THIRTY-FOUR

Somewhere deep inside the Machine, Lucifopolis, Gray Timeline; Luciprex IX, MMMMMMMXXVI

Blue Mercury thought he was prepared for the transition to the Gray timeline, but he wasn't. If anything, the air of oppressiveness was worse than he remembered.

If you've never been to another plane, it's hard to explain how it's possible to just *feel* when something is off. It's not the air, or the light, or the smells, or the scenery, although the perceptions of all those things are affected as well—it's the energy of the place. There are those on the Mundane plane—mediums and ghost hunters and the like—who claim to be able to sense "bad energy," and like most unverifiable assertions, those claims are mostly nonsense. Living things do, however, have an innate ability to sense and respond to interplanar energy, although this relationship is almost entirely on a subconscious level. Most people are no more aware of the interplanar energy that flows around them than a fish is aware of water. If you take a fish out of water, though, it will quickly deduce that something is very wrong.

Something was very wrong on the Gray timeline.

Blue Mercury and Balderhaz found themselves in a concrete building that resembled a parking garage, lit by strings of dim incandescent bulbs hanging from wiring that looked like it dated from the 1930s. The bulbs barely augmented the gray light filtering in through a series of grimy windows that lined the wall to their left. Through the windows they could make out a dingy gray-brown sky hanging over a desolate brown-gray plain. Several fires burned on the horizon, emitting plumes of black smoke that added to the haze. To their right, massive rusted steel pipes and other conduits of indeterminate composition or purpose ran from floor to ceiling and wall-to-wall. A deep rumbling sound could be heard somewhere beneath them, occasionally punctuated by the screech of metal or the chugging of some machine. The air was dank and smelled like burning garbage and mildew.

"I think I've changed my mind about staying here," said Balderhaz.

"I hear you," said Mercury. "Let's blow this thing and go home."

"Where is the... oh." Balderhaz turned to find something resembling a steamer trunk on its side behind him. A dinner plate sized dish was mounted on top of it, casting the ellipse-shaped portal on the ground. Other than the fact that it seemed to be made of wood, brass and other low-tech materials rather than stainless steel and plastic, and that its display was an ancient-looking monochrome monitor, it looked almost identical to the portal generator Balderhaz had built.

"Cool," said Blue Mercury. "It's like the steampunk version of our portal generator."

Balderhaz nodded, regarding the device. "I have to admit," he said, "Lucifer has style." He traced a conduit from the base of the portal generator to a manifold on the floor from which protruded a great many other pipes and wires. "That's the connection to the interplanar energy capacitor," said Balderhaz. "You see how they've modulated the ambient flow with an array of superconductive coils? Somewhere they must have a hell of a condenser to get the temperature down to a level that would permit—"

"Yeah, super-impressive," said Blue Mercury. "Can you blow it up or not?"

"I'm not sure I could keep this place from blowing up if I tried," said Balderhaz, studying the mass of pipes. "The way this thing is designed... it's a one shot deal. This facility has got to be the size of a small city, and the whole thing is a giant death trap. There are a hundred different things that could cause this thing to blow sky high."

"We just need one," said Blue Mercury. "Whatever's the quickest."

Balderhaz nodded. "If I reverse the polarity on the compressor override, the flux nebulizer should overheat, causing a chain reaction that'll wipe this place off the map. No more portals from Gray timeline."

"Do it," said Mercury.

As he spoke, a door opened in the far wall, and a man burst through, holding a dark brown bottle that appeared to be half-empty. He was wearing the same sort of dingy, ill-fitting clothing Gray Mercury had been wearing, but on his head was a conical paper hat. He seemed completely oblivious to the presence of Blue Mercury and Balderhaz. He stumbled into the room, a young woman, similarly dressed, right behind him.

"Wooooooo!" yelled the man. "We did it! He's really gone!"

"We're free!" cried the woman. "The Machine worked! I only wish Granny were alive to see it."

The man nodded, suddenly somber. "Many people have died in the service of the Machine. But now it is done, and Lucifer is gone. We can honor the memory of our ancestors by living our—hey! Who are you?" The man had finally noticed the two visitors.

"Hey there," said Blue Mercury. "Don't mind us. We're just going to, um, blow up your life's work."

The two looked at each other and shrugged. "Okay," said the man.

"You don't mind?" asked Blue Mercury.

"I never thought I would live this long," said the woman, who couldn't be over thirty.

"None of us expected to see this day," said the man. "And frankly, I think we all expected Lucifer to rig this place to blow up before he left. I guess he got distracted. We're a little overwhelmed by the thought of actually having a life after the Machine."

"Well, you won't if you don't get out of here. How long till the place blows, Balderhaz?"

"Fifteen minutes, give or take."

"Is there anyone else in this building?" Blue Mercury asked.

"Just a few other technicians," said the man. "Lucifer fired most of the workers when construction was finished. He only kept us around to finish programming the Machine."

"Get everyone out," said Blue Mercury. "You've got less than fifteen minutes."

"How many minutes are in a lucifon?" asked the woman.

227

"Uhhh…" said Blue Mercury. "How many lucifons are in a day?"

"86,423," said the man.

"Okay," said Blue Mercury. "That means…" He thought for a few seconds, doing the math in his head. "…you should probably just get everybody out of the building as fast as you can."

"Lucifer that," said the man. "Come on, Lucifressa. Let's get out of here!"

"Last one out the building is a Mercury!" yelled the woman.

The two ran out the door, giggling.

"I fucking hate this place," said Mercury. "Are you done yet?"

"Almost," said Balderhaz. "Just have to shut down the portal generator—"

Blue Mercury frowned. "Is that safe? What if we get stranded here?"

Balderhaz shrugged. "Should be no problem to reactivate it," he said. "I have the coordinates."

"I know, but…"

"You said to pick the fastest way to blow it up," said Balderhaz. "This is it. I just have to shut it down for a second, reverse the polarity on the compressor override, and then flip it back on."

"Fine," said Blue Mercury. "Do it. This place is creeping me out."

Balderhaz tapped a few keys and the portal winked out. He walked a few feet away, turned a valve 180 degrees, and then walked back to the keyboard. He tapped another series of commands and the portal reappeared. "See?" he said. "Easy."

"Let's go," said Blue Mercury. "If I never come here again, it'll be too soon."

Blue Mercury stepped on the portal and was gone.

CHAPTER THIRTY-FIVE

The rubble of the BOX, just outside Elko, Nevada; April 29, 2017

Something was wrong.

Not wrong on the same level as the Gray timeline, but wrong nevertheless: the building was missing. More accurately, it seemed to be reduced to a large number of piles of smoking rubble. Blue Mercury looked around to see small fires burning in several places.

"What the hell happened?" Blue Mercury said to Balderhaz, who had just materialized behind him. "It looks like a bomb went off."

"Uh-oh," said Balderhaz. "I think maybe it did."

"How long were we gone? Five minutes? Why would the FBI blow up the building?"

"To stop Lucifer from going back in time," said Balderhaz.

"Lucifer's in custody. Along with all the other demons."

"Not on this timeline he's not," said Balderhaz. "Look." He pointed at a tall, lean figure coming toward them in the dim light.

"No," said Blue Mercury, watching the tall man approach. "No, no, no."

"Hey there," said the tall man, whose uncannily familiar face was now clearly visible in the flickering light of a nearby fire.

"No, no, no, no, no," said Blue Mercury. "No."

"What's gotten into him?" asked the tall man, looking at Balderhaz.

"You're the third alternate version of himself he's met today," said Balderhaz.

"I'm losing my mind," said Blue Mercury. "Nothing makes any fucking sense anymore."

"So," said the tall man. "Is he a future version of me? Am I a future version of him? What's the deal?"

Blue Mercury wandered off through the rubble, pounding himself on the forehead with his fist.

"As far as I can tell," said Balderhaz, "You're parallel versions of each other. Let me ask you this: did I flip a quoin recently?"

"Sure," said the tall man. "To determine whether I should stop myself from going back in time or not."

"And what was the result?"

"Weren't you there?"

"Yes and no," said Balderhaz. "Humor me."

"Tails," said the tall man. "So I didn't interfere. I let myself go back in time. Then Special assfucking Agent fuckface Burton decided to bomb the building. He wrecked the portal generator, Lucifer got away, and I barely got this out of there in time." He held up the shard. "Then you showed up."

"Amazing," said Balderhaz, nodding slowly. "Let me ask you another question. What's your favorite color, and don't say red or blue."

"Uhhh… green, I guess?"

"Good," said Balderhaz. "You're Green Mercury."

"Sweet!" cried Green Mercury. "Like the Hulk! So are you saying that he—" Green Mercury motioned toward Blue Mercury, who was still shuffling aimlessly through the rubble. "—is the heads version of me? The one who did interfere with himself going back in time?"

Balderhaz shook his head. "No, that would be Red Mercury. He's back on the Blue timeline."

"Why is Red Mercury on the Blue timeline?"

"Causal anomaly," said Balderhaz. "Do you have Tiamat's miracle detector on you?"

"Sure," said Green Mercury. He removed the device from his pocket and handed it to Balderhaz. "What do you need it for?"

"I should be able to use it as a WAWAW device," said Balderhaz, tapping at the screen.

"A wow-wow device?" Green Mercury asked.

"WAWAW," said Balderhaz. "Where And When Are We? Every place and time on every plane has a unique energy channel signature, like a fingerprint. By looking for minor variations in the energy channels, I should be able to pinpoint exactly where and when we are. Aha! Just as I thought. Wrong timeline."

"Wrong for you, you mean."

"Yes. It's right for you, of course. Green Mercury on the Green timeline. We just ended up in the wrong universe."

"How did you get here?"

"We had to go through a portal to the Gray timeline to shut down a portal generator there. I reopened the portal to return to the Blue timeline, but we were in a hurry so I truncated the coordinates to three decimal places. That level of precision should have been more than sufficient, but I forgot about the possibility of interference from a proximate timeline. Foolish error."

"You tuned to the wrong channel."

"Something like that," said Balderhaz. "It's fine, though. Just forget we were ever here. We'll go back to the Gray timeline, fix the coordinates, and then return to the Blue timeline. Mercury!"

Blue Mercury turned to look at Balderhaz, half in a daze.

"Time to go!"

Blue Mercury nodded and shuffled back toward Balderhaz, rubbing his scalp with his hand.

"Hold on," said Green Mercury, rubbing his chin. "Maybe there's a reason you're here."

"Yes," said Balderhaz. "Imprecise coordinates and proximal timeline interference."

"No, I mean... what happened to Lucifer on your timeline? The Blue timeline?"

Balderhaz shrugged. "Red and Blue Mercurys stopped him from going back in time. The police have him now."

"Ah, you see?" said Green Mercury excitedly. "You stopped him on your timeline, but I failed on mine. And since Burton blew up the portal generator, I have no way of going after him. But you have a perfectly good portal generator on your timeline!"

Balderhaz scowled. "You want us to bring our portal generator to this timeline so you can go back in time and stop your Lucifer?"

"Exactly!" cried Green Mercury.

"No," said Blue Mercury. "No, no, no. We need that portal generator to transport Lucifer and the others to Heaven."

"You can have it back," said Green Mercury. "I just need it for a minute."

"I don't like it," said Balderhaz. "Once you start borrowing problems from other timelines, there's no end to it."

"Easy for you to say," said Green Mercury. "You happened to be on the timeline where everything worked out."

"Oh yeah," said Blue Mercury sardonically. "Everything's fan-fucking-tastic over on Blue timeline."

"Don't be a dick," said Green Mercury. "Just let me borrow your portal generator for one minute. You know I'd do it for you."

Blue Mercury groaned, still rubbing his scalp with his hand. "Balderhaz, how much time do we have on the Gray portal generator's self-destruct clock?"

"About ten minutes."

"Can you stop it?"

"Sure," said Balderhaz. "By blowing up the building."

"That would rather defeat the purpose," said Blue Mercury.

"You rigged your portal generator to blow up?" asked Green Mercury.

"Not our portal generator," said Balderhaz. "The one Gray Lucifer built. We didn't think we were going to go back there."

Blue Mercury sighed. "So," he said, "the question is: do we have time to return to Gray, reset the Gray portal generator with the Blue coordinates, take the portal from Gray to Blue, grab the Blue portal generator, take the portal back to Gray, reset the Gray portal generator coordinates to Green, bring the portal generator here, reset the coordinates to caveman times so Green Mercury can go back and stop Lucifer, drag the Blue portal generator back to Gray, reset the Gray portal generator coordinates to Blue, and take the Blue portal generator back to Blue before Gray blows?"

"I don't see why not," said Balderhaz. "But I still object on philosophical grounds."

"You should have objected before you split the universe in two," said Green Mercury.

"Fair enough," said Balderhaz, with a shrug.

"Why did I ever get involved with this crap?" Blue Mercury said. "I was perfectly happy building Twinkie ziggurats. Okay, if we're going to do this, let's do it. Everybody ready?"

Balderhaz and Green Mercury nodded.

"Time for some advanced timeline-hopping," said Blue Mercury. "Balderhaz, you first."

Balderhaz took a deep breath, stepped onto the portal and disappeared.

Blue Mercury turned to Green Mercury. "You'd better hope you don't screw up our universe as well as yours," he said.

"Man, I can see why they call you Blue Mercury," said Green Mercury. "You're a real downer."

"Just get on the portal."

Green Mercury took a step onto the portal and disappeared. Blue Mercury sighed and followed.

Once they were back on the Gray timeline, Balderhaz shut down the portal and began tapping at keys. After a minute or so, Blue Mercury began to get nervous. "What's taking so long?" he asked. "If that thing explodes while we're here, we're going to be blown apart *and* be stuck in the worst place ever, and yes, before you ask, I'm including Chuck E. Cheese."

"Your chattering isn't going to help," said Balderhaz. "This is the most difficult part. Once I get these coordinates entered, the rest is cake. Relatively speaking."

Blue Mercury bit his tongue while Balderhaz finished entering the sequence. Once again, the portal appeared on the ground in front of them.

"Okay," said Blue Mercury, "Everybody through."

This time Green Mercury went first, followed by Blue. Balderhaz brought up the rear.

They found themselves back inside the portal facility, which Blue Mercury was relieved to find in more-or-less the condition they'd left it.

"Um," said Special Agent Burton, staring at the three men who had just materialized. "I noticed you've brought yet another Mercury with you. Did you at least shut the portal generator down?"

"Long story," said Blue Mercury. "No time to explain. We need the portal generator."

"Not a chance," said Red Mercury. "That thing is the only way we have of getting Lucifer, the other Lucifer, and Tiamat out of here. What's with Brown Mercury?"

"I'm Green Mercury," said Green Mercury, brushing the dust off his shirt.

"Suit yourself," said Red Mercury. "But you can't have our portal generator."

"Technically it's *my* portal generator, since you're an interloper," said Blue Mercury. "And we've already had this discussion. Green just needs it for a minute."

"I'm with Mercury," said Burton. "Er, Red Mercury. You can't take the portal generator."

"Zip it, Burton," said Green Mercury. "Nobody cares what you think."

Blue Mercury nodded.

"At least tell me what you need it for," said Red Mercury.

"We can discuss it while Balderhaz is working," said Blue Mercury. "Help us get this thing through the portal."

"I'm not helping you with anything until you tell me what's going on," said Red Mercury.

"Look," said Blue Mercury. "I get where you're coming from. You hate doing something just because you're told it's the right thing to do. I'm the same way. And frankly, I don't like this any more than you do. But in this case, it's your more experienced self asking you to trust him, the way you asked me to trust you about not going back in time."

"You kind of got screwed on that deal, though," said Red Mercury.

"So you owe me," said Blue Mercury. "In any case, it's two Mercurys against one, and the clock is ticking. For once in your life, just do what you're told."

"I'll explain everything once we get to the Gray timeline," said Green Mercury. "Trust me."

"Fine," said Red Mercury. "Then let's go."

"You're going with them?" asked Burton in disbelief. "And leaving me here with all of these...demons? And no portal generator?"

"We'll be right back," said Blue Mercury. "I hope."

Blue Mercury and Green Mercury picked up the portal generator and set it down on the open portal. After a moment, it vanished. Green Mercury stepped onto the portal and vanished as well, followed by Blue Mercury.

"If I don't come back," said Red Mercury, "tell Christine... well, whatever you tell someone when you're about to jump to an alternate timeline where everything is sorrow and misery forever. You'll think of something." He stepped onto the portal and disappeared.

CHAPTER THIRTY-SIX

Inside the Machine, Lucifopolis, Gray Timeline; Luciprex IX, MMMMMMMXXVI

"This is a terrible idea," said Red Mercury, once Green Mercury had explained their plan. The three Mercurys were waiting in the grim gray room of Lucifer's Machine while Balderhaz reprogrammed the portal generator to take them to the Green timeline.

"That's what I said," replied Blue Mercury.

"Me too," added Balderhaz, not looking up from the portal generator display.

"Then why are we doing it?" asked Red Mercury.

"I'm not sure we have a choice," said Blue Mercury.

"How do you figure?"

"Think about it," said Blue Mercury. "The three of us split off from each other less than an hour ago, reckoning by my time at least. Before our timelines split, there was just a single timeline."

"Wow," said Green Mercury, nodding thoughtfully. "That's a good point. If Lucifer succeeds in rewriting history on the Green timeline, he succeeds on *all* of our timelines."

"Because before the split, there only was one timeline," said Red Mercury. "Shit. Okay, I'm on board. But even if this works, how are we going to foil his plan? Lucifer has almost taken over this plane half a dozen times, and this time through he'll have all the experience he didn't have the first time. He knows exactly which agents in Heaven he can turn, who will betray him, the whole Heavenly leadership structure, how they're going to build the planeport... how exactly are we going to stop him?"

"I've been thinking about that," said Green Mercury. "I think I know a way we can get the upper hand. The portal generator has a builtin range limit due to the size of the shard, right? It can only hold a certain amount of interplanar energy."

"One point two billion Balderhazes," said Balderhaz, still tapping at keys. "Give or take."

"Right," said Green Mercury. "But we have two portal generators and two shards."

"Slap me with a spatula and call me Meredith," said Blue Mercury. "You want to leapfrog back in time."

Green Mercury grinned and nodded.

"I must be the slow one of the family," said Red Mercury, frowning, "because I'm not following you at all." It struck him as odd that there could be such a stark divergence in the thought processes of the three Mercurys. Intuitively, it seemed that they should always be completely simpatico. But the slight variations in their respective histories, as well as varying motivations, had resulted in this weird situation where sometimes they were completely in sync and other times—like now—he could have no idea what the other two were talking about. Was it evidence of free will, or just of the unpredictable nature of his own thought processes?

"Simple," said Green Mercury. "When Balderhaz gets the portal open to the Green timeline, we drag the Blue portal generator through. Then we set the Blue portal generator's coordinates for the Gray timeline—"

"And then drag the Gray portal generator through to the Green timeline," said Red Mercury, suddenly back in sync with his counterparts. "I see what you're getting at."

"Right," said Blue Mercury. "So then we have two portal generators and two shards on the Green timeline. We open a portal with one of them to sometime in the recent past, and drag the other portal through, with the other shard. As long as the shard is uncharged, there shouldn't be a problem taking it through a portal."

"And the we set the second portal generator's coordinates for as far back as it will go," said Red Mercury.

"No," said Green Mercury. "We set the second portal generator's coordinates for the current time. That way, we can drag the first portal generator through to our stopover point, so we'll once again have two portal generators."

"Got it," said Red Mercury. "*Then* we set the second portal generator's coordinates for as far back as it will go. We go through the portal to caveman times and take the first portal generator through with us."

"Right," said Blue Mercury excitedly. "If all goes well, we should arrive in caveman times before Lucifer gets there. We can be ready when he shows up. And since we'll have brought a portal generator with us, we can return to the present time when we're done. We aren't dependent on somebody here keeping a portal open for however long it takes us."

"Exactly," said Green Mercury.

"This is," said Red Mercury, after a momentary pause, "without question, the most absolutely batshit crazy plan that anyone has ever come up with in the infinite histories of every plane in the multiverse."

"So we're agreed then?" asked Green Mercury.

"Hell yes," said Blue Mercury. "Let's do it."

"Balderhaz," said Red Mercury, "did you get all that?"

"Sure, sure," said Balderhaz absently. "Leapfrogging back in time to prevent somebody from stopping things from happening that have already happened. Pretty tame stuff. Okay, it's ready. Everybody through. Chop-chop!"

The portal to the Green timeline had reopened, and the three of them went through, taking the Blue portal generator with them. They appeared at the scene of the destroyed facility to find themselves surrounded by black-garbed men and others in uniforms. Special Agent Burton approached.

"What on God's green Earth is going on?" Burton asked. "I saw the second Mercury show up, then the first one vanished, and now there are *three* of you!"

"No time to explain," said Green Mercury. "We have to leapfrog back in time to stop Lucifer."

"Balderhaz," said Blue Mercury, "are you going to be able to open a portal to the Gray timeline in time?"

"It's going to be tight," said Balderhaz. "Time is moving at the same rate on the Gray timeline as here. The Machine could blow any second. Whoever goes through will be lucky to make it back, with or without the portal generator."

"Who's going through?" asked Red Mercury.

"I'll do it," said Green Mercury. "This is my timeline. My Lucifer."

The other two Mercurys nodded.

"Okay," said Balderhaz. "It's ready." The familiar blue-white ellipse of the portal once again appeared on the ground. "Try not to get yourself blown up."

Green Mercury nodded and took a step onto the portal. In a split-second, he was gone. For a few seconds, those assembled simply stared at the glowing ellipse on the ground.

"By the way," said Red Mercury, "What happens if the Machine blows up while the portal is open?"

"Well," said Balderhaz, "the stabilizers should absorb most of the energy, but with an explosion that size…"

"Will the blast come through?" asked Blue Mercury.

"It might," said Balderhaz with a shrug.

"Is it safe for my men here?" asked Burton.

"Safe as anywhere," said Balderhaz. "If the blast comes through, it's going to destroy the shard. And if that happens…" He trailed off, making an explosion gesture.

"Mmm, banana bread," said the two Mercurys together.

A moment later, Green Mercury reappeared, dragging the other portal generator behind him.

"Shut it down, Balderhaz!" cried Blue Mercury.

"I'm on it," said Balderhaz, furiously tapping keys. A few seconds later, the portal faded.

"Whew," said all the Mercurys together.

"Now what?" said Burton.

"Now we save the world again," said Green Mercury.

"How long will it take to set the portal to caveman times?" asked Blue Mercury.

"Not long," said Balderhaz. "But that's not the tricky part. The real challenge is going to be setting the second portal generator to go farther back. The Gray portal generator hasn't been adapted for the shard. So we're going to have to use the Blue portal generator to go back first, then cannibalize it for parts and bring the parts along with the Gray portal generator and the second shard back, then adapt the Gray portal generator in the field, so to speak."

"Is that even possible?" asked Red Mercury. "Disassembling the Blue portal generator while it's active?"

240

"I just have to remove Drekavac's adapter," said Balderhaz. "The portal will remain active for a few minutes after the shard is disconnected. It'll be tight, but I can do it."

"And what happens if something goes wrong?" asked Blue Mercury. "Like, if you forget a part?"

"Then we'll have to either manufacture the part or wait. Depending on the part, waiting might be simpler."

"Wait?" asked Green Mercury. "For what?"

"For us to build the portal generator. Then we can cannibalize our own portal generator to get Lucifer's to work."

"That would defeat the purpose," said Red Mercury. "We'd have gone back in time only to end up in the present. We'd have to figure this out all over again."

"Yes, but the second time we'd know what mistakes to avoid," said Balderhaz.

Green Mercury sighed. "Well, if it's our only option," he said.

"We should only go back a few days, then," said Red Mercury. "That way, if something goes wrong, we won't have to wait very long."

"But..." began Blue Mercury, thinking this over. "If we had done that, we would know about it. We would have seen ourselves suddenly appear in the portal generator facility a few days ago."

"So we're doomed to fail," said Blue Mercury.

"Or create another alternate timeline," said Balderhaz. "But I wouldn't bet on it. Time is stubborn. It doesn't like to split unless it has no choice."

"Can we please stop anthropomorphizing time?" Red Mercury said. "Time hates that."

"What if we go farther back?" asked Green Mercury. "Not thousands of years, in case something goes wrong and we need to wait for the present to fix it, but sometime before we built this place. Then there'd be nothing here but desert. We could show up, jerry rig the portal generator, and be on our way."

"Nobody would ever know we were here," said Blue Mercury. "Not even us."

"So there's no paradox," said Red Mercury. "I like it."

"Pick a safe margin," said Blue Mercury. "Like four years. After all the Apocalypse nonsense but before Tiamat started causing problems again. And well before we ever thought about buying this property."

Balderhaz nodded. "No problem," he said. "I'll set it for four years on the dot." He went back to work.

Burton didn't look happy. "I was hoping to get your help with Tiamat and the others," he said, looking at Green Mercury, whom he apparently identified by the dirt stains on his clothes.

"Probably should have thought about that before you put her on the FBI payroll," said Green Mercury. "Fortunately for you, I've been dealing with Tiamat for a while now. Just ply her with flattery until we get back and I'll take care of her. Right now, Lucifer is the bigger threat."

"All three of you are going?" asked Burton. "Is that really necessary?"

"We're in this together," said Red Mercury. "Fate, or something, has thrown us together, and we're going to see this through."

The other two Mercurys nodded, having apparently come to the same conclusion.

"I wonder if we should—" started Red Mercury.

"No," said Blue Mercury.

"What?" asked Green Mercury. Then, realizing what Red Mercury had been about to say, added, "Oh."

"You know," said Burton, "We don't all share a single brain. Anybody want to clue me in on what's happening?"

"They're wondering if we should tell… people… before we go back in time," said Blue Mercury. "The answer is no."

"What if we never come back?" asked Green Mercury.

"What if we do?" asked Red Mercury.

"Look," said Blue Mercury. "The fact is, there are two Christines on two different timelines, one here and one on the Blue timeline. There are three of us, and we can't even agree which Mercury goes with which Christine, if such a thing were possible, which it isn't, because we're angels. We're going seven thousand years back in time and we have no idea if any of us will come back or when. What exactly do you geniuses plan to say to her?"

Red Mercury and Green Mercury looked at each other and shrugged.

"Exactly," said Blue Mercury. "It was obviously a mistake to bring her back here in the first place. But now she's here, and we're going back there to prevent someone from preventing all of this from ever having happened, and everything is so fucked up that I'm not even sure what the point is, but it certainly isn't going to help things to start getting into blubbery goodbyes."

"Damn, dude," said Red Mercury. "I can see why they call you Blue Mercury. You're a real—"

"Yeah, Green Mercury already made that joke. Hilarious. Can we go now?"

Balderhaz glanced at a gauge on the box connected to the portal generator. "The shard is charged," he said.

"No use standing on ceremony," said Blue Mercury. "Balderhaz, let's do this."

Balderhaz nodded. He tapped a series of keys and once again the portal appeared.

"Tell me again where you're going exactly?" said Burton.

"Right here," said Red Mercury. "Four years ago. If all goes well, we should show up again right here in a few minutes. Then we'll drag our portal generator back to four years in the past. And then from there, we'll go back another 7,000 years."

"I hope you know what you're doing," said Burton.

"Not a chance," said Red Mercury.

The other two Mercurys dragged Gray Lucifer's portal generator to the portal that had just opened. "Ready?" said Green Mercury.

"Somebody give me a hand with this," said Balderhaz. He was busy disassembling the shard adapter apparatus.

Red Mercury helped him finish taking it apart.

"Okay, quick!" said Balderhaz. "It won't stay open much longer."

Green Mercury and Blue Mercury pushed Gray Lucifer's portal generator onto the portal and it disappeared. Green Mercury stepped onto the portal and disappeared as well, followed by Blue Mercury.

"Hey, Burton," said Red Mercury, as he stepped toward the portal. "Tell Christine…"

"What?" said Burton.

Mercury thought for a moment. "Well, tell her not to lose hope, I guess."

He stepped onto the portal and was gone.

CHAPTER THIRTY-SEVEN

Mentzel Ranch, just outside Elko, Nevada; April 29, 2013

Red Mercury found himself on a small plateau ringed by a dozen electric lanterns on poles. The plateau he remembered: they'd had to level a large area of ground before building the portal generator facility. But the electric lanterns were inexplicable. Why would someone have put up lanterns in a remote area of the desert in the middle of the night? This whole area should be uninhabited.

The portal generator and the various adapter parts Balderhaz had brought through sat on the ground to his left. The other two Mercurys and Balderhaz were standing a few feet in front of him, and at first he thought they were speaking—but then he realized what he was hearing was the low murmur of an astonished crowd. They were not alone.

"Hey!" called a voice. "Who are you?" It was the voice of a teenage boy. His body was barely visible at the edge of the penumbra of light cast by the lanterns, but his blond hair shone in the dim light. There were obviously more people out there, judging by the sound, but only this one boy was within range of the lanterns. Odd.

The three Mercurys, at a loss to explain what was happening, turned toward Balderhaz, who simply shrugged. "Don't ask me," said Balderhaz. "I'm a master of the occult secrets of the multiverse. People confuse the hell out of me."

"Are they campers?" asked Blue Mercury. "Hunters, maybe?"

"What's with the lights, though?" asked Green Mercury.

"Are you sure you got the coordinates right?" asked Red Mercury.

"Of course," sniffed Balderhaz. "Four years in the past, exactly."

"I'm going to try talking to them," said Green Mercury. "Balderhaz, get to work on that shard adapter. We need to be ready to leave if this goes south." Balderhaz nodded and set to work.

Green Mercury turned and walked to one of the lanterns, removed it from its pole, and held it out in front of him. He cleared his throat and said, "Is this planet Hooston?"

The boy remained silent. The crowd murmured uncertainly in the dark beyond the lanterns.

"Um, what?" said the boy after a moment.

"I asked if this is planet Hooston," said Green Mercury. "It's a joke."

"Oh," said Lucas. "I, um, don't get it."

"Can't you see the kid is like twelve?" said Blue Mercury, coming up next to him. "When *Superman II* came out, he wasn't even..." He trailed off and the two exchanged glances. Then they said, in unison, "Wait, what's the date?"

"April 29," replied Lucas.

"The year!" cried Green Mercury. "Tell me the year!"

"Um, 2013," said Lucas.

"Then it worked," said Red Mercury.

"That was the easy part," said Green Mercury.

"Why are you people on our land?" said Balderhaz.

"It's not ours yet," said Green Mercury.

"Get out of our yard!" yelled Balderhaz, ignoring him.

"Balderhaz, can you please get to work?" said Green Mercury.

Balderhaz grumbled something and went back to assembling the shard adapter.

Green Mercury held the lantern out in front of him again, peering at the throng of people that was slowly beginning to gather around the plateau. "Say, what's going on out here?" he said.

"Some kind of campout?" asked Blue Mercury.

"Um, it's a kind of religious thing, I guess," said the boy. "Supposed to be the end of the world. But I think it's over now."

"Oh yeah," said Red Mercury. "The big Apocalypse scare. I almost forgot."

"Where did you guys come from?" the boy asked.

"Not *where*," said Blue Mercury. "*When*."

"We're from the future," said Red Mercury. "But don't worry, we don't intend to stay long. This is just a pit stop."

"We'll be out of your hair in a jiffy," said Green Mercury. "And you can get back to your apocalyptic ritual. Although, spoiler alert: the world is still here four years from now."

"We can't go on," said a man who was approaching from behind the boy.

"Sure you can," said Green Mercury. "Seriously, we'll be gone as soon as we get the shard adapter connected to the portal generator. Twenty minutes, max. Then you can get on with your primitive dumbfuckery. Not that I'm judging."

"You killed our leader," said the man. "First Prophet Jonas Bitters. I'm his brother, Noah. Technically I'm Second Prophet, but he was entrusted with divine secrets to which I am not privy. We can't continue the ceremony without him."

"Well," said Red Mercury, "That sucks. Usually the portal generator will adjust its target location to avoid solid objects. The universe must have had it in for your leader."

"If it's any consolation," Green Mercury said, "killing him was an accident. We honestly thought this whole area would be uninhabited."

"Who are you people?" demanded Noah Bitters.

Green Mercury, still holding the lantern, walked to the edge of the plateau and stepped off. Gasps went up from the crowd, but Green Mercury floated gracefully to the ground, landing a few paces in front of the boy. The other two Mercurys stepped off a moment later, floating to the ground as well.

"Behind me," said Green Mercury, holding up the lantern, "is the famed inventor Balderhaz."

Balderhaz gave a wave from the plateau.

"My name is Mercury," Green Mercury went on. Then he moved the lantern in front of Blue Mercury, on his left, and said, "This is my friend Mercury." He moved the lantern in front of Red Mercury, on his right, and said, "And this is my other friend Mercury."

The people in the crowd had begun to cautiously converge on the four men. They spoke amongst themselves in hushed tones, obviously in awe at the mysterious manifestation—and particularly at the three identical men with silver hair.

"Is one of you Jesus?" shouted someone in the darkness, and from the encouraging murmurs that followed, it was clear that he wasn't the only one wondering this.

"It can't be Jesus," said someone else. "There are three of them, and they're all the same!"

"Demons!" cried a woman to their left. "False gods!"

"No!" growled an older man near the front. He turned to face the crowd. "Don't you people know your Bible? We are witnesses to the return of Jesus and the Prophets! He pulled a small, tattered book from his back pocket and took a moment to find a particular page. He cleared his throat and then read aloud:

"After six days Jesus took Peter, James and John with him and led them up a high mountain, where they were all alone. There he was transfigured before them. His clothes became dazzling white, whiter than anyone in the world could bleach them. And there appeared before them Elijah and Moses, who were talking with Jesus. Peter said to Jesus, 'Rabbi, it is good for us to be here. Let us put up three shelters—one for you, one for Moses and one for Elijah.' Then a cloud appeared and covered them, and a voice came from the cloud: 'This is my Son, whom I love. Listen to him!' Suddenly, when they looked around, they no longer saw anyone with them except Jesus."

"It's Jesus, Elijah and Moses!" a woman near him shrieked. "And…"

"Balderhaz," called Balderhaz, still working on the adapter.

"It's Jesus, Elijah, Moses and Balderhaz!" the woman cried. "Reverend Jonas was right after all! He sacrificed his own life so that Jesus could return!"

Noah Bitters nodded, rubbing his chin. "The Transfiguration is said to be a foretaste of the Second Coming. Perhaps it is true."

"But which one is Jesus?" asked someone else.

"Demons!" cried someone else. "False gods! Stone them!"

The three Mercurys and Balderhaz traded glances, not certain whether it was better to try to communicate the truth or to push the Second Coming angle. These people were obviously predisposed to believe that something either very wonderful or very terrible was happening; it didn't seem likely that they would be satisfied with the explanation that they were angels on a time traveling pit stop. This is why the scripture writers used metaphors and parables, Red

Mercury thought. If anybody tried to explain the actual truth to such people, they'd never understand it. And really, was the Second Coming thing really so far off from the truth? They were, after all, a trinity of angels (plus Balderhaz) on a mission to save the world from Lucifer. If it kept these people happy long enough to allow Balderhaz to install the shard adapter on the portal, what was the harm?

The murmuring in the crowd had intensified; as far as Red Mercury could tell, those assembled were evenly divided on whether the three Mercurys were prophets or demons. It didn't seem to occur to any of them to ask the newcomers themselves for clarification on the matter.

"And look!" a man yelled from somewhere on their left. "They brought the Ark of the Covenant!" He was clearly referring to the portal generator. Excited murmurs and chatter followed.

"Okay," said Green Mercury, having evidently decided things had gone far enough. "This isn't what it looks like. I'm not sure what it looks like exactly, but whatever it is, it isn't that."

"I admit it's an odd coincidence, us showing up like this," added Blue Mercury, "and maybe there's some kind of weird synchronicity involved, but trust me, we're not what you're waiting for."

"So you *are* demons!" yelled a woman near the front. This was followed by an assortment of gasps, boos, and chattering.

"No," said Green Mercury. "We're not important. As disappointing as the fact may be, our arrival here has no particular significance. We just had to stop here on the way to somewhere else. We'll be on our way shortly."

"Don't leave us, Jesus!" cried a woman to their right, addressing Green Mercury.

"What the hell?" said Red Mercury, turning to face Green Mercury. "Why do *you* get to be Jesus?"

"I call Moses," said Blue Mercury.

"We're not doing this," said Red Mercury. "And Elijah's Kung-Fu is more powerful than Moses' anyway."

"You can't be serious," said Blue Mercury. "Moses parted the Red Sea."

"Elijah raised the dead," said Red Mercury.

"One time," said Blue Mercury.

"How many seas did Moses part?"

249

"As many as he needed to. People died around Elijah all the time and he didn't do shit."

"Demons!" shouted someone in the crowd. "They're going to drag us all to hell! Don't look at them!"

"That's actually a good idea," said Green Mercury. "Everybody stop looking at us. Hey, what are you doing here?" He had just noticed Balderhaz had come up next to him.

"Portal generator is ready," said Balderhaz. "I'm just waiting for you guys to stop chattering."

"Let's get out of here," said Red Mercury.

"Agreed," said Green Mercury.

"Well, it's been fun," said Blue Mercury, "but we need to be on our way."

"Don't leave us, Jesus!" the woman called again.

"Look," said Green Mercury, "I'm not Jesus, and these guys aren't Elijah and Moses."

"But if we were," muttered Blue Mercury, "my Kung-Fu would be stronger."

"Can we just go?" said Red Mercury.

"Yes," said Green Mercury. "Let's go."

The four of them floated back onto the plateau as the crowd continued to scream an unnerving combination of supplication, adoration, and malediction. As they walked back to the portal generator, they saw a middle-aged woman scampering away down the slope of the plateau.

"Hey!" Red Mercury shouted. "What are you doing?" But the woman disappeared into the darkness without a sound. The woman seemed strangely familiar, he thought. He wondered if the others had noticed the same thing. She looked almost like—

"Okay, let's see what this baby can do!" Balderhaz hollered. He began tapping away at the keyboard. While the crowd continued to yell and murmur below, the portal flickered to life in front of them.

"Caveman times, here we come!" yelled Blue Mercury. But as he stepped toward the portal, the edges of the ellipse began to blur and expand outward.

"Um, Balderhaz," said Red Mercury. "What's going on?"

The ellipse continued to grow, inching closer to their feet.

"The portal's unfocused," said Balderhaz. "That should be impossible. I know I installed the—"

250

"I got a relic!" cried a woman's voice in the dim light below. "From the Ark of the Covenant!"

Looking down, they saw it was the woman who had been near the portal generator a moment earlier. She was holding a small, cylindrical part in her hand.

"Uh-oh," said Balderhaz.

"That bitch stole a part!" cried Red Mercury.

"The focusing reticule," said Balderhaz. "This could be interesting."

"Does she look familiar to you?" asked Blue Mercury. "Because I swear, if I didn't know better—"

But before he could finish the thought, the portal's edge reached their feet. In a blink of an eye, they were gone.

CHAPTER THIRTY-EIGHT

Somewhere in North Africa; c. 5,000 B.C.

The three Mercurys, along with Balderhaz, found themselves on a familiar African plain—familiar except for the glaring absence of the massive domed structure of Eden II. Assembled in a rough semicircle around them were several hundred people, who were standing around, blinking in the sunlight, speechless or whispering quietly in awe. The young blond kid was still standing at the head of the crowd, in relatively the same place he had been when they had disappeared, but Noah Bitters was nowhere to be found.

The Mercurys stared at the assembled masses in disbelief.

"Um, Balderhaz," said Red Mercury. "When are we?"

"Seven thousand years ago," said Balderhaz. "Give or take. The miracle detector is still orienting itself."

"I thought we were going back to the present day first," said Blue Mercury.

"That was the plan," said Green Mercury. "We were supposed to get the other portal generator and bring it back with us."

"Oh," said Balderhaz. "Whoops. Those people distracted me."

"Yeah, about that," said Blue Mercury. "We seem to have taken those people with us."

Balderhaz looked around, as if noticing the cultists for the first time. "Huh," he said. "Unfocused portal."

"Oh, shit," said Blue Mercury. "We've transported a bunch of crazy people back in time."

"And we have no way to return them to the present," said Green Mercury.

The other two Mercurys nodded as they realized what he was saying: there was no portal in sight. It must have closed after they went through.

"The portal generator probably overheated," said Balderhaz. "Without a focusing reticule, the energy surge would have overwhelmed the capacitor. That thing is probably just a heap of melted metal and plastic. Or will be, in seven thousand years."

"So we're stuck here," said Blue Mercury. "With all these nuts. Fantastic."

"Do these people look familiar to you?" asked Green Mercury.

"You mean other than that chick who sabotaged our portal generator?" said Blue Mercury. "She was the spitting image of Tiamat. Where is she, anyway? Did she get sucked back in time with the rest of them?"

"I don't see her," said Green Mercury. "But check out that girl in the front." He was pointing to a brown-skinned teenager with long, curly black hair. There weren't many children in the crowd, but a small group of them had gathered around the brown-skinned girl, as if instinctively turning to her for safety. Several of the children, obviously frightened by their trip through the portal, had begun to cry, and the girl was methodically, authoritatively reassuring them.

"Okay, now that's just weird," said Blue Mercury.

"It's her, right?" said Green Mercury. "I'm not imagining it."

"It's Michelle," said Red Mercury. "It has to be."

"And that guy, over here," said Green Mercury, pointing at a balding man to their left. "Isn't that Uzziel?"

"Holy crap," said Blue Mercury. "It is. And there's what's-his-name. The dim one. Nisroc."

"What the hell is going on?" asked Red Mercury. "Why do so many of these people look like angels?"

They stood for a moment, regarding the baffled congregants. The immediate shock of being transported through a mystical portal seemed to have given way to a general confusion. A few people seemed to be trying to determine where they were, but many more were looking around in puzzlement as if they had lost someone. After a moment, it became clear that the entire crowd hadn't been sucked through the portal. Noah Bitters, for one, seemed to have been left behind. He had been standing right next to the blond kid, and now he was gone. Those who had been closer to the portal generator seemed to have been more likely to be sucked through; the crowd grew progressively sparser as distance from the epicenter increased. Those who had come through were mostly men—had the portal generator discriminated? No, thought Red Mercury. More likely it was the result of attempts to get the women and children away from the rift that had torn their leader apart.

"Uh-oh," said Balderhaz again.

"Now what?" asked Green Mercury. "What else could possibly go wrong?"

They turned to see Balderhaz staring at the miracle detector. "The energy signature is off," Balderhaz said. "Losing focus on the portal must have drained some of the energy. We didn't go back as far as we were supposed to."

"So when are we?" asked Red Mercury. "Did we beat Lucifer here or not?"

"The amount of available interplanar energy gradually decreases over time," said Balderhaz. "It's known as the Balderhaz coefficient. By calculating the Balderhaz coefficient, I can pinpoint exactly when we are." He closed his eyes and moved his mouth silently for several seconds while they waited. "Well," he said, "we beat Lucifer."

"Great!" said Blue Mercury. "How long until he arrives?" asked Blue Mercury.

"As near as I can figure," said Balderhaz, "about an hour."

"You have to be shitting me," said Green Mercury.

Balderhaz shrugged. "At least we beat him here."

"What are we supposed to do in an hour?" asked Blue Mercury.

"What were we going to do in four years?" asked Red Mercury.

"Warn the other angels," said Green Mercury. "Get them prepared."

"Well, go ahead," said Blue Mercury.

"These people aren't angels!" cried Green Mercury. "They're just… people!"

"They're what we've got," said Blue Mercury.

"Maybe the real angels are around here somewhere," said Red Mercury.

"I don't think so," said Green Mercury. "I just tried to raise Heaven on angel band."

"And?" asked Red Mercury.

Green Mercury shrugged. "Try it yourself."

The other two Mercurys and Balderhaz took a moment to concentrate, then regarded each other with frowns on their faces.

"Nothing," said Red Mercury.

"Less than nothing," said Balderhaz.

Blue Mercury nodded. "No noise, no signal from other planes. Just... nothing."

"It's like the system hasn't been set up yet," said Green Mercury.

"Yeah," said Blue Mercury. "Weird."

They knew that somebody must have configured the system that allowed angels to communicate telepathically across great distances and even across planes, but they couldn't remember a time when angel band hadn't existed. It was just part of the background of the multiverse, something they could always count on. And now it was gone.

"What happened?" someone said. "Where are we?" They turned to see the blond boy approaching. Several others, evidently still not sure whether the Mercurys were to be feared, worshiped, or both, hung a few steps behind, watching the boy.

"Thanks to the meddling of one of your idiot members," said Green Mercury, "you've all been transported seven thousand years into the past."

"Don't blame me," said the boy. "My parents dragged me to that stupid thing. So what's the deal? Are you guys, like, actual demons? Why are there three of you? My name is Lucas, by the way."

"Long story, Lucas," said Blue Mercury. "We're not demons. We're... well, we're not demons. We're three different versions of the same person. Alternate universes, you know."

"And you all have the same name?"

"We're all Mercury," said Green Mercury. "I'm Green, he's Blue, he's Red."

"I'm Balderhaz," said Balderhaz.

"He's Balderhaz," said Green Mercury. "We've teamed up to travel back in time to stop Lucifer from rewriting history. And now you and your dumbass friends get to play too."

"Whoa," said Lucas. "Lucifer? Like, the actual Devil?"

"Yeah," said Green Mercury. "Don't get too excited; he's kind of a douchebag. Where are your parents, Lucas?"

"Pretty sure they're still back in Nevada or wherever. I'm fine with it. They're lame."

"Um," said Red Mercury suddenly. "What's that?" He was pointing at a bright glint of sunlight in the distance. The four of them stared at it a moment, trying to figure out what sort of prehistoric structure could be reflecting that much light.

"A building?" asked Blue Mercury.

"Made of glass?" said Green Mercury. "Nobody had the technology to make sheets of glass in 5,000 B.C."

"Well, we'd better check it out," said Red Mercury. "If the people who built that thing have the technology to make glass panes, maybe they can help us against Lucifer."

"We'd better hurry," said Green Mercury. "Because we're not the only ones who have noticed it." He was right: the people gathered around them had begun to turn and stare as well. Whatever it was, it didn't belong here, and they knew it.

"All right," said Blue Mercury. "Let's go."

"I'm coming with you," said Lucas.

"No, you're really not," said Red Mercury.

"Hold up," said Green Mercury. "One of us should stay here and watch these people. They could get eaten by a lion or something."

"They're twenty-first century Americans stuck in 5,000 B.C.," said Blue Mercury. "They're all going to get eaten by lions eventually."

"I'm not," said Lucas.

"Denial is one of the symptoms," said Green Mercury.

"Of what?" asked Lucas.

"Of early onset getting eating by a lion," replied Blue Mercury.

"I'll stay," said Green Mercury. "You guys check it. Come on, Lucas, help me keep these idiots from getting eaten."

Lucas didn't look thrilled, but he seemed somewhat gratified to be asked for help. He and Green Mercury walked toward the group, most of whose members were now staring at the shining object in the distance. A few had even begun to walk toward it.

"Okay, everybody, gather round!" yelled Green Mercury. "Let's do a headcount and see how many of us made it through. You over there, please stay with the group. There will be plenty of time for wandering off and being eaten by lions one you're all accounted for."

The stragglers began returning to the group.

"What's happening?" yelled a young woman holding a baby. "What is this place?"

"I'll explain everything in due time," said Green Mercury.

"Looks like he's got things handled here," said Red Mercury. "Let's go."

Blue Mercury and Balderhaz nodded. The three of them set off across the plain toward the mysterious object in the distance.

CHAPTER THIRTY-NINE

It was a massive blue crystal pyramid, at least five stories tall. The Eye of Providence. There was only one like it in the multiverse, and it was supposed to be in Heaven. Red Mercury, Blue Mercury and Balderhaz stood staring at it from about a hundred feet away.

"So," said Red Mercury, "why is the Eye of Providence here?"

"No idea," said Blue Mercury. "Are those monkeys?"

Several hunched-over humanoid figures were moving about the base of the pyramid, occasionally stopping to pound on the sides of the pyramid or give one of the other figures a shove.

"Apes, technically," said Red Mercury.

While they watched, a dark, vertically oriented rectangle appeared in the center of the pyramid's base, rapidly growing larger until it was the size and shape of a doorway. A figure, seemingly human, appeared in the doorway and stepped outside. The door slid shut behind him.

The figure shook a fist at the simians roughhousing around the pyramid and yelled something in a strange language. The apes barked back at him, standing tall and waving their hands over their heads. The man, not appearing the least bit intimidated, took a few steps toward the apes. It was hard to judge sizes at this distance, but he didn't appear to be a large man. The apes, now more agitated, moved to surround him.

"Should we do something?" asked Red Mercury.

"Let's see how this plays out," said Blue Mercury.

Red Mercury shrugged. Balderhaz, for his part, had lain down on the dirt and gone to sleep.

One of the apes stepped forward from the circle. He jumped up and down, howled, beat his chest, and bared his teeth at the man. When he was finished, he took a step back. The man stepped forward and did a near perfect imitation of the ape's war dance, complete with bared teeth. Then he took a step back as well.

The ape who had challenged the man had some sort of non-verbal exchange with the other apes, then took a step forward again. He bent down and picked something up, then waved it over his head. It looked to be a bone, perhaps a femur.

The man nodded excitedly and beckoned to the ape. When the ape just stared at him, the man found another bone and picked it up. Then he repeated his war dance again, pounding his chest and growling at the ape. At the end of it, he swung the bone as if bringing it down on someone's head. The ape, seeming to catch on, howled and ran at the man, drawing the bone back over his shoulder. The man dropped his bone and pointed his finger at the approaching ape. Then there was a flash of light and a loud pop, and the ape was lying on its back on the ground.

The man made the beckoning gesture once again, to the ape who had been standing next to the one who was now prone. The other apes turned and fled, screaming. The man shrugged and stepped back to the spot on the pyramid's base where the door had appeared. He leaned in and waved his right hand over an area of the pyramid's surface just to the right of the door. For a moment, some sort of control panel seemed to appear. The man did something at the panel and the door slid open again. He went back inside the pyramid, and the door closed behind him.

"Well, that was odd," said Blue Mercury.

"Indeed," said Red Mercury. "Come on, Balderhaz. Let's go."

Balderhaz got up from his nap and they walked the rest of the way to the pyramid. There was no sign of a door or any other imperfection in the base of the structure. It appeared to be a solid pyramid made of translucent blue crystal. A few feet from the base lay a dead ape, its charred body still smoking.

"It's the Eye of Providence, right?" said Red Mercury. "It has to be."

"I never knew the Eye had a door," said Blue Mercury. "What do you think is inside it?"

"If I had to guess," said Red Mercury, "I'd say a guy who kills monkeys with lightning bolts from his fingers. Hey, Balderhaz, did you know the Eye of Providence has a door?"

Balderhaz shrugged.

"Should we knock?" asked Red Mercury.

"I guess?" said Blue Mercury.

Red Mercury banged his fist on the wall, but very little sound escaped the marble-like surface of the pyramid. After a few seconds, though, the section of the pyramid folded out again, and the man stepped outside, yelling incomprehensibly and shaking his fist. When he saw the two Mercurys and Balderhaz, he stopped with his fist in the air and frowned. "Zhee khaw hawanagatha!" he growled.

"Um," said the two Mercurys.

"Hawna keezhaza na nani," the man said, and took a step toward Blue Mercury with his hand out.

"Whoa," said Blue Mercury, taking a step back.

"Zhee?" said the man, puzzled. Blue Mercury glanced at the dead ape.

"Zawkah!" said the man, and burst into laughter. He made a horizontal hand-waving gesture, which seemed to be the equivalent of head-shaking.

"Better just let him do what he wants to do," said Red Mercury.

"What if he zaps me?" said Blue Mercury.

"Exactly," said Red Mercury. "Let him do what he wants."

Blue Mercury sighed and made what he hoped was a conciliatory gesture toward the man.

"Kweenah zha na heenaw," said the man, and took a step toward Blue Mercury again. He held his hand up to Blue Mercury's chest, just below his left collar bone. "Zheenakwah!" the man cried after a moment, and pulled his hand away.

"Look," said Blue Mercury. "We don't want any trouble. We just—"

"You've ruined everything!" cried the man. "Do you have any idea how much this project cost?"

"Uh," said Red Mercury. "You speak English."

"I do now," said the man. "I tapped into your... er, there's no word for it in English. Call it your soul. Also picked up this awful drunken bar fight of a language you call English. Good grief, did you know that you people have three different words for *snot*, each one stolen from a different language? Explain yourself!"

"Well," said Blue Mercury, "*Snot* is straightforward, but a bit crude-sounding for some. Doctors like to use fancy words like *mucus* because it helps to justify their salaries. As for *phlegm*, there's no explaining the Greeks."

"I meant explain what you're doing here," said the man coldly.

"Oh!" Blue Mercury exclaimed. "Right. We traveled back in time to stop Lucifer from rewriting history. I'm Mercury, by the way. So is he. There are three of us, actually."

"I'm Balderhaz," said Balderhaz.

"Also," said Red Mercury, "We should probably tell you about the thousand or so people back that way a mile or so. You see, we had a bit of a—"

"I know all of this already," said the man. "It was in his—" he waved vaguely at Blue Mercury "—soul-thingy."

"Then why did you ask what we were doing here?" asked Red Mercury.

"I didn't," said the man. "I demanded that you explain yourself. By what right have you meddled in the Ontological Skein?"

"The what?" asked Blue Mercury.

"The fabric of the universe," said the man. "Clearly you manifested a causal anomaly or you wouldn't be here. Where is it?"

The two Mercurys glanced at Balderhaz, who reached into his pocket to produce a small silver disc: the quoin.

"There it is," said the man. "The proverbial wrench in the machine. The fly in the ointment. The burr in the saddle. The straw that broke the camel's back. The monkey in the middle. You know, I'm actually starting to like this language. Now ain't that a kick in the pants? I'm Zhanakza, by the way. You can call me John. Blazes, it's hotter than two squirrels fucking in a wool sock out here. Are you gents thirsty? Where are my manners? You may have broken the universe, but that's no excuse for rudeness. Come inside, please."

John stepped toward the pyramid and waved his hand over an area to the right of where the door had appeared. Something like a keypad appeared on the pyramid wall, with three rows of three symbols each. They looked vaguely like Egyptian hieroglyphs. John tapped a series of eight symbols in quick succession and the door slid open. Cool air wafted out from inside. The three angels glanced at each other nervously.

"Please," said John. "If I was going to kill you, I'd do it out here with the ape. I mean, I wouldn't do it with the ape. I'd do it with my finger, out here with the ape. Professor Plum with the candlestick in the library. Such a strange language. Anyway, I just had my floors done. Please, come inside."

Blue Mercury reluctantly walked inside, the other two following. John tapped an icon on the wall just inside and the door closed behind them.

They found themselves in a large marble entryway with walls paneled in cherry wood.

"What is this place?" said Red Mercury. "I never knew the Eye of Providence had an inside. This is the Eye of Providence, right?"

"Never heard it called that before running into you gents," said John. "Its official name is Ontological Outpost 73221. My people have thousands of them set up to document any ontological developments."

"Your people?" said Blue Mercury.

"I use the term loosely," said John. "We're a race of sentient beings from what you might call another universe. We exist outside of time and space. You could call us the Eternals."

CHAPTER FORTY

"Wait a minute," said Blue Mercury. "You're one of the Eternals? I thought…."

The two Mercurys glanced at each other.

"You thought you met some before," said John. "I read your memories. It's possible the people you met were manifestations of the Eternals. Reality is a funny thing. Some entities have what you might call echoes, manifesting themselves in different ways in different times. We Eternals try to remain in the background, but inevitably we affect what we observe. Since your reality began with one of our experiments, it's not inconceivable that the people you met at the dissolution of it were echoes of us. In any case, your memory of reality seventeen thousand years from now is just a phantom of what might have been. I'm going to have to shut down this outpost, so none of what you remember having happened in the future will ever happen. This way, gentlemen." John walked in front of them, leading them through the entryway. He opened the door and escorted them into a luxurious sitting room furnished with plush leather couches. "Please, have a seat," John said. "What would you like to drink? I can get you… well, literally anything you can imagine."

"I could use a beer," said the Mercurys together.

"Chocolate milk, please," said Balderhaz.

"Back in two shakes of a lamb's tail," said John, disappearing into another room.

"What do you think he meant by that?" asked Blue Mercury. "Not the lamb's tail thing, I got that. I mean the part about shutting down this outpost?"

"He's going to deactivate the Eye somehow," said Red Mercury.

265

"So what happens to us?" asked Blue Mercury. "This planet? I thought the Eye of Providence sustained the whole universe."

John walked back into the room, bearing a tray with two icy beer steins, a glass of chocolate milk, and a teacup. "It goes away," he said. "More precisely, it will never have been. Obliterated. Here you go, gents." He handed them each their respective beverages, then took the teacup for himself, setting the tray down on a table next to him. Balderhaz guzzled his chocolate milk and the two Mercurys took several swallows from their beers. John took a sip from his tea and continued, "It's clearly a disaster anyway. I mean, look at you. Two different versions of the same immortal entity traveling back in time to stop another immortal entity from erasing history. Ridiculous. Time travel is bad enough, but meddling with the Ontological Skein? It's a mess! Why bother with causation at all if this is what you're going to do with it? How the hell did you all get to be immortal in the first place?"

"We're angels," said Red Mercury.

John chuckled. "Of course," he said. "Silly question." He took another sip of tea.

The two Mercurys frowned at each other, not sure how to take this.

"I think," said Blue Mercury after a moment, "we're a little unclear on who you are exactly, and what you're doing here."

"Oh," said John. "Sorry. If you don't mind retiring to another room, perhaps I can show you. This way, please." He got to his feet and made his way toward a closed door. The two Mercurys and Balderhaz, still holding their glasses, followed.

John tapped an icon to the right of the door and the door slid open. The four of them walked into a large room that was dark except for the dim luminescence of the bluish-white floor tiles. In the center of the room, visible only because of the contrast with the floor, was a sort of pedestal, about chest-high, with what appeared to be a glass dome, about the size of a half-basketball, on top. John walked to the pedestal and waved his hand over the globe. Suddenly a brilliant display appeared overhead, a chaotic kaleidoscope of images, some large, some small. Some appeared to show planets or galaxies, others showed jungle scenes or fish swimming in the ocean; others seemed to be graphical representations of data— stacked blocks of varying colors or interlocking blobs reminiscent of a Venn diagram. About a third of the images were completely unidentifiable, ranging from vaguely fractal patterns to things that resembled abstract paintings. The ceiling of the room appeared to be domed, so the display took up most of the area above chest-level, like a small planetarium. Around the base of the dome was a series of several dozen icons resembling those on the entry panel to the Eye.

"This is the inner sanctum of the Outpost," said John. "The Iris of the Eye, if you will. A bit overwhelming, I know. Give me a moment." He pointed at one of the icons at the base of the dome and it lit up. He then made a sweeping motion with his hand and the entire display was swept clean. They were left in darkness except for the glow of the floor and the icons around the base of the dome. He pointed at another icon and suddenly the display was filled with what appeared to be an aerial photograph of a desert landscape. In the middle of the display was a small blue pyramid.

"That's the Outpost," John said. He moved his fingers over the display and the landscape shifted down until the blue pyramid was at the top edge of the display. He pointed his finger at what looked like a swarm of insects on the bottom of the display. "And those are your pals." He pinched his fingers together on the swarm and then drew them apart, and the display zoomed in on the group. They could make out Green Mercury standing in front of the crowd. John touched an icon at the bottom of the display and suddenly the room was filled with the sound of Green Mercury addressing the crowd.

"—am not stalling," he was saying. "I just think it would help us all get to know each other if we each said who our favorite Gilmore Girls character is. Personally, I'm abstaining from the question on the grounds that—"

Green Mercury's voice was cut off as John tapped the sound icon again. "And here's a view from a bit farther away," John said, putting his hands on either side of the display and then making a motion like slamming cabinet doors. The display zoomed out until the people and the pyramid receded into tiny dots and then disappeared. The beginnings of a mountain range came into view on the left and a river cutting through the desert on the right. John made the cabinet-closing gesture again and the display zoomed out even faster. Soon a body of large field of blue appeared on the right, and as the view continued to recede, the coastline of eastern Africa became identifiable. Several seconds later the curve of the Earth became visible, and soon they were looking at the planet as if from a hundred thousand miles in space.

"How are you doing that?" Red Mercury asked. "Some kind of satellite?"

"Extrapolated perspective," said John. "You could call it the God's eye view." He jabbed at an icon on the bottom of the display and then made the cabinet-closing motion once more. Earth continued to recede, but more slowly, and the several other planets came into view.

"The perspective is off," said Blue Mercury. "Earth shouldn't be that big compared to the other planets."

"It's a logarithmic map," murmured Balderhaz.

"That's right," said John, nodding. "Think of it as series of concentric circles. Rather than showing all parts of the universe on a linear scale, each circle represents a field of view several orders of magnitude larger than the one before it." While the Earth remained stable in the center, the planets receded from the edges, forming a spiral around the Earth. Soon a field of stars crept onto the display from the outer edges. "That's the outer ring of our Milky Way galaxy," said John. "Then the Perseus Arm." They watched as the stars moved toward the center, forming a ring around the hazy mass of stars enveloping the solar system. "And here come the neighboring galaxies." Several masses, most some variation on a glowing spiral, crept onto the display. "There's Andromeda, and that's the Large Magellanic Cloud. And then the more distant galaxies." Many more tiny spirals and other glowing forms came into view. "And then the rest of the cosmic web, a ring of cosmic microwave background radiation, and finally a ring of plasma around the outside. Gentlemen, I present you the entire observable universe."

The three angels stared for a moment, awed by the sight.

"And now say goodbye," said John. "Because you've mucked it all up."

CHAPTER FORTY-ONE

"You're blaming us for mucking up the entire universe?" said Red Mercury. "That seems a little harsh."

"If the shoe fits, wear it." said John. "The proof is in the pudding. He who smelt it dealt it. You've broken the causal schema of the universe. The universe is made of pretty resilient stuff, but it can only be stretched so far. You've torn a gaping hole in the Ontological Skein, and we're stuck with it. It's as simple as that."

"I get what you're saying," said Blue Mercury. "Trouble in paradise. We messed up history by going back in time. In a perfect world, this never would have happened, but sometimes bad is bad."

Red Mercury nodded. "We're walking on a thin line here," he said. If this is it, let me know. But you know, I'd like to believe that the heart of rock and roll is still beating. That's the power of—"

"Please stop," said John. "You broke the Ontological Skein by both going back in time and not going back in time. It's a miracle you're even here."

"Fine," said Red Mercury. "We broke your skein thing. But you can't seriously tell me that's somehow going to screw up stuff in the Andromeda galaxy. That's got to be, like, millions of light years away!"

"You're missing the point," said John. "Once you've broken causality, there's no limit to how fast light can travel. Hell, once causality is broken, there's no reason that it even has to remain light if it doesn't want to. If there's no causality, a photon could suddenly turn into a giant purple chicken, and there's not a damn thing you can do about it."

"But causality isn't broken," said Blue Mercury. "I'm willing myself to speak and words are coming out of my mouth. The sound waves are traveling through the air, your ears are picking them up, and then you're reacting to what I say. That's all cause and effect."

"It's not *completely* broken," said John, "but it's damaged. And that damage is going to spread, like cancer. Eventually it could even spill over into other universes, and then I'll lose my job for sure."

"What *is* your job, exactly?" asked Red Mercury.

"I'm an observer," said John. "The Ontological Observation Society sets up these outposts to gauge the effects of ubiquium on nothing."

"I'm sorry," said Blue Mercury. "You said you gauge the effects on nothing?"

"Of course," said John. "If you start with something, it skews the experiment. We build outposts like this one and put them in the middle of nowhere to see what happens."

"You mean that literally," said Red Mercury. "The middle of nowhere."

"Obviously," said John. "This is basic ontological engineering. Nothing is simple, really. A child could understand it. It takes a while, but eventually some sort of causal scheme tends to manifest itself. In the case of this particular universe, it was what you would call the big bang."

"You caused the big bang?" Blue Mercury asked.

"Are you listening to anything I'm saying?" said John. "No, I didn't 'cause' the big bang. Causation didn't take hold until after the big bang."

"So how long have you been here?" asked Red Mercury.

"Meaningless question," said John. "Time didn't exist before the big bang either."

Blue Mercury frowned. "But how can there *be* a before the big bang if time started with the big bang?"

"There wasn't," said John impatiently. "That's my point."

"Okay," said Red Mercury, "but you're saying you've been here *since* the big bang?"

"Well, yes," said John. "But you have to understand that time works differently inside the Outpost. Existence is largely determined by observation, so if no one is around to observe something happening, it doesn't actually happen. The Outpost in effect observes everything, but insulates me from becoming quantum entangled in every event that happens in the universe."

"Like a tree falling in the woods," said Red Mercury.

"Exactly," said John. "In the absence of observation, the tree makes no sound, but if you had placed a recording device near the tree, you'd have a recording of a tree falling. The Outpost insulates me from becoming entangled in every miniscule event in the universe, so for me they don't actually happen. Mountain ranges rise and fall around me without me being aware of it. But if I wanted to go back and view the complete history of the creation of a particular mountain range, the Outpost has the recording at my disposal. So although I've been here for billions of years, it hasn't felt nearly that long."

"Hold on," said Blue Mercury. "You're saying that time passes faster outside the Eye? How long have we been in here?"

"Relax," said John. "I synched the dimension we're perceiving as time inside the Outpost with the passage of time outside about 80,000 years ago. Switched to real time, you might say. About the time the apes showed up."

"The apes have been out there for 80,000 years?" asked Red Mercury.

"Not *those* apes, obviously," said John. "A different batch. The first ones evolved into homo sapiens. I don't know what the deal is with apes and alien monoliths. Eventually they show up and start hitting each other with bones. It's not always apes, of course. Sometimes it's transdimensional beings of oscillating phase energy. Man, I could tell you some stories. The point is, once the apes or their equivalent show up, I know shit is going to start to happen. Sentience. Consciousness. Observation. Perception. All the big names in ontological engineering. Unfortunately, the manifestation of consciousness is sometimes associated with a breakdown in causation, which is what we have in this case. There's nothing for it but to shut the whole thing down."

"Just to be clear," said Blue Mercury, "you're claiming to have created the universe."

"Creation is a causal term," said John. "Your language lacks the words to describe what it is I do. I monitor the outpost. The outpost observes-and-brings-into-being reality. But it's not a causal relationship. Time and causation themselves flow from the Outpost. They take many forms, but generally reality settles on three or four dimensions. Sometimes it gets stuck at one, which is pointless. Two dimensions is dull as dishwater too. Once you get above four dimensions, observation gets tricky because causation becomes muddled when the dimensions start folding back on each other. The best of all possible worlds, so to speak, is when you've got three predominant dimensions with a fourth acting as a sort of organizing force."

"Three dimensions of space, plus time," said Balderhaz.

"Precisely," said John. "Once you've got setup like that, it's only a matter of the fourth dimension before consciousness arises, which is when things really start to happen. Sentient minds are capable of observation, and observation gives rise to being. Once there are enough points of observation to keep the universe going without the Outpost, I would normally shut the eye down so it could be redeployed elsewhere. Or nowhere, more precisely. Unfortunately, consciousness sometimes starts getting it into its head to start meddling with the causal schema, which can result in damage to the Ontological Skein. And if that happens, I'm under strict orders to shut down the universe."

"But that's insane," said Blue Mercury. "You can't obliterate the entire universe at the first sign of problems."

"I didn't," said John. "The Outpost's sensors went crazy a few hours ago, by your reckoning of time, so I knew something was going to happen. I don't shut things down until I know the risk."

"Hold on," said Red Mercury. "You said you exist outside of time. So shouldn't you have known this was going to happen from the beginning?"

John shook his head. "Being outside of time is not the same thing as being omniscient. When I observe your universe, I have to interact with it on its own terms. Yes, I could move forward on the time axis, but that skews the results of the experiment. If I went looking for causal anomalies in the future, I would just end up causing causal anomalies in the future. Fortunately, my sensors can pick up energy patterns that correlate with anomalies, so I can prepare for them before they happen. I made a backup of the universe at the point where the sensors began to pick up trouble, so I could revert to it in case the damage got out of hand. Observe." John made a wiping motion with his hand and the display disappeared except for a semicircle of icons near the outside. He tapped one of the icons, which looked suspiciously like a file folder.

The folder appeared to open, and an image of Earth popped out of it, filling the center of the display. John tapped on the Earth and suddenly they were looking at the same desert plain they had been observing earlier—except both the blue pyramid and the people were missing.

"This," said John, "is what the universe would look like if you had never shown up. It's only a simulation, of course. This version of the universe doesn't actually exist, but I could deploy it if I wanted to." For a moment, his finger hovered over an icon at the bottom of the display that looked like a volcano erupting, or maybe a fountain spewing water. But then his hand dropped to his side.

"Looks fine to me," said Blue Mercury.

"Where's the Outpost?" said Red Mercury.

"I had to subtract it from the simulation," said John. "That's the problem. This version of the universe is relatively stable, but only because the Outpost is missing. The Outpost exudes what you might call the force of being, preventing the universe from regressing into nothingness. At this point, it's essential to the universe's existence. This universe isn't self-sustaining yet. It only looks stable because I'm feeding it artificially. Watch." He reached up and tapped a small blue pyramid on the bottom of the display and the icon turned gray.

As they watched, the display became grainy, eventually getting so bad that most of the image was obscured.

"What's wrong with the video?" asked Red Mercury.

"Nothing," said John. "That's what's going to happen when I redeploy the pyramid."

Soon they were just staring at a blank field of dull gray. The Mercurys shuddered in unison.

"Gentlemen," said John, "you just watched a universe regress into absolute nothingness."

CHAPTER FORTY-TWO

"But why?" asked Red Mercury. "Why does the universe disintegrate? It seemed perfectly fine."

"Not enough points of consciousness," said John. "If you'd appeared a thousand years later, the local tribes might have grown to the point where the universe could rest on their shoulders, but we're not quite there yet. Existence depends on observation. You need a critical mass of sentient observers to sustain a universe."

"So leave the Outpost active for a while longer," said Blue Mercury.

John shook his head. "Keeping an Outpost active in a universe where causation has begun to break down is like giving steroids to a cancer patient. You just feed the cancer."

Balderhaz nodded. "You can't deploy the universe without the Outpost because it's not self-sustaining, but you can't deploy it with the Outpost, because the Outpost exacerbates the breakdown in causation."

"Between a rock and a hard place," said John. "Between the devil and the deep blue sea. Scylla and Charybdis. Out of the frying pan—"

"We get it," said the Mercurys together.

"But your simulation showed a stable universe at first," said Red Mercury.

"Because, as I said, I was keeping it alive artificially," said John. "I added a minimal flow of ontological energy, just enough to keep it going but not enough to feed the causal anomaly. Think of it as putting a throttle on the flow. The simulation is being fed the equivalent of roughly one one-thousandth the output of the Outpost."

"Can you duplicate that effect in reality somehow?" asked Blue Mercury. "Throttle down the flow of energy from the Outpost?"

John shook his head again. "It doesn't work like that in reality. The Outpost is inside the universe. Imagine a radioactive heating element in a closed, insulated room. You can channel the heat with fans and ducts as much as you like, but you have no control over the amount of heat generated. All that heat is going to end up in the room, one way or another. This simulation depends on there being a controllable source of energy *outside* the universe."

"Multiple universes," said Balderhaz. "One with the Outpost, and others without. The alternate universes act as safety vents for the universe with the Outpost. The energy is split across a thousand different universes, so the each get enough to sustain them without feeding the breakdown in causation."

"I'm not authorized to create multiple universes," said John.

"Who gives a shit what you're authorized to do!" cried Blue Mercury. "Would it work or not?"

"Theoretically," said John with a shrug. "But I can't do it."

"You mean you won't do it," said Red Mercury.

"The Ontological Observation Society has strict rules about these things. One failed universe is a mark on my record, but it's not the end of the world, so to speak. But if I set up a thousand different universes and something goes wrong... the shit hits the fan. The pooch is screwed. You can't unring that bell. There's no way to contain the damage at that level. It could spread across the entire multiverse. No, I'm afraid it's out of the question. I've got a few housekeeping chores to do, but then I'll be shutting this place down."

"The hell you will," said Blue Mercury, getting to his feet. "We've given you a perfectly reasonable solution, and you won't even consider it. At least get your bosses on the phone or however you communicate with them."

"There's no point," said John, getting to his feet and staring coldly at Blue Mercury. "The rules are very clear. A causal breakdown of this magnitude necessitates a full abort. I'm not going to waste my superiors' time on something like this. So if you gentlemen are finished with your beers, I will see you out."

Red Mercury stood as well, and the two of them towered over John for a moment. John chuckled.

276

"Before you get any ideas about overpowering me and taking over the controls," he said, "remember what I did to that ape."

"We're not apes," said the Mercurys together.

John laughed. "No, you're *angels*," he said. "Immortal beings with mystical powers. Guess where your powers come from, Heckle and Jeckle?"

The Mercurys exchanged glances.

"That's right," said John, holding his hands in the air. "This place. The Outpost. Your so-called 'Eye of Providence.' And guess who controls the Outpost? Tell you what, gents. Why don't you try using your hocus pocus on me and see what happens."

The Mercurys said nothing. Balderhaz remained seated, watching the exchange, holding his empty chocolate milk glass in his lap.

"How about this," said John. "A simple test." He pointed his finger at Balderhaz, and the empty glass jumped out of Balderhaz's hands. Balderhaz gave a small yelp and sat up straight. The glass floated toward John, pausing to hover between him and the two Mercurys. "Fill this glass with water," he said.

"From this angle?" said both the Mercurys simultaneously.

"You're as childish as you are predictable," said John. "Too challenging? How about shattering the glass? Surely you can manage that."

The Mercurys made no response.

"I have to do everything myself," said John. "It's fine, I've been doing it for six billion years." He snapped his fingers and there was a sudden crack. The glass had shattered into dozens of little pieces, which floated before their eyes.

"Whoa," said Red Mercury. "He broke a glass."

"It's a metaphor for his career," said Blue Mercury.

"Very amusing," said John, as the glass shards—with the exception of two large, jagged pieces—fell to the floor. The two remaining shards floated toward the two Mercurys, one toward each of them. The Mercurys tried to step backwards, but found their feet stuck to the floor. The shards moved toward their necks, stopping only when the jagged edge began to bite into the skin of their respective throats.

"One thought from me—not even a motion, just a thought—and you're both dead. Forever. Because I control the Outpost, and the Outpost is the source of your immortality. I don't know how you managed to tap into it in the first place; some kind of glitch in the causal matrix. But it doesn't matter. I can shut it off with a flip of a switch. Ooh, I have an even better idea! The two of you fight to the death. Two Mercurys enter, one leaves!"

"That's not much of a prize if the universe is going to evaporate twenty minutes later," said Red Mercury.

"We'll do it," said Blue Mercury, glancing at his counterpart, "if you agree to try Balderhaz's universe-splitting idea. Let the universe live, and we'll fight. To the death."

Red Mercury looked at Blue Mercury grimly, but said nothing. Blood dripped from his throat where the glass shard pressed against it.

"Interesting!" said John. "Two identical beings fighting to the death for the fate of the universe. Except, of course, you're not truly identical, are you? Red Mercury cheated Blue Mercury out of a chance at happiness." He took a step toward Blue Mercury, regarding his face curiously. "I can see why you're so eager to kill him."

The Mercurys remained silent, staring at John.

"I'll tell you what," said John. The shards of glass moved away from their throats, and the other broken pieces of glass leapt into the air. The pieces fused together into a glass once again. Then the glass morphed into a crystal hummingbird, which buzzed away. "Out of respect for your fighting spirit, I will seek an audience with my superiors regarding the fate of your universe."

"Great," said Red Mercury. "Get them on the phone right now and we'll make our case."

"Out of the question," said John. "I must visit the headquarters in person. Your bodies would never even survive the translation into pandimensional form. Don't worry, it won't take long. Only about an hour in your time. And then I will give you an answer. But don't get your hopes up, the rules are quite clear in this case and I have no reason to believe my superiors will grant an exemption. But if nothing else, you will have an hour to prepare for your obliteration."

"Gee, thanks," said Blue Mercury.

"It's the best I can do," said John. "I'll see you gentlemen out and then be on my way. Follow me, please." He clapped his hands and the display disappeared. The two Mercurys and Balderhaz reluctantly followed him out of the room and back through the entry way.

"So," said Blue Mercury, "assuming your bosses say no, what happens next?"

"From your perspective, the Outpost will simply cease to be. In reality, it will never have existed at all. And shortly afterward, nothing else will either."

"How shortly?"

"Hard to say. Milliseconds, probably. If you're lucky you might get a second or two of existence, depending on the aggregate observational power of every conscious being. But it doesn't matter, because even that time will never really have happened. There will be no mark left of this universe anywhere. Even my backups will have to be erased; can't risk bringing the ontological impression of a faulty causal schema back to headquarters. The only thing that will remain is my own notes and my memories. Well, thanks for stopping by, gentlemen. I'll be back in an hour to pronounce the fate of your universe."

John opened the door and the three filed out. Blue Mercury glanced at the area on the pyramid wall where the keypad had appeared as he walked by.

"Don't get any ideas," said John. "I'll be changing the combination before I leave. And the Outpost will be set to self-destruct in the case of a mis-entered code. One wrong key and the Outpost—along with your universe—goes kablooey. So sit tight, say goodbye to your friends, make your peace with… whatever. I'll be back before you know it." The door slid shut, with John inside.

"Now what?" asked Red Mercury.

Blue Mercury shrugged. "We wait to die, I guess," he said.

"Man, did we land on the right name for you," said Red Mercury.

"Whatever," said Blue Mercury. "Let's go tell Green Mercury the exciting news."

The three walked away from the pyramid across the desert plain.

CHAPTER FORTY-THREE

"Son of a bitch!" Lucifer cried as he materialized on the prehistoric desert plain. "How do you keep getting ahead of me?"

"Well," said Green Mercury, turning to face him. "It helps that there are three of me."

"And who the hell are all these people?" Lucifer asked, noticing the crowd that Green Mercury was addressing. The crowd, in turn, stared speechlessly at Lucifer.

"Just some folks we picked up in the desert," said Green Mercury. "Not angels or anything."

Lucifer regarded the crowd curiously. "Are you sure?" he said. "Because a lot of them look familiar."

"I thought the same thing," said Green Mercury. "But trust me, they're just a bunch of knuckleheads waiting for the Second Coming. Whatever you're planning, it's not going to work. There are no angels here, nobody to manipulate. If Heaven even exists, it's inaccessible from here. And there's no angel band. Try it yourself."

Lucifer concentrated a moment, and a frown crept over his face. "This isn't right," he said.

"Disappointing, isn't it?" said Green Mercury. "You expected somebody else to have done the heavy lifting before you got here. They set up the angelic hierarchy and you slip in and corrupt it. But there's no hierarchy here. Nothing to corrupt. If you want to build an empire, you're going to have to do it from scratch."

Lucifer thought for a moment. "No matter," he said. "It's just as well there's no competition."

"Competition is the least of your worries," said a voice from in back of the crowd. The crowd parted to reveal Red and Blue Mercury returning with Balderhaz.

"You weren't joking," said Lucifer, stunned. "There really are three of you." He shook his head and regained his composure. "It makes no difference," he said. "You still won't be able to stop me. Soon this entire plane will be mine!"

"Go for it," said Blue Mercury, as the three approached. "You've got about forty-five minutes."

"What's that supposed to mean?" asked Lucifer.

"It means," said Red Mercury "that before the ink is dry on your global despot business cards, this whole universe is going to vanish. You see that?" He pointed to the glinting in the distance. "That's the Eye of Providence, also known as Outpost 73221. It sustains all of reality. In less than an hour, it's going to disappear, and take the whole universe with it. None of this—none of us—will have existed."

"Damn it," said Green Mercury. "And our *Gilmore Girls* convo was just starting to get interesting."

Lucifer chuckled. "What an absurd bluff. The three of you and Mr. Crazypants travel 7,000 years back in time and this is the best you can do?"

"Check it out yourself if you like," said Blue Mercury. "Or go nuts with your world domination schemes. We won't try to stop you. Either way, this is it. Game over."

Lucifer scowled. "Well, that's no fun," he said.

"So that really is the Eye of Providence?" Green Mercury asked, squinting at the horizon. "Shouldn't it be in Heaven?"

"Apparently not," said Red Mercury. "All of reality seems to have been the result of some sort of experiment by extradimensional beings. We broke something when we both did and didn't go back in time, so they're shutting it down."

"Who is 'they'?" asked Lucifer. "You talked to someone?"

"Yeah, a guy named John. Kind of a dick. He's checking with his superiors right now, but he basically said there's no hope for appeal. When he gets back, he's going to redeploy the Eye and then everything goes away."

"Ridiculous," said Lucifer. "I'm going to go see this thing myself." He turned and started off toward the pyramid.

Green Mercury sighed. "Should we try to stop him?" he asked.

"I don't see the point," said Blue Mercury. "He can pound on that pyramid all day and it's not going to change anything. Well, he can do it for about forty-five minutes anyway."

"But this John," said Lucas, who had been listening from a few feet away. "He said he's going to come back with a verdict?"

"That's right," said Red Mercury.

"Then we should all go there," said Lucas. "Maybe he'll be more sympathetic if he has to look us all in the eye."

Red Mercury shook his head. "I don't get the impression that John's a real sympathetic kind of guy. He sees universes created and destroyed all the time."

"And kills apes," said Blue Mercury.

"Well, we can't just give up," said a woman's voice. They turned to see the woman who was the spitting image of Tiamat. The Mercurys looked at each other and shuddered.

"Do what you like," said Blue Mercury. "I'm done trying to fix the past. I've been hopping from one timeline to another all day, and this is where it's gotten us."

Red Mercury nodded. "Me too," he said. "I'm out."

"Well," said Green Mercury. "I at least want to see this guy who's pronouncing our doom."

Red Mercury waved his hand dismissively.

"Attention, everyone!" yelled Green Mercury. "We're going on a field trip to the shiny thing. Everybody follow me."

There was some confused mumbling from the crowd, but ultimately everybody followed Green Mercury. It was unclear how much they had heard or understood about what the Mercurys had been saying. Most of them still seemed too dazed and overwhelmed to make much sense of anything.

Red Mercury and Blue Mercury watched as the crowd made its way toward the glinting in the distance. "Should we go after them?" Blue Mercury asked after a moment.

"Why?" said Red Mercury.

"You know, end of the world. Doesn't seem like a good time to be alone."

"We're not alone," said Red Mercury. "We have each other."

The two exchanged distasteful glances.

"Yeah, okay," said Red Mercury. "Let's go."

CHAPTER FORTY-FOUR

"How did you get inside?" asked Green Mercury. He and the other Mercurys, along with Lucifer, Lucas, the woman who looked like Tiamat, and a few of the other cultists stood in a rough semicircle, staring at the pyramid. Most of the other cultists hung back, too afraid to approach the strange monument, while a few walked around it, banged on it, or even tried—without much luck—to climb up the sides.

"There's a door in the center of this side," said Blue Mercury. He took a step forward and waved his hand over the side of the pyramid where he'd seen the control panel appear. It took him a few tries, but ultimately the nine icons reappeared.

"Weird," said Lucas. "It's like a combination lock. You'd think these extradimensional beings or whatever they are would come up with something... I don't know, fancier."

"Pattern recognition security is easy to fool," said Balderhaz. "Irises, fingerprints, voices, faces... just analog patterns that can be duplicated. Code-based security is much harder. Nine characters, eight digits. That's nine to the eighth possible permutations. Just over forty-three million possibilities. At five seconds per permutation, it would take seven years to try them all."

"We have about half an hour," said Green Mercury.

"It's worse than that," said Red Mercury. "A wrong combination will cause the Eye to self-destruct, taking all of us with it."

"And even if we could get inside," said Blue Mercury, "we don't know that we could figure out how to take control of it."

"I think I can figure it out," said Balderhaz. "That gooey interface in the Iris seemed rather intuitive."

"It doesn't matter," said Red Mercury. "We can't get inside. And in any case, John will be back in half an hour. We can't fight that guy."

"I could take him," said Lucifer.

"Good luck with that," said Blue Mercury. "He controls the Eye, which is where you get your power. And he's got powers that make angels look like these dumbasses." He waved his hand to indicate the crowd behind them. "He could kill you just by looking at you."

Lucifer swallowed hard. For a moment, everyone was silent.

"I, um, have an idea," said Balderhaz. "But I think it might be insane."

"Oh God," said Blue Mercury. "If *you* think it's insane, I'm afraid to even ask."

"Shoot, Balderhaz," said Green Mercury. "It can't possibly make things any worse."

"Well," said Balderhaz. "What if we could try *all* the combinations?"

"We can't," said Red Mercury. "And if we did, we'd all be annihilated forty-three million times."

"Forty-three million, forty-six thousand and seven hundred nineteen times," said Balderhaz. "But we'd succeed once."

Blue Mercury threw up his hands. "How the hell are we going to try every possible combination in twenty minutes? Unless you're planning on duplicating us a bunch more times, it's... oh."

"No," said Red Mercury, realizing where Balderhaz was going. "No more universe splitting."

"What do we have to lose?" asked Green Mercury.

"Everything!" cried Blue Mercury. "John's going to be back in a few minutes. Let's say there's a one percent chance that he was able to get approval to keep our universe going. Not great odds, I'll grant you, but still a thousand times better than you'd get with Balderhaz's plan."

"Four hundred thirty thousand times better," said Balderhaz.

"See?" said Blue Mercury. "Even Balderhaz knows it's insane."

"Any of you jerks plan on telling me what the hell you're talking about?" asked Lucifer at last.

"A quoin," said Red Mercury. "A quantum coin. Show him, Balderhaz."

Balderhaz held out his hand, revealing the silver disk.

"It's like a coin, but it taps into quantum mumbo jumbo something," said Blue Mercury. "The point is, the outcome is completely unpredictable. Not determined."

"Truly random," said Lucifer. "Pure chaos. I like it!"

"But there are only two possibilities with a coin," said the woman who looked like Tiamat. "Not forty-three million."

"We'd need to flip it a bunch of times," said Green Mercury.

"Twenty-six times," said Balderhaz. "We'd get a random output of a binary number twenty-six digits long. A string of ones and zeroes, basically. Ones for heads, zeroes for tails. Then we convert that number to a four-digit base base-nine number. Translate the digits one through nine to the hieroglyphs on the panel, and we have our combination."

"We have *a* combination!" exclaimed Blue Mercury. "A combination that is almost guaranteed to be wrong!"

"But we'd be doing it on forty-three million different universes," said Green Mercury. "Right, Balderhaz?"

"Theoretically, yes," said Balderhaz. "And in nearly all of them, we will be obliterated. But on exactly one, we will succeed."

"Remember earlier," said Red Mercury, "When I said our timeline-hopping plan was the most batshit crazy plan of all time? Turns out I was wrong by several orders of magnitude. That plan was basically a midnight trip to Arby's compared to this. This is like Salvador Dali and Hunter S. Thompson on a peyote trip crazy."

"I say we do it," said Lucifer.

"Yeah, because you're a psychopath," said Blue Mercury.

"I don't like it either," said Green Mercury. "But I also don't like leaving the fate of the universe up to some bureaucratic assholes."

"We should let people vote," said an older man in the group, who looked eerily like a seraph named Cravutius.

"No, we shouldn't," said Red Mercury. "We're not leaving the fate of the universe up to a bunch of end times nutjobs. Particularly ones who are only here because one of them stole a part from our portal generator." He glared at the Tiamat lookalike, who glared back.

"There's no time for organizing a vote with all these people anyway," said Lucifer. "We need to make a decision now. I think we should do it."

"Me too," said Lucas. "It's worth a try."

"No it isn't!" yelled Blue Mercury. "This is why people buy lottery tickets. They don't understand statistics. Help me out here, Balderhaz."

Balderhaz shrugged. "I kind of want to try it."

Blue Mercury sighed. "Of course you do. You're insane too."

"I'm with Blue Mercury," said Red Mercury. "We wait for John to come back. It's by far our best chance."

Green Mercury nodded. "I'm inclined to agree. I don't like it, but there's no sense throwing the universe away on a one-in-forty-three-million shot."

"So all the Mercurys are in agreement," said Lucifer. "What a surprise. But they only get one vote."

"We're not voting!" yelled Blue Mercury. "This is not even a serious question. Even if the odds of John getting us a reprieve are one in a million, it's still way better odds than trying to pick an eight digit combination completely at random!"

"I think it's the principle of the thing," said the Cravutius lookalike. The Tiamat lookalike nodded.

"What principle?" demanded Red Mercury. "The right to make ridiculously terrible decisions?"

"Well yeah," said Lucas. "I mean it's our universe. Shouldn't we get to decide?"

"The kid makes a good point," said Lucifer.

The Mercurys let out a simultaneous groan.

"You realize he's literally Satan," said Blue Mercury to the humans in the group. "He wants to destroy the universe."

"What an absurd and offensive thing to say," said Lucifer. "You wound me, Hermes Trismegistus!"

"Lay off the theatrics, Lucifer," said Green Mercury. "These people deserve to know the truth. You've been trying to destroy the world for thousands of years."

"I haven't the faintest idea what this man is talking about," said Lucifer. "I just want to give the combination thing the old college try. Sounds like fun."

"Seconded," said the Tiamat lookalike.

The Cravutius lookalike nodded. The others in the group still seemed unsure, but the Mercurys remained the only ones arguing against the idea.

"You know what?" said Blue Mercury. "Screw it. Do what you want."

The other two Mercurys nodded slowly in agreement. "I suppose it's only fitting that the universe be wiped out in an orgy of irrational thinking," said Green Mercury.

"Yeah, I'm out too," said Red Mercury. "Balderhaz, if you want to try it, go for it. Better hurry up, you've only got about twenty minutes."

Balderhaz nodded. "Okay, blond kid, grab that stick."

Lucas grabbed the twig Balderhaz was indicating.

"I'm going to flip the quoin twenty-six times. If I say heads, you draw a one in the sand. If I say tails, you draw a zero. Got it?"

"Yeah, I think I can draw ones and zeroes."

"Don't be a smartass. No mistakes. You have to do it perfectly."

"No mistakes," said Lucas. "Let's do this."

"There are more possible quoin permutations than there are door combinations," Balderhaz said, "so if we get an invalid permutation, we have to start over. Okay, here we go." Balderhaz flipped the quoin and caught it. "Heads. That's a one."

"I know," said Lucas, drawing a one in the sand. "Just say heads or tails. I got this."

Balderhaz flipped the quoin again. "Tails," he said.

Lucas drew a zero.

"Heads. Heads. Tails. Heads. Heads. Tails."

As Balderhaz called out each succeeding toss, Lucas made the corresponding mark in the sand. A minute later they were looking at a twenty-six digit long string of zeroes and ones.

"Now what?" asked Lucas. The others stood in a circle around him and Balderhaz, and more of the cultists were joining them, curious about what was happening.

"Now everybody shuts up while I convert this to base nine," said Balderhaz. He wagged a finger in the air as if writing, his lips moving silently. Then he scratched a four-digit number in the sand below the number Lucas had written. He did a few more mental calculations and then wrote another twenty-six digit string of ones and zeroes below that. He looked up at the group. "Does everybody agree that the top number and the bottom number are identical?"

There were nods and murmurs of assent.

"Good," he said. "Mercury, go to the door."

"Which one?" said the Mercurys in unison.

"The one in the pyramid," said Balderhaz.

The Mercurys looked at each other. "I'll do it," said Red Mercury. The other two nodded. Red Mercury walked to the area on the pyramid where the door had appeared and waved his hand, revealing the control panel. Finding his hands were shaking, he took a deep breath to calm himself. "Ready," he said.

"One to nine, left to right and then top to bottom, got it?" said Balderhaz. "Just like a telephone."

"Got it," said Red Mercury.

"First number is four," said Balderhaz.

"Four," repeated Red Mercury. "That's the first icon on the second row."

"Correct," said Balderhaz.

"Done," said Red Mercury, tapping the icon.

"Second number is three," said Balderhaz.

"Third icon on the first row," said Red Mercury.

"Correct," said Balderhaz.

"Done.

"Third number is eight," said Balderhaz.

"Second icon on the third row."

"Correct."

"Done."

"Third number is six," said Balderhaz.

"First icon on the second row."

"Correct."

In this manner, they went through the remaining digits, checking each one as they went.

"Done," said Mercury, after tapping the eighth and final digit. "Any last words?"

No one spoke. There was nothing to say. If they had entered the wrong combination, then nothing mattered anyway.

"Just as well," said Mercury. "And now, we reap the whirlwind. Goodbye, everybody. It's been a hell of a ride." He pressed the enter button.

CHAPTER FORTY-FIVE

The door slid open. Red Mercury was so shocked that he almost passed out.

"That... can't happen," he said. "It's impossible."

"No," said Balderhaz, walking up next to him. "Just highly improbable."

"But the odds..." Red Mercury said.

"The odds were one to zero in favor of success," said Balderhaz. "There was a one hundred percent chance the correct permutation would be selected."

"No," said Blue Mercury, approaching from behind. "They were forty-three million to one against."

"Incorrect," said Balderhaz. "They were forty-three million to one against for any given permutation. They were one to zero in favor for all possible combinations."

"But the odds that we would pick the right one..."

"Were also one to zero in favor," said Balderhaz. "If we didn't pick the right permutation, we wouldn't be here to ask the question.[11] So the odds of any group of beings in our situation being the ones who picked the right permutation are one to zero in favor. Before we entered that particular permutation, alternate versions of us existed who picked every possible permutation. Once we entered the correct code, though, all possible versions collapsed into this one. Us."

---

[11] The strong anthropic principle states that the universe can't exist without consciousness. This is not to be confused with the strong misanthropic principle, which states that the universe exists to screw with us.

"You mean they were obliterated," said Green Mercury. "Forty-three million other versions of us, just vanished as if they had never been."

"Semantics," said Balderhaz. "For all practical purposes, those alternate versions of us *were* us. The only difference was that they picked different permutations of hieroglyphs. But those permutations were dead-ends, impossibilities. They led to oblivion, which is simply another way of saying they couldn't happen. So they didn't. And here we are."

"You knew this would happen," said Red Mercury.

"I suspected," said Balderhaz.

"I can't believe that worked," said Lucas. The Tiamat lookalike and the others regarded the open doorway with awe.

"It shouldn't have," said Lucifer glumly. "Forty-three million to one. Ridiculous."

"Sorry, Luce," said Blue Mercury. "Better luck next time."

"Okay, let's not waste this chance," said Red Mercury. "Balderhaz, let's go. Blue, you too. We're going to need all of us to figure out how to work the Iris. Green, keep an eye on things out here."

"Yeah, yeah," said Green Mercury.

Blue Mercury followed Red Mercury and Balderhaz into the Outpost, closing the door behind him.

"How much time do we have?" said Blue Mercury, as they walked down the hallway toward the sitting room.

"About ten minutes, I think," said Red Mercury. "You think you can figure this thing out by then, Balderhaz?"

"I don't have a clue," said Balderhaz.

"What," said Blue Mercury. "No reassuring 'the odds are one to zero in favor' talk?"

"Not applicable," said Balderhaz. "We're on virgin territory here."

"Fantastic," said Red Mercury. "We survive forty million to one odds just to get inside and find you don't know what the hell you're doing."

They crossed the sitting room and opened the door into the Iris. They walked across the glowing floor and approached the pedestal, the two Mercurys moving aside as Balderhaz regarded the glass dome.

"If this thing is password-protected," said Blue Mercury, "I'm going to punch myself until I pass out."

"Do me first," said Red Mercury.

"You got it," said Blue Mercury.

But as Balderhaz waved his hand over the dome, the chaotic assortment of images appeared once again. Balderhaz cleared it as John had done, and then brought up the display of their universe, which currently showed only the blue pyramid and several hundred people gathered around it. Green Mercury seemed to be arguing with Lucifer.

"Ugh," said Blue Mercury. "What's that about? Should we help him?"

"No time," said Red Mercury. "We'll have to deal with it later."

Balderhaz did something and the view of the Eye shrank to a fraction of its size.

"Gaaahhh!" cried Blue Mercury. "Don't do that!"

"Calm down," snapped Balderhaz. "I'm just making the display manageable." He tapped another icon and a view of the desert without the Eye appeared. He shrank this one too, and dragged it next to the other. He made another motion and a second display, identical to the one he had just brought up, appeared next to it.

"How are you doing that?" asked Red Mercury. "You don't even speak this language."

"Good UI design," said Balderhaz. "Also, I'm a genius. Now shut up." He paused a moment, staring at the three little windows. "Okay, so I've figured out how to duplicate universes," he said. "And the little fountain icon deploys them. But that doesn't do us any good if none of the universes are self-sustaining. Or if this one is unstable, for that matter. So the question is, how do I set this universe to vent ontological energy to the others?"

The three of them stared at the display for a moment.

"Well," said Blue Mercury, "we know John artificially set up an energy flow to his backup universe. Can we view that setting somewhere?"

Balderhaz nodded and tapped the window holding the initial backup. The display once again filled the screen. After trying a few icons with unsatisfactory results—including one terrifying blinking red warning dialog that showed something that looked like a giant shrimp tossing a chicken in a wood chipper—he happened upon one that brought up a sort of settings window.

"There," said Red Mercury. "That blue pyramid. That's the energy source."

"And that slider-looking-thing next to it is the energy level," said Blue Mercury.

"Fine," said Balderhaz, "but that doesn't... aha!" He tapped on an icon below the pyramid, and another window popped up, showing a series of smaller windows. Several of them appeared to be pictures of some kind of landscape. The one on the far upper left was a desert scene with a blue pyramid in it. Hundreds of what looked like tiny insects moved around the outside of the pyramid. "It can't be this simple," said Balderhaz. He tapped on the picture with the blue pyramid and the window vanished. The simple blue pyramid had now been replaced with the picture he had just selected.

"Brilliant!" cried Red Mercury. "You've selected this universe as the energy source for the backup!"

"And look," said Blue Mercury. "The energy level slider is halfway over. It defaulted to splitting the Eye's output fifty-fifty between the two universes."

"Hmm," said Balderhaz. "But look at this." He pointed to a line of red hieroglyphs below the energy level, which seemed to be a sort of warning message.

"Is that saying it's unstable?" said Blue Mercury.

"That's my guess," said Balderhaz. "Too much energy. John had that slider pretty far down on his simulation. Probably less than one percent."

"Try dragging the slider down until those scary red frogs go away," said Red Mercury.

Balderhaz tried it, but he dragged it too far, and the warning message was replaced with another, even longer and scarier message.

"You've turned the scary red frogs into terrifying red turtles," said Blue Mercury. "I don't think that's an improvement."

"I'm doing my best!" Balderhaz snapped. "It would be easier if I could read the... oh." He tapped a box above the slider, which currently held a series of seven hieroglyphs. A series of nine hieroglyphs appeared below it. Below this were three larger hieroglyphs. Together, the two rows seemed to comprise a sort of virtual keyboard for entering numbers into the box.

"We've seen two of those three bottom symbols before," said Balderhaz. "The first one is 'enter.' The second one is 'cancel.' And the third is…"

"Erase," said Red Mercury. The hieroglyph looked vaguely like a cloud raining on some kind of tablet.

"Right!" said Balderhaz. "And the ones in the row above it are digits."

Blue Mercury nodded. "Base nine," he said. "Just like the code panel for the door."

Balderhaz closed his eyes for a moment, as if trying to picture the panel. Then he opened them again, looked at the number, and frowned. "There are too many symbols," he said. "That one on the left isn't on the door panel."

"Maybe it's a zero," said Red Mercury. "The door panel only went from one to nine."

Balderhaz shook his head. "No, it went from zero to eight. I converted from index zero to index one to avoid confusion with the ordinal numbers. Otherwise, the first number would have been the—"

"We trust you," said the Mercurys together. "Let's move on."

Balderhaz continued, "In a base nine system, the digits go from zero to eight. Nine would be represented by a one and a zero. It has to be some other mathematical symbol."

"Decimal point," said Blue Mercury.

Balderhaz's eyes lit up. "Yes!" he cried. "But it's not a decimal point. It's a radix point. Okay, let's try for about one percent. If I erase everything in the box and just put one of these tree-looking things in there… hmm."

"Still unstable," said Red Mercury.

"Gotta go lower," said Balderhaz. "Thank the Eternals for the radix point. And thank them for left-to-right oriented numbering too. That could have gone either way." He erased the tree, inserted the radix point, which looked a little like a man with a long nose peeking over a wall, and then tapped the last symbol on the right.

The message remained.

"Still too much energy," said Balderhaz. "No worries. We just replace this sickly sheep with this one-legged robot and… voila!"

The red message disappeared.

"Stable," said the Mercurys together. "Now what?" asked Red Mercury.

"Going to check the lower end of the scale, just to be safe." Balderhaz deleted the one-legged robot character and replaced it the one to the left of it on the keyboard, which looked a bit like an upside down eagle.

"Gaaahhh!" cried Blue Mercury. "Terrifying turtles!"

"Okay, radix point upside-down eagle is too low. If we reduce the energy level that far, the universe will fall apart. So the optimal value is somewhere between radix point upside-down eagle and radix point—"

"Balderhaz," interrupted Red Mercury. "Not to tell you your business, but we don't have time for this level of precision. Stable is good enough."

Balderhaz frowned but nodded. "Okay, radix point one-legged robot it is."

"Now what?" asked Blue Mercury.

"Now we do some math," said Balderhaz. "We've got radix point one-legged robot as an optimal energy level for each individual universe. That's point eight in decimal. The maximum value of that slider appears to be three sickly sheep, which equates to… seven hundred twenty-eight. Dividing seven hundred twenty-eight by point eight, we get…" Balderhaz closed his eyes for a moment. "…nine hundred ten."

"I have no idea what any of that means," said Red Mercury. Blue Mercury nodded.

"It means we need nine hundred ten universes to get the optimal energy distribution, assuming…"

"Assuming what?" asked Blue Mercury.

"Well, assuming no energy loss in transit, and about a thousand other things I don't have time to figure out. We're just going to have to assume all those factors are within the margin of error."

"Cool," said Red Mercury. "It's not like the fate of nine-hundred and ten universes hangs in the balance or anything."

"John said he'd reduced the energy flow to roughly a thousandth of the pyramid's output," said Blue Mercury. "So that jibes. Now what?"

"The universe we currently occupy is the energy source, and we've got John's backup and a copy. So I just need to make nine-hundred seven more copies."

"Better get moving," said Blue Mercury. "Because John's going to be back any minute."

Balderhaz nodded. He duplicated the backup the way he had the first time, and then did it again. And again.

"You've got to be kidding me," said Red Mercury. "There's no faster way to do it?"

"I'm sure there is," Balderhaz said, "but the instructions are in Martian, so why don't you pipe down and let me work?"

The two Mercurys backed off as Balderhaz continued the incredibly dull and time-consuming process of copying universes. A few minutes in, as the Mercurys were pacing the perimeter of the Iris, a flashing red warning message appeared overhead.

"What's that?" the Mercurys said together.

Balderhaz frowned. "I don't know," he said. "It seems to be an unrelated subprocess."

As they stood there, pondering the meaning of the strange message, a luminescent bluish-white circle appeared on the floor on the other side of the pedestal from Balderhaz. As it solidified, the message on the display changed, turning green.

"Incoming!" cried Red Mercury. "It's a portal!"

While Balderhaz continued to furiously copy universes, the two Mercurys ran toward the portal, diving headlong toward the half-materialized form of John.

They were too late. John's form solidified a moment before the Mercurys reached the portal. He held up his right hand, and suddenly the Mercurys were suspended in mid-leap, inches away from him.

"What in the name of all that's eternal is going on here?" John asked, a stunned look on his face. "How did you two get in here?"

"Kind of a funny story," said Red Mercury, still hanging in mid-air. "We used the—"

"The quoin," said John. "I should have known. Hey!" He had noticed Balderhaz. "Get away from that! You don't know what you're doing!" As he spoke, Balderhaz flew backwards, slamming into the wall behind him. Stunned, Balderhaz sunk to the floor.

John stepped to the podium, staring at the display overhead. "What is this? You've made hundreds of copies of my backup universe. What did you think you were going to do with all of these?"

Another warning began flashing on the display.

"Blast it!" John growled. "You can't have nine hundred active universes open at once. You've overrun the compile buffer."

"That sounds bad," said Red Mercury. "Is it bad?"

"Too much ontological strain on the Outpost's systems," John said, reaching his hand toward the glass dome on the pedestal. "Nobody move. The slightest jolt could cause an uncontrollable—" John screamed as something like lightning arced from the glass to his hand. The overhead display went black and John slumped to the floor, unconscious.

CHAPTER FORTY-SIX

"Forty-three million to one," Lucifer grumbled again. "We shouldn't be here. None of this should be here."

"Take it easy, Lucifer," said Green Mercury, standing guard in front of the Eye. "I'm just as upset about existing as you are, and you don't see me being a big baby about it."

A few dozen cultists, including Lucas, the Cravutius lookalike and the Tiamat lookalike, gathered around them in a rough semicircle. Most of the cultists seemed to have some idea that something momentous was happening inside the pyramid, but were unclear on the details, to say the least. Some of the people had gathered in groups to babble apocalyptic theories to each other; others continued to inspect (or try to climb) the pyramid. A few particularly dim bulbs had started whacking each other with bones. Those gathered around Green Mercury and Lucifer seemed mostly content to listen in on their conversation in the hope of obtaining some insight into what was happening. These people were disappointed. The mood of the crowd was surprisingly upbeat, however—due in part, no doubt, to a low pressure zone that had moved in, bringing with it cooler air and some cloud cover.

"Admit that I'm right," said Lucifer. "Admit that we shouldn't be here."

"I admit the odds appeared to be against it," said Green Mercury. "But here we are. It's the eternal existential dilemma: why am I here?"

"You think it was destiny or fate or something, don't you?" said Lucifer. "Maybe it was God's will that we survived. Is that what you think?"

Green Mercury sighed. "I honestly don't have any idea. I guess I still believe there's some reason for us to exist, though, yes."

"Then let's try it again."

"What?"

"Let's try another combination."

"We know the correct combination. It's penguin on fire, crashing spaceship, upside-down eagle, one-legged robot, guy with—"

"You said there's a reason we're here," Lucifer interrupted. "There's a reason we picked the right combination. If that's true, then we shouldn't be able to pick the wrong combination. God wouldn't let us survive forty-three million to one odds just to let us vanish into nothingness a few minutes later."

"You're nuts, Lucifer. We're not trying another combination. We know what would happen."

"Do we?" asked Lucifer. "Wouldn't God stop us, if there is a God? Why would he let all of creation lapse into oblivion?"

"He won't, because we're not trying another combination. See, God just saved the universe. Problem solved."

"Step out of the way, Mercury."

"Not a chance, Lucifer."

"Move or I'll move you."

"You've got to be kidding me, Lucifer. Not even you can be this spiteful and nihilistic. We just survived forty-three million to one odds. I have no idea if this universe-creation plan is going to work, but it deserves a chance, doesn't it? Just let things be for once. Accept the possibility that we're going to actually get through this. That means more world domination schemes for you. You used to love world domination schemes."

Lucifer thought for a moment. "You know," he said, "you're right. I hadn't thought of it that way. How am I going to impose my will upon billions of people if the universe doesn't exist? Okay, we'll do it your way. I'll just go sit over here with the future subjects of my unquestioned dominion over all reality and..." He suddenly stopped and darted toward the pyramid.

Green Mercury, anticipating the move, shoved him aside. Lucifer stumbled and smacked his forehead against the pyramid wall several feet from the panel.

"Damn you, Mercury," growled Lucifer, rubbing his head. "Get out of the way!"

"Not going to happen," said Green Mercury.

Lucifer got to his feet and charged Green Mercury. Green Mercury tried to dodge, but was too slow. He and Lucifer thudded to the ground. Lucifer got up first, but Green Mercury grabbed his ankle and pulled, causing Lucifer to fall on his face. Green Mercury scrabbled forward and climbed on top of him, pinning him down. "Yield!" Green Mercury yelled.

"Mmph!" said Lucifer, his face in the sand. Their audience had now grown to more than a hundred people, watching the contest with great interest.

Mercury grabbed the blond hair on the back of Lucifer's head and pulled. "Yield?" he said.

"Yield," moaned Lucifer.

Mercury got up and gave Lucifer a kick in the ribs. Lucifer groaned. "Get away from the Eye," he said. "You get within a hundred yards of it again and I'll break a boulder over your head."

Lucifer scurried away on his hands and knees, like a frightened animal. The crowd parted for him as he fled. "It's not fair, you know," Lucifer said, getting to his feet and brushing the dirt off his knees.

"Cry me a river," said Green Mercury, wiping his brow with the back of his hand. The air had cooled a bit, but it was still warm and the humidity seemed to have gone up. He wished it would rain. He hadn't had a chance to clean off since diving into the dirt to save the shard from the bunker buster. And eventually the cultists were going to need water, which meant a lot of transmogrification.

"Oh, I didn't mean for me," said Lucifer, a smile playing at the corner of his mouth. "I meant for you. It's unfair that you have to try to outwit me with that feeble little brain of yours."

"What are you blabbering about now?" said Green Mercury, wiping his brow.

"Don't worry," said Lucifer, backing away from Green Mercury. "It will hit you eventually."

In the distance was a low rumbling sound, and suddenly Green Mercury realized why the weather had changed so abruptly. While Lucifer had been distracting him with talk and amateur attacks, he'd been amassing clouds overhead—thunderclouds. Green Mercury had been struck by lightning before, and it wasn't an experience he was keen on repeating.

Lucifer must have seen realization dawn on Green Mercury's face, because he suddenly turned and ran. Mercury launched into a sprint, diving at Lucifer's legs just as a blinding flash lit up the sky. If he was going to be hit, Lucifer would be as well. He could only hope the cultists were far enough from the strike to be unharmed.

A deafening boom sounded as the two hit the ground. Green Mercury's ears rang from the sound and every hair on his body seemed to be standing at attention, but he and Lucifer were both unharmed. The lightning had missed them. The two of them turned to see what had happened. Many of the people who had been closest to the Eye were now lying on the ground, dazed, but no one looked seriously injured.

"The pyramid!" somebody yelled. "It hit the pyramid! Look!"

Something did indeed seem to be happening with the pyramid. The top several feet had taken on a pulsing orange glow, almost as if it were on fire.

"It's just lightning," said Lucifer. "It's got to be able to handle lightning."

"You would think so," said Green Mercury. "It's been around for billions of years. This can't be the first time it's been struck by lightning."

But the orange glow seemed to be intensifying and spreading to the rest of the pyramid.

"Something is wrong," said Green Mercury, getting to his feet.

Lucifer stood up next to him. "Yes," he said, a hint of excitement in his voice. "Very, very wrong."

"It's some kind of power surge," said Green Mercury. "We need to get everybody away from the Eye. Hey, everybody! Get away from the pyramid!"

A few of the dazed and confused cultists turned to look at Green Mercury, but most were transfixed by the sight of the pyramid, which was now almost entirely engulfed by the orange glow.

"Run!" yelled Mercury. "It's going to..." He trailed off, realizing that he had no idea what it was going to do. In any case there was little hope of getting anyone to run away from the mesmerizing sight of the transfigured pyramid, and probably no chance of any of them getting safely away. If the pyramid exploded, it would take the rest of the universe with it. Might as well just sit and watch the show.

"Burn, baby, burn," said Lucifer, staring gleefully at the Eye, his face aglow with orange light.

"There is seriously something wrong with you," said Green Mercury. "What happened to you to make you such an asshole?"

"This is what I was born for," said Lucifer. "I've waited for this for seven thousand years. To see everything gone. Erased, as if it never was. Where is your God now, Mercury? Sleeping, perhaps? Out for a stroll?"

But Green Mercury wasn't listening. He simply stared at the Eye, taking in the sight. It was beautiful in a way, he thought. The whole pyramid was now glowing orange, aflame with an energy it seemed powerless to contain. If this was the way the universe ends, he thought, I'm ready for it. Blasted apart by ontological energy, overwhelmed by the power of Being itself. He and everyone else here would become too real to exist. It seemed appropriate.

A wave of energy swept out slowly from the Eye, engulfing the cultists and everything around them. As it approached Green Mercury, he glanced at Lucifer, who was still gleefully anticipating his own doom, along with that of everyone else. Green Mercury couldn't help laughing. The great Lucifer and all his plotting had been reduced to this: literally rooting for absolutely nothing. For all his cleverness and charm, Lucifer was an empty suit—more than that, an empty shell, like a snakeskin left behind by a molting snake. Nothingness personified.

And what about me? thought Green Mercury, as the wave struck him like a blast of hot air from an open furnace. Am I an empty suit as well? What good have I done, considering how everything ended up? None at all, I suppose. For the most part, I was just a leaf on the wind, a bubble of mercury pulled one way and then another by forces I didn't understand, and still don't. And yet, somehow I don't believe that all is for nothing. There is still hope, I think, even when all else is oblivion. And there is some small value in what I am, and who I have been. Mercury, he thought to himself. I'm Mercury.

And then there was nothing.

CHAPTER FORTY-SEVEN

Both Mercurys fell to the floor with a thud. The Iris was dark except for the glow of the floor tiles.

"What the hell happened?" asked Red Mercury. "Balderhaz, are you okay?"

There was no response. The two Mercurys got to their feet and made their way to the pedestal. John was lying on one side of it, face up, spread-eagled on the floor. Balderhaz was curled in a corner on the other side. Something resembling a swirling yin-yang symbol appeared overhead.

"Progress indicator?" Blue Mercury asked.

"Maybe it's rebooting," said Red Mercury.

"Let's hope," said Blue Mercury. "How's John?" He went to check on Balderhaz while Red Mercury inspected John.

"Unconscious," said Red Mercury. "Whatever advantages he has over us, he doesn't seem to be immune to electric shock."

"Same here," said Blue Mercury.

"Hopefully Balderhaz comes around first," said Red Mercury. As he spoke, the display lit up overhead once again. It looked the same as it had when it shut down: several hundred little windows showing copies of the backup universe had appeared.

"Is it done?" Blue Mercury asked. "Did Balderhaz make enough copies of the universe?"

"Dunno," said Red Mercury. "How do we deploy them?"

"Beats me," said Blue Mercury. "Try that swirly galaxy thing."

"I'm not trying anything," said Red Mercury. "I'm waiting for Balderhaz to wake up."

There was a sound like a scream from somewhere outside the Iris. It was followed by a cacophony of clattering and crashing.

"What the hell is that?" Blue Mercury asked. "Did somebody get inside?"

"I'll check it out," said Red Mercury, heading for the door.

"No, don't check it out!" said Blue Mercury. "I need someone to keep an eye on John!"

"I'll be right back," said Red Mercury. He exited the room, closing the door behind him.

On the floor on the other side of the pedestal, John groaned.

"Shit!" said Blue Mercury, scanning the series of hieroglyphs at the bottom of the display. Which one of them would deploy the universes? The three-legged cat? The melting ice cube? The stapler being eaten by a snake? None of the icons meant anything to him. "Balderhaz!" he yelled, giving him a nudge in the side with his toe. "Wake up!"

But Balderhaz didn't wake up. John began to pull himself to his feet. Outside the room, the crashing and banging and yelling continued.

Blue Mercury didn't know what to do. He'd always been a loner, but he'd grown accustomed to having another version of himself (or two) to bounce ideas off. Now he had to decide the fate of the universe alone. He could run around the pedestal and give John a kick in the head to try to buy himself some time, but having another minute to stare at the indecipherable icons wasn't going to do him any good. Balderhaz might come around eventually, but he showed no signs of rousing, and Balderhaz's guess probably wouldn't be any better than his own. So, pick an icon, he thought. Quick, while I still have control over my limbs. But which one? Iguana on a stepladder? Log cabin floating on a pond? Banana peel windsock?

Then he saw it. An icon that looked like a glass apple. It didn't make any sense; there was no logical reason for the glass apple to be the deploy icon. It probably wasn't even really a glass apple. But it was the right button. It had to be.

"Get... away... from that..." John groaned, pulling himself to his feet with the pedestal.

Blue Mercury pointed at the red apple, and it lit up. An indecipherable message popped up. Three digits of it were numeric; he recognized them from the door code panel. The Iris was asking him if he was sure he wanted to deploy all nine hundred ten universes. There were two options, one of which he didn't recognize. The second one was the 'cancel' button. He pointed at the one he didn't recognize. The display went dark again, except for the whirling yin-yang.

"What... did you do?" gasped John.

"I'm not entirely sure," said Blue Mercury, "but I think I just created 910 universes, give or take."

The display came alive again, this time with a message in green.

"What does it say?" asked Blue Mercury.

"It says," John said, looking from the message to Blue Mercury impassively, "that the operation was a success."

"Woohoo!" cried Blue Mercury, then suddenly became very serious. "Please tell me that means you're not going to erase them all."

"My request for an exemption was rejected," said John. "I'm to shut down this universe immediately."

"Okay, but the situation has changed," said Blue Mercury. "Now there's—"

"However," John went on, "the situation has changed, so it behooves me to reassess matters." He tapped a series of icons, bringing up various windows displaying graphs and charts, which he spent several seconds reviewing. "It would appear," he said at last, "that the universes are stable."

"It worked!" Blue Mercury cried. "Balderhaz, it worked! So there's no need to shut them down, right?"

"From the perspective of my superiors," John replied, "the situation has not changed. These universes were not authorized to be brought into being, and this project and all dependent universes are to be shut down immediately."

"But the—"

"But there has been a complication," John went on. "Any time a universe is annihilated, a UG-473 must be filled out, in triplicate. That's thirty-six pages of paperwork *per universe*. For a total of—"

"Thirty-two thousand, seven hundred sixty pages," murmured Balderhaz from the floor.

"That's correct," said John. "And the Iris keeps a record of all deleted universes, so unfortunately there is no way around this chore, assuming the Outpost is returned to headquarters according to protocol. Of course, occasionally a causal breakdown is so severe that it infects the Outpost itself, requiring that the Observer, shall we say, scuttle the ship."

"You're going to leave the Eye here?" Blue Mercury asked, helping Balderhaz to his feet.

"I don't seem to have much choice. It's either that or spend the next three years doing paperwork. The Outpost will be on autopilot, of course. I'll disable the door so no one can enter. It will remain only as an energy source to power the universes you've created."

"It's much appreciated," said Blue Mercury.

"Don't thank me," John snapped. "You're lucky the weight of the bureaucracy is on your side. I have half a mind to annihilate the lot of you, just out of spite."

Suddenly the door slammed open and Red Mercury, looking dazed and haggard, stumbled in. "Um, guys?" he said. "I could use some help out here. Lucifer has gone insane."

CHAPTER FORTY-EIGHT

A man came into being, motivated only by the thought of destruction. He had no name, no past, and no plans. His first thought was: this should not be.

But what is *this*? He wondered to himself. And he answered: *all of it*.

In this inchoate state, he was not fully aware of himself as a person, nor of the world around him, as he could not decipher the signals transmitted to his mind by his senses. He was merely a mind surrounded by something that was not-mind. And yet, even in this state, he yearned for something that was not. More precisely, he yearned for all of it, both mind and not-mind, to be obliterated. Oblivion was what he craved. But the craving itself mocked his desire: the stronger it became, the more of it there was to wish away. The mockery drove anger, and the anger mocked him as well.

Where did all this come from, he thought? The mind and the not-mind, the yearning and the anger. The Source, he thought. But what was The Source?

A phrase came to him: the Eye.

The Eye was watching him, even now, mocking his anger and his yearnings. The Eye was the source of it all, the mind and the not-mind. Yes, he thought, destroy the Eye and the rest goes with it. Oblivion.

He got to his feet, some sort of primitive muscle-memory reasserting itself despite his lack of awareness. I am in this body, he thought. This body was given to me by the Eye, so that it could see itself from the outside. But to do this, the Eye had to send a part of itself away. In the Eye's vanity, it made a mistake: for with this body I can not only observe the Eye; I can also destroy it.

The Eye was not far away, relative to the body's mode of movement. It had taken the form of a blue pyramid several times as tall and as wide as the body. The pyramid was not perfect, though: in the side facing the body there was a dark rectangle, just large enough to permit the passing of the body inside. A door, thought the man. The Eye has grown careless. I shall enter the Eye and destroy it from the inside.

The man began to walk slowly, deliberately across the surface between him and the Eye. He was vaguely aware of other bodies around them—hundreds of other people who had also come into being, some of them just waking up. These people did not matter. Soon they would not be, along with everything else. He walked past the other bodies to the door of the pyramid and went inside.

He found himself in a sort of entryway. There seemed to be no one inside. No other bodies to meet him. He sensed no intelligence within; no mind inside the Eye. He was disappointed. He wanted the Eye to know its doom had arrived. Words came to him.

"YOUR DOOM HAS ARRIVED!" he screamed.

Nothing seemed to happen. The man continued through the entryway into the next room, which was nicely appointed with leather couches and chairs.

"YOUR DOOM HAS ARRIVED, EYE!" he screamed. Still there was no response.

He picked up one of the chairs, finding it surprisingly easy to lift. Some part of him was aware that he was channeling energy from the Eye itself in order to lift the chair. The thought made him angry. He threw the chair against the wall, and the chair splintered into pieces. He felt better. It felt good to destroy. He picked up one of the couches and did the same thing. When he had destroyed all the furniture in the room, he moved on to the next room, which was large and whose walls were lined with wood shelves. On the shelves were items he recognized as books. A word came to him: library.

The thought of destroying a library filled him with glee. Much better than destroying chairs. Books had entire worlds inside them. Fire, he thought. Fire is the way to destroy books. I can use the energy from the Eye to make fire. He pulled a book off one of the shelves and began to concentrate. The energy became heat, and the heat manifested itself as flame.

"Hey there," said a voice.

Startled, the man dropped the book. The flame went out. He scowled and looked toward the source of the voice. It was another body—a man. Taller than his own body, with silver hair on top. A strange man.

"I will destroy it all," said the man.

"Fire is good for that," said the tall man.

The man nodded uncertainly, not sure if this man intended to help him or hinder him. "Fire good," he said.

"Indeed," said the tall man. "You don't recognize me, do you?"

"You are tall man," said the man. "Other body, not mine."

"Ah, so you've heard about me, then," said the tall man. "Yes, I'm known in several universes for being tall man, other body, not you. Some call me Mercury. Say, how about we step outside and discuss this plan you have for destroying it all?"

"No," said the man. "Stay inside the Eye. Destroy the Eye. Destroy it all."

The tall man sighed. "So this is what's left of you, eh, Lucifer? Your memory and personality are completely erased, and yet the urge to destroy persists. It's kind of pathetic, to be honest with you."

"Tall man not help destroy," said Lucifer.

"Tall man not help destroy," said Red Mercury. "I'll tell you what, though. There's a place called the Iris, just down here. It's the nerve center for the Eye. If you want to destroy it all, that's where you want to be."

"Nerve center," said Lucifer. "The Mind for the Eye."

"Exactly," said Red Mercury. "Just follow me and I'll take you there."

Lucifer regarded Red Mercury suspiciously for a moment, but then nodded. "Tall man take me there."

"This way," said Red Mercury, leaving the library through a door on the opposite side. Lucifer followed him. Together, they took a circuitous route through the innards of the pyramid, passing a dining room, a kitchen, a study, various laboratories and workshops, and many rooms whose purpose was impossible to determine at a glance. Finally, they ended up in a sort of entryway.

"The Iris is right through that door," said Red Mercury, pointing to an open door through which bright light was pouring. "That light is the, um, reactor core."

Lucifer took a few steps toward the door, then stopped and looked around at his surroundings. "Not inside," he said at last. "Outside. Tall man, other body trick me!" He turned and let out a furious scream.

But the tall man was nowhere to be seen.

CHAPTER FORTY-NINE

"Lucifer started out insane," said Blue Mercury.

"That's what I'm saying," said Red Mercury. "I think... I mean, never mind. The important thing is that he's lost it. Like, really lost it. He's all of the bad parts of Lucifer without any of the intelligence or charm. Hyde without Jekyll. The Hulk without Bruce Banner. I tried to trick him into going back outside, but no dice. I think he's tearing up the kitchen now."

There was a scream and a crash from somewhere outside the Iris.

"How did he get inside?" asked Blue Mercury.

"Reboot opens the door," said John. "Safety measure."

"Yeah, it seems really safe," said Blue Mercury. "Hats off to the engineers for that one."

"Eventually he's going to find his way in here," said Red Mercury. "I'm not sure we can stop him without causing serious damage to the Eye. John, I realize you've washed your hands of this whole business, but we could really use your help here."

"I'm forbidden to raise a hand against any sentient creature," said John.

"We saw you zap an ape to death!" Red Mercury exclaimed.

John shrugged. "He was right on the edge."

As he spoke, the door to the Iris crashed open. Lucifer staggered in, his eyes wild. "YOUR DOOM HAS ARRIVED!" he shrieked. The two Mercurys turned to face him. Balderhaz backed against the wall. John remained at the pedestal, calmly tapping icons, as if oblivious to the crazed demon in the room. Lucifer charged the pedestal, and the Mercurys braced for his attack. When he was a couple steps away, though, a portal suddenly opened in front of him and he vanished. The portal closed as quickly as it had opened.

"I can, however," said John, "trap him in an alternate universe."

"Nice!" exclaimed Blue Mercury. "Where'd you send him?"

John shrugged. "One of the universes you created. This one." He pointed at a window on the display. "I picked it at random."

"Well done," said Red Mercury.

"What happened to him anyway?" said Blue Mercury. "Why'd he flip out like that?"

"Apparently," said John, examining the display, "the Outpost was struck by lightning. Wouldn't ordinarily be a problem, but the system was already overwhelmed from you overloading the compile buffer with your nine hundred universe trick. There was a momentary burst of ontological energy. Wiped out Lucifer's memory while intensifying the core attributes of his soul-thingy."

"Making him an even bigger asshole," said Red Mercury. "What about Green Mercury and the others?"

John brought up the display of the pyramid and its surrounding. From this distance, the cultists seemed to be dazed but unhurt.

"They look okay," said Red Mercury.

"Undoubtedly their memories have been affected as well," said John, bringing up some sort of graph on the display. "And there may have been other... changes."

"So it's over," said Blue Mercury. "The universes are saved, and insane Lucifer is no more."

"Hmm," said Red Mercury.

"What?" replied Blue Mercury.

"Well," said Red Mercury, "Don't get me wrong, I'm glad he's gone. He could have done a hell of a lot of damage from inside the Eye. But..."

"You feel a little bad for that universe."

"Yeah," said Red Mercury. "I mean, it doesn't stand a chance. Eventually Lucifer is going to come to his senses, and he's going to be just as dangerous and evil as he was here. If there are no angels in that universe, he's going to be in charge of the whole universe soon enough. The Earth part of the universe, anyway."

"And there's no guarantee he'll stay there," said Blue Mercury. "If he manages to build a portal generator..."

The two Mercurys traded glances. "Shit," they both said at once.

"It's the Gray timeline," said Balderhaz. "I suspected as much."

John nodded. "So it would seem. What you remember of the Gray timeline is consistent with it being the universe in which I trapped Lucifer."

"That means one of us has to go there to stop him," said Blue Mercury.

"We can't stop him," said Red Mercury. "He takes over the whole plane. We already know that."

"But we're the resistance," said Blue Mercury. "Things would have been even worse there without us. Without Gray Mercury, I mean. And if Gray Mercury hadn't been there when we accidentally opened a portal to his universe, he wouldn't have been able to warn us to shut down the portal. If Gray Lucifer had come through at that point, there's no telling what might have happened. One of us has to go."

"Why us?" asked Red Mercury. "What about Green Mercury?"

They looked at the window that was still showing the cultists staggering about, obviously confused. After a moment, they located Green Mercury, who was standing alone, scratching his head and staring at the Eye.

"If he's in as rough a shape as Lucifer, he's not going to be much help. I'm sure we could toss him into the Gray universe and he'd figure it out soon enough, but it seems like a nasty trick to play on him."

Red Mercury nodded. They were silent for some time. At last he said, "You realize what this means, right?"

"Seven thousand years on the Gray timeline. And then…"

"Yeah. So… we flip the quoin?"

Blue Mercury shook his head. "No more universe splitting. No more leaving things up to chance. I'll go."

"What?" said Red Mercury. "Why?"

"Free will," said Blue Mercury. "If I choose to go and you choose to stay, it proves we're not just copies of each other. We're individuals."

"Bah," said Balderhaz. They ignored him.

"Anyway, it's my destiny. I'm Blue Mercury. One of us had to take the sad ending, and it's me. It just fits."

Red Mercury frowned. "You're contradicting yourself," he said. "Is it your choice or is it your destiny?"

"Both," said Blue Mercury. "Frankly, I don't envy you. At least I know what's in store for me, and there's an end in sight—even if it's seven thousand years away. You're stuck having to figure out your own fate."

"I'll manage," said Red Mercury.

"We always do," said Blue Mercury. He turned to John. "Would it be possible for you to open another portal to the Gray universe, just for a second?"

John regarded him for a moment. "You're certain you want to do this?" he said. His voice revealed for the first time something that sounded like sympathy.

"Yeah," said Blue Mercury. "I've thought it through. Somebody's got to be the foil for Gray Lucifer, and somehow I always knew it was going to be me."

Red Mercury regarded his counterpart for a moment but said nothing.

"All right," said John. "Give me a moment."

"Oh, and one more thing," said Blue Mercury. "Balderhaz, eventually you're going to figure out how to travel between all these different universes. That is, I assume it will be you. Somehow I doubt there's another Balderhaz out there. Someday you'll even build a planeport connecting them all. But you are to forget all about the Gray universe. I don't want Lucifer's hellhole infecting the rest of the planes. No portals to the Gray universe, ever. Nobody outside this room ever knows it exists. Do you understand?"

Balderhaz nodded. "As good as forgotten," he said sadly.

"Thanks," said Blue Mercury. "You'll see me soon enough."

A glowing circle appeared on the floor next to them.

"Well, I guess this is it," said Blue Mercury. "Once I step on that portal, I'll be Gray Mercury."

Red Mercury shook his head. "No," he said. "You'll be Mercury. You always were. Just as much as I, and probably more."

"Thanks, man," said Blue Mercury. "Coming from you, I'll take that as a compliment, considering you're a raving narcissist." The two Mercurys grinned and clasped hands for a moment. Then Blue Mercury stepped onto the portal and was gone.

CHAPTER FIFTY

"Well, thank God that tiresome bastard is gone, eh?" said Red Mercury. Balderhaz shrugged.

"Strange," said John.

"It's a defense mechanism," said Red Mercury. "I miss the other me just as much as you guys do."

"What?" said John. "No, I'm referring to this." He pointed at one of the little universe icons, and it grew to fill the display.

"All I see is desert," said Red Mercury. "It looks like all the other universes we created."

"That's exactly it," said John. "It looks just like them, but this doesn't appear to be one of the universes you created. Not intentionally, anyway. The timestamp predates by several minutes the moment you accessed the Iris."

"One of the universes we created with the quoin survived," said Balderhaz.

"When we tried the combinations, you mean?" said Red Mercury.

"The timestamp fits," said John, frowning. "It came into being at the exact moment the door to the Outpost was opened."

"But all the other combinations were supposed to have resulted in oblivion," said Red Mercury. "There was only one possibility for success, and we took it. There can't be another universe created at that moment."

"Unless it was somehow able to stabilize on its own," said Balderhaz. "Without the help of the Eye."

John nodded. "It should be impossible, but that's the only explanation."

Red Mercury rubbed his scalp with his hand. "So forty-three million or so different versions of us each tried a different combination. The combination we tried worked, letting us into the Eye. Forty-three million combinations didn't work, resulting in the destruction of the Eye. In every other case except for one, the destruction of the Eye resulted in the end of the universe. But by some fluke, this universe survived. How?"

"Consciousness," said Balderhaz. "Observation. It's the only thing that can sustain a universe."

"That's right," said John.

"But all the other universes had the same number of conscious entities," said Red Mercury. "The result should have been the same in all of them. You said it yourself, John. There wasn't enough consciousness to sustain a universe."

"Consciousness is a funny thing," said John. "It's not easily quantifiable. The Iris estimated the chance of this universe being self-sustaining without the Outpost were virtually nil, but given forty-three million chances, it's not inconceivable that some particular combination of consciousnesses in this universe allowed it to become self-sustaining."

"So even though every universe was identical," said Red Mercury, "the conscious beings on that one were able to bring about a different result. That sounds like evidence for free will."

"Bah," said Balderhaz. "Just quantum randomness. It means nothing."

"Perhaps some unquantifiable feature of consciousness made the universe possible," said John. "Or perhaps it was merely a fluke, as Balderhaz indicates. In any case, it's not likely to be a very interesting universe."

"Why do you say that?" asked Red Mercury.

"It has the bare minimum consciousness needed to sustain it. No active connection to the Outpost, which is the source of all being. I wouldn't be at all surprised if the whole universe withers and dies eventually. At the very least, I would expect it to be a terribly mundane place."

Mercury found himself laughing.

"What?" said John. And then a look of realization came over face. "Oh, I see. It's your so-called 'Mundane Plane.'"

"Not so mundane after all," Red Mercury observed. "As it seems to have been the result of nigh-impossible fluke of reality."

John shrugged. "Its genesis aside, it's going to be a hell of a dull place. The laws of physics are going to be nearly immutable. Very little possibility for miracles to occur. In any case, I'm afraid the matter will remain academic. It's time for me to cut my losses with this debacle. I'll escort you gentlemen outside and then be on my way."

John walked to the door and Red Mercury and Balderhaz reluctantly followed.

He led them out of the Iris, through the entryway, and outside, where the cultists lay, sat, or stood around. Some of them spoke to each other in hushed tones, but most were silent, staring at the pyramid or puzzling at their surroundings. A few simply held their hands in front of their faces, as if seeing them for the first time.

"They've all lost their memories," said John. "The energy of pure being will do that to you. The specifics of experience fade, leaving only one's essential nature."

"The soul-thingy," said Balderhaz.

"Correct," said John.

But as Mercury surveyed the crowd, he realized the energy wave had done more than that. Many of the cultists had been physically changed in some way—some looked older, some looked younger, some seemed taller. The only commonality was that nearly all of them looked healthier and more robust than before.

"They've changed," said Red Mercury.

"Another side effect of ontological energy," said John. "It tends to make things more of what they are. Better representations of themselves. You might call them Platonic ideals of human beings."

"More human than human," Balderhaz murmured.

"So this is how it happened," said Red Mercury, looking from one cultist to the next. "They were just human beings after all. Ordinary people transformed into—"

"Angels!" cried a voice to their right. They turned to see a tall, thin, blond man getting to his feet. He was holding something in his hand that glowed bright orange. The man seemed at once foreign and familiar to Red Mercury, like the twin brother of someone he had once known. As they watched, the man began to float in the air, holding the shining object in his hand. The ersatz angels turned to gape at him. "I am the Light-Bringer," the man said. "Behold!"

"The shard," said Balderhaz.

"Hmm," said John, craning his neck to look at the pyramid. "A chip got knocked off the peak by the lightning."

"This can't be happening," said Red Mercury. "It's that damn kid. Lucas." But he wasn't a kid anymore. He'd been transformed by the ontological wave, made more than he was. Red Mercury couldn't believe he hadn't noticed the similarity before. Lucas was Lucifer.

"I understand that you are confused and frightened," Lucas-cum-Lucifer went on, "but there is no reason for you to fear. We angels have been brought into being to safeguard the newly created universe, and I, Lucifer the Light-Bringer, am your ruler!"

"Where is he getting this shit?" Red Mercury asked.

"Delusion," said John. "Fabrication. Who knows? It may be remnants of memory, or his mind attempting to rationalize his situation. Probably some combination thereof."

"Or he's realized that everyone else is as clueless as he is, and he's bullshitting them."

"Also a possibility," John acknowledged.

"Where are we?" the Cravutius lookalike, who now looked even more like Cravutius, asked.

"Why, this is Heaven, of course," Lucifer said. "This pyramid behind me is the source of all reality, the Eye of Providence. Around this pyramid we shall build a great celestial city, from which we will oversee every plane of existence. And then we shall build a hub connecting all of the planes!"

"A planeport!" yelled Balderhaz, suddenly excited.

"Yes!" said Lucifer. "A planeport connecting all the planes!"

"Seriously, Balderhaz?" Red Mercury said. "You know he's full of shit, right? Doesn't this strike you as familiar? We've been through all of this before."

Balderhaz shrugged. "I just want to build stuff," he said.

Mercury sighed. It figured, somehow. Balderhaz's mind existed only to solve problems, to engineer solutions. He had no long-term memory to speak of. He lived in an eternally renewing present. Balderhaz always was, and always would be.

"But who are we?" asked a young woman. "How did we get here? I don't remember anything."

There were nods and murmurs of assent.

"Do not be afraid," said Lucifer. "It's perfectly normal to be a bit confused. Fortunately, I know all of your names, and I have a purpose in mind for each of you!"

"What's my name?" asked the woman.

"You're, um, Gabrielle," said Lucifer.

"And me?"

Lucifer thought a moment. "Izbazel," he pronounced.

"What about me?"

"Nisroc."

"Me?

"Cravutius. Tiamat. Uzziel. Ramiel. Scalzi. Konrath." Lucifer was no longer waiting to be prompted; he was just pointing at people and making up names off the top of his head. Mercury shuddered as he realized he was mouthing the names along with Lucifer. When he got to Balderhaz, he paused a moment, as if unable to come up with an appropriate name.

"I'm Balderhaz," said Balderhaz.

"Of course," said Lucifer. "Balderhaz. My planeport engineer."

Balderhaz smiled. Red Mercury sighed. Lucifer pointed his finger at Red Mercury, who shook his head. "Skip me," he said. "I'm not here."

Lucifer shrugged and moved on. He pointed to Green Mercury, who had just wandered forward out of the crowd. "Ophiel," he said.

Green Mercury frowned. "I'm Mercury," he said.

"Whatever," replied Lucifer, and moved on. "Malcazar, Gurien, Ederatz, Shamalaz..."

"He remembers," said Red Mercury.

"Fragments," replied John. "The faintest of impressions. A name, little more."

"I remember this," said Red Mercury. "I remember being him."

John nodded. "This is all in your memories," said John to Red Mercury. "It's faint, but it's there. When consciousness first arises, it has difficulty organizing its experiences into memories. So this seems familiar to you, but your earliest clearly defined memories stem from much later. After Lucifer's hierarchy is established and the Celestial City is built."

Lucifer had gotten to a woman carrying a baby, and seemed momentarily stumped. "Laylah," he said, pointing at the woman. "And, um, Perpetiel."

Mercury laughed. "So Perpetiel really was a baby all along. He got stuck that way, for eternity. Never had a chance to grow up." When Mercury managed to tear his gaze off Perpetiel, he noticed that several of the others present had begun to float as well. One man had managed to lift a rather large boulder over his head and now seemed terrified of dropping it. They were realizing that whatever they were, they were not ordinary human beings.

"So Lucifer is in charge of everything?" Mercury said, turning back to John. "I don't remember that part."

"Only at first, from what I can gather of your memories. It didn't take long for others to see through his bullshit, as you say. Michelle, for one. And Tiamat. They're already skeptical. They form the Senate as a check on his power, and ultimately kick him out of Heaven. At least, that's what happened last time."

"Heaven," said Red Mercury, looking around him. "It's just another universe."

"The proto-universe," said John. "All the others are copies of it, without the Outpost."

They watched for some time as Lucifer continued to pull names out of his ass. Green Mercury remained standing, with a puzzled expression on his face, taking in his surroundings.

"Poor bastard is going to have to do it all over again," said Red Mercury.

"It's all new to him," said John. "His memory has been erased."

"Not all of it," said Red Mercury. "Traces remain. I know. I lived it. I always knew there was something before. A promise of something more than this life. Something lost."

John shrugged. "Everyone feels like that," he said. "Well, it's time for me to go. Better luck this time around."

Balderhaz nodded, obviously excited about the idea of building his planeport.

John turned to go back into the Eye.

"Hold on," said Red Mercury. "You can't leave me here. I can't do this again. There's already a Mercury here. This universe doesn't need two of us. I'm superfluous."

"What do you want me to do?" asked John, frowning. "I can't return you to your time. No time travel. We can't risk another causal breakdown."

Red Mercury shook his head. "No, I'm not asking for that."

"Then what?"

Red Mercury turned to Balderhaz. "You'll be okay here without me, right, Balderhaz?"

"Hmm?" said Balderhaz. "Oh, sure. You're right over there." He pointed to Green Mercury.

Red Mercury nodded and turned back to John. "Oblivion," he said. "Annihilation."

John frowned at him. "You're asking me to annihilate you?"

"Yes," said Red Mercury. "I can't take it anymore. Being immortal was bad enough, but now this? Having to go through it all over again, knowing what's going to happen? No thanks."

"It doesn't have to be the same thing all over again," said John. "Nothing is written in stone at this point. You could change things. It's none of my business, of course, but with what you know now… you could rule this entire plane."

"No," said Red Mercury. "They will have to figure it out on their own. I'm not going to endlessly relive the same life just to fix whatever mistakes I made last time around. I did the best I could. Green Mercury will do the best he can. I'm out. Can you do it or not?"

John nodded. "If oblivion is what you want, I can oblige you," he said.

"Good," said Red Mercury. "Let's get this over with."

CHAPTER FIFTY-ONE

The rubble of the BOX, just outside Elko, Nevada; April 29, 2017

Christine stood amid the wreckage of the facility, along with Jacob, Suzy, Eddie, and several federal agents. Burton had let them out of the trailer to wait for the Mercurys' return as a show of good faith, but it had been nearly four hours since they and Balderhaz disappeared.

"I guess they're not coming back," said Christine, watching the inert portal generator. "They never even said goodbye."

No one spoke for some time. There really wasn't anything to say.

Special Agent Burton approached the group, sliding his cell phone into his pocket. "Just got word from Washington," he said. "A PR team is on its way to handle the press. I'm to have my technicians disassemble the portal generator and have its parts shipped to a lab in Colorado somewhere."

"It won't work in Colorado," said Eddie. "It has to be on an energy nexus."

"Yeah, well, it's going to be in a hundred pieces anyway," replied Burton. "The FBI doesn't want it put back together until they understand what all the components do."

"That could literally take a thousand years," said Eddie. "Reverse engineering this sort of technology? You might as well poke at an octopus' brain with an egg beater to see how it swims."

"Those are my orders," said Jacob. "The demons will be loaded into a prisoner transport truck with the Balderhaz cube and sent to a secret prison."

"What about us?" said Suzy. "Are you still going to need our help finding the other angels?"

Burton shook his head. "My task force is being disbanded. Apparently the powers that be are 'looking to go a different direction.'"

"What does that mean?" asked Suzy.

"It means they think I've fucked this all up. Which I have. My informant turned against me, I was taken hostage, I got several good men killed, and all I have to show for it is a bunch of idiot demons—sorry, BIOs—that couldn't hatch a diabolical plan to take over a Taco Bell if their lives depended on it. They might give me another shot if I could apprehend the ringleader, but apparently he's not going to be around for another seven thousand years. My only chance is if your friends show up with Lucifer on a leash, and it's starting to look like they're not coming back at all."

Christine bit her lip. The others remained silent.

"Sorry," said Burton. "It's been a long day. The technicians will be here shortly to take the portal generator apart, but I can try to delay them for an hour or so."

"It won't matter," said Jacob. "If the Mercurys come back, they won't be using this portal generator. They'd have to open a portal from their end."

"I thought they were going to come back and get this portal generator," said Suzy. "Isn't that what you said, Special Agent Burton?"

"That was my understanding," said Burton. "But frankly I gave up trying to understand this universe hopping business."

"It makes sense," said Eddie. "That way they could leap frog back in time and always have a portal generator with them. But it shouldn't have taken them this long."

"Something must have gone wrong," said Jacob. "Either they never made it to the stopover point, or something happened to prevent them from coming back to the present to get the portal generator."

"Well, we know they didn't get stuck four years in the past," said Eddie. "Because if they had, they'd be here now."

Suzy nodded. "Maybe they changed their minds about returning here, and decided to go all the way back on their second jump."

"If they did," said Eddie, "then they have no way to get back to the present."

"Only if they let the portal close," said Jacob. "If they left it open, they could still get back."

"Not back to now," said Eddie. "They could get back to four years ago."

"Close enough," said Jacob.

"No," said Eddie. "Because if they came back anytime between four years ago and the present, well... then, where are they?"

"Laying low?" offered Suzy. "Maybe they decided to go into hiding for four years to keep from screwing up stuff that had already happened?"

"Could be," said Eddie. "But they went back in time four hours ago, from our point of view. So they couldn't be trying to prevent anything that has already happened from their point of view. We're three hours into their future. If they're here, what are they waiting for?"

Nobody spoke for some time.

"You know," said Suzy at last, "three of them were a bit much to take, but I have to admit I'm going to miss the big guy."

Jacob, standing next to her, put his arm on Suzy's shoulder. She didn't resist.

"Hold on," said Christine. "Mercury split the universe when he did and didn't go back in time, right?"

"Yes," said Eddie. "That's why there were two Mercurys. Well, three."

"And starting from four years ago, both of them are equally valid futures, right?"

"Hmm," said Jacob. "Interesting point. They may have accidentally returned to the other universe. And if they have no portal generator there, they wouldn't be able to get back here."

"Is there any way to know?" asked Suzy.

"Sure," said Eddie. "We could go there."

"I'm under strict orders not to let anyone use the portal generator," said Burton.

"Of course you are," said Jacob. "And also, you're a—*unck*—coward."

"Excuse me?" said Burton.

"All three Mercurys could be over there right now," said Jacob. "And if they are, that means they stopped Lucifer from rewriting history. But we'll never know, because you have 'strict orders.' So I guess we'll all just—*unck*—live in constant fear of being annihilated from here on out."

Burton glared at Jacob. Then he looked at the three FBI men standing nearby. "Gentlemen," he said. "Go check on our prisoners."

"Yes, sir," said one of the men. The three of them marched off.

"You know how to work that thing?" he said to Jacob.

"I can do it," said Eddie. "I've watched Balderhaz. Piece of cake."

"All right," said Burton. "I go through. No one else. If I'm not back in five minutes, shut it down."

"What do we tell the FBI?" asked Christine.

Burton shrugged. "The fuck do I care?" he said. "If I'm not back in five minutes I'm either dead or trapped in an alternate universe. Tell them I left to be a roadie for Linkin Park."

Eddie went to the portal generator and turned it on. He selected the coordinates Balderhaz had entered for the Blue timeline and a moment later, the familiar glowing blue ellipse appeared.

"So I just step on it," asked Burton.

"That's all there is to it," said Eddie. "Be back in five minutes or you're stuck there."

Burton nodded. "All right," he said. "See you shortly." He stepped on the portal and disappeared.

Christine, Jacob, Eddie and Suzy waited silently for him to return. Three and a half minutes later, he reappeared on the portal, looking no worse for wear. Eddie went to shut down the portal generator.

"Wait," said Burton. "There's somebody else coming." He cupped his hands together. "Rogers, Dexter!" he yelled. "Get over here." The two agents came running.

Those assembled watched as another figure materialized on the portal. Christine was holding her breath.

It was Lucifer. He was wearing a crimson robe with flared lapels and an odd-looking pyramid-shaped hat that seemed to be made of velvet.

Christine let out a heavy sigh.

"Curse you and your black cubes of mundanity, alternate version of Special Agent Burton!" cried Lucifer. "You shall rue the day you interfered with my conquest of the other version of this plane!"

"What the...?" Jacob said.

"Put him with the others," said Burton to the other two FBI agents.

"The Mercurys weren't there either," said Burton. "But they had an extra Lucifer on their hands. I said I'd be glad to take him."

"Curse you, alternate Burton!" shrieked Lucifer, as Dexter and Rogers dragged him away.

"Is that even the real Lucifer?" asked Eddie. "He seems... different."

"He's from some other alternate universe," said Burton. "Probably doesn't have a clue about our Lucifer's plan to erase history. But it doesn't matter. He calls himself Lucifer and matches the description of the BIO of that name. By the time my bosses figure out he's just some fruitcake refugee from a screwed up universe, I'll be the head of my own division."

"Well, it's really great this is going to be a career stepping stone for you," said Christine.

"I'm sorry," said Burton. "I was hoping they'd be over there too. But they aren't. The good news is that if I still have a job, I can probably use all of you. Particularly you, Eddie, since you're a BIO."

"Angel," said Eddie.

"Right," said Burton. "An angel. But I could use the rest of you as well, since you've all had some fairly extensive experience with angels and Heavenly politics."

"We'll think about it," said Suzy.

CHAPTER FIFTY-TWO

Christine and the others were transported by the FBI to Salt Lake City, where Burton had reserved rooms for them. He apologized for the length of the drive; evidently all the decent hotels within twenty miles of the portal facility had been gobbled up by members of the media. The luxury was mostly wasted on Christine, though; she was so exhausted after the night's events, she could have slept on the floor of the portal generator facility. That is, if it hadn't been blown to a million pieces. Or had that been a dream? She thought she remembered an explosion, but the whole experience had been so surreal that she couldn't be sure.

She slept for ten hours and then got up and took a long shower. It was her first for either three months or seven thousand years, depending on one's perspective; either way, it felt very, very good. She brushed her teeth and got dressed in shorts and a t-shirt—the toiletries and clothing courtesy their FBI chauffeur, who had had the foresight to stop at a twenty-four hour truck stop for some basic necessities. The shorts were too large and the t-shirt read NO PANTS ARE THE BEST PANTS, but as least she wasn't wearing seven-thousand-year-old clothes anymore. Those went in the garbage.

Once she felt more or less human, she went down to the lobby. It was now mid-morning and she wasn't sure if she was expected to check out at eleven. Perhaps Burton or their FBI escort had told her, but if so, she had been too hazy to retain such details. The cheerful front desk clerk informed her, however, that the room had been reserved for two more days. Good. She had no idea what she was going to do when those two days were up; she had no money, no identification, no transportation, no home. She supposed she had no choice but to go to work for Burton's task force, but at least he'd had the decency to give her three days to consider alternatives—like hitchhiking to Vegas and becoming a stripper. Hopefully more options would present themselves to her addled brain after she'd had a couple of cups of coffee.

Coffee!

She had forced herself not to think about it for the three months she was in prehistoric Africa. Along with hot showers, it was one of the things she missed the most. For a moment she considered continuing her abstention, but then the odor wafting over from the restaurant adjoined to the lobby caught her nostrils and she came to her senses. She walked over to find Jacob and Suzy already in a booth. It figured. Those two had forged an immediate connection. Good for Jacob, she thought. She liked Jacob okay in a platonic sense, but as hard as the universe had tried to get them to end up together, it just wasn't going to work between them. Even when he was the last man on Earth—well, the last man who spoke English, understood the value of flossing, and didn't think the sun was three hundred feet away—she just couldn't see it happening, and she suspected Jacob felt the same. She was reluctant to interrupt their chat, but Suzy noticed her and waved her over. Christine walked over and sheepishly sat down next to her, across from Jacob.

"Good morning," said Jacob. "Nice to sleep in a bed, isn't it?"

"Oh God, yes," said Christine, noticing a carafe in the center of the table. "Is that...?"

"Coffee," said Suzy. "I made them bring a whole pot."

"You are my favorite person in this universe," said Christine, pouring herself a cup.

Jacob and Suzy traded glances but said nothing.

"Oh, stop," said Christine. "I didn't mean it like that. I mean, I miss the big jerk, just like you guys do. But, well, he's an angel. And sort of a jerk, as I mentioned. Anyway, I just get the feeling that his time on this planet... this universe, this plane, whatever... that his time here is done. Like, the world needed somebody like him at this particular moment, and now the moment is passed. This probably isn't making any sense. Where's Eddie?"

"Outside," said Suzy. "Talking to Burton."

"About what?"

"Tracking down angels, I suspect," said Suzy.

Christine frowned. "I'm not sure I like the sound of that."

Jacob shrugged. "Eddie's feeling is that the FBI—and probably agencies of other governments—are going to be working on trying to track down and recruit angels anyway, and if we're involved, we might be able to keep them from starting another interplanar incident."

"Sounds like you're sold on the idea," said Christine.

"Well," said Jacob. "It would mean a fresh start with me and the FBI. I don't really have a lot of career options after going AWOL and getting mixed up with all this Apocalypse stuff."

"Me neither," said Suzy. "With Mercury gone, I'm unemployed. And probably unemployable."

"I'm not judging," said Christine. "If you guys think you can do some good for angel-human relations, go for it."

"What about you?" asked Jacob. "You've seen more of the multiverse than any human being alive. I'm sure Burton would love to have your help as well."

"Yeah, well," said Christine. "I don't imagine I have much choice."

"You could give it a few months," said Jacob. "Until you're back on your feet, at least. Then maybe get back to that novel you were writing."

Christine shrugged. "My manuscript is lost seven thousand years in the past. I'd have to start all over. I don't know, maybe sitting alone in a cubicle somewhere in Washington, D.C. is a fitting end to all of this. You can only fight bureaucratic stupidity for so long. Eventually everyone is assimilated."

Jacob and Suzy were silent for some time.

"Morning, everyone," said a man approaching their table. It was Special Agent Burton. Eddie was right behind him. "I hope you all got some rest and had some time to think about my offer."

"Excuse me," said Christine, getting up from the table.

"Everything okay?" asked Eddie.

"Yeah, fine," said Christine. "I just need to get some air."

"No worries," said Burton, as he sat down next to Jacob. "We'll wait for you."

Christine nodded and began to walk away. Eddie came after her.

"Hey," said Eddie, putting his hand on her shoulder. "I know you and I have never been, like, close, but I just want you to know that I understand."

"You understand what?" asked Christine.

"The story," he said. "Somewhere along the way, we lost the plot. Things got so crazy there with all the time-travel and universe-hopping that after a while it seemed like nothing was ever going to make sense again. But it's human nature to believe in the power of the narrative. The flow of cause and effect, actions and consequences. So through it all, we keep hoping that it's all going to make sense eventually. That everything is going to come together."

"Happily ever after," said Christine.

"Exactly," said Eddie.

"But real life isn't a story," said Christine. "There's no beginning, no middle, no end. Just stuff happening, for no reason. And then you go work in a cubicle until you die."

Eddie shook his head. "No," he said. "There's still hope. There's always hope. Just because we don't see the end, it doesn't mean there isn't one. Things will get back to normal, yes. Life will go back to being mundane. But mundane can be wonderful, if you want it to be."

Christine smiled at him. "Do you really believe that, Eddie?"

"I try to," said Eddie. "Every day, I try. As hard as I can."

"Try for me too, okay, Eddie?" said Christine. "I'm not sure I can do it anymore."

Eddie nodded. "I will."

"Thanks, Eddie," she said. "You're a good guy. A good angel."

Eddie grinned.

"Go keep an eye on our pal Burton," said Christine. "I don't trust him."

"Will do," he said. He smiled at her once more, then turned and walked back to the table.

Christine walked out through the lobby and went outside. It was a beautiful day, sunny and in the seventies, with just a slight breeze. Salt Lake City was a nice place, she thought. A beautiful city the people here had carved out of the wilderness. Like Heaven on Earth. No, better than that. She had seen Heaven, and she preferred Salt Lake City.

I could live here, she thought. Maybe get a job in a little coffee shop or something. I don't need much. But then she sighed as she remembered that even that modest dream would require more than she had: she couldn't very well apply for a job wearing a shirt that read NO PANTS ARE THE BEST PANTS, and in two days she would be homeless. Even getting replacement driver's license was going to be a challenge in her present circumstance.

So as she strolled through downtown Salt Lake City, she resigned herself to going to work for Burton, as a "BIO consultant," whatever that meant. Burton was going to be disappointed if he thought she had any special insight into the minds of angels. To her, angels were just people, albeit people who had been given the ability to bend the laws of physics. They had all the same faults as any other people. Some were vain, some were foolish, some were power-mad… and some were just downright unreliable. She envied those who could still believe in angels the way she once had—angels who had all the answers, who did the right thing unwaveringly, and who would swoop in and save you when you needed it the most. For all the wondrous things Christine had seen over the past months, that was an illusion that was no longer available to her.

After a circuitous walk through the downtown area, Christine found herself on the opposite side of a small municipal park from the hotel, and decided to cut through it. As she neared the other side of the park, she could see the hotel in the distance and was struck by an overwhelming sense of melancholy. She didn't want to go back there. Not yet. She found a bench next to a small pond and sat down. The others would be waiting for her, wondering where she had gone. But that was okay. They could wait five minutes longer. Just five minutes. And then she'd go back to normal life, whatever that was.

"Hey," said a man's voice behind her. "Want to see a card trick? I'd bend a spoon, but I don't have any of my trick spoons with me."

Christine turned slowly, not believing her ears. It couldn't be. It was impossible. A very tall man with silver hair was walking toward her. "Speaking of which," he went on, "you wouldn't happen to have a deck of cards, would you?"

She stared at the man for several seconds, unable to make herself speak. At last she managed, "Mercury?"

CHAPTER FIFTY-THREE

"One in the same," said Mercury, walking around the bench toward her.

"One *and* the same," Christine corrected.

"Ah, okay," replied Mercury. "Cool, I was hoping there'd be someone in this park who could correct my grammar. What do I owe you?"

"How the hell did you get here?" Christine asked.

"I walked," said Mercury, taking a seat next to her. "Same as you."

"No, I mean, I thought you were trapped seven thousand years in the past."

"I was."

"Then how did you get here? And don't say you walked, or I will slap you."

Mercury grinned. "I kind of like it when you slap me. In answer to your question, I got to the present time in the usual way: I waited."

"You waited," said Christine flatly. "For seven thousand years."

"That's right," said Mercury.

"Would you care to elaborate?"

"Well," said Mercury, "the first five thousand years were pretty dull. But folks in Sumeria started digging irrigation ditches, which I realize doesn't sound that exciting, but stick with me, because once the city-state of Eridu was formed, it didn't take long for a trade route to—"

"Hold on," said Christine. "I realize that you've been around a long time. But you're not just saying you've been around since prehistoric times; you're saying that you've now lived through all of human history *twice*."

"All of human history so far, yes," said Mercury. "I had John drop me off on the Mundane Plane just a few minutes after it split off from the... you know what, the details aren't important. The key point is that yes, I've lived through it all twice."

"But... why?"

Mercury shrugged. "The alternative was oblivion," he said.

"I think I might have gone with oblivion," said Christine.

"I almost did," said Mercury. "But then I remembered something."

"What?"

"That I told you not to give up hope," Mercury said. "I couldn't choose not to be when I knew you'd be here waiting."

Christine just stared at Mercury for a long time. At last, she said, "You waited seven thousand years for *me?*"

"Well, you and hot dog stuffed crust pizza," said Mercury. "But yeah."

"That's... unbelievable," said Christine.

"Actually," said Mercury, "it's a fairly logical progression from the other types of stuffed crust pizza, if you think about it."

Christine realized she was grinning like a crazy person, and she didn't care. "You know what, Mercury? You can make dumb jokes all you want, but you're not going to ruin this moment. You waited seven thousand years for everything to happen all over again, just so that you could meet me here at this moment. You went through the great flood, the fall of the Roman Empire, the Crusades, both world wars... wait, why didn't you kill baby Hitler?"

"I made a pledge not to interfere in history," said Mercury. "Also, the line of time travelers waiting to kill baby Hitler is insane. You're much better off trying to kill baby Leopold II. That guy was a serious asshole. But no, it wasn't my place to meddle. I let things happen the way they happened, for better or worse. I only used my foreknowledge of events once, to buy three hundred shares of a company called Quicksilver Fabrication, under the name Marcus Uittenbroek. And I only used my angel powers a dozen or so times, only to save lives, and even that almost got me in serious trouble. For the most part I've just lived a normal life, keeping to myself.[12]

---

[12] Savvy readers will note that if this instance of Mercury coexisted with his alternate self, then both Mercurys were mortal during this time, as I previously

Figured if Jesus didn't use his powers to get down from the cross, I could manage."

"You saw Jesus on the cross?"

"Well, no," said Mercury. "I heard about it after, though. I did meet him once, a few years before."

"Really? Did he say anything to you?"

"Yeah," Mercury replied. "He said, 'Don't lose hope.'"

"He did not!"

"Swear to God," said Mercury. "Of course, he said it in Aramaic."

"Did you say anything back?"

"Yeah, like an idiot I said, 'you too!' Doesn't even make any fucking sense. 'You too!' I panicked."

"Did he know? About you, I mean?"

"Hard to say," replied Mercury. "I like to think so."

"Did you ever meet the other you?"

Mercury shook his head. "I avoided myself. Was rarely even on the same continent."

"And you never stopped by to see me either. Even when I was in ancient Africa."

"No," said Mercury. "Thought it best not to interfere."

"Wow," said Christine. "This is all so amazing. But what happened to the other Mercurys? And now that I think about it, how do I know you're the real Mercury?"

"We're all real," said Mercury. "I'm the one called Red Mercury, but Green and Blue were Mercury too. Are. Well, Green is. Sort of. Can I explain this later? It's kind of complicated."

"Sure," said Christine. "But can I ask one more question?"

"Shoot."

"How did you know you'd end up on a timeline where I came back from ancient Africa? I mean, isn't there a universe where you prevented yourself from going to get me?"

---

established that only one instance of an individual can be immortal on a given plane at a given time. If it makes you feel better, you can assume that Red Mercury remembered this and asked John to implement some kind of override using the miraculous powers of the Eye, and that I did not mention this development until now because it would have completely wrecked the flow of this very poignant and pithy final chapter. In fact, what the hell are you doing reading footnotes at a time like this? Get back to the story!

"I knew I'd end up on where you were," said Mercury, "because that's where I belong."

"Oh my God," said Christine. "You had no idea, did you?"

"Honestly," said Mercury, "it was a crapshoot. I've been trying to figure it out for seven thousand years, and I'm still not sure it makes any sense. I'm just glad I'm here with you now."

"Me too," said Christine, smiling.

"So what do you want to do?" asked Mercury. "The future is finally here, and it's ours for the taking."

"Let's fly to the Azores and do nothing for a thousand years," said Christine.

"I knew I liked you," said Mercury. "Shouldn't we tell your friend back at the hotel? Suzy and weird guy and what's-his-face?"

"Nah," said Christine. "Let them wonder. They're just going to try to recruit you for their stupid angel task force team thing anyway."

"Sounds boring," said Mercury.

"Incredibly boring," Christine replied, getting up from the bench. "Pick me up."

Mercury scooped her into his arms and she threw her arms around his neck.

"So," he said. "We're just not going to talk about your shirt?"

"No, we are not," said Christine.

"Fair enough," said Mercury, and leapt into the air.

"Strange how paranoia can link up with reality now and then."

— Philip K. Dick, *A Scanner Darkly*

ONE

"That's a really big sheep," said Erasmus Keane, his observational powers functioning as flawlessly as ever.

The woman in the lab coat nodded curtly. "He's a Lincoln Longwool," she said. "Largest breed of sheep in the world." She had introduced herself as Dr. Kelly Takemago, Director of Research for the Esper Corporation. We were standing in her lab, a vast white room filled with the low humming of vaguely terrifying machines that hung from the ceiling like colossal clockwork bats. Poised in the middle of the room was the sheep in question, which Keane and I were regarding with professional interest. The sheep, in turn, was regarding us. It didn't appear impressed.

Keane, holding his chin in his hand, began walking around the sheep in a stooped posture that reminded me of a waddling duck. The sheep was nearly as tall as he was, and was looking back at Keane with scientific detachment. It was hard to say which was the odder-looking specimen, the quadrupedal area rug standing in stoic silence on the tiled floor of the lab or the lanky, balding biped creeping awkwardly around it.

"Can I touch it?" asked Keane, after completing his circumnavigation of the creature.

"Of course," said Dr. Takemago, seeming mildly annoyed at the question. "The sheep doesn't bite. They're very docile creatures."

Keane reached out nervously, his hand gradually disappearing into the beast's lush fleece. He gave an excited yelp, which startled Dr. Takemago but had no appreciable effect on the Longwool's equanimity. "You gotta try this, Fowler," he said. "It's like sticking your hand into Narnia."

I demurred.

"They produce the heaviest and coarsest fleece of all the long-wooled sheep varieties," said Takemago, as if reciting from an encyclopedia article. "That isn't why the Esper Corporation keeps them, of course. This one is male. There are two others. John and Paul are downstairs."

"John and Paul?" I asked. "What's this one's name, Ringo?" There was a tag on the sheep's ear, but all it had on it was the number eight.

"Mark," said Dr. Takemago.

I nodded, as if that had been the other possibility.

"Biblical, not Beatles," mused Keane. He continued, "'All the nations will be gathered before him, and he will separate the people one from another as a shepherd separates the sheep from the goats. He will put the sheep on his right and the goats on his left.'" He grinned at me, as if expecting recognition of some sort. I shrugged noncommittally.

"That's from Matthew," he went on. "The apostle, not the sheep."

I turned back to Dr. Takemago. "So the missing one...?" I ventured.

"Mary," replied Dr. Takemago.

"Of course," I said. "And did Mary by any chance have a little lamb?" Very unprofessional of me, I know. But you can't lob a softball like that at me and expect me not to take a swing.

"No," said Dr. Takemago, without cracking a smile. I couldn't tell if she was irritated by the joke or if the subtlety of my wit eluded her. I got the impression that Dr. Takemago didn't go in much for jokes. She was short and stocky, and wore her straight black hair cut so short that it required a constant effort to remind myself that she wasn't a twelve-year-old boy. Her expressive range seemed to encompass only detached bemusement and mild irritation.

"So they are sterile?" asked Keane, now with both of his hands sunk deep within the long-suffering animal's fleece. The sheep bore this indignity with aplomb.

Dr. Takemago shook her head. "No, in fact the plan was to breed them. Unfortunately, Mary is the only female of the group."

"And she's been missing since yesterday?" I asked.

Dr. Takemago nodded. "Mary was gone when I arrived, shortly after seven. The security system had been overridden. The cameras

348

didn't catch anything. All of the animals wear a GPS tracking device on their collars, but Mary's stopped transmitting at 4:29am, while she was still in the lab. Whoever did this knew what they were doing."

"Who else has access to the building?"

"To the building? Several hundred people. But the research area is only accessible to about fifty."

"We'll need a list," I said. "As well as details on your security system."

"Of course," said Dr. Takemago.

"You've called the police?"

Dr. Takemago was silent for a moment. "The executives didn't feel that the police would appreciate the nuances of this case."

I nodded, as if this were a perfectly reasonable answer. Keane had extracted his hands from the fleece and was holding them in front of his nose with a slightly revolted expression on his face.

"You said you don't keep the sheep for their wool," I remarked. "Why do you keep them?"

"Genetic research," Dr. Takemago said.

I raised an eyebrow at her. Now she was being downright evasive. After a moment she sighed. "Organ transplants," she said. "The idea is to raise genetically modified sheep specifically for the purpose of being hosts for organs that can be transplanted into humans. Livers, kidneys, even hearts and lungs. This is confidential, of course."

Just at that moment the sheep let out an impassioned bleat that sent a shiver down my spine. It sounded precisely like the frightened cry of a small child. I turned to see Keane kneeling in front of the sheep, staring intently into its eyes. The sheep backed away, appearing frightened.

Dr. Takemago didn't look pleased. "Stop spooking the sheep, Keane," I said, by way of mollifying her. I had no real hope of having any effect on Keane's behavior.

Keane continued to stare, and the sheep retreated, bleating its horrible bleat.

"What are you doing, Mr. Keane?" demanded Dr. Takemago.

Keane didn't answer, continuing to stare at the terrified sheep. Then he stood up and turned to Dr. Takemago. "I have taken measure of this sheep's soul," announced Keane. The room was silent except for the low hum of the machinery for some time before I realized that Keane wasn't planning to elaborate.

"And…?" I asked at last.

Keane remained silent for several seconds more. "Inconclusive," he said at last. With that, he wandered to a corner of the laboratory and began staring at the wall. Dr. Takemago shook her head, clearly dubious about the Esper Corporation's decision to hire Keane to find their missing sheep.

"He's an unconventional thinker," I explained without enthusiasm. "But he gets results."

"One thing needs to be made clear," said Dr. Takemago, turning to face me. "The Vice President of Research and Development left instructions to be cooperative. But hiring a two-bit private investigator to locate the missing specimen seems misguided, and frankly Mr. Keane's attitude is doing exactly nothing to allay those concerns. That sheep is absolutely critical to the life-saving research Esper Corporation is doing, and if it isn't found—"

"Phenomenological inquisitor," I mumbled.

"Excuse me?"

"Mr. Keane doesn't like being called a private investigator," I explained. "He prefers the term 'phenomenological inquisitor.'"

"Delusions of grandeur too," noted Takemago coldly. "In what way does a 'phenomenological inquisitor' differ from a two-bit private investigator?"

I was ready for that one. "Phenomenology," I began, "is the philosophical study of the structures of experience and consciousness. The methods of a phenomenological inquisitor differ from those of a typical investigator in that the phenomenological inquisitor regards each case as a matter of resolving the tension between the appearance of things and things as they actually are. Further, the phenomenological inquisitor does not limit his understanding of the 'real' to merely physical phenomena, accepting that consciousness, memory and experiences are no less real than, for example, chairs, automobiles, or—" I glanced at the sheep—"farm animals." I had this speech memorized, but I liked to occasionally improvise depending on the situation. Returning to the script, I went on, "Finally, the phenomenological inquisitor differs from a scientist in that he does not attempt to isolate himself from his subject or to observe reality under artificially created laboratory conditions, preferring to seek out apparent anomalies and explore them on their own terms rather than reduce them to preexisting categories."

"That sounds like bullshit," said Takemago.

I shrugged. To be honest, it sounded like bullshit to me too.

"Any idea who would want to steal your sheep?" I asked.

"The most reasonable hypothesis?" said Takemago. "One of the other biotech companies. Competition in this industry is cutthroat. Mary represents the culmination of a decade of top-secret research."

I frowned. I was no scientist, but something about that didn't seem to jibe. "You think they're going to dissect Esper's sheep to learn its secrets? Wouldn't it make more sense to steal the research? Not to mention that it's a lot easier to smuggle out a terabyte of data than to kidnap a sheep."

Dr. Takemago nodded. "Security is looking into the possibility that research data was stolen as well. Stealing Mary may have been only one part of their plan."

"Be sure to contact us if you find anything out," I said. "If we're going to solve this case, it's vital that you not withhold any information."

"Of course," Dr. Takemago said, after a slight hesitation. I glanced at Keane to see if he had picked up on it, but he was oblivious, seemingly transfixed by the wall of the lab.

"What about someone needing an organ transplant?" I ventured.

Dr. Takemago shot me a dubious look.

"You said these sheep are engineered as hosts for organs intended for transplant. What if someone was desperate for a transplant, and couldn't get an organ through legal channels for some reason?"

"Not a chance," said Dr. Takemago. "Anybody with the resources to pull off a theft like this could easily have gotten hold of a black market kidney."

I furrowed my brow at her.

"Black market trade in human organs from the Disincorporated Zone is well-documented. It wouldn't be difficult for a motivated person with adequate resources to get their hands on a viable human kidney." She was right of course, but something about the way she said it creeped me out. Takemago had a strange, clinical way of speaking that made me feel a little like I was conversing with a machine.

"What about a liver?" I asked. "Nobody's going to sell their liver on the black market."

"No one's own liver, no," Dr. Takemago said.

I nodded. She was right. You could get anything in the DZ, if you had the money. "Still," I said, "it would help if we knew a little more about the potential uses for a sheep like Mary."

"There seems to be a bit of a disconnect here, Mr. Fowler," she said. "There are no 'uses' for a sheep like Mary. Her only value is as a subject of research. This is undoubtedly a case of corporate espionage. If the involvement of a 'phenomenological inquisitor' in this matter is unavoidable, then that's where such a person's efforts should be directed."

"Humor me," I said. "When you say that the organs are meant for transplanting into humans, do you mean that the sheep actually have human organs inside them?"

"More or less," Takemago said. "Its heart, kidneys, and liver are designed from a subset of chromosomes common to sheep and human beings, so they can be transplanted from one to the other with minimal complications."

"Minimal complications," I said. "Not no complications." I watched as Keane spun around and approached the sheep again. He sank his hand into the top of its fleece once more, and the sheep gave a quick bleat as it felt his presence. Dr. Takemago frowned, clearly agitated.

"There's always the risk of complications with any transplant operation," she said, her eyes on Keane. "Particularly cross-species—even if the animal is specifically designed for the purpose. That's why it makes no sense to steal a sheep like Mary for her organs when one could more easily purchase a human organ on the black market. It's always better to stay within the same species, if at all possible. Not to mention that these sheep are still experimental. There's simply no advantage to harvesting organs from a sheep."

"Then why breed them in the first place?"

"Because," Takemago explained irritably, "Esper Corporation isn't selling organs on the black market. The idea is to supply usable organs through legitimate channels, without anybody having to die in the process."

"Except for the sheep," I said.

"Of course," said Takemago to me. "But better a sheep than a human being."

I nodded. "Why do you use such a large breed of sheep?" I asked. "Even allowing for the volume of its fleece, that one has to weigh close to three hundred pounds. I would think its organs are too large to fit inside a person."

Takemago nodded, still watching Keane anxiously. "Another reason it wouldn't make sense to harvest organs from Mary. But in answer to the question, Esper uses several different breeds. These specimens are all experimental. Size is one of the easiest variables to control. Once the problem of organ viability has been solved, the next step is to breed a version with a mass approximating that of an average human being. What are you doing, Mr. Keane?"

Keane seemed oblivious to the question. He was running his hands through the sheep's fleece, pulling away loose fibers and regarding them with apparent fascination.

Dr. Takemago turned to me. "What exactly is Mr. Keane doing?" she demanded.

I watched Keane impassively for a moment. "Woolgathering," I said, eying Dr. Takemago for her response. Crickets.

She continued to watch Keane for some time, clearly agitated. Her hands were clutched in fists at her sides. I saw her lips quivering as if she were preparing for a confrontation. She took deep breath and said, "Mr. Keane, you have had adequate time to observe that sheep. If you have no other questions, I am going to have to ask you to leave."

Keane mumbled something incomprehensible.

"Excuse me?" said Dr. Takemago.

"I said, 'You'll do no such thing,'" Keane remarked.

"Oh?" said Dr. Takemago, rising to the challenge. "And why is that?"

"Because I'm your only hope to keep your job."

Dr. Takemago snorted derisively. "And how is that, Mr. Keane?"

Keane sighed. He straightened, facing Dr. Takemago, his hands tucked behind his back. "Other than the three of us and Mark here," he began, "this lab—which could easily accommodate twenty or more scientists and technicians—is empty. Not even a wrangler to help you with the sheep. I can't imagine all of your research has ground to a halt simply because one of your subjects has gone missing, which means that the lab has been intentionally cleared of personnel for some reason. Not on your orders, I assume."

Dr. Takemago didn't reply.

Keane went on, "It's possible that they're trying to hide the theft of the sheep—or some other detail about the case—from the other employees, but that seems unlikely. They aren't going to be able to keep the sheep's disappearance under wraps for long, and you haven't told us anything that I couldn't have learned from any low-level employee. Speaking of which, my fee is high enough that ordinarily when I'm hired by a corporate client like Esper, I'm met by one or more board members. Corporate officers uniformly possess an exaggerated sense of their own understanding of the strategic business realities affecting a case. This leads them to believe that I couldn't possibly solve the case without their input. But rather than being called into meeting with the Vice President of Research and Development, who ostensibly hired me for this case, I was directed to speak only to you, a lowly researcher. No offense."

Dr. Takemago scowled.

"And then there's the fact that nobody has called the police. Perhaps, as you intimate, this is because the matter is too sensitive to be handled by the civil authorities. Or perhaps it's because your superiors didn't see the need."

"What is your point, Mr. Keane?" demanded Dr. Takemago.

"My point, Doctor, is that your bosses have already determined who is responsible for your missing sheep. They set up this meeting with the sole purpose of seeing how you would react—to see if you would attempt to steer us away from suspecting you. This room is monitored, I assume. I'd wager the VP of R&D—assuming he really did hire me—is watching us right now. You'll be followed when you leave the building as well. If you don't incriminate yourself during this meeting, they're hoping to spook you into making a mistake, like trying to contact your co-conspirators."

Dr. Takemago's mouth had fallen open in shock. "But I… I didn't—"

"What your superiors fail to take into account is that if you were the sheep thief, you'd have anticipated suspicion and surveillance. In fact, given that you're the obvious prime suspect, you'd likely have planned a strategy of misdirection, deliberately inviting suspicion in order to demonstrate your innocence and utter guilelessness. If you had conducted this heist directly under your superior's noses, as it were, the last thing that would spook you into making a mistake is some eccentric detective poking around your lab, asking silly questions. This is one of the hazards of being an eccentric detective, by the way. Clients tend to rely on my reputation while discounting my ability. Esper hired me not to solve this case, but to put on my dog-and-pony show in your lab in order to flush you out. In addition to being completely misguided and doomed to fail from the outset, there's one major flaw with this plan."

"I didn't steal the sheep," said Dr. Takemago.

"No," Keane said. "You didn't."

"How do you know?" I asked.

"Do you see this sheep?" asked Keane, walking over to Mark and patting it gently on its head. "The poor thing is terrified."

"So?" I asked.

"Sheep are herd animals," said Keane. "They hate being separated from their herd. It's a little hard to tell, but this beast is having the sheep equivalent of a panic attack right now. Simply because it's standing alone in this lab, a place where it's probably been a hundred times before."

The sheep let out a low bleat, and Keane scratched its ear comfortingly.

I held up my hands, indicating I wasn't following.

"Well," he said, "imagine how Mary feels. She's in a strange place, alone, separated from her flock. "She must be out of her mind with fear."

I was about to interject, asking if he was going to get to the point sometime this week, but then I saw Dr. Takemago bite her lip, and I caught a glimpse of the picture Keane was painting.

"Dr. Takemago's surly demeanor is a cover," said Keane. "She loves these sheep. She empathizes with them. You can tell by the way she fidgets when I approach it. It pains her to see poor Mark standing here alone in the lab, being harassed by a strange man.

Maybe at first they were just research subjects, but she's come to have strong feelings for them. She would never willingly remove Mary from her herd. I suppose it's possible that she assisted the thief under duress, but it's hard to imagine what sort of leverage the thief might use."

"The usual, I suppose," I offered. "Threaten her family, or—"

Keane shook his head. "Dr. Takemago tends to avoid eye contact and personal pronouns, engages in the bare minimum of personal grooming, lacks social graces, presents a virtually asexual affect, and demonstrates an abbreviated range of emotions. These characteristics, along with her chosen career in a highly technical, specialized scientific field, indicate that she possesses traits of autism and social anxiety disorder. I expect she has no friends and no close family. This job is her entire life, and those sheep are the closest things she has to friends. To get Dr. Takemago to betray her employer and cause suffering to one of her sheep, the thief would have had to threaten to take away something she values more than her job and her research subjects. There isn't any such thing."

Dr. Takemago stared at Keane with something that was either annoyance or awe.

"So," I said, "this whole meeting has been a waste of time."

"Not at all," said Keane. "We've accomplished two important tasks. One, we've eliminated Dr. Takemago as a suspect and saved her job. Two: we've demonstrated that I'm the only person in this building smart enough to find the real thief." Keane craned his neck back and addressed the ceiling. "So," he said, "if it's all the same to you, I'll get to work on that."

Want to read more?
The Big Sheep will be available from booksellers
everywhere on June 28, 2016!

Review this Book!

Did you enjoy this collection? Please take a moment to leave a review on Amazon.com! Reviews are very important for getting the word out to other readers, and it only takes a few seconds.

More books by Robert Kroese you might enjoy:

"Mercury Begins" (short story)
Mercury Falls
"Mercury Swings" (short story)
Mercury Rises
Mercury Rests
Mercury Revolts
Schrödinger's Gat
City of Sand
The Foreworld Saga: The Outcast
Distopia
Disenchanted
Disillusioned
"The Chicolini Incident" (short story)
Starship Grifters
The Force is Middling in This One

Coming Soon:

The Big Sheep (June 28, 2016)
The Last Iota (January 2017)

31064882R00226

Made in the USA
Middletown, DE
16 April 2016